To Fredd♡

JUST WHAT I ALWAYS
Wanted

Nancy Roman

JUST WHAT I ALWAYS
Wanted

NANCY ROMAN

Dedication

To my parents, who told me I could do anything.
And to my husband, who believes I can.

Chapter 1

BACK IN MY TWENTIES, I was married for a while. I remember one day. We're having a cook-out in our backyard. My husband is standing at the barbecue with a long fork, and he's laughing. I see him in an apron, but that must be my imagination. Two other couples are over. The men are standing in the charcoal smoke, and the women are lounging in those long webbed chairs that you can buy everywhere, even the drugstore. We are all drinking pina coladas, which is the only thing I have learned to make in the blender that Aunt Lorraine gave us as a wedding gift.

I remember that one day. It was the only day I thought it was nice to be married.

When we finally decided to divorce, the discussion went something like this:

What's-His-Name: "Marsha in Payroll has much better boobs than you. I think I am going to live with her instead."

Me: "Okay."

The actual conversation was a little longer than that. It lasted three years. But it was basically the same conversation for the whole three years, except that I didn't say my line until the last day.

I found I didn't miss him at all. And I was glad that I had been married, for two reasons. First, because I get to use the phrase, "my ex" in a sentence once in a while, which makes me sound like I am full of life experiences.

More importantly, I kept the house. I paid him for his half, or rather, his equity, which was about three tenths of one percent. I like my house. It's small but with lots of windows and even a sunroom in the back. It's very cheerful, especially without him.

Once my ex was gone, I didn't have much money, but over the course of the next several years, I replaced every stick of furniture we had bought. So everything is mine, and there are no sweaty marks anymore. I never saw a man sweat like he did. It's funny that I never noticed that when we were dating. But after we married, it was uncomfortably clear that every place he sat was always damp. He'd get up from a chair and the upholstery or the wood or the leather or heaven help me, the vinyl, would be wet from his sweaty butt. I began to avoid the places he liked to sit. I replaced throw pillows on a monthly basis. When I went to my sisters' houses, I would wait for either of their husbands to get up, and then I would jump into the empty seat like I was playing musical chairs. I wanted to see if all men were as sweaty, but no. It was just mine. I replaced our mattress the day he moved out. I paid extra for same-day delivery. The things he didn't touch much were a lower priority, but eventually, even the lamps and the draperies went. I repainted too, as he often leaned against the walls.

I lost touch with my ex-husband very quickly, but I heard from Carol at the supermarket that he and Marsha didn't last long. I think he was on a holy quest for stupendous knockers. If I ever needed to get in touch with him, say if I needed an alibi for back in the 80s, like for the Wells Fargo robbery or something, I think I would look in Las Vegas.

Considering how broke I was when we divorced, I now have quite a bit of money, even though I wasn't in cahoots on the armored car robbery.

I'm no miser. In fact, my sister Mary Ann says that I spend money like a drunken sailor. She means that I pay too much for a haircut. Mary Ann gives me one of her disapproving snorts when she sees me right after a salon visit.

"I look as good as you; in fact, I look just like you," she says, "and I go to Cut'N'Go. Eight bucks and out the door—and no tipping."

Mary Ann doesn't look just like me. She looks like my mother, who went to Cut'N'Go for about forty years. I think that a really good hairdresser would not be working at Cut'N'Go, but would work in the classiest salon in a very rich town, where one makes good money plus big tips. So I drive to West Hartford and empty my wallet.

And good shoes too. I'm not talking designer shoes that cost more than your mortgage payment. But I won't look like Payless. I have nice clothes, an account at the dry cleaner where they know me by name, a BMW, and real china and silver.

So it's as surprising to me as it is to Mary Ann that I have found myself at fifty with a huge nest egg.

Not having children probably accounts for a good deal of my accumulated wealth. I had no sneakers or braces or video games or college tuitions. Then of course there's my job.

Just like that guy—who someday I'll look up—said, it's amazing how successful you can be by just showing up. I wasn't rushing off to PTA meetings or basketball games or school plays, or worrying about whether little Tiffany was letting the neighbor's boy look up her dress. I didn't have doctors' appointments every week or someone down with a cold or giving me one.

So I was at work every day. I met every deadline, and I had time in the evening to straighten up my office and make sure I was prepared for the next day. That's all it takes. Most people's lives are such a mess, and their attention so scattered that just being reliable is enough to make you shine at the office.

I turned fifty the first Friday in April. The night before, right after work, I went to my hairdresser's.

"Instead of just getting rid of the gray, let's do something fun," I told her.

"I can cut it so that it brings out your curl just a little more. A little wild."

"Wild. Yes, yes, yes. And how about some highlighting? For drama, you know. Not subtle."

"Really?" she asked.

Oh, really. I left that place looking ten years younger and full of drama, and not subtle.

I stopped at Monty's, about three doors down from the salon. This is where I have always bought my clothes. They're nice; well-made; classic. I walked in and looked around. The spring season was strong for pinstripes and sweater sets. Every season at Monty's is strong for pinstripes and sweaters sets. I walked out.

Next door is a store called, simply, 'Lovely'. I've stopped there once in a while. The clothes there are mostly imported from India and Mexico. They are gossamer, beaded, feminine. I had never tried anything on in that store. But I've let the delicate material run through my fingers.

"Hi," said the salesgirl, "I'm Miranda". She was about twenty. With her emerald green dress Miranda was wearing four necklaces, seven bracelets, earrings like chandeliers, and a little red jewel glued to the middle of her forehead. She wore sandals, and given the cool weather, socks decorated with purple cats.

"You look great," I said. "I want to look like the fifty-year-old version of you. You know, not trying to look like a teenager, but looking sort of like an artist."

"Right this way," she said. "Have you come to the right place! I know exactly what you need."

And she dressed me in a tiered skirt in gauzy Indian cotton, made from three shades of royal blue, the deepest at the bottom. There were little mirrors and wooden beads embroidered into the hem. She added an aqua tee shirt.

"That's all you need in the summer," she said, "with a turquoise necklace. For now, you need to add a sweater." And she brought me a plum crocheted sweater, with silver buttons shaped like tiny animal crackers—a lion, a giraffe, an elephant.

"Adds a little whimsy," she said, as if the ruffled skirt with mirrors was a bit too staid.

Miranda disappeared again, and a moment later returned with her triumph. "Here's the necklace I had in mind." And she fastened it around my neck. It was a triple strand of turquoise and silver, randomly-shaped beads born to dance together.

She sold me a couple of wooden bangles and a big silver watch. She threw in some tiny turquoise earrings "on the house," but of course I had already spent more than a week's take-home.

"Shoes," she said. "Look, no offense, but you said you didn't want to look like a teenager, so although you can wear sandals pretty soon, right now you just can't add socks like

5

me. Go next door to Griswold's. They've got brown leather boots in the window... lace-up. Go right now, in this outfit, and come back and show me.

"Wow," she said when I returned wearing the entire ensemble, boots included. "You're pretty tall, and now you look leggy too. You can really carry this off. You look like an artist."

"Or a dancer."

"Or a poet," Miranda laughed. "What are you, really?"

"An accountant," I said.

"Not any more."

And she was right.

I wore the outfit the next day. My curly hair, my mirrored skirt, my fiftieth birthday. I ran up the stairs to the second floor to drop off my forms at Personnel. Then I rode the elevator up to the seventh floor. I threw my sensible camel-hair coat across the desk, ran my fingers through my curls, and gave a flounce to my skirt. I strode down the hall to my boss's office.

Lynne was on the phone. The first picture her kid ever drew of her must have had a phone attached to her head. I regarded the frame on her desk. I had suspected for quite some time that the picture of her kids so prominently displayed might actually be one of those photos that just comes with the frame. She probably had different kids' pictures in her wallet—whatever came with the wallet. But of course that wasn't fair. Lynne certainly loved her kids... I mean, why else would she go through three nannies in the last four years?

"Jesus, Cynthia," she said, hanging up. "What's with the get-up?"

I smiled. Not dismayed. "My new look," I said. "My happy look."

"But perhaps not the most appropriate executive attire…" she warned.

"Yeah, well it doesn't matter now. I've got these forms for you. I already dropped off a copy at HR. I'm taking my early retirement."

"You're what?"

"Early retirement. I've hit the threshold. Twenty-five years of service and fifty years old."

"Are you sure?" Lynne asked.

"Oh, yeah, I'm definitely ready."

"No, I mean about qualifying. I don't think you have twenty-five years in."

She didn't mention that I didn't look fifty. I let it pass.

"I do. My twenty-fifth was back in September. But it's okay. I mean, I know we didn't have a party, and I didn't get a plaque like Sharon and Bob got last year. But I didn't hold it against you that you forgot." I smiled a sweet smile. "You were a little swamped back in the fall. The budget problems and all."

Lynne's face turned pink. "Oh, Cynthia, I think you may be making a big mistake. Fifty's awfully young to retire. You won't get a lot of pension without building up another ten years."

"I appreciate your concern. But I'm okay. Remember back last March, when the stock peaked during the takeover rumors? I cashed in my options."

"But Paul recommended that we don't. That it wouldn't look good at Corporate."

"I did anyway."

"Well," Lynne said, a bit more red-faced. "You are full of surprises. What will you do with yourself?"

I smiled. The first sincere smile I had given her that day, and very probably the first sincere smile I had ever given her.

"I have absolutely no idea."

Chapter 2

I MAY HAVE HAD NO IDEA of what I would do, but everyone else certainly did. The advice streamed in from every possible source, from my friends at work to the lady at the dry cleaners. They all knew exactly what to do with my retirement. I didn't mind all the advice. Since I had no opinions of my own, I took to asking everyone and writing all suggestions down in a notebook with Tweety Bird on the cover. I surveyed for one month.

The recommendations basically fell into three categories:
1. *See the World*
2. *Move to Florida*
3. *Play Golf*

Numbers two and three were often given in combination, but you could do one without the other, so I gave them separate identities.

Of course, 'See the World' had lots of subcategories. They were all quite fascinating. The old hippie with the long gray hair who works on the left side of the counter at the post office felt that I should see America first, especially the Grand Canyon and the Mississippi River. I liked both those ideas, but the greenish skinned guy who worked the right side of the counter was adamant that Europe was the place to go, Paris first. "No, Barcelona," said some pony-tailed person behind me in line. "Barcelona is the most romantic city in Europe." Which then started an argument between several postal patrons on romance in Europe. "Didn't you see that old movie about the Bridge of Sighs in Venice? The one with the girl who now has a middle-aged bosom but still the pretty face?" "Vienna. No question." "Any Greek island on a sunny day."

Then there were those, minority though they may be, that held for China, or Bali, or perhaps even South America. My image of South America was Butch Cassidy's Bolivia, so that suggestion ended up quite low on my list.

The main problem with 'See the World' was that as a full time retirement pursuit it would eat up the actual retirement dollars pretty quickly. I could swing one two-week trip per year, so with a probable twenty-five good years in me, I'd have a nice long list of wonderful places to see before I ever got down to Bolivia. But it also left me fifty weeks of the year to do something else.

For obvious reasons, everyone in New England detests winter. So Option 2—'Move to Florida'—was a very common suggestion. I'd been down to Florida a few times in January myself, and I had to admit that the absence of icy roads, freezing toes and chapped lips was not too bad.

My mother has lived in Florida for the past sixteen years. I love my mother dearly of course, but I have found that my love for her has grown even more dear with 1,114 miles between us.

And as for Golf, it is practically a religion down there, and pretty popular in Connecticut too. I play a couple of times every summer, and enjoy it very much. Golf could perhaps consume a retirement if living someplace warm. But then again, I loved my little house. And it was in Connecticut.

✐

My friends at work were in denial. I didn't kid myself though. I knew that only Gwen, my soul mate in Accounting for the past nine years, would really miss me, and maybe Lenny, who seemed to have a mild crush on me that he had not and would never act on. Everyone else expressing deep sorrow at my departure was really grieving for something else. Most I think just mourned the loss of stability. Change was vocally celebrated at Heritage Insurance as the essence of corporate culture, but secretly was greatly feared. I was as much a fixture as the coffee machine or the copier repairman, who seemed to live permanently in the Finance building. I was just supposed to be there.

The employees of Heritage Insurance—Heretics, Gwen and I called them—fell into two categories. First, there were the family folk, the staff who worked hard enough to keep their jobs, but would rather be home with the kids. In mission statements and at corporate functions, Heritage exalted the 'work/life balance'. In reality, family folk were despised.

For the other group of Heretics, mostly executives or soon-to-be executives, my departure put in question the very rationale for twelve-hour days, gall bladder attacks, and children who were strangers. They took full briefcases, laptops, and blackberries on what they called vacations. But if you could leave, and your life went on, and Heritage went on without you, well…what was the point?

I belonged to this second group of Heretics because I simply had nothing better to do. I moved with no apparent speed or design up the ranks of Finance. For the last ten years, I had a satisfactory plateau position, projecting cash flow. I had complex models that day-by-day predicted the cash, lots of it, coming in from premiums, mortgages and investments, and the cash going out, for claims (as little as possible) and for big expense accounts (as much as possible). I could predict this daily for one year, and monthly for three years. I could probably go out annually for another twenty-five years, if anyone had ever asked.

I was very good at this. It didn't really matter however. My models could be literally right on the money, or on the far side of completely stupid, and there were no consequences. It didn't matter how accurate I was. It only mattered that my reports were on time.

I had lunch almost every day with my best friend Gwen. Like me, Gwen had a critical yet somehow meaningless job in Finance. She analyzed long-term contracts. She took future dollars and discounted them to present day dollars, and took present day dollars and projected them into future dollars. She did this all day long, and she was serious about it with her boss, and dismissive the rest of the time.

Gwen was upset that I had not confided in her about my retirement.

"Well," I said. "I thought we would both cry every time we looked at each other, so I figured to keep that at a minimum."

"But now I have so much crying to catch up on. I'm way behind," she said completely dry-eyed.

We sat at Wah Lung and, as she did every day, she took an elastic band off her wrist (where she always kept one) and wrapped it around and around the end of her chopsticks, first around one stick, then around the other, then around both, making a little hinge. After years of eating Chinese, she never attempted to use the chopsticks without her little rubber assistance. It was as if she never intended to become good at it, and that was perfectly acceptable to her.

We liked Wah Lung because it was fairly horrible so there were never any Heretics there.

"What will you do when you retire?" I asked her.

Gwen was only forty-four and had only worked at Heritage for nine years, and so she had a long way to go. I saw this as an advantage because she could really give some imagination to the answer. I didn't figure I would get 'Florida' from her.

"You know what I'd love? I'd love to go to Art School, and take sculpture or life drawing. I'd carry a big portfolio and have a little paint on my cheek—on a cute spot of course—and I'd have a professor who looked like Al Pacino."

"Wow," I said. "That's really good. How much would you hate me if I stole your fantasy?"

"Steal away. By the time I retire, Pacino will be dead. And Jim and the kids will still be dragging me along, just assuming that I like all those boy things." She smiled in the way that said she was okay with life's disappointments. "I think at seventy I'll still be standing in the aisle at Home Depot while Jim sorts through the drill bits for a five-sixteenth when they've all gone metric."

"Can I still have lunch with you even though I'm retired?"

"Okay," she said.

"Do you think you'd ever go to Florida and play golf?"

"Sure," she said. "When I'm eighty."

On my last day of work, there was no big party or testimonial. Nobody gave me a watch or sang "For she's a jolly good fellow" or whatever it is they sing right now, probably some song that rhymes 'duty' with 'booty'. They did have a nice cake, though, which ensured a decent turnout.

And that was it. I got up the next morning and didn't go to work. I retired.

✐

My second day of retirement, I told my family. I had not mentioned it during my full four weeks' notice. I come from a long line of dedicated workaholics.

My father died at fifty-seven, keeling over the lathe at the factory where he had worked since the day after high school graduation. The doctors found cancer everywhere inside him. They figure he must have been in incredible pain for a very long time. He had never missed a day of work, never even punched in a minute late. He had changed the oil in my mother's car the Saturday before he died.

My mother took three days off for the wake and the funeral, and went back to work, inspecting springs in the same factory where Dad had worked. She worked until mandatory retirement at age sixty-five, then moved with her twin sister Lorraine to Florida, where, no kidding, she got herself a paper route. She's been delivering newspapers every morning at five-fifteen for the past sixteen years.

My mother simply could not comprehend retirement. But I didn't have to worry about breaking the news to her. I had sisters.

I told my sister Mary Ann over the phone. My relationship with Mary Ann was conducted mostly by phone. She only lived twelve miles away, but we had gotten into a comfortable habit of never looking each other in the eye without a family intermediary nearby.

Her reaction was exactly what I expected. She was terrified.

"Can't you tell them you've changed your mind? That you made a horrible mistake?"

"But I don't want to," I said. "I want to retire."

"You can't possibly have enough money to live on for thirty years or more...what if you live to a hundred?"

"That would be a shame, I guess."

"You know what I mean. You don't want to be destitute. Eating dog food."

"I hear Alpo is the most flavorful."

"Stop turning it all into a joke. There must be some way you can get your job back. Maybe you can tell them that you had a hormone imbalance that affected your judgment."

"Well, that would certainly make them want me back to analyze their cash."

"Cynthia, you had a fantastic job. The best job anyone in the family ever had. How can you just give it up...just like that?"

"It wasn't 'just like that'—I worked there for twenty-five years. I think I had a pretty good idea of whether I liked it or not."

"You'll never get a job like that again."

"But I don't want a job like that again. If I do ever work again, I want to do something entirely different. Maybe I'll clean swimming pools or plan weddings. Maybe I'll just want to sit at home and read."

"Now I know you're crazy. You can't do that. No one in our family can stay home."

"Well, you've got a point there," I said, trying to placate her so that I could get off the phone, and she could get my mother on speed-dial and do my dirty work for me. "Look, I'm really happy and excited about this. I'll find something wonderful to do. Don't worry."

"But it's what you are!"

"No, it's what I do. And I'm not going to do it anymore."
I changed the subject. "You know," I said, "I'm going to give
away all my business suits. Would you like to come over and
try some on?"

"Really?"

"Yeah," I said. "We'll have dinner. Just the two of us."

"That would be really nice," said Mary Ann. She paused.
"Angela too, of course."

"Of course," I said, as neither of us really wanted to be
alone together.

The next morning I bought a small oak table at a second
hand store, and dressed it up with my grandma's rose-covered
tablecloth. I added two wicker chairs with pale yellow
cushions, and arranged them by the window in my sunroom.

That afternoon, I sat at my little table, checking the birds
in Sibley's book and drinking oolong tea and eating organic
oranges wedge by wedge. Trying out retirement.

D.J. came to mow the lawn. D.J. was my neighbor's kid.
He was eighteen, and he'd been mowing my lawn since he was
twelve. Now that I was retired, I certainly could do it myself,
but I hated to let him go. Besides, I loved how he mowed
the lawn. Even as a little kid who had to reach up to push
the mower, with his legs far back for leverage—even then, he
mowed like a dream. He made perfectly straight swaths, with
ever so gentle curves around my two little trees.

I watched him; he was an artist. His overlap between
the rows was no more than two inches. The grass height was
perfect, not left too long, not stubby and scorched, and the
grass was green and no crabgrass dared grow. The mower
made quite a racket, and yet it felt completely quiet watching
him. It was kind of ...soothing.

I sipped my oolong tea, and enjoyed the drone of the motor and the fragrance of the grass drifting into the sunroom. D.J. was probably at it for a good half-hour before I realized that he wasn't alone. Sitting right below me on the steps to the sunroom was a young girl.

She was somewhere between thirteen and sixteen. She had the same long straight hair of every girl her age, held up in back with one of those toothy butterfly clips. Her jeans were unhemmed, and dirty at the heels from being dragged around behind her every day like reluctant puppies. Though it was quite warm, she wore a hoodie with "Juicy" written across the back. I only caught a glimpse of her face now and then, when she turned to watch D.J. as he pushed the mower over by the fence. She was without any color in her cheeks whatsoever. Pale eyes too, rimmed thickly with black. Her little pudgy hands gave away her youth. She still had fat baby fingers, and her nails were short and decorated with glittery and badly chipped blue polish.

A few minutes after I noticed her, she noticed me. Her shoulders suddenly stiffened in the recognition of being watched. She turned around and looked up into the window, her lips tight and her eyes narrow, her sullen glare just a few felonies away from an FBI wanted poster.

I smiled and she frowned back. I took three bottles of spring water from the fridge. Like everyone else in the world, I had forgotten that you could drink water right from the tap.

I went out the sunroom door, squeezing by her on the steps, and sat down next to her. I handed her a bottle of water, and put the other two on the bottom step.

"Are those both for D.J.?" she asked.

"Yes."

"Well that figures. He gets two."

"He's working," I said. "You're sitting."

"Whatever," she said and pulled her sleeve down over her hand, using the ribbed cuff as leverage to open her bottle.

"Are you dating D.J."? I asked.

She kind of snorted. "Oh yeah. We're going steady. We're a-courtin'."

"I apologize for being old. Are you and D.J. hooking up?"

A disdainful snort. "No. I'm just hanging out."

"No school today?" I asked, although the bus had stopped here this morning and picked up the whole troop of hollering kids.

"The seniors got out at noon. D.J. has a class trip, leaves tonight, and so he wanted to get your lawn mowed so he'd have extra money."

"That certainly makes sense. For D.J., that is. You're not a senior."

"Yeah, I'm missing Study Hall. I'm missing Art Appreciation. I'm missing Hygiene."

"School is more boring that watching D.J. mow the lawn?"

"Fuck, yeah," she said. Then her surliness faded for just a second. "I don't know. There's something about the way he mows. He's so straight and careful. It's kind of … soothing."

Chapter 3

I ARRIVED AT CHURCH THAT SUNDAY one minute late. I slid into the pew where Angela had saved me my regular space, and she gave me one of her benevolent but reproachful looks.

But Mass had started so there was no scolding, and we had our nice quiet time together. I went to church solely to watch her pray. I knew what grace was by the serenity in her face.

Angela was the middle child. Two years younger than Mary Ann and year older than I. She was blond and cream-skinned, with full soft lips, unlike anyone else in the family. Maybe unlike anyone else in the world. She had a light around her like in holy pictures. Like a halo. Sometimes I could tell by the way her husband and her children looked at her that they could see it too.

Angela prayed and sang and took communion, while I received my full share of blessings by being next to her. Holiness by association.

After Mass, I followed her to her house in my own car, where we made Sunday dinner together as usual. She didn't mention my retirement, although I was certain Mary Ann must have told her.

I knew I should have told Angela first but I was afraid. Angela was the only person in the world whose approval I ever needed.

We made chicken with mashed potatoes and gravy, and green beans and cornbread. Even now that her kids were adults and not too likely to groan over brussels sprouts, we always prepared food on Sunday that everyone loved. We wanted only contentment and happiness for Sunday dinner.

John came in from the garage where he spent most of his life, and Angela's kids pulled up in strikingly similar maroon SUVs. Karen and Michael and their spouses, both named Sean. We had gotten to calling them Sean-Boy and Sean-Girl, as a kind of takeoff on the Waltons, and although the kids were too young to get the reference, they seemed to take it in good enough humor. Michael and Sean-Girl had a five-month-old son. When they were expecting, Angela confided in me that she hoped that they'd name the baby Joseph, after our father. She had always regretted that she hadn't named her own son after our dad.

"Tell them," I said.

"Oh no, I just couldn't," Angela had replied. "I mean, it would only result in unhappiness. Either they'd name the baby Joe because I asked, and they'd resent it, or they wouldn't, and they'd feel guilty."

So Angela said nothing, and even though I was tempted quite a few times to drop a hint to Michael (which would have to be a very large hint, since men don't seem to catch anything subtle), I managed to respect Angela's wishes. And they named the baby Max. Angela has a least two friends who have dogs named Max.

We had a nice loud normal dinner around the kitchen table, with the men talking to the men, and the women talking to the women. John went back to the garage, and the kids went to the den with the baby. I heard the basketball game come on.

And Angela and I had our conversation over the dishes. Angela had quite a good dishwasher, but we hardly ever used it on Sundays. She washed and I dried as we had for the last forty years. For all our lives, all our confidences were exchanged over the sink. I knew which of her boyfriends were good kissers, and what technique I should use to shave my legs, and she knew that Paul Deacon called me Ape-Girl, and that I had shoplifted a lipstick once, and how in high school I rolled up my waistband to make my skirt shorter as soon as I was out the door. And we also knew each other's deep hurt of rejection and delight of true love.

"I've retired," I said, as she handed me the gravy boat.

"So I hear," she said. "Are you happy?"

"Yes!" I said. She was the only one so far who asked me that. "I'm seeking opinions on what to do with all my new spare time."

"Well, I know you'll figure it out. You'll do something wonderful. You'll be something wonderful. I've been waiting for you to do more than add numbers for twenty-five years."

"Like what?"

Angela didn't look at me but instead looked through the window over the sink and into her back yard.

"See that orange cat?" she said.

I leaned near her. "Yeah, sitting like a king on your porch. Did you get a new pet?"

"No, it's the neighbors'. His name is Riley. He sits on his own back porch all morning, but when the sun moves off, he comes over here and sits on our porch. The whole purpose of his existence is to follow the sun and make his own life as pleasant as possible."

"So you think in my retirement that I should be like Riley?"

"No. You've already been Riley for way too many years. No," she said. "No. Don't be the cat. Be the porch."

There was no use in asking Angela what she meant. For as long as I remember, Angela spoke in parables, in fables, in metaphors. She never explained herself.

"What the heck is that supposed to mean?" Mary Ann would say. Or I would. Or sometimes even Mom and Dad.

But Angela never explained.

I remember the first story she ever told me. I was seven and she was eight. She was reading from her book of Aesop's Fables. The Grasshopper and the Ant. On the next to the last page, during the hard winter, the Grasshopper has asked the Ant for something to eat.

"Why come right in, said the Ant," Angela recited. "I've enjoyed your singing all summer, and it always cheered me up while I was working so hard. Your singing made my work easier, and the least I could do to repay you for your wonderful gift is to share my harvest with you. Why don't you stay all winter?"

"That's not what it says," I protested. "That's not how the story goes."

"That's how it goes in my edition," Angela replied. I can still hear her saying "my edition" in her eight-year old voice.

The phone was ringing when I got home from Angela's. This was more than my mother being aware of my schedule. She could, with complete accuracy, also tell you what I was wearing, and, in a pinch, could probably tell you every item in my hamper and every dish in my sink that should have been in their respective washing machines.

"You're retiring?" she hollered in my ear.

"Hi, Mom," I said. "Yeah, "I've got a great pension, and I figure it's time to do something fun."

"God help me, but I just can't understand how I begat such a reckless kid," she said, just as if I had quit school at sixteen to join the circus, rather than earning both an undergraduate and graduate degree, and then working twenty-five years for the same company, and with an attendance record to rival my dad's, to boot.

"I know, I know." I commiserated with her on my flightiness. After all, I did get a divorce twenty-two years ago.

"I suppose you'll want to come down here," Mom said. "I can do over my little sewing room and you can have a bedroom here with Lorraine and me."

Now that certainly surprised me. Here was a woman who knew her children so well she could tell you the exact amount of change in our purses, by denomination, and she had completely missed the boat.

"Oh Mom, that's a really wonderful idea. But I thought I would stay in Connecticut. At least for a while."

"Okay," she said, very quickly. "You know, I'm doing ceramics now too, and I've got my macramé and everything in the sewing room…but you know we'd love to have you."

And she surprised me again. The relief in her voice was so obvious. My mother had a life of her own; it didn't revolve around me. And I was filled with affection for this old lady who would invite me to live with her, but was glad I said no.

"Aunt Lorraine wants to say hello."

And Aunt Lorraine didn't surprise me. She said the same thing she'd been saying at least once a week for twenty-one years.

"You need to find a husband."

"Right," I said. "Do you have any that you don't want?"

"Yeah," she cackled, sounding in her twinship exactly like my mother, only with a cigarette and a highball. "I got four of them."

Chapter 4

M Y SISTERS WERE HAPPY TO come over the very next evening to raid my closet.

I made dinner first, the special type of dinner we had when there was no one else around. Specifically, we didn't have dinner at all. We had desserts—apple and blueberry pies warm from the oven, which we ate a la mode. The three of us ate the better part of both pies.

After dinner the girls picked me clean. They tried on outfits and threw them on the bed and on the floor, like we did playing dress-up when we were kids. Mary Ann hogged the full-length mirror, and so Angela kept climbing up on my bed, balancing clumsily on the mattress, checking herself out in the dresser mirror.

"I love this," Angela said, balancing wide-legged on the bed, wearing my black Ann Klein suit and sweat socks. "It will be perfect for PTA nights. I'll intimidate all those moms who think I just don't understand their little Ashley."

"What do you think?" said Mary Ann in a gray pin-stripe pantsuit. Do you think it's too much?"

"You look great," I said. "Take the lavender silk blouse with that."

"Well, I promise to take good care of it. And remember, we're just borrowing these things. You'll go back to work and you'll want them back."

"Cynthia's not going back to work," Angela said. "And she can't have this back. It's already my favorite outfit."

We filled the back seat of Mary Ann's car with skirts and slacks, blouses and jackets—with shoes and scarves and earrings to match, and the girls drove off.

My closet was empty except for the most forlorn (or tiny) of my office clothes.

I made the trip the next morning to the battered women's shelter, bringing them everything but a few pieces that were in such horrible condition that they would only make battered women feel worse. Except for my jeans and sweaters, and the new outfit from Lovely, I saved only one article of clothing—a leather skirt, size six. There was a time, albeit of short duration and long ago, when I was sexy.

With my closet bare of all those sensible suits, I went back to Lovely. Miranda was there, and so was the owner, who had graduated from the Ronald McDonald School of Cosmetology. I had a wonderful splurge. I didn't even have to spend any of my retirement money, since I had also received a nice big check for five-and-a-half weeks for accrued vacation. So I bought flouncy skirts and beaded belts, lace blouses and crocheted sweaters and thick silver jewelry. I bought a tapestry tote in antique ivory, and moved everything out of my sensible black Coach handbag right in the store.

When the owner was out of earshot, Miranda also directed me to their competition.

"There's this store out in Watertown," she whispered. "They carry lots of this same stuff, and some that's even sweeter. And their prices are great. I buy lots of cool dresses there—I just don't wear them here."

The next morning I went to the tiny bedroom that I used as an office, with my computer and file cabinets all organized with my paid and unpaid bills and tax returns. I took all my Accounting textbooks from the shelf in the bookcase and threw them in the trash.

Chapter 5

THE WEATHER TURNED WARM EARLY. Sunday dinner at Angela's moved outdoors and became hotdogs and hamburgers. No one complained that there was no big sit-down dinner. Even John set up a work table outside of the garage and tinkered in the filtered sunlight under the big maple.

We had a good crowd that Sunday. Besides Angela's crew, Mary Ann and her husband Frank had come, and three of their four kids, and assorted grandchildren.

With finger foods and paper plates we had no dishes to wash, but at the end of the day Angela and I stood over the sink anyway, needlessly washing the plastic forks and spoons.

"Well, I think your pores are open," Angela said as we were finishing up.

"What?"

"Remember, when we were kids, Mom wouldn't let us go outside in winter if we had just bathed? Because 'our pores were open'."

"Yeah. I never understood that. What kind of germs get inside your pores?"

Angela turned and leaned against the sink. "I always thought that it was wonderful—to have your pores open. To be able to absorb the world right through your skin." She smiled. "Imagine how wise you'd be."

"I guess."

"Well, you've had a month to do nothing, to let your pores open up, so to speak. So, being open, you'll recognize what it is you're supposed to be."

I laughed. "Is someone sending me a sign from heaven?"

Angela frowned. "Go ahead—snicker. There are signs around us every day. But we are just not open to them." She took the towel from my hand. "But you are... your pores are open."

"Okay, okay," I said. "I'll look for the sign."

It didn't placate her. She knocked on my forehead the way Mary Ann used to when I was being a dense little kid.

"You don't have to look. It'll be right there."

On Friday, D.J. showed up just before 3:00. Although he lived just two houses down, he parked his truck out front and unloaded the mower.

The sullen girl was with him again, and she sat down on the steps as she had last week, and put herself in the lawn-mowing trance, as did I. I let myself just enjoy the enveloping din and the clean straight lines for several minutes, then I got up and got four bottles of water. I walked out and put two on the bottom steps and two by the girl's side.

"Geez," she said. "There must be a sale at Stop and Shop."

It was extremely hot, but she was again dressed in the same Juicy sweatshirt. Her face had more color this week— pink from the heat.

She took a long swig of water, and let some drip down the front of her shirt. She held the cold bottle up to her forehead. The gesture made her suddenly look older than I had first thought, but a second later the image was gone and she was a very little girl again.

She reached into her backpack and took out a pack of cigarettes. She shook one loose rather clumsily. A new habit.

I have a talent. Well, Talent is probably not the appropriate word. Certainly not Gift. An Ability. A Perception. I don't use it much since it usually is not welcome. But I pulled it out now.

"So when is the baby due?" I asked.

She recoiled like I had struck her, but recovered almost immediately. Her eyes turned into narrow kohl-lined slits. She turned the open water bottle upside down, letting the water pour down the steps, stood up and stomped off to the truck. With gestures so overblown they would have made Bette Davis laugh, the girl threw her bag in the back of the truck, whirled around to face me, and dramatically lit her cigarette. Then she climbed in and sat in the wavy heat of the cab. She rolled down the window just slightly to knock the ashes off her cigarette. But I noticed she was just letting it burn down; she never put it to her lips.

I waited until she flicked the butt out the window. I walked over to the truck and opened the door.

"It's way too hot in there," I said. "You'll have a stroke. And you're missing the best part—D.J. is about to go around the trees. Come in and watch from the sunroom."

I turned around and walked back to the house, trying not to look behind me. I remember Angela doing the same thing when Michael misbehaved in the supermarket. And sure enough, the girl slowly slid out of the truck and followed me in a practiced nonchalance.

I scooped up her unopened water and brought it in, though I put it back in the fridge and got her a cold one. We sat in my yellow-cushioned chairs, silently watching D.J. cut gentle curves around the trees.

When the main feature was over, I spoke. "I'm Cynthia Breault. What's your name?"

She looked away. I half-expected her to turn her little imaginary key with fingertips to her lips.

"Shannon Miller," she finally said.

Well, that kind of exuberant response deserved a reward, so I went to the fridge and got two Popsicles. I could say that I keep them for when my sisters' grandchildren come over, but they are for me. I love Popsicles.

She chose the cherry. We sat and sucked on our Popsicles while D.J. took out the weed-whacker and trimmed around the fence.

"I don't like this part," I said. "There's something mean about it."

Shannon didn't respond, but she sucked slower, so perhaps she was considering it.

All the muffled noise from outside stopped. D.J. picked up his shirt hem and wiped his face. This, I could tell, was the highlight for Shannon. He strolled to the door.

"Don't you rat me out," Shannon hissed. But the menace of her threat was undermined by the cheerfulness of her bright red Popsicle lips.

I gave her a serious nod of conspiracy. D.J. came in – flushed, sweaty—radiant actually, if you could use that word for a boy. He was at that moment the healthiest person on the planet.

"All done," he said. He considered the two of us sitting there, the empty Popsicle wrappers and sticks like the evidence of a decadent orgy. "Hey," he said, "You two hitting it off?"

We both answered at exactly the same time. "No," said Shannon, but she was drowned out by my loud, "Absolutely."

Shannon went to the kitchen and came back with a popsicle for D.J. I was both impressed and aggravated. Impressed that she had the good manners to offer D.J. what we had obviously been eating. And aggravated that she had the bad manners to help herself to a stranger's freezer. I concentrated on that little generous spark.

And I was curious to know more.

"Shannon and I have decided to make cookies for you next week."

"Great," he said, though the suspicion level rose in his voice. It wouldn't take much familiarity with Shannon to doubt her enthusiasm for cookie-making. "I like chocolate chip. With nuts."

"Perfect," I said. "Shannon, what kind of cookies do you like?"

"Oreos," she said. She smirked. As she followed D.J. out the door, she turned back to me and stuck out her cherry tongue. And gave me the finger.

It was sweet not to have to shop on the weekend. I waited until Tuesday to find the store that Miranda at Lovely had told me about. I had neglected to get the name of the shop, but there's really only one commercial street in Watertown. I figured I'd recognize it.

Watertown is a secret little gem in Connecticut. The state has lots of picturesque towns with quaint Main Streets that the tourists flood in the summer and the shopkeepers survive through the winter by visiting each other. But Watertown is off the list, and it seems the inhabitants like it that way. It has a nice Main Street, but not quite as quaint as the tourist towns, and it appears that there might be some kind of ordinance that ensures that they don't get too 'special' and start attracting out-of-towners.

I drove slowly down Main Street looking for a shop that might fit Miranda's description. In between the hardware store and jewelry store was a shop called Maya Maria. The parking in front was parallel, and although there was space enough for two cars, I didn't even try it. I can't parallel park. I couldn't do it in high school driver's ed, and I haven't tried it since. I figured that if I could get to fifty and never have to parallel park, I could probably get to eighty without needing it. I drove two blocks further to the CVS drugstore (which was probably erected to ensure the town didn't get cute) and parked in their lot. Signs warned "CVS Customers Only," so I went in and bought some toothpaste.

I walked back the two blocks and stopped and looked at Maya Maria's window. There was a beautiful embroidered purse, and a shiny red slicker and a big umbrella with purple polka-dots, but also a mannequin wearing only a silver blouse. Her bottom half, only partially hidden by the umbrella, was bare.

I went in. Clothes were hung on the racks in no order— not by color or by style or by size. The racks were sparse, but the disorganization made them look messy anyway. A girl sat on a stool behind the counter, reading a romance novel.

"Hi," I said. "I'm told this is the place to come for cool clothes."

She reluctantly looked up from her book. "Well, our inventory's a little down right now. But look around," she added, not helpfully.

"Where are the raincoats like the red one in the window?" I asked.

"That's the last one. It's a size two."

"Are you getting any more in?"

"Um," she said. "I don't know."

"Look, is the owner around?"

"No. She's gone."

"When do you expect her back?"

At that the salesgirl finally put down her book, got off her stool and leaned over the counter, beckoning me closer with a come-here gesture.

"No one knows," she said. "Maria—that's the owner—she took off two months ago with some guy. It was like two weeks before we even knew what had happened. At first her husband kept saying she went to see a sick relative. Then he finally told us that she just took off. He doesn't know if she's coming back. He asked us to try to keep the shop open for a while. Just in case, you know."

"That's why you're down on inventory?"

"Yeah," she nodded. "Maria had ordered most of the summer stuff, but a lot of it is sold now, and no one knows whether to order some more...or even how to. I figure we'll close up pretty soon."

"Wow," I said.

I walked around the store, examining everything in light of this information. There were some heavy sweaters from Peru that should have been put away for the winter. There were a few beautiful sheer skirts from India, but only in extra-small and extra-extra large. A couple of shelves held Mexican pottery and hand-blown glass vases and a decent coat of dust.

In the back of the store were some large baskets. One basket had umbrellas, a few in their tightly bound state look liked the polka-dot type in the window. One opened into a red umbrella strewn with white tulips, dancing in the rain.

Another basket held scarves, thrown one over the other, some folded, many not. I rummaged through the pile, and found a large scarf with red gondolas riding through the Venice canals. I took the red-and-white umbrella and the scarf over to the display window. I removed the purple umbrella, and opened the tulip umbrella near the red raincoat. Then I took the scarf and tied it, pareo-style, around the naked mannequin. It would probably be hours before the clerk looked up from her book and wondered why the window looked different.

When I left the store, I stood on the street and contemplated the shop window for quite a while. I went back into the store.

"Do you have a phone number for the owner's husband?" I asked.

The next day, I took out my Tweety Bird notebook and turned to the page where I had copied the name from the business card that the clerk had handed to me. *Benson V. Shelter, Donovan & Shelter, Attorneys-At-Law.* I wondered what the V was for. For a lawyer, maybe Versus.

I called. "Benson V. Shelter, please," I said to the woman who answered the phone. "My name is Cynthia Breault," I told her. "I would like to speak to Mr. Shelter about Maya Maria."

A minute later he picked up. "Ms. Brown?"

"It's Breault," I said, "Cynthia Breault. B-R-E-A-U-L-T, but pronounced Bro, like in 'Hey, Bro, wassup?'"

There was no polite chuckle. Oh well.

"I'm told you're calling about Maya Maria. Are you a customer, or a vendor?"

"A customer, sort of. Umm…I was in the shop yesterday, and I think I could help you get that store back on its feet."

"You could, huh? Help me?" His voice was a big raw bruise.

"Look," I said. "Can I come by? Talk about it?"

There was silence for several long seconds. "Yeah, all right." I could almost see him run his hand through his hair in that resigned way that men do when they are giving in to a woman. "How about at the end of the day? 6 PM. Do you know O'Hara's?"

A little tavern on Route 4, O'Hara's had been spiffied up last year, and now was cozy instead of dilapidated.

"I'll be there," I said. "I'll be wearing a bright yellow sweater. You can't miss me."

"I'll wear a suit. Medium gray. You can't miss me."

Well, well. A little humor after all. I gave him the chuckle that he had withheld on my bit of wit.

It was dark in O'Hara's, especially coming in from the brilliant late afternoon sun. As my eyes adjusted I saw six men, five of them in suits that could be gray. One guy sat in a booth facing the door and gave me an almost imperceptible head nod. So I strode over in my yellow sweater, pretending I was still a businesswoman in a gray suit.

"Hi," I said. "Cynthia Breault." And I slid into the booth opposite him.

Benson V. Shelter was a tall (at least he appeared so, sitting down), slim man, probably about forty. His hairline hadn't receded at all, sending a conflicting signal between the youthful hair and the stress-lined brow beneath it. He had a big Magnum PI mustache that had gone out of style at least a decade before, but sort of looked like it belonged there.

"Well," I started right in, "Have you been in the shop recently?"

"No," he said. "I was over there a few weeks ago, but lately I've just called the girls once a week to find out their hours, and I send them their checks."

"It's pretty bad," I said. He scowled at me and I could see a wave of defensiveness pass between us over the table. I smiled quickly and shook my head lightly to push it away. "Don't get me wrong. It's a beautiful store. And you had wonderful merchandise for summer—it must have been wonderful because it's all gone."

He nodded just a little, like the way he had acknowledged me when I walked in. He must be a terrible poker player.

"No one has reordered," I continued. "No one has cleaned either. The floor is dirty, the shelves are dusty, and you are beginning to get a nice collection of fly carcasses in the window."

"Okay," he said. "I'll go over there and talk to the girls." Mr. Problem-Solver.

"Come on. What are you paying them? A dollar over minimum wage? Where are they supposed to get any initiative? The problem is not the clerks—it's the management. You don't have any."

"And you are going to supply that?"

"Sure. I can get the place clean and stocked with beautiful things. I can make sure the store opens when it should and that the customers are pampered a little. It's all you need."

"And where did you get all this experience?"

"I don't have any. None. Nada. I'm an accountant, retired."

He smiled then. It may even have been genuine, but with lawyers it can be a little hard to tell.

"Look," I said. "You need a manager. Maybe just temporarily," I added, to keep him from clouding over again. "You can go out and find someone with experience. And that's okay, if you want to do that. But the thing is, I'm here and I want to. I like fixing things and I have a newly acquired interest in fashion."

"Do you have a plan?"

37

"A hazy one. I'll figure out the vendors and get some merchandise delivered right away. From what I understand, the key to retail is to get the inventory sold before you have to pay for it... I hope the bills have been paid and the credit's still good?"

"Yeah, I've paid all the bills."

"So I'd go in tomorrow and order. Then I'll clean. It should be pretty easy with the store so empty."

"So, Cindy...can I call you Cindy?"

"You can, but you'd be the only one."

"No nickname?"

"Nope. Just Cynthia."

"So, Cynthia," he started again. "What do you want for your services?"

"Double what you pay the clerks. And five percent of the gross sales."

"What? You want a cut?"

"A commission. It's in your best interest after all. You only have to pay me a lot if the store's a success."

Benson V. Shelter looked down at his hands, then back up at me. "So why would I care? If the store's a success, I mean. Why shouldn't I just close down?"

"You can. And maybe you should. But you haven't yet." He looked down again, and I spoke to his forehead. "I know that your wife is...away. But here's the way I see it. If she comes back and you want her back, you can give her this wonderful store that you've taken care of for her in her absence. But...if that doesn't happen, and she doesn't come back or you don't want her back, then you have a successful store that you might be able to trade in the settlement for something that you really do want."

He laughed then, but it was not a very happy sound.

"Have you ever thought about law school?" he asked.

"No, but I'll write it down." And I took out my Tweety Bird notebook and added it to my long list.

I got a puzzled but much nicer laugh. He took out his key chain, removed a key and slid it over to my side of the booth. He kept his finger on the key and looked me in the eye for the first time.

"One month," he said. "I'll give you one month."

I held his gaze while I thought fast. I'd won staring contests before, but I was twelve.

"One month? To do what? Show a profit? Not lose more than you're already losing? What?"

"To convince me I shouldn't close, I guess."

"Three months," I countered.

"Two."

"Two."

Benson V. Shelter took his finger from the key and I picked it up.

"So here's an important question," I said. "Where do I park the car?"

Chapter 6

---❦---

I ARRIVED THE NEXT MORNING JUST before ten, maneuvering into the tiny parking space that Benson V. Shelter had directed me to in the alley behind the store. I waited in my car until after ten though, and walked around to the front entrance instead of using my key. I didn't want to alarm the salesgirl, as she didn't know I was coming.

It was a different girl. Thirty or so, dressed in the kind of clothes that Maya Maria sold, if there had been anything to sell. A loose-fitting sundress of a burgundy Indian cotton, with a sleeveless tee in pale yellow underneath. Pretty and modest.

"Hi," I said, walking up to the counter. "I'm Cynthia. Mr. Shelter has hired me to look after the store for a little while."

Her jaw tightened. "Maria's not coming back?"

"I really don't know. But it's been an awfully long time."

And she started to cry. It unnerved me; I didn't anticipate confronting a friend.

"I'm sorry," she said, grabbing a tissue from under the counter. "I just keep telling myself it's just an extended vacation. That any day now she'll be back."

"You could be right," I said. "I'm going to try and keep the store as nice as possible, so she'll be happy when she comes back."

"Okay," she said. She smiled a little. "I'm Kate."

Kate took me into the back room. Except for several stacks of big baskets, the shelving for merchandise was as bare as the store. One corner of the room was set up as an office, with desk, computer, a file cabinet and a small bookcase with catalogs.

"The password's Maya," said Kate.

I spent the next couple of hours exploring the computer and the file cabinet. I found some old financial statements where the store looked okay, if not spectacular. Most useful to me were all the old invoices, sorted neatly by vendor. Maria had three main vendors—all importers, which was good news for me since I didn't know one thing about bringing goods into the country. There was an importer who brought in clothes and baskets and pottery from Mexico and Latin America. Then there was one for the same type of products from India and Southeast Asia. And one jewelry importer with merchandise from all over the world. Perhaps I could run a nice little shop with just those three vendors, at least for a while.

I matched this year's invoices to the items in the catalogs. No wonder everything was gone. What Maria had ordered was beautiful.

Kate and I spent the afternoon, unfortunately uninterrupted by a single customer, deciding what to buy. I wanted some summer merchandise right away, so as not to miss the whole season, but I concentrated on the most inexpensive items, since we'd probably have to mark them down by the end of June. We poured over the catalogs and drew up a list of bright sundresses and embroidered skirts and blouses, and even a couple of bikinis. Then I got on the phone with the vendors and explained our emergency. They agreed to ship as much as they could by the end of the day, with the rest to follow within two days.

That done, Kate and I spent the afternoon housecleaning. Kate dragged around the dust cloth half-heartedly at first, but when she saw that I was serious, and as the shop began to look better, she added a tiny speck of enthusiasm.

At the end of the day, we had a clean floor, dustless shelves, no flies, three large shipments pending, and $64.80 in the till.

Chapter 7

Early Saturday morning, I packed a box with odds and ends and drove over to the shop. I struggled a little with the back door key, and left my stash in the dark hallway as I ran my hands along the walls, searching for the light switches, which, it turned out, Shaquille O'Neal had installed.

I got to work on the window. I dragged the old-fashioned mannequin from the window, and gave her a time-out in the corner of the storage room. Then I made three trips carrying armfuls of the big baskets. I stacked them in the window pyramid style, and from my own stuff I added bright rolled-up beach towels in the top three, so they stood sticking up from the basket like colorful French breads. Out went the red raincoat and umbrella.

By that time Kate had strolled in. I sent her out to the street to check out the display.

"It's pretty nice," she said. "But Maria was going to send back those baskets. They weren't what she ordered."

"Well, we've got almost forty of them, and not much else to sell. We have baskets and tee shirts and scarves. So today we are going to sell baskets and tee shirts and scarves."

There were quite of few pretty tees but they weren't displayed very well, as they were all folded neatly on shelves against the wall, So I had Kate take them down, and hang them on the rack right in the front of the store, moving the heavy sweaters to the back.

"Maria likes all the tees folded, not hanging," said Kate.

"Right… But we've got to fill up all these racks."

We also got the steamer out and freshened all the scarves and hung them on hangers.

From my box, I unpacked coconut-scented candles and pretty soon the smell of old llamas from the Peruvian sweaters gave way to something that vaguely approached suntan lotion.

The young girl I met the first day arrived. "Weren't we going to return those baskets?"

"Heather, this is Cynthia," Kate explained.

Heather paused. "Don't I know you from someplace?"

And customers came in. Not a lot, but a few. By eleven-thirty, I caved on the baskets, and we marked them down to three dollars over cost. At the end of the day, we had sold nine of the baskets, five pastel tees, and one scarf; there was $348.95 in the register.

"Pretty lousy," I said, filling out the bank deposit slip.

"Are you kidding?" said Kate. "We had more customers in the store today than we have had in weeks."

We were just getting ready to lock up when the phone rang.

"Maya Maria," I said self-consciously.

"Hi," the voice said. "It's Ben."

Ben? I didn't know anyone named Ben. "I'm sorry," I began.

"Ben Shelter," he said.

Oh, Benson V. Shelter. "Hi, Ben," I said, and the two women picked their heads up immediately.

"How is it going?"

I thought about the fifty-seven days left. "We had a good day today," I said in my most cheery voice. "Quite a few customers. And I've got a lot of merchandise coming in on Monday, I hope."

"Well that's great," he said, but he didn't sound great. In fact, he sounded distinctly put out.

Oh shit, I thought. It's been three days and I'm telling him I can do better than his wife. And he'll find out soon enough I barely covered the cost of the merchandise, let alone my salary. I toned down the enthusiasm. "Well maybe not great," I said, "but we're all doing our best to hold it together."

It sounded lame to me, but the girls smiled and Ben seemed to buy it. "That's good," he said, "You know, I have to be up in that area for a meeting on Monday. Will you be there if I drop by about noon?"

"The store won't be open but I'll be waiting for the UPS delivery. So come on over. And bring the checkbook."

I thought Mass would never end. I couldn't wait to tell Angela all about the store.

For this early in June, it was a scorcher, and Angela, John and I sat under the maple and drank iced tea. It was too hot to cook. I suggested that we just have ice cream sundaes instead. John gave Angela a look that plainly said, "Your sister is out of her mind." John hasn't missed a meal since he left his mother's breast. So he stood over the hot grill, tending hamburgers that we didn't want. We listened to the hiss of the grease hitting the coals and just enjoyed the quiet heat. Michael and Karen and the two Seans had gone into New York for the weekend to see a play and walk around the city. Angela was babysitting for Max, and he sat on a blanket and played with some kind of toy that looked like a frog with wheels. He mostly sucked on it, but once in a while he slapped it to the ground. This seemed to please him.

We ate our hamburgers plain, since no one felt like making the walk to the kitchen for the ketchup and pickles. We just ate them to eat, dropping the paper plates on the grass to be picked up later. Maybe when the sun went in. Or if we got lucky the ants might carry them off.

John asked me (already knowing the answer) when was the last time I changed my oil.

"Why, the last time you did it for me of course," I answered, and he happily went off to take care of it. "I'll pay you for the oil," I called after him.

"You certainly will," he said.

"He doesn't have to do that," I said to Angela.

"Oh, please," she said. "He needs it. Everything's all caught up here. A lot of guys would be ecstatic to have no chores, but I think John is on the verge of clinical depression. Yesterday, I put the baby's spoon down the garbage disposal just to give him something to do. I'm figuring to pull the cord off the toaster tonight."

Max managed to hit himself on the nose with the frog-car, but it was too hot for a tantrum. He just let the tears roll down his face with his mouth silently open. I picked him up and kissed him, trying not to cuddle him too tightly. He held me by the v-neck on my blouse and soon fell asleep.

"You were absolutely right," I finally said to Angela. "I saw the sign almost immediately." And I told her about Maya Maria: about Maria's disappearance, and how I convinced Benson V. Shelter to let me run the store; and changing the window and selling stuff that had been ordered by mistake. "It's perfect for me," I said.

"That's nice," Angela said.

"Nice? How about my destiny and all that? Shouldn't you be thrilled for me, and of course smug that you predicted it?"

"It's very nice. I think it must be quite satisfying to go into a place like that and be creative and see immediate results. Very satisfying," she repeated.

"But why aren't you excited for me? Are you trying to tell me that I got the wrong sign?"

"I'm not saying that. I just think that there's something special for you out there, and it probably doesn't involve overpriced baskets."

"Oh, come on, be happy for me," I pleaded.

"I am," Angela said. "Because this will probably be fun for a while, and maybe it will lead you to what you are really meant for."

"Is my life a waste if I'm good at selling clothes? What if this is just what I always wanted?"

Angela smiled in that serene way that makes me want to kiss her on the top of her head. She leaned back in her lawn chair and said to the sky, "What was the best Christmas present that you ever got?"

"The Snow White doll. No question."

"Do you remember the story of the Snow White doll?"

"Just vaguely," I answered, although I knew the story like I knew my prayers. But, oh, to hear it again, especially Angela's version.

"Well," she began, "that was the year that Mary Ann and I both had whooping cough. Mom wouldn't leave us, not for a minute. It was just before Christmas, and she couldn't shop. She had to send Dad out to buy the presents. Dad, who was hard pressed to buy a birthday card for Mom. Remember the time she sent him out for more bows for the Christmas presents and he came back with Hanukkah bows? Mom was beside herself, but he said that they were very pretty and on sale too, and so the Christmas presents that year had red and green paper and blue and white bows...that may have been the same year. Anyway, she gave him our Christmas lists that we had written to Santa, and told him to do his best.

"On Christmas Eve, it got to be quite late before Mom and Dad started putting our presents under the tree. Mary Ann got the right side, near the piano, and I was on the left, near the door, and your presents were right in the middle, right under the center of the tree. Mom counted every present and made sure we all got exactly the same number of gifts. 'They'll count,' she said, and you know we always did. She actually put away one present for Mary Ann that she saved for her birthday, so it would all be even-steven. She put out books, and games, and lacy socks, and ribbons, and a little horse with hair you could comb for Mary Ann, and a pogo stick for me. Remember that pogo stick? That was my all-time favorite.

"After everything was laid out and looked so beautiful, Mom sat admiring it all. Then she saw what was missing. 'Where's Cynthia's doll?' Mom asked Dad. 'What doll?' he said. 'Look at all this great stuff!' But no, Mom said, 'Cynthia has to have a doll. She just has to have a doll.' Well, you were five years old. You had never had a Christmas or a birthday without a doll.

"And Mom made Dad go out again late Christmas Eve to find a doll. It wasn't like now, where there're huge stores all open twenty-four hours. No, everything was locked up tight, and Dad drove around the deserted town looking for any store that might be open. And he finally saw a light. It was Noveck's Pharmacy, and they were open for ten more minutes.

And he bought the Snow White doll. And he came home with this doll, and Mom gave him cocoa. And took away your crinoline slip and gave it to you for your birthday, so it would all still be even.

"The next morning was the best Christmas we have ever had. Dad had interpreted our lists very liberally, and so we got what we had asked for, but in very unexpected ways. Mary Ann had wanted a Liberace record and a jigsaw puzzle, but she had written it on one line, and Dad actually found a jigsaw puzzle of Liberace. And I got real seashells, when I had asked for seashell barrettes. Oh, we were delighted! And you! You saw that Snow White doll and it was full-blown love. And when you opened the box and took out the doll, you saw that the cardboard scene behind the doll lifted out. And guess what was behind the cardboard? Why it was all the seven dwarfs. Dad had thought he bought one doll—but he bought eight!"

"I'll love those dolls till the day I die."

"Do you remember what you said when you saw them? You said, 'This is just what I always wanted.'"

"It was true."

"But you had never seen those dolls before. How could they be just what you always wanted?"

"Because I didn't know it until I saw them."

"Exactly," said Angela.

She extended her hand towards me and flipped her palm up with a deliberate flair, in that gesture that says, 'See?' But I didn't.

Angela sighed and peeled herself off the lawn chair. She picked up the paper plates and our iced tea glasses and went in. Watching her from behind, I could see the outline of the chair's webbing across her thighs, and it made me suddenly aware of how hot and uncomfortable I was. I squirmed in my seat to try to get unstuck. Max protested with a little sing-song whine, and I bent down and kissed his hair. He reached up sleepily and put his hand on my cheek.

We sat there for a long time—hours and hours or minutes and minutes, I'm not sure—Max's little hand caressing my cheek, my lips to his damp curls. I was filled with some remote long-forgotten emotion. When I finally looked up, Angela was watching us from the screen door. She was crying.

Chapter 8

$\mathcal{I}$ KNEW THE UPS TRUCK WOULDN'T come until after ten. But just in case, I got to the shop a little early. It was six forty-five.

I turned on the computer. While it booted up, I examined a photographed taped to the wall. There were the women from the store—Kate and Heather. And with them was a woman who must be Maria. She was about thirty, much taller than the other women, and thinner, with long sheets of dark luminous hair on either side of a spectacular face. She didn't look like she belonged in the picture—it was like someone had pasted the portrait of an Aztec princess in the middle of a photograph of Ellis Island.

Since our cleaning, and our few little sales on Saturday, there was hardly anything left in the store. I wandered around, needlessly straightening the remaining hangers. It seemed that everywhere I turned there was a mirror. I saw the same restless person that I had examined late last night.

I had come home from Angela's sticky and irritable. Annoyed that Angela hadn't shared my enthusiasm for the shop, I had paced through the rooms in my little house, pointing out to myself all the tasteful and chic decorating. I took my new clothes from my closet, laying them on my bed in coordinating ensembles. I have a talent, I said aloud, and this is going to be fun.

I didn't sleep well, and I found myself at midnight and again at four A.M. staring at my middle-aged face in the bathroom mirror. There really should be an emergency walk-in clinic for gray roots.

The computer beeped me back to the present. Kate had tried to show me how to enter products into inventory when we priced the baskets on Saturday. But the process was too much like accounting, and I had tuned out almost immediately. Instead, I had watched her type with her long hard scarlet nails, thinking that it must be a skill in itself to type with your fingertips a good inch away from the keys.

So now I was at a loss, and I had hundreds of items due to arrive momentarily, if you consider momentarily being four hours or so. I spent the morning slowly entering, swearing, deleting, and re-entering all the orders I had telephoned in last week.

The uniformed UPS guy showed up about 11:40.

"Do you want me to stack them in the usual spot?" he asked.

"Sure," I said, and he left them in the middle of the hallway.

I lugged them all into the back room. It took me five minutes to find the box cutter, and another two to open the first box. Fearful that I would cut through the box and right into the clothes, I made the most tentative of cuts, barely denting the tape. When I finally opened the first box, I saw that there was eight inches of packing paper between the box and the merchandise, so I tore into the other boxes in a flash.

Well, it was almost as good as the Snow White doll. Dazzling dresses, skirts, shirts in summer sorbet colors. I tore off the plastic and shook loose each tightly wrapped surprise, piling the treasures on the shelves and floor.

A raspberry-pink sundress tempted me. I pulled it on over my t-shirt and jeans, and walked out to the front of the store to admire myself in the three-way mirror. Benson V. Shelter was standing at the front door peering in.

I held up a finger to signify 'just a second', and I ran to the back and struggled out of the dress. It snagged on my jeans and caught in my hair. I hurried back to the door, raking my fingers through my disheveled hair.

"Sorry," I said. "The new stuff's just come."

"So I see," he said, handing me a long black binder and a small paper bag. I gave the bag a little questioning shake.

"Sandwiches," he said. "I figured we could do the checkbook over lunch."

He followed me to the back room, and I dragged a second chair over to the desk. He handed me a sandwich, warning, "Don't get any crumbs on the merchandise."

"Never," I agreed. And we ate our tuna sandwiches over the old-fashioned hardbound checkbook, while he took me backwards in time to where Maria had recorded everything in her curly handwriting, then forward through his sharp staccato slant.

"You can see that she advertised quite a bit back then," he pointed out. "But except for the Sunday paper, I've just sort of let it drift. The girls put the cash receipts into the night deposit, but I haven't done much else besides pay them and the rent. I think we've lost a lot of money in the past month or so. The cash deposits cover the paychecks but not the rent."

"Well, you've recorded all the deposits, so along with the check stubs, I'll figure out what the loss is, and what you need to break even." Suddenly I felt like an accountant again, and it stuck on me, like the sundress snagged in my hair.

"Everything is really beautiful," I said, trying to get back to my new persona, nodding my head in the direction of the piles of new clothes.

"Yeah, well... at the risk of spoiling the fun, and being a tattletale too, let's just say that Kate spends more than her take-home."

"Okay, I'll try some self-control, but it won't be easy. I already know I have to have that pink dress."

"From what I saw from the door, I can't say that I blame you."

I suddenly felt embarrassed. "Speaking of Kate," I started. "Yes?"

"Um, she's a nice person, and she's worried. I don't want to pry into your personal life, but if you know where Maria is..."

Benson V. Shelter looked up from the desk to the photograph on the wall. He held the last bite of his sandwich in mid-air.

"Let them know she's okay. She's in Florida."

"Jesus," I said. "Why does everyone go to Florida?"

"To play golf, I guess. To play golf with my former business partner."

"Excuse me?"

"You know, Donovan & Shelter. Maria's in Florida with Roger Donovan."

"Shit," I said, even though I didn't know either of them and hardly knew Ben.

"No kidding." He let his fingers drift back to Maria's curly handwriting in the checkbook. His touch on her signature reminded me of something. He sighed. "I don't hear from them, but other people at the office do. I'll let Maria know that she should call Kate. I'm kind of surprised that she hasn't already, but then again, how much more surprised can I be?"

Ben extended his pointed finger to my face. I flinched reflexively. "Mayo," he explained, and wiped it away, touching my cheek in exactly the same place that little Max had. Max's gentle caress—that's what I was reminded of when Ben traced Maria's signature.

Chapter 9

BEING THE YOUNGEST OF THREE girls, I grew up without any first-hand experience of power. I played at being the baby, and getting my sisters to spoil me, but decision-making was scarce. I went last in games that I didn't choose, wearing second-hand clothes chosen for someone else.

At Heritage, I kept my head down and siphoned a smattering of independence by being the only one who actually wanted to do my job. But not power. I handed off my schedules and someone else (maybe) made decisions.

So it was a bit of a rush to discover that this simple retail job gave me more power than I had ever wielded. Because I chose everything in the store, no matter what someone bought, they bought something I chose. I decided what everyone should wear, just by carrying it. It was strangely gratifying.

Although it didn't always turn out as expected. That very first week, a customer bought a perfectly beautiful outfit that looked dreadful on her. I kept reappearing in the dressing room with clothes better suited to her nice middle-aged body, but she bought a mini that gave her knees like cauliflowers and a blouse stretched so tight across the chest that the seams screamed in fear.

"This is all one-hundred percent cotton," I said. "Organic cotton. There could be some shrinkage."

"That's not a problem," she laughed, surprising me that she could take a breath, "when you're as petite as I am."

She swung her bag jauntily as she went out the door. She may have been happy, but I was aggravated. I hated the prospect that she would tell anyone where she got the outfit.

But I was not half as mad at her as I was at the gorgeous young girl who came in and bought my raspberry sundress. I was crazy about that dress, and I was completely annoyed that it could look that good on someone else. I showed her the same dress in saffron, but she insisted that shade was not flattering on her, which I knew.

I took Friday off. I wasn't even sure the girl would come, but I found myself surprisingly disappointed when I woke to rain. I stood at the kitchen window like I had at ten when thunderstorms threatened my first Girl Scout sleepover. If I counted to one hundred, the sun would come out. If I counted to two hundred.

And it did. About eleven, the sky brightened. I resumed my spot at the window again, willing the grass to dry up.

They came a little after noon. Shannon stayed in the truck while D.J. unloaded the mower. He stood on the front lawn with his hands on his hips, more like a father than a boyfriend. Finally the door opened and she climbed out. Climbed wasn't the right word—she just slowly slid down the side of the truck till her feet touched the ground. D.J. took

Shannon by the hand and led her across the grass and up to the porch. He went back for the mower. I heard her say, "What an asshole"—and I assumed she meant D.J., but it certainly could have been me.

I didn't have to wait for her to knock. She opened the door and strode in.

My anticipation turned to irritation.

"Well, hi," I said. "I guess I didn't hear you knock."

"Guess not," she said.

I let it go. "We promised D.J. some cookies."

"Whatever," she mumbled. Shannon's heavily rimmed eyes looked back at the door.

I took out cookie sheets and turned up the oven. I handed her a towel.

"What?" she asked.

"Wash your hands."

Shannon mouthed a swear word, but went to the sink and let a few drops trickle over her fingers.

The lawnmower clamored, and Shannon dropped the towel and went to the sunroom. She watched D.J. cut the first path through the grass. She didn't smile—I hadn't seen her smile ever—but she looked slightly less angry when she came back in.

"Do you think there are contests for lawn mowing?" she asked.

"I don't know. Do you think we could get D.J. to enter?"

"Probably not. He just wouldn't see the point."

"Which would be?"

"To show them," she said, and with her finger she drew a star in the flour I had sprinkled on the cutting board.

I gave her the little log of dough I had prepared. "See this chocolate dough? We'll cut cookies and later add our own icing. Did you ever make homemade Oreos?"

"Yeah, I'm the fucking cookie elf. I live in a tree."

I ignored her profanity.

"Cut them about this thick." I demonstrated with a couple of slices and stepped aside.

Shannon frowned and sliced off cookies with the kind of awkwardness that comes from a fear of knives. I mixed up fresh dough for chocolate chip cookies for D.J., and I watched her arrange her slices on the cookie sheet. They were too close together, but I kept my mouth shut.

I put her batch in the oven and handed her the bowl of the chocolate chip batter. "Stir in the chips and the walnuts, and you can drop these on the cookie sheet with a spoon."

Shannon poured out a handful of chocolate chips from the bag and popped them into her mouth. She poured a few into the batter. Then she held the bag up and poured some more directly into her mouth. She looked into the bag.

"This doesn't look like enough," Shannon said.

"Then stop eating the ingredients."

She poured most of the remaining chips into the batter, and then shook the rest of the bag onto the table where, she lined them up and ate them one by one.

"Seriously," she said. "We need another bag."

"We certainly do not," I said, taking the first batch out of the oven

"Damn," she said, eying the first batch. "They're all stuck together." She quickly moved the dollops of chocolate chip dough around the second cookie sheet, giving them more room. "Better," she murmured under her breath.

"So," I said. "Have you told your parents yet?"

"That I'm making cookies?"

"That you're pregnant. Does your mother know?"

Shannon gave me a nasty scowl. "My mother?" Let's just say Mom's not around."

"Where is she?"

"Prison probably."

"What?"

"I'm joking. Sort of."

"And your dad?"

"My DAD? "There's only about three kids in the whole town who have a dad. Jesus, get with it."

"Well, then where do you live? With relatives?"

"Hell, no. I wouldn't go there for a million dollars, even if they begged, which they don't. No, I'm in the State pen—you know, foster care. Only I've had it with foster families. I'm living in a group home now. Decision House. Oh, it's swell. We make cookies every day."

"Do you hear from your mother at all? Can you write her?"

Shannon put down the spoon. "Look, she said. "The State kicked her out for being a bad mommy. She licked the batter off her finger. "About ten years too late if you ask me." She regarded my horrified look. "What? Mommy sucked. I can take care of myself."

"What about D.J.?"

"What about him? She looked at me puzzled for a second, then her brow cleared. "Oh, you think he's the daddy. Well, he's not. He's a nice guy."

"How long have you known him?"

She suddenly softened. She looked almost sweet under all that makeup.

"It was fucking weird. I was hanging out at the Green and these assholes were really bugging me. They were making nasty remarks and they kept bumping me on the shoulder until I was almost backed up against the fence. Then D.J. was there, and he goes, 'Hey, are you messing with my girl?' to these fuckers. I mean, I didn't even know D.J., except of course that he's a big shot and I sort of know his asshole sister. But anyway, these dudes just backed right off, and no one has bothered me since. I asked D.J. why he did it, and he says, 'I don't know. I just hate those pricks.' That was all there was to it. And so I just hang around, and D.J. lets me, although sooner or later he'll be asking me to take a hike. But I give him a little head now and then—even though he doesn't even ask—so he might let me stick around."

"I thought you said he was a nice guy."

"Well, yeah, but a guy. An eighteen-year-old guy. Jesus, do you think he's going to turn down a blow job because he's nice?"

My opinion of D.J. plummeted. But she had a point.

Shannon continued. "He'll go off to college though, and he won't need me. College girls give head all the time."

"You don't sound too broken up about it."

"Hell, everyone leaves."

I handed her the icing tube. "See," I gave it a squeeze. "Squeeze here and the icing comes out. You can put a little on the cookie and then put another cookie on the top to make the Oreo."

Shannon squeezed out a dollop the size of a golf ball. "Oops. Wait, wait, I got it." And she made a nice little flower in the middle of the cookie. I watched her as she carefully, seriously placed icing on the cookies. A little "S" and then an "H." She's just a kid after all, I thought, spelling her name out in sugar. And then the next letter was an "I".

"Cute," I said, as she finished the profanity and started on a better one.

"How did you know?" she asked, as she licked off a "K" that looked too much like an "R".

"You can't re-do one that you licked," I said. Eat the whole thing and start over."

"But how did you know? I don't look at all pregnant. No one knows."

Now usually I downplay any of the eerie aspects of my talent. I make it matter-of-fact and say that it's in the eyes, or some reassuringly normal explanation. But I figured that Shannon would probably like it on the spooky side, so I gave her the exaggerated version.

"I've always been able to just see a baby inside someone. Until I was seven, I thought that everyone could. It was Thanksgiving. We had my father's family over, my aunt and uncle and my grandparents. And after grace, we went around the table and each of us had to say what we were thankful for."

"Jesus, what crap. Were you puking up the turkey?"

"No. It was nice."

"It was bullshit."

"Cut that out. It WAS nice. Anyway, when it was my turn, I said, 'I'm thankful that Aunt Marjorie is going to have a little baby.' Everyone gasped. My Aunt Marjorie was forty-three years old, and had been married for over twenty years. She had never been able to get pregnant. Not even close. And my father started apologizing and saying that I was just a kid and didn't mean to hurt anyone's feelings. Aunt Marjorie started to cry, but happy tears. She said that it was her turn to say what she was thankful for. And she said, 'I'm thankful that I am going to have a little baby.'"

"And did they tie you to the bed and call the exorcist?"

I laughed. "Just about. Everyone thought it was wonderful and that I was very creepy."

"And your old aunt had a baby?"

"Yes, my cousin Sheila. She's in her forties now. One of those broad-in-the-beam nurses that wears white pants with an elastic waist and a smock with cute little ducks on it. She's very sweet."

I reached up to the shelf near the sink. I brought down two pink angels with holes in their heads for salt and pepper. "My Aunt Marjorie gave me these that Christmas. She said that one angel was to keep me safe and one angel was to keep her baby safe."

"Too bad they couldn't keep her baby out of bloom-ass pants."

"Sheila was the first time I ever told anyone. But I always know. Women in my family are afraid to come over."

"You know what's kind of weird? How some people try and try and can't get pregnant. And other girls, like me, who don't know shit, can have two beers and a thirty second screw and there you go. Do you ever think about that?"

I looked away. "Yes, I do."

The lawnmower suddenly went quiet. We quickly finished putting lids on the dirty Oreos, so no one would know what they were eating. D.J. came in and his wet grassy smell mingled with the sweet cookie aroma.

"I like them best with the chocolate still melty." He ate several right from the warm sheet. "Not bad," he said to Shannon, and she nearly smiled.

We packed up almost all the cookies in two bags, one for D.J. and one for Shannon.

"You don't have to give me too many," she said, "I already ate all the broken ones."

"You can bring them to the other girls at the House," I suggested.

"Fuck, no. Not unless you have some cyanide."

I picked out a few cookies for myself. From the spot where I remembered what she had spelled out, I took a half dozen, one half of Shannon's best word. I took M-O-T-H-E-R.

As they were about to leave, D.J. said, rather too loudly, "Thank you, Cynthia," nudging Shannon at the elbow.

"Thank you, Cynthia," Shannon parroted. Then she asked cryptically, "Have you ever sometimes seen it, but then the next time, it's gone?"

I thought about Heritage's finance secretary, whose affair with the married V.P. went from romantic glances to angry voicemails. "Sometimes," I answered.

"Well, guess what? You may get another chance," she said.

Later, cleaning up the bowls and spoons, I noticed that on my knickknack shelf there was only one pink angel.

Chapter 10

*I*T HAPPENED EXACTLY THE WAY that Shannon had described. Except that I was thirty-two at the time, about twice Shannon's age. I don't consider that a great distinction, given that there is no age limit on the lack of judgment brought on by a couple of beers.

It probably would have been more understandable, or at least a more interesting story, if it had been a famous movie star, or at least a senior executive like in the case of the sad finance secretary. But it was just one of a dozen identical PC troubleshooters—pizza-eaters, we used to call them, since they had pizza delivered to the office every single day. This pizza-eater had seduced me at the company Christmas party. I was behind him in line at the bar, and he ordered seven Heinekens. "If you make it eight, I'll help carry them," I offered. "Oh, but I am a talented guy. I can carry all eight." And he did. And so I was seduced. We went out to my car, where he wriggled my pantyhose down from under my little leather skirt, and we fumbled around for the same thirty seconds it had taken Shannon, and, as she said, there you go.

I had been divorced several years at the time. I had hardly even dated since, and I hadn't even realized that I missed it. I was mortified that I had to search the Heritage phone directory to remember his name. I recalled that it was something charming and European, like Ernesto. I was close. It was Bob.

After my initial panic, I found I was tremendously happy. I worried a bit that I could be denying a child to a guy who might actually want to be a father. I saw him in the break room a few weeks after my pregnancy test. When I caught his eye, he placed his hand tenderly on the arm of the girl he was with and looked away. So either Bob was a nice guy who had a momentary lapse and was truly committed to this chubby nearsighted fellow pizza-eater, or he was a cad that would seduce her too with his irresistible technique. That was the end of my guilt.

I was not daunted by the idea of raising a baby myself. In fact, I was delighted. Since I didn't need the financial help, I saw no benefit in fathers except perhaps providing a set of eyes now and then so mothers could go to the bathroom by themselves.

At the end of February, my boss of that year sent me to a seminar on capital budgeting. It was not really my domain; it was his, but I certainly couldn't blame him for skipping that one. I flew to Philadelphia and sat for ten hours, listening to presentations on digital technology and returns on investment. And the snow started. All flights were cancelled, and I checked into the airport hotel. In the lobby store, I bought contact lens solution and an outrageously priced t-shirt to sleep in. The World Wrestling guys were stuck in the same hotel, and I rode the elevator with platinum-mulleted musclemen. I got off on a floor not mine, and walked down a flight so none of those scary-looking guys would see me enter my room.

I hung up my suit, turned on the TV, and lost the baby. I miscarried in Philadelphia during a rerun of Mary Tyler Moore. I layered two facecloths in my panties, put my suit back on, and a cab took me in slow slippery motion to the hospital. I spent the night in the "quiet" area of maternity, the last room at the end of the hall that had no crib or baby decorations.

There was no one to call, since I had not yet told anyone.

Chapter 11

NGELA WAS RIGHT. I DIDN'T have to be on the lookout for the sign. It came stomping into the store in tap shoes with floodlights and a drum roll.

It was two weeks since we had received all the new merchandise at Maya Maria. We had a decent amount of business the Saturday before, and the customers must have spread the word that we had some great choices, while other stores were already going into leftover mode. While I wouldn't exactly call it a parade, we were steady and busy, and the bar code reader kept the beat with the reggae music that Heather chose for the day.

By late morning I had already come to the realization that there were very few, if any, women left in town—perhaps in the state—who wore a size Small. The Mediums, the Larges, and even the Extra-Larges were bought and restocked from the backroom with regularity, while the Smalls and the Petites still hung in the original spots, with all of the extras still in boxes. It was obvious that ordering the same number of articles in each size had been a mistake.

I thought about my alternatives. I could advertise in the middle school newspaper, although it appeared that most junior high kids were already bigger than their mothers. I looked at the seams on a few of the skirts, wondering if it was possible to take two Petites and make a Large. Maybe I could do an online ad on the pro-anorexia web sites I had been reading about. That would probably mean shipping merchandise to Los Angeles, which appeared to be the hotbed for eating disorders. Of course shipping charges would be minimal for stuff this tiny.

We had a lull at noon, and I went into the back room to steam out the few Larges we had left. A few minutes later, Kate came in.

"Heather's holding the fort," she said, "so I can have some lunch. She'll holler if it gets busy."

Kate took a yogurt out of the tiny refrigerator we kept by the desk. She removed the foil top and delicately licked it clean. She stirred the yogurt. She stirred and stirred, looking at the cup but not really seeing it. She'd have butter in a few minutes, I thought.

"Do you have something on your mind?" I asked.

She stopped stirring.

"Maria called me last night."

"Oh," I said. "Is she all right?"

"I guess. She's in Florida."

I tried to make my face look surprised. "Really?"

"Yeah. She's there with a guy who works with Ben. Roger Someone. He has a boat."

"Did she seem happy?"

"I don't know." Kate frowned and shook her head. "I just can't figure it out. She says she's working in a boutique. I mean, she had a lawyer here; she had a boutique here. Did she leave for a boat?"

We peaked that afternoon about 2:00. Then traffic slowly diminished until we had just single customers here and there. Both Kate and Heather hinted broadly that it was a shame that I had to pay them when it was so quiet. They both had dates.

"Okay," I said, finally giving in about 3:30. "One of you can leave now and the other at 4:30, and I'll handle the last hour and close up."

"No problem," said Heather. "I'll stay another hour and Kate can go. I can use another hour's pay, since Kevin's kind of broke."

So Kate gave her a hug and me a wave and flew out the door.

"I figured Kate needed to go early," explained Heather. "You know, the older you are, the earlier the date you have, but the longer it takes you to get ready. It's…what's that word?"

"Ironic," I offered.

"Yeah, ironic."

"But don't you think that's a bit of a generalization?"

"No, it's a fact. If you were going to a movie, and there was a show at 7:00 and at 9:00, which one would you go to?"

"Okay, probably the seven."

"Right. And would you go without doing your makeup and hair, and changing your clothes, and making sure you had a nice sweater in case the theater's cold, and cough drops in your purse, and going early to get a good parking place?"

"Okay, you win."

Christ, I thought. If I ever have a date again, I'll have to go to a matinee, and start getting ready right after breakfast.

❧

By 5:00, I had no customers, and I made myself busy by checking the racks, and rearranging the jewelry. I was coming in from the storage room with an armful of shopping bags when the door banged open accompanied by a scream. It was literally a scream, since the door had slammed against a baby carriage whose occupant was in the throes of a great tantrum. A young woman struggled to hold the door while trying to clear the wheels of the carriage and maneuver the monstrosity into the store. I remembered carting Angela's Michael in one of those tiny, light umbrella strollers. I guess the product security police had decided that those flimsy contraptions were unsafe, but I had never dumped Michael on his head. We had managed just fine. I felt a little sorry for this mother trying to steer her lace-edged Humvee.

"Let me help," I said, as I held the door and picked up the front of the carriage.

"Thanks," she said. The woman was young, and red-faced from a combination of freckles, exertion, heat, and frustration.

"She's been crying for an hour, and I've been running around like crazy. The christening is tomorrow, and I've been getting all the stuff for the party. I was just about to head home and collapse, but I saw that pretty outfit in the window…I realized I don't have anything to wear for tomorrow."

"The turquoise skirt and lace top?"

"Yes. They're beautiful." She frowned. "The baby is at her limit. Sorry to subject you to her fit, but maybe I could just try it on quickly?"

"Don't worry, there's no one else here. I'm not bothered by a few tears," I said through the incredible screeching. I

71

grabbed pieces for the girl to try on. I hung them in the dressing room, Mediums up front, and the Larges hanging behind, so she wouldn't have to be embarrassed asking me for a larger size.

"Just leave the baby here," I said, although it was clear that she didn't really have a choice, since the carriage wouldn't fit through the aisle. "I'll watch her."

"Don't pick her up," she warned as she closed the curtain to the changing room. "She's going through that phase where she hates strangers."

So I stood by the carriage, looking through the mosquito netting at the purple-splotched wailing infant. Her legs and arms were stiff with anger as she alternately shrieked and gasped.

How much worse could it be? I thought as I lifted the netting. The baby's eyes were shut tight and she didn't see it coming, so it startled her when I picked her up. She stopped. Just like that. She put her head down on my shoulder and let out an enormous and very adult sigh.

"Oh no, what's wrong?" The woman came rushing out from the dressing room, shocked by the silence, skirt unzipped and blouse half buttoned. She stopped and stared.

I figured this could be unpleasant. I'd observed that lots of mothers are really quite pleased that their babies won't go to strangers. I didn't want to injure her pride, or worse—imply that she was a bad mother, letting her baby scream when I could soothe her so easily.

But the woman wasn't mad. Her shoulders relaxed and she let go of her open blouse. "It's a miracle," she said.

I smiled, "Oh no. I just surprised her, and she decided she was ready to give up."

The baby tucked her face into my neck.

"It's more than that," said the woman. "Look how happy she is."

"I wear lavender cologne. Babies like it."

"No, you have a way. You're just a natural mother. It's hard for me," she admitted, "I'm so nervous all the time, I think I make her worse."

"That's because you have all the responsibility,' I said. "I just have to hold her for five minutes. You have her for life."

The woman smiled then. She zipped her skirt and looked in the mirror. "I love this," she said.

As I wrapped her purchase in tissue, I added a small bottle from the shelf near the register. "Lavender cologne," I explained. "On the house."

"Thanks, she said, "You must have very happy children."

I let it go. "What's her name?" I asked as she tucked the baby back into the carriage.

Drum roll.

"Shannon," she said.

Chapter 12

SUNDAY WAS D.J.'s GRADUATION PARTY. I had been mildly surprised when I received the invitation. I was one of Robert Frost's good-fences kind of neighbors. I waved from my porch, and discussed the weather from my car. If that skinny little boy hadn't pushed his big mower into my yard years ago, I probably would still be referring to D.J.'s parents as Mr. and Mrs. Carmody—which I would have only known from their mailbox.

I had stopped at the big box store on the way home on Saturday, wandering down the aisles looking for an appropriate gift for a teenage boy off to college. I had no idea what D.J. was interested in, except of course what Shannon was offering. I bought a gift certificate and a dictionary and left the store with a nostalgic sorrow for the little boy that I had watched grow up without getting to know at all. I recognized the self-pity in my sadness. And a strong undercurrent of shame.

"You look confused," Angela remarked as we left Mass on Sunday morning.

"I saw the sign," I said. "And I'm not sure I'm happy about it."

Angela sat abruptly on the big limestone steps, nearly causing an avalanche of devout parishioners escaping the church. I sat down next to her, ignoring the unchristian glares of impatience.

Angela smoothed her skirt. She turned up the hem a bit, looking at the tiny perfect stitches. Mary Ann must have hemmed it for her.

"Why do you think there were so many empty lifeboats on the Titanic?" she asked.

I smiled. "Because it seemed safer to stay with the big boat."

"You're getting good at this," she said. She stood and looked down at me. "Sometimes staying where you are is the most disastrous thing you can do. Only the dangerous choice can save you."

I waited until there were half a dozen cars in the driveway. I shook away the remnants of self-pity that were telling me that no one would notice if I didn't show up. I may not know many people at the party, but there was one I certainly wanted to see.

Shannon was standing by the edge of the swimming pool. She was wearing a skimpy bikini in an orange print that turned her skin a grayish white. She was completely dry but shivered anyway despite the humid day. Her shoulders were hunched so far forward that her breasts hugged each other. Her discomfort surprised me. Here was a girl, demonstrably promiscuous, trying to disappear.

She saw me and straightened a bit. She put on a tough-girl face and jumped into the pool. As she pulled herself up at the side of the pool, I was enormously relieved that she still had the aura of pregnancy. And a tiny but visible belly.

I exchanged pleasantries with vaguely familiar neighbors and strangers who looked like one or the other of D.J.'s parents. All the while I watched Shannon interact with the other kids. Or rather, not interact. She hung back from the others. On the edge of the group but not part of it. Her eyes followed D.J. but she didn't stick by him either. Every once in a while, Shannon would catch me watching her; she'd move a little closer to the other kids and tilt her head as if they were speaking to her.

"Weird, huh?"

I turned. It was D.J.'s sister. I recalled her name after a second; Celeste.

"Sorry?"

"Weird. She's weird." She nodded in Shannon's direction.

"I don't know. She seems like all the other kids."

"Are you kidding? She doesn't even have a bathing suit. That's mine," Celeste continued. "My mother lent it to her. And she's as white as can be. Does she ever go outside?"

"She sits outside when D.J. mows my lawn."

"Dressed like it's February, I bet. I just don't get what D.J. sees in her. She doesn't smile. She doesn't laugh. She doesn't even talk—and I mean she doesn't even talk to D.J."

"Is she your age? In your class?"

"Yeah…although maybe she's stayed back a couple of times. I wouldn't be surprised."

I felt like I needed to come to Shannon's defense. "I've talked to her quite a bit. She's very bright. And friendly. I think she's just shy."

"Shy my ass," said Celeste. "I've seen her shove her breasts in D.J.'s face."

"Well, aren't you affectionate with your boyfriend?"

"D.J. is not her boyfriend," she hissed. "Look at him. He hardly even notices her. Do you know what my mother says? My mother says she's like a stray dog, following the only person who doesn't kick her."

I looked at Shannon, who was picking tiny bits of bread off her hot dog roll and dropping them in the pool. "Your mother may be right."

I called my friend Gwen as soon as I got home.

"Is Jim home?" I asked. Gwen's husband worked at the Department of Children and Families.

"Sure," she said, sounding a bit confused. "Is there a problem?" she guessed. "Did you witness some abuse or something?"

"Oh no, it's nothing bad. I just need some advice."

"Then why don't you come over? We can have dinner."

"Would you like me to bring it?"

"Pepper steak for me, Kung Pao for Jim, and a poo-poo platter for the boys," she answered instantly.

Angela better be right about this, I thought. The Titanic is much too terrible a metaphor if she's wrong.

A half-hour later, the kids were in the family room with the tray tables and the latest Spiderman movie, and Jim, Gwen and I were seated around the kitchen table.

"Here's the thing," I said, drawing absent-minded circles in my rice. "I know a young woman who is pregnant, and I want to adopt her baby."

Jim and Gwen simultaneously dropped the food that they had balanced in their chopsticks.

"Wow," said Gwen.

I shrugged.

Jim looked at me. "How old are you?"

"Fifty."

"It's not going to happen," he said bluntly.

"But what if she wants me to have the baby?" I lied.

"Private adoption is illegal in Connecticut. You have to be approved by the State. And the State is not going to approve a fifty-year-old to adopt an infant."

"But I know three women raising their grandchildren."

"That's different. They're relatives. The State makes exceptions for family."

"You know I'm a good person. I was meant to be this baby's mother. Can't you help get the State to make an exception for me?"

"Cynthia, I do know you're a good person. And that's why I wouldn't want to get your hopes up. There are tons of couples, *young* couples, who've been waiting for years to get a baby."

Gwen reached across the table and touched my hand.

"Honey," she said. "You'd be a terrific mother. But a baby—at fifty?"

"I can do it."

The two looked into my eyes as if they were trying to discover how I could have become so delusional. I reassured them. "If you think I'll break my hip or something, I can hire help. I'm pretty rich."

"I've been in this job a long time," said Jim. "And here's what I really think: I think you are capable and loving *and young*. But no one will let you do it. But there's an alternative—a good one. As hard as it would be for you to adopt a baby, well, it would be incredibly easy for you to adopt an older child.

There are so many kids out there just waiting. You could have your choice in about a minute."

I looked down and saw that I had drawn a star in my fried rice. A fat tear dropped into the very center. I had really known all along what the Sign had meant.

"I've already met her." I said.

Chapter 13

━━━━━━━━━⟡━━━━━━━━━

I SAT AT THE DESK AT Maya Maria's on Monday morning trying to put together financial statements. It was useless. The numbers were all meaningless. It was more than them not making sense, although they certainly didn't. They meant nothing to me. I didn't care.

Jim and I had talked at length the night before. He had never been to Decision House, where Shannon lived, but he had heard of it. "Derision House" he said they called it. "Where the abused go to abuse each other." Not that it was any worse than any of the group homes in Connecticut. Unfortunately, it was typical. Six or so older children –all of the same sex—living with a surrogate parent or two and maybe an assistant. The kids were always a mess. In and out of foster homes with increasingly disastrous results, until they could no longer be foisted upon anyone. So they got dumped into group homes with other unmanageable kids. You'd think the kids would bond for some small comfort, but that never happened. Unless you counted the way they ganged up on one another. They fought, they stole, they tormented each other. And it went on until they were eighteen and thrown into the world, each of them carrying nasty scars and the worst interpersonal skills imaginable.

"So with the hundreds of older kids waiting for a home, that's where you've found the one you want?" Jim said.

"I'm afraid so," I said, and didn't tell him that she was the pregnant young woman whose baby I wanted. It just seemed prudent at the time to keep the two stories separate.

So now, instead of sales profitability, my mind raced with questions and possible scenarios. How do I approach Shannon? Would she find the idea reprehensible? Knowing what her life was like made me think that she would leap at the chance to live with me. But she was a tough kid.

And then there was my family. Angela might think it was a great idea. But my mother. And Mary Ann. Just thinking of Mary Ann and Shannon having a dinner conversation on a Sunday afternoon brought me some wry amusement.

But the biggest fear was what my life would be with a kid as screwed up as Jim had described. Shannon was every adjective in Jim's list—hostile, rebellious, deceptive, suspicious. Managing a little boutique was so easy. But then again, I'd circle around to Shannon with the tip of her tongue pressed to her top lip as she concentrated on her cookie designs. There was something in there. And there was a baby in there.

Certainly I could handle a few years of Shannon, and find a way to keep the baby when she left.

I wanted the baby I lost in Philadelphia.

"Hi," said Ben, startling the bejesus out of me. "The back door was open."

"Sorry. I was lost in thought." I added, "Working on financials, of course" while I quickly toggled back to the spreadsheet, hoping he didn't see that I had been searching 'parents murdered by adopted children'.

Ben handed me the bag with the sandwiches and walked out to the front of the store.

"Looks nice," he said.

"Sales have been pretty good. I'm trying to figure out if they're good enough to turn a profit for you."

"A profit for somebody." He took out his sandwich and took a vicious bite that seemed to be a surrogate for someone's head. "She lets it go to hell," he mumbled, mostly to himself, "but now she's so damned concerned."

"Does Maria want the store back?"

"I don't think she knows. But she doesn't want anyone else to have it. She called me fuming about never giving me permission to sell the store."

"That's okay. Maya Cynthia sounds pretty dumb."

"What? You've changed your mind too? You don't want the store?"

"Ben, I never wanted to own the store. I just wanted to straighten it out. I'm a born straightener, and it seemed like such a waste to see it fall apart. And I thought it would be fun."

"Is it? Fun?"

"Sure," I said, brushing aside how meaningless I thought it was a few minutes ago. "But what about you? You said, 'two months and I'll probably close it down.' Well, one month is about gone. So is it you who've changed your mind?"

"When Maria left I hated this store. A few years ago the firm defended an arsonist. Got him off. So I thought maybe I could hire him. But now I like that I might be saving it." He crumpled his sandwich wrapper. "Proving something, I guess."

"You can fix something she broke."

"Yeah, that's a big part of it. But you know, I kind of like it here."

"Must be the fancy lunches," I said.

Chapter 14

THE NEXT FRIDAY I COAXED Shannon into staying for dinner.

We baked a cake. Or rather, I baked a cake while she sat in the sunroom, eating popsicles and watching D.J.

"I need to rearrange the furniture in the living room," I lied. "Stay and help me and I'll pay you."

"How much?"

"Ten dollars."

"Fat chance," she said.

"Fifteen."

"Maybe. What are you having for dinner?" Shannon asked. "I think my shit is actually turning orange and curly from all the macaroni and cheese."

"Gee," I said, "That's what I was going to make."

Shannon bent over and stuck her finger down her throat

"Okay," I said. "Just kidding. How about pork chops and applesauce and a salad?"

"I could stand it."

I took out the lettuce, tomatoes, radishes, a cucumber and a green pepper, and put them on the cutting board. I handed Shannon the salad spinner. "Get to it," I said.

"What the hell is this?"

"A salad spinner."

"A what?"

I took the head of lettuce, pulled off a few leaves and rinsed them in the sink. I put them in the salad spinner and pulled the cord. The inside bowl spun around and when it stopped, I opened the cover and handed the bowl to Shannon "Clean and dry," I said. "Perfect."

"A dryer for lettuce? Are you kidding me? Just how spoiled are you?"

"It was a gift," I explained. "But it works. I like it."

Shannon made a disgusted face, but she was already rinsing lettuce and filling the bowl. "How did I ever live without one?"

"That's why they call you underprivileged."

And she smiled. She shut if off immediately, but I saw it. I figured I might actually have a chance.

I got two peelers from the drawer. I gave her one for the cucumber and I started peeling apples with the other. We stood side by side over the double sink. She watched me from beneath her lashes.

"Doesn't applesauce come in a jar?"

"Sure, if you want gooey sugary crap."

"Yeah, that sounds good."

"No. Not good. Fresh applesauce is easy, and it tastes wonderful. And there's a bonus too—it makes the house smell really nice."

"You know," she said, "if you were out of clean underwear, I bet you could put your panties in the salad spinner. Do you ever do that?"

I let it pass.

We ate in silence. Silence except for a little hum as Shannon unconsciously accompanied herself in her chewing. Good thing my expectations were low.

As she gnawed at the last little bits in the curve of the bone, I finally started.

"Shannon, I have a proposition for you."

"Shit," she said. "I knew it. You're a lesbian or something, right?"

"No. Not that kind of proposition. A plan. An idea."

"What?"

"How would you like to live here?"

"Yep, that's what I thought. A dyke."

"No. No. Please. Not a dyke. A mother."

"What?"

"A mother." I took a long breath and launched. "Look, Shannon, I don't really know that much about your life. But it doesn't take a genius to guess that you've heard more bullshit in fifteen years than I have in fifty. So I can't give you a load of how much I love you or want to change your life or save your soul or whatever. I don't love you. But for some reason, God only knows why, I do like having you around."

Shannon moved back in her chair. Her eyes were flat. She put her spoon in her mouth and clamped her jaws tightly around it. There were too many years of rejection for Shannon to believe even this minimal level of affection. I would never get to her this way. I started again.

"Okay. Rock-bottom truth. I want a baby. And you have one. So here's the deal: I want to adopt you. I'll be your mother, and that way I am the baby's grandmother."

Shannon stopped sucking on her spoon and held it up, regarding her reflection.

"You want my baby."

"Yes, I want your baby. And in return you get a really nice home—with your own room and good food and new clothes, and someone who'll be decent to you."

"And when you kick me out, you keep the baby."

"What are you, sixteen? You'll be in the foster care system till you're eighteen. Two years. Two years of the same crap. The group home with broken furniture; nasty kids stealing your stuff; no privacy; macaroni and cheese five days a week. Or you can stay here instead for those two years. And yes, I'll keep the baby when you're ready to go out on your own. Not kicked out. Ready."

"I'm fourteen," she said.

Shit. I thought it was going to be a miracle to stand her for two years. "All the more reason," was what I actually said. "You'll never be able to stand Decision House for four years."

"Shit," she said.

"Did I tell you that I manage a clothing store? You'll get a fantastic wardrobe."

"Of old lady clothes like you wear?"

"These are nice!"

"If you're ninety!"

"Now you're just being mean. But okay, I get it. You don't have to shop at the same stores as me. You get to choose your own clothes. Anyway," I added, "I'll probably only work there a few more months."

"How come?"

"Because I'll stay home and take care of the baby while you're in school."

"Christ," said Shannon. "What the hell are we supposed to do for money? Do you think you'll get rich on the foster care payment?"

"Shannon, I'm a little bit rich already. And there won't be a foster care stipend. This is an adoption. For real. Permanent."

"How rich is a little rich?" Oh, I definitely got her attention.

"Not mink coats and trips to the Riviera rich. But if I don't go crazy, I don't have to work if I don't want to."

"Raising kids is expensive," she told me, sounding for all the world like Mary Ann.

"Well," I said. "There goes the Ferrari."

And she laughed, but her eyes darted involuntarily to the window, as if she expected to see the repo man towing off my imaginary sports car. Every once in a while I glimpsed a naïve little girl.

She drained her milk and wiped her mouth with the back of her sleeve. Then she wiped her sleeve against her pants leg. I thought she might wipe her pants leg by getting down on the rug, but she pushed back her chair and said, like a proper real estate agent, "Well, let's see the rest of the house."

So we left the dishes on the table and I gave her the formal tour. The cushy flowery sofas keeping each other company in the living room, the dining room that I never used, that looked never used, and the little bedroom near the first floor bathroom.

"This would be your bedroom," I said. I loved this room, with its French country look of pale blue and butter yellow. Lace curtains of ivory matched the ivory eyelet quilt, and the sunflower pillows were sweet but not silly.

"Hm," she said, and she nodded her head at intervals slowly turning around the room. Counting.

"Ten by twelve." I said.

Shannon peeked into the bathroom, "Yup," she said, but I wasn't sure what she had confirmed.

We went upstairs. There was a full bath at the landing, with a bedroom on either side. She stepped first into the bedroom that I had converted into my small office.

"I'll make this into the baby's room," I said. "I'll move the computer downstairs so you can use it too."

She touched the keyboard hesitantly, the way a non-musician might touch a piano. She walked back through the hallway and into my bedroom. She stood motionless for a long time, much longer than she had in the downstairs bedroom that I had offered her as her own. Shannon studied the room like it was a mystery she could solve. I tried to look at it through her eyes, wondering what the sage wallpaper and the pale silver bedding could tell her about the person I was. Peaceful, maybe. I suddenly wished there was more energy here, but perhaps tranquility might be appealing to a casualty of domestic terror.

She walked up to the bureau and put her face down to the level of the photograph that stood in a silver frame. She had her hands behind her back—a child fearful of breaking something precious. My mother and father and the three of us girls squinted at her in the bright sunlight. We wore our Easter Sunday best of more than forty years ago. "Which one is you?" she asked.

"The little one."

"Little?" She sneered, but not maliciously. "Maybe age-wise. You didn't miss too many meals back then." She took one finger and carefully touched the top of my Easter bonnet. "I have to go to the bathroom," she said, and ducked into the bath and locked the door.

"I'll be downstairs," I said loudly, and left her to her exploring. I was sure that she was already into the medicine cabinet, and the linen closet would follow. She was probably trying a few shades of lipstick right now. I didn't have any serious prescriptions, so I left her to it. It didn't bother me; I would do exactly the same thing.

I had picked up the dinner dishes and stacked the dishwasher before Shannon reappeared. Her lips looked like she had recently rubbed them hard with Kleenex, and her eyelids had a definite sheen.

"Would you like dessert?" I said. "I have lemon coffee cake."

"I'll miss curfew," she said, even though I was positive she had never thought of curfew once in her entire existence.

"Okay, I'll take you back," I said. I almost said 'home' and maybe I should have—to push the contrast. I wrapped up a slice of cake and placed it gently in a small bag. "For later," I said.

She went into the living room and moved a throw pillow from one side of the sofa to the other. She held out her hand.

"Fifteen dollars."

I paid her.

I drove her back to the group home. It was a silent trip, and she leaned as far away from me as she could, staring out the window with her forehead on the glass.

I pulled up to a big old house with peeling paint and a cracked front window. The grass was brown and trampled, and there was a McDonald's wrapper on the sidewalk. Two girls about Shannon's age were sitting on a dilapidated couch on the porch. Shannon got out of the car, and in unison, they each gave her the finger.

"Shannon," I said, as she was about to close the car door. She leaned in, and she got two-for-one in that gesture, because she could listen to me and waggle her butt at the girls at the same time. "Think about it. What could make my house worse than this?" I asked.

"Yeah, well," she said. She looked me in the eye for the first time that night, and she said, "You would expect me to be, like,…grateful."

I laughed then. "Honey," I said. "You're a teenager. No one in the world expects you to be grateful."

"Okay," she said.

Okay? Okay what? Okay that she didn't have to be grateful? Okay that she would think about it? Okay to everything? The adoption? But she had already slammed the car door and run into the house, making a wide circle around the girls on the porch, but not so distant that she couldn't wave her dessert at them.

I drove away. It started to rain that misty stuff that the wipers drag and smear. The wiper blades taunted me all the way back to the house. "O-Kay. O-Kay. O-Kay."

Chapter 15

FRIDAY NIGHT'S HALFHEARTED DRIZZLE TURNED into serious rain on Saturday. I wasn't running an ice cream parlor or a ski slope, so I drove to the store unprepared for the unpleasant and boring impact of weather upon retail sales.

It seems that people who want to shop go to the mall when it rains. They obviously didn't come to Main Street and run between the shops. The few customers who came in dripped on my beautiful merchandise and then refused to try anything on. I guess they didn't want to peel off the wet things only to put them back on again. I put one of the tulip umbrellas in the window, and pulled the basket with the rest of the umbrellas by the door. Two customers dropped their soaked umbrellas right in the basket as they walked in. I moved the umbrellas back to the original spot.

And that was about all I did the whole day. Move the umbrellas and move them back.

I sent Heather home early and just sat behind the counter. I thought that maybe Benson V. Shelter would stop by. I could use a tuna fish sandwich. So far though he had only come by on Mondays. He seemed like one of those guys whose behavior was steady. Monday, a tuna sandwich. Tuesday, meat loaf. Wednesday discover that your wife had run off with your partner. Thursday, leftover meat loaf.

❦

We had the whole family at Angela's on Sunday. The weather had cleared and took away the worst of the heat, and the dry sunshine lifted everyone's mood. Angela's daughter Karen seemed especially happy. She was skipping in some kind of ring-around-the-rosy with Mary Ann's two-year-old granddaughter.

"What do you think?" asked Angela. "You can read pregnancy while the sperm is still meandering."

"Don't make me spoil her surprise," I said.

"Yeah, that's what I thought," she said.

At the picnic table, Mary Ann uncovered my lemon cake, and eyed the missing slice.

"Did you indulge for breakfast?"

"Yeah," I said. "No putting one over on you."

When Mary Ann went in for the coffee, I recognized the opportunity to casually introduce my plan.

"I didn't eat the cake," I said to Angela. "I shared a piece with a friend."

"Benson V. Shelter?" Angela had an amazing memory. And a galloping imagination.

"No, not Benson V. Shelter. It's a little strange, but I've made friends with this teenager. She's really sweet and she's had a hard life." Well, the hard life part was true anyway.

Angela laughed. "A sweet teenager? Isn't that one of those, what-d'you-call-it, oxymorons? Like Military Intelligence?"

"Come on," I said. "Your kids were great. Karen was a sweet teenager."

"*MY* Karen?" Angela said in the voice that parents use when they are about to tell you some horror story. There's a lot of pride, I noticed, in stories about how terrible your kids are.

"Did I ever tell you," she continued, "that Karen had her belly button pierced when she was sixteen? I had absolutely forbidden it, and then she comes home with this hole. In the cute little belly-button I gave her nourishment through. She had a ring studded with rhinestones. My god, I thought John was going to have a stroke. I don't ever remember seeing him so mad. Oh, except maybe that time the mice ate through the new ignition wires on the Thunderbird."

"But she turned out all right. No harm done."

"You're right. No harm done. Except of course for the raging infection and the doctor bills."

When I got home, Shannon was sitting on my back steps. "Come on in," I said.

She sat down at the kitchen table. From her jeans pocket she took out a piece of paper torn from a spiral binder. She tore off the tiny ragged tabs one by one and made a little pile on her left. I leaned against the refrigerator and waited until she had torn off the last one.

"Well?" I said.

"I have a list."

"Let's hear it."

"One," she said, with her finger on the actual number one she had written and circled. "I want to redecorate the room."

"But that room is beautiful!"

"Jesus, you're defensive!" she said with surprising perception. "I'm not attacking your precious room. I'm sure your old Grandma thinks it's really cute and all, but I'm a kid. If you really want me to live here, shouldn't it look like a kid's room? Is it your room, and I'm just staying there, or is it my room?"

"It's your room. You can redecorate. New paint, bedding, curtains. Not new furniture. And the paint can't be black."

"Okay." Shannon said. "Two. I need a cell phone, my own TV, and my own computer."

I thought about a conversation I had overheard in the market a few days before. One mother was telling the other that she used a GPS system to track her daughter's whereabouts through her cell phone. "Yes to the cell phone," I said. "But I get to pick it out. Yes to a TV, because I don't think we'll want to watch the same stuff ever. But no to your own computer. I told you I would put my computer where we can both use it."

"But maybe I want to use it in private."

"Yeah. That's why you can't."

"Do you think I'm going to start some chat with an old pervert?"

"I sure do."

"Can the TV have a built-in DVD player?"

"Okay," I said. She gave me a smug smile, and I knew then that she had only asked for the computer to get the TV.

"Three. An allowance."

"You can have an allowance, but I expect you to earn it. You can help with the cooking and the dishes and the housework. How much do your friends get?"

Her eyes darkened, and her business-negotiation façade faded a little. Shit, I thought, this kid doesn't have any friends.

"We'll find out the going rate," I said quickly. I opened the refrigerator, took out the ham and bread and mustard. I put a sandwich down near her little pile of shredded paper. This is how kids got fat. When mothers see hurt, they feed it.

Shannon took a bite. Her finger traced the number four but she skipped it. "Next," she said. "Can I have a car when I'm sixteen?"

I sat down across from her. "Not unless you're working and you buy it for yourself. And pay the insurance. And no working full time. You have to graduate from high school."

"Okay," she said readily. She obviously had thrown that in just to see how much she could get. "What happens then?"

"When? When you finish school?" I asked. "What do you want to do?"

"Get the fuck out of town."

"But then what? What happens once you are out of town?"

"I don't know. Get a job or something."

"Well, here's something for your list. When you graduate from school, I am willing to give you a stake to get you started with whatever you want to do. Maybe you want to think about some kind of professional training. You could go to hairdresser's school, or learn data processing, or culinary arts or something. Think about it."

"I get money when I finish school?"

"Yes. Provided the baby stays here."

"How much?"

"Twenty thousand dollars."

"Can I have a pencil?" she asked. I handed her the pen I keep by the phone, and she drew a big star in front of her last number.

"This is going good," she said. "Can I have highlights?"

"You want a highlighter pen?"

"No, highlights for my hair."

"Sure," I said.

She checked off number four. She had two numbers left, but I couldn't read them upside down.

"I want to name the baby."

I considered it. "You can name the baby but I have veto rights. The name you pick has to be okay with me. I'm not raising a kid named Hiawatha or Slash."

"But what if I can't find a name you like?"

"There are thousands of names out there. Surely you will find one that we can both agree on."

"But we have to find two."

"Two? Are you having twins?"

"No," she laughed. She put her finger on the only unchecked number. "It's for the dog!"

"Dog?"

"Yeah we have to have a dog. First, 'cause I've never had a pet and I always wanted one. And second, because we need it. For protection."

"We need protection?"

"Shit, yes." She leaned over the table, better to impart her fourteen-year-old wisdom. "I mean, someone could come by here. Say they were looking for some meth or coke or something. Something you didn't have, but they thought you did. Someone could, like, grab you by the hair and pick you up right by the hair. Then they could throw you down the stairs and kick you. And all the time you were telling them that you didn't know where it was. But they could be a lot bigger than you, and you couldn't even stop them. Then they could lock you in a closet, and you might be there for, like, all day before someone found you. And then when you finally got found, the people who found you would be all mad because you wet your pants in the closet. But you couldn't help it." She nodded in agreement with herself. "Oh yeah, we need a dog."

Holy Mother of God, I thought.

Shannon got up and took the sandwich half she hadn't finished. When she closed the door behind her, the disturbed air scattered her little pile of torn paper. I scooped the tiny pieces into my hand. Then the door re-opened and she poked her head back in.

"What the fuck is culinary arts?"

Chapter 16

———◆———

BEN SHOWED UP ON MONDAY empty-handed. I felt a surprising rush of disappointment, which was quickly replaced by embarrassment. I felt like a fool in my raspberry sundress and my extra poufy, youth-attempted hair.

"Hey," said Ben, "No offense, but could we go down the street and have lunch? You know, in real chairs, with a table and everything?"

"Sure," I said, somehow even more embarrassed.

He signed the six checks I had written out, and I flicked off the lights as we locked up. I was going to go out to lunch and take the afternoon off, in that delightful aimless way young women do.

As I walked up the block with Ben, I took in how very tall he was. I was quite tall myself—always standing in the back in group photos, maybe even bending my knees a little so I fit into the picture. But Ben walked with his head and shoulders first, and they were about eighteen inches ahead of me.

"Did you play basketball as a kid?" I asked.

He laughed and leaned in his giraffe way towards me.

"Everyone asks me that. And coaches and short guys were always asking me to try out for whatever team. But just because you're tall doesn't necessarily mean you have any athletic skill. I can't dribble the ball without hitting my foot, and I can't block shots without fouling everyone within four feet. About all I can do is stand there and look tall."

"Well, you can change light bulbs and get stuff off the top shelf."

"I certainly can."

"I can dust the top of the refrigerator."

"We've got talent. No doubt about it."

He opened a thick brass door and ushered me in, ducking his head with exaggeration.

It was a bakery, with a few scratched tables lining the wall on one side. The chairs were mismatched metal. But I guess a step up from the store's back room.

"The best tuna salad in Connecticut," Ben said. "Maybe the world."

"So I've seen," I said, and we ordered exactly the same thing he had been bringing me the last few weeks, down to the sesame seed hard roll.

"How do you know this little bakery so well?" I asked, and regretted it instantly. He seemed so relaxed today; why did I have to bring up a subject that would certainly include Maria?

But it wasn't the case.

"I come here often because I have a client up here."

"A big case?"

"No. Not a case. I have conservatorship for an old guy. He's in a nursing home. I'm only legally obligated to watch his estate, but what good is keeping his property cared for without making sure he's cared for?"

"I'm not sure I'm following."

Ben wiped mayo off his mustache.

"Last year, when I first took over the estate, I went to see the old man in the nursing home. I didn't exactly like what I saw. It occurred to me that if you have no family, if the staff thinks no one cares, they tend to neglect you. So I stop by about once a week and make sure the nurses see me. And now the old guy is dressed in clean clothes, and shaved, and he doesn't smell anymore."

I sipped my tea and regarded this good-hearted lawyer. No wonder his suit looked old.

"He must be glad to have you."

"Oh no, I'm glad to have him. Do you know what this guy did back in the fifties, who his boss was? He worked for Albert Einstein. No kidding. Einstein."

"Wow."

Ben put down his sandwich and leaned toward me, his face full of joy.

"I mean, think about it. It just blows me away. Physics and philosophy. But you know what amazes me the most? The ordinary stuff. That this old guy had lunch with Einstein, just like I'm having lunch with you. He rode in Einstein's car, for God's sake."

"He must have a million fascinating stories."

"Yeah, he must."

Ben read the puzzlement on my face.

"Harry's stories are pretty much locked up inside him. He's usually a little vague. On good days, he mostly talks about Oprah Winfrey. He's quite smitten with her."

"That's such a shame."

He shook his head. "I know. But just because he can't share his Einstein stories with me doesn't mean he doesn't have them. He's had experiences I will never have. I'm happy to go and talk about Oprah with a man like him."

"I met her once," I said.

"Oprah?"

"Yes. I saw her at O'Hare. She had this beautiful silky scarf that was about to slip off her coat. So I caught it for her. She had her hands full, so I tied it to her handbag."

"It figures that it would have something to do with clothes."

"I hadn't thought of that. But you know, I've always been observant when it comes to fashion—even if I didn't do anything about it until recently. Oprah's scarf was a deep violet with gold fringe. Striking."

"Well, I hope Oprah was appreciative."

"Definitely. You can tell your friend Harry that she's got the most lovely manners. And she's tall. Not like us of course, but tall."

"I'll tell him. He'll be quite excited. Imagine knowing Einstein and preferring Oprah."

I wasn't that surprised to see Shannon waiting on the back steps when I got home. It was kind of nice having someone there to greet me. She reminded me of a puppy, until I remembered that I had actually promised her one. I wondered if there was a way I could get out of it.

"Here," Shannon said as I unlocked the door.

She handed me a business card. It was soft and limp in the way that paper gets when you hold it in your hand a long time. The corners were frayed and grimy.

"It's the social worker. Melissa Rodriguez. You need to call her first. Let's call her today, and then you can give me money to get my hair done."

"Hold on," I said, hooking my handbag on the back of a chair. "Let's think this through."

"You changed your mind. Fuck. I knew it." Shannon grabbed the card out of my hand and headed back out the door.

"Wait. I didn't change my mind. I just want to make sure we say the right thing. To make it as easy as possible."

Shannon turned and I saw the disappointment in her eyes before she set her face back in its impenetrable defense.

"This is not necessarily going to be easy," I said. "I don't want them to say no."

"They won't say no. They'll be so glad to get rid of me, they won't ask a lot of questions."

This is exactly what Gwen's husband Jim had said. But I thought there was probably a lot more to it. You can't just go to the State Kid Store and pick out a teenager.

"It's their job to watch out for your best interest—to protect you," I said, and Shannon snorted and rolled her eyes.

"Oh yeah, they've done a super job of that so far."

"And then there's all the red tape and paperwork. Has anything ever been easy to get from the State?"

"No shit. I can't even get my teeth cleaned without about a zillion forms."

"Right," I said. "So let's sit down and plan this out."

Shannon sat down in the same chair she took when she had dinner with me, when she brought me her list of demands. At home when we were kids, we always had our places at the table, and never even thought of taking a different seat. Family habits were nice, and I was seeing my first one for my new family. I smiled at Shannon, but of course she didn't smile back.

"So," I said, "What's this Melissa Rodriguez like? How long has she been your social worker?"

"Two years," said Shannon. "That's like centuries in social work years. These guys come and go. Usually go."

"And what is she like? You know how to work her, I'll bet. What does she like to hear?"

Shannon frowned. "She's not as easy as the last one. Before Melissa, I had Monica. She was one of those weepy types, who like saving people. I could get her to agree to anything if I gave her a hug. But those kind never last. They either end up in the loony bin or they marry someone rich and don't work anymore. But Melissa, she's one of those tough ones who never trusts you."

Like you, I thought.

"She told me a while back that her job is easier if she just figures that all the kids are lying all the time."

"So she's going to be skeptical…we can't lay it on too thick."

"Yeah, she'll never believe you if you give her a load of crap like how much you love me or shit like that."

"So what do we say?"

Shannon got up and opened the refrigerator. I found myself a bit annoyed at this presumption. It wasn't going to be easy to share the house after all these years. She took out the milk.

"That's probably not …"

"Fuck," she said, putting her nose to the carton. "How long has this been in here?"

"I don't drink that much milk. I was going to pick some up this week."

She looked at me with disapproval. "And you want a baby in this house?"

"Well, I didn't think she'd be here today!"

Shannon took a bottle of spring water and sat back down.

"Back to Melissa," I said. "Do you think she would buy it if we just tell her we're lonely and we want each other's company?"

"I'm not lonely," Shannon said instantly. "Maybe you are, but not me."

"Okay," I said.

"But...she'd believe me if I said that you had a nice house, and I'll get my own room and a television."

"Which is true."

"Yup."

"Okay. This is good. Let's stay close to the facts. I want to take care of you. You want a better lifestyle and you'll get it from me."

"So let's call her."

I hesitated. I didn't want to tell her to keep the pregnancy a secret, although I needed her to. If the social worker knew that Shannon was going to have a baby, everything would get very complicated. Perhaps there were rules that would make it impossible for me to adopt Shannon. They might encourage her to have an abortion. And they might question my motives.

But if I didn't mention the pregnancy, and Shannon did, well, that could be disastrous. Melissa Rodriguez would know that my intentions were as dishonest and dishonorable as they were. If Shannon spilled the beans, she'd ruin any chance of having this plan succeed. But I couldn't bring it up with Shannon either. I was afraid to make it so obvious to her that she had that kind of power.

I said, as casually as possible, "What about the baby?"

"None of her business," Shannon said.

I took a breath, and jumped off the high dive into the rocky shallow water.

"Let's call," I said.

We got voice mail. "Naturally," said Shannon. So I left a message that I had become friends with Shannon Miller and would like to speak to Ms. Rodriguez as soon as possible.

"If she calls you first," I said, "Stick to the script."

"Trust me," she said.

❧

Melissa Rodriguez called that evening.

"What did Shannon do?" she asked.

"Nothing," I said. "Nothing wrong, that is. I met her a while ago. I like her."

"No one likes her," said Melissa.

"I do," I said. "I'll admit she's not everyone's cup of tea…"

There was a guffaw on the other end. I didn't think that anyone actually guffawed since Charles Dickens' time, but there it was.

"Look," I said, with indignation creeping into my voice. "I do like her. Don't ask me why. I'm fifty years old, single, financially secure. I've never had any kids. I like having Shannon around. In fact, I want to adopt her."

"Where do you live?" Melissa Rodriguez asked. "I'll be right over."

❧

I thought about calling Shannon, driving over to Decision House and bringing her here right away. She could handle this better than I could, I thought.

But I sat in Shannon's designated kitchen chair, and waited alone for the social worker to arrive. I heard a coughing engine pull into the yard, and a young woman slammed the car door and marched up the front walk.

Melissa Rodriguez was barely out of college. She was pretty in a severe way; 'hard' my mother called it. She wore a brown cardigan buttoned up to her throat despite the warm evening. Her blue jeans were about a half-inch too short, and her woven sandals displayed very knobby toes. Her jaw was locked and she had her hair pulled back so tight her eyebrows must hurt.

I smiled warmly. "Come on in. Can I get you some coffee or something?"

"Black."

We sat in the living room, and she pulled a file and a pen out of the enormous handbag that was capable of holding her whole life.

"How did you meet Shannon?" she asked, pen poised.

"Her boyfriend mows my lawn. We started talking one day, and I just felt drawn to her."

"She talks to you?"

"Sure," I said. Just as I was tempted to paint the rosiest picture possible, Melissa pursed her lips and narrowed her eyes, reminding me that she knew Shannon already. "She's not exactly bubbly, but she does talk. Sometimes if I distract her—with a task or something, she opens up a little."

"A task?"

"You know, making cookies or peeling vegetables."

"She makes cookies?"

"Yes, she does." The young social worker stared at me like I said Shannon could fly. "She writes dirty words in the icing," I added, and Melissa nodded and the throbbing in her jaw relaxed a bit. She put down her pen.

"I'm sorry, but I have to ask," she said. "Are you gay?"

I was surprised, but then again, Shannon had asked the same thing. The world had changed in some significant way while I was minding my debits and credits.

"Don't apologize," I said, "I know you have to ask. No, I'm not gay. I'm not sexually interested in Shannon, or any other fourteen-year-old for that matter. If I were looking for romance, I would be looking for some nice middle-aged man, not too chubby, who's kind to his mother. Oh, and maybe he would have a cottage at the beach."

"That sounds really nice," Melissa said, her tight shoulders dropping a fraction.

"Yeah," I agreed with a sigh. "Anyway, back to Shannon. I really want her. I want to be her mother."

"Do you know what adopting a teenager is like? A troubled teenager?"

"No, I don't. I don't know anything about teenagers at all, troubled or otherwise. But I like her, and to be honest, the house just feels empty now when she isn't here."

"I can't let you read her file—not yet—but let me tell you a thing or two about Shannon. She has attachment disorder, like many abused and neglected kids. She won't open up to you. She won't trust you. She'll never love you."

"That could be. But I'm pretty irresistible." I smiled, and I almost got Melissa to do the same. "I know her life has been awful, and she's badly scarred. But it seems to me that I can make her life a little better for a couple of years, and I want to."

"Why don't you try foster parenting for a while?"

Foster parenting. Jesus. I was better prepared for the sexual question than this one. How could I respond to such a reasonable suggestion? Foster parenting was certainly the most practical option—except in my case. I needed to be related to the baby. I sipped my coffee, striking a pose that I hoped signified that I was seriously considering it, all the while foraging for possible ways to reject it.

"I don't know," I finally said. "How many foster homes has Shannon been through?"

"A ton."

"She won't believe in it. She'll consider me just another temporary caretaker. She'll keep her guard up and never let me in. She'll always be waiting for the end. You said yourself that Shannon can't trust anyone. For once in her life I want her to see that someone is committed to her. She's not a car I can test drive. I'm not going to return her in sixty days. She has to know I'll stick by her, or we'll certainly be doomed."

Melissa Rodriguez leaned away from me, as if giving herself a little more space to absorb this strange information.

"What does Shannon think? Have you discussed this?"

"We have. I think Shannon feels she can manipulate me and that's appealing to her." Melissa leaned forward again, nodding slightly, and I knew I was on track. "She wants her own bedroom, and a TV, and a puppy, and an allowance, of course. All the normal teenage self-centeredness. But I see something else too. She's afraid. Afraid she'll be disappointed again. I can't do that. I don't want to even start if you don't think it can happen."

She put down her pen. Melissa Rodriguez looked at me and gave me a remarkable, slow sweet smile.

"It can happen," she said.

I called Decision House. The girl who answered said, "Oh, I'd be thrilled to get Shannon for you," and I waited for seven minutes while I heard screeching that might have been music and might have been murder. I hung up and called back. The line was busy.

I grabbed my bag and drove over there. Shannon came to the door, summoned by an older woman who looked as if she had materialized out of an Alfred Hitchcock movie. She has a kind face, I told myself; it's just the porch light.

Shannon and I went out to my car, and leaned against the hood.

"Melissa Rodriguez was just at my house," I said. "She said yes."

"I told you they'd be glad to get rid of me," Shannon said without a trace of the excitement that I was feeling. "I already made an appointment at the hairdresser. Tomorrow. I was going to come by first thing, but now that you're here—can I have eighty dollars? Plus tip."

Chapter 17

WEDNESDAY WAS THE FOURTH OF July, so I spent Tuesday at the shop marking down everything for Thursday. I hated to put these beautiful things on sale so soon after they had arrived, but no one paid full price after the Fourth. I never had in my whole life.

As I took the red pencil to the price tags, I obsessed about the baby. It wouldn't be long before Shannon started to show. I had to convince the social worker that I was committed to Shannon before the baby became obvious. Then I would profess worry and doubt, but in the end, I'd decide that I wanted them both. I wondered how far along Shannon was, and how soon I could get her to a doctor to find out. Maybe I'd have a baby by Christmas. Too bad for Snow White and the Seven Dwarfs.

About 4:00, the telephone rang; it was Melissa Rodriguez.

"Sorry to bother you at work, but I wanted to get in touch before the holiday," she said. "I saw Shannon today."

I waited. Either the game was over or just beginning.

"Shannon pretty much confirmed what you said. I mean, she didn't come right out and tell me that she thought you were a pushover, but she did say that she thought you were a lonely lady who didn't suck as a cook. She said, and I quote, 'Cynthia thinks she can win me over, but it ain't gonna happen.'"

I thought Shannon might have gone a little overboard playing the tough kid. "So she doesn't want to live with me?" I said, trying to sound hurt and disappointed.

"Oh, on the contrary. She says that your house is a million times better than the group home. And she can't wait till she gets a regular allowance."

"But you think it's a bad idea."

"I didn't say that. Shannon also said something that shows me she's not quite as mercenary at heart as she pretends. She said, 'Cynthia is going to quit her job to be a mother.'"

Oh Jesus, she just couldn't help herself. Maybe I could strangle her right after she gives birth.

But Melissa interpreted that sly statement in a strangely positive way. "She believes you are committed to her," she said. "I'm going to help you make it happen."

"That's wonderful. I'm so happy."

"There's a ton of paperwork, and everything takes forever. We have to get started right away. Can I come over Thursday evening?"

"Certainly. Come anytime. Should Shannon be here?"

Thankfully, Melissa said no. "This is all background stuff. We'll go faster with just the adults."

"Great. I'll see you then," I said.

"By the way," said Melissa, "Did you pay for Shannon to get her hair done today?"

Shit. "Yes, I'm afraid I did. I probably shouldn't have."

"It's okay," said Melissa. "But I'd be careful in trying to buy Shannon's affection. She'll definitely encourage you to try, but to quote Shannon, it ain't gonna happen."

When I got home from work Tuesday evening, Shannon was waiting for me on the back steps. It took me an extra second to recognize her. She had dyed her hair black—witch black, Elvis black. Her pale skin took on a greenish cast under the funereal curtain.

"I need a phone," she said. "Do you know how hot it is? How long it took me to walk over here?"

"Hello to you too," I said in my own mother's sarcastic-mom voice. "It's certainly hot, but I don't believe for a second that you walked here."

"I might have had to, if D.J. wasn't home. And I could have passed out or something."

"You could have called me from the group home."

"Oh yeah, right. And have all the other little asshole bitches hear every word about our plans."

I tried to resist commenting on her hair, but the mom voice took hold.

"I thought you were going to get highlights," I said.

"I did," Shannon replied, and gave her hair a TV-shampoo-commercial toss. In the sunlight, I could see gleams of purple and blue, like ribbons of oil in a parking lot puddle.

"Hmm," I acknowledged. "Does D.J. like it?"

"Yeah," she said. "He said you were going to freak out."

It startled me that D.J. would express concern on how I would react.

"Did you tell him about...our plan?"

She held up her thumb and forefinger about an inch apart. "I told him I was *this close* to convincing you that I should move in."

It was an interesting spin on the situation that I wasn't sure I liked, but it would work for now.

I held my own thumb and forefinger even closer. "This close. Melissa called. We're going to start the paperwork on Thursday."

"Good," said Shannon. "You can drive me back."

My family was planning its traditional beach outing for the next day. I wasn't prepared to foist Shannon on them yet—I mean, introduce her to her new loving family. But I knew it had to be soon, so as I drove her home, I reluctantly asked Shannon if she wanted to go to the beach with us tomorrow.

"No way," she said. "D.J. is bringing me to a party with all the cool kids."

"Okay," I said quickly before she could change her mind. I felt guilty right away. I thought about how horrible she looked in that borrowed orange bikini, and despite the warnings from Melissa, I asked Shannon, "Do you need a new bathing suit?"

"My bathing suit days are over. My belly's starting to stick out."

Something close to affection took hold of me. Shannon actually had turned down my bribe. "You don't have to hide it for too much longer. I want you to be healthy and happy."

"Let's stop at the cell phone store," she said.

Chapter 18

------------◆------------

As I HAD EVERY YEAR since birth, I spent the Fourth at the beach with my family.

Years ago, there were cars with my grandparents and Aunt Marjorie and Uncle Nick and cousin Sheila, and our car with Mom and Dad and us three girls, followed by Aunt Lorraine and whoever her husband was at the time. Now the caravan consisted of Mary Ann and Frank and Angela and John riding together, and most of the kids and grandkids in their own cars. I usually drove alone, so I could leave when I'd had enough. Often I was ready to go home long before anyone else.

I remember driving down to Rhode Island before cars had air conditioning. When the rolled-down windows and the speed of the car created the only breeze we had. The roar of the engine and the oncoming traffic left conversation to brief shouts. And there were years when we drove in pouring rain, my father leaning towards the wipers. My mother would turn back to us girls and reassure us, "You just wait, the sun will be shining at the beach." And sometimes it was.

We certainly didn't have to worry about the weather this day. The sky was sharp blue, cloudless. I had the air on lightly, the radio off, the windows tight. I drove in silence. My last quiet drive for a very long time, I thought.

We arrived quite early; we needed to all park alongside each other—it had never been otherwise. Mary Ann went down from the parking lot with one blanket. She had inherited from my father (not by virtue of being the oldest but rather the bossiest) the job of picking the spot. She set the blanket down like the flag planted on the moon, and gave us a toot on my Dad's old penny whistle. And then we trekked in single file, each carrying as much as we could, with Karen back at the car guarding the overflow: blankets and umbrellas, chairs and coolers, beach bags and diaper bags, boogie boards and pails and shovels and beach balls and one big kite.

By the time we set up we were red-faced and sweaty. The kids were already running in that tiptoe way down to the water's edge.

"Stop! Wait!" cried Mary Ann. "Sunscreen first!"

Mary Ann was obsessed with sunscreen. She always started with the smallest baby and worked her way up, slathering lotion on arms and legs, faces and backs. She held each wriggling kid by one skinny arm, greasing him until he was slippery enough to slide out of her grasp. Then she'd start on the adults. She'd have the women hold up their hair as she rubbed lotion into necks that would never see the sun. For the men, no back was too hairy, no belly too embarrassing. With so many of us, by the time she had finished with her husband Frank, it was time to start on the baby again. We tolerated this because we loved her; it was the closest she could come to an embrace.

On this day, watching the now-grownup kids play in the water with their own children, all the previous beach holidays seemed to crowd together like the nearly identical umbrellas nodding to each other in the sun. I had believed that I spent those days playing with the children, but now it was clear to me that I had been as much on the periphery then as I was at this moment. Waving from the blanket; the benevolent aunt.

But it wasn't too late. I watched Angela swing Max through the surf. I could do that too. I had enough energy for a baby. Shannon might even turn out to be a help. Maybe not.

In the middle of the afternoon, I found myself alone with Angela. The kids were back in the surf with the grandkids. At the water's edge, MaryAnn re-started her lotion procedure with the baby. Frank and John, discovering after lunch that one cooler was empty, went off to the wharf to see if they could fill it with lobsters or clams.

Angela and I lay side by side on the green army blanket. The sounds of surf and squealing children and crackling radios receded in the heat, as if the sun's penetration into my skin dominated all the other senses.

Angela's fingertips touched mine.

"Okay," she said. "What's up with you? You're way too quiet. What are you trying not to tell me?"

I had been nervous about this moment, but now I felt calm—ready to share my secret.

"Remember the girl—Shannon—I told you about, the one who has been hanging around the house?"

"Sure."

"Well, she's moving in with me."

"Really? Wow."

"Actually, it's a lot more than that. I'm adopting her."

"My God."

"I know—I can hardly believe it myself, but it's really happening."

"My God," Angela said again. She propped herself up on her elbows and squinted at me. "How old is she?"

"Fourteen."

"My God," she said, stuck. "This happened so fast. She must be wonderful."

"Um, she's fourteen. She's kind of a brat. But I'm crazy about her in some strange way," I added.

"Cynthia; a mother," she said to herself, trying it out. "What drew you to her? Does she remind you of someone? What does she look like?"

I thought about it for a minute. I skipped over the blue-black hair. Maybe I could get her to dye it back before she met the family.

"To tell you the truth, she sort of looks like me at that age. Only much sadder."

Angela smiled at the memory, and lay back down. "You mean, she looks like you the summer you discovered Leonard Cohen."

I laughed. "Yeah, exactly. Only her sadness comes from more than listening to depressing music."

"A hard life?"

"Shannon doesn't talk much about it, but the few things she has said would straighten your hair."

Angela was quiet for a while.

"What do you like best about her?" she asked.

I raised my arm and laid it across my eyes, as if shielding myself from the sun. I didn't want Angela to see me lie when I didn't say, 'her baby.'

I found it difficult to see Shannon apart from the baby she was giving me. I tore through my thoughts as quickly as I could to uncover something I might like about her.

"Her attitude," I finally said. "Don't get me wrong; there are lots of times when she's downright nasty. But she's tough, and sharp, and funny. And she's completely uncensored. I like not knowing what outrageous thing she'll say next."

"Kids are the reason the word 'fresh' is both positive and negative."

This wasn't so hard after all, I thought. I concentrated again on feeling the hot sun on my forearms.

"So," Angela said after a while, "So what does Shannon like best about you?"

"My money."

Angela laughed. "No, seriously."

"No. Seriously." I replied ruefully. "She's quite openly pleased that she won't be poor anymore, and she plans to spend as much as possible in the next few years."

"But she must like you. I'm mean, you're really so sweet. She must see that."

"I think she's mystified by me. She watches every move I make. I think she's waiting for me to hurt her. And she's completely bewildered by my alien normal life."

"Well, I'm happy for you. I can't wait to meet her."

"Don't set your expectations too high."

Angela leaned back and closed her eyes against the sun.

"Once upon a time," she started, and I turned on my side towards her, so I could watch as well as listen to her story, "there was a lady in Germany who had a reputation for Black Forest Cake. She made the best black forest cake in all of Germany. She was renowned for this cake. The bishop came to her one day and asked her to make black forest cake for the church's Christmas celebration. Of course, she said. I'll make you the best cake you have ever had. On Christmas morning, she began to make the cake. She took out the big tin jar where she kept the flour and it was empty. Completely empty. She had never checked to make sure she had all the ingredients.

Now it was Christmas and all the stores were closed, and she had promised a black forest cake."

"Like Dad and the Snow White doll," I said.

"Yes, like Dad," said Angela, "except there was no Noveck's Pharmacy to save the day. So the woman looked into her cupboard to see what she might be able to do instead, and she found she had twenty Hostess cupcakes."

"Oh come on," I complained. "Hostess cupcakes in Germany?"

"Quiet," she said. "Of course they have Hostess cupcakes in Germany. She had four children and she had twenty cupcakes for their school lunchboxes the next week. So she took the Hostess cupcakes and made sort of a pyramid, sticking them together with strawberry filling. Then she covered them with a tremendous layer of strawberries and whipped cream. She took the concoction over to the church and the bishop served it after high mass. Everyone knew she made the best black forest cake in Germany, and everyone raved about this particularly amazing black forest cake. It was the best black forest cake they had ever eaten. And they all wondered how the woman had managed to get the whipped cream into pockets throughout the delicious cake."

Chapter 19

———◆———

SHANNON WAS RIGHT. THE STATE of Connecticut was only too happy to say goodbye to her.

It's not that there wasn't a truckload of paperwork. But on every page, there was always some criteria that didn't apply to teenagers, some requirement that was waived for teenagers, some checklist that we could just skip, because, well, this was a teenager.

Shannon called on her new cell phone early in the evening, when Melissa was just taking forms out of her bag, to tell me that D.J.'s idiot sister, Celeste, got an allowance of $20.00 a week, and she didn't do anything at all to help around the house, except maybe to dust accidentally because her fat ass swiped all the furniture as she walked around. "Mm," I said, as Melissa watched curiously.

Despite how simple the process seemed, or maybe because of it, I found myself increasingly anxious. My fingers trembled as I read an adoption brochure while Melissa copied the family tree from my bible. This leaflet described in detail the ten-week intensive instruction that preceded even temporary custody. This was terrible. Shannon was probably more than ten weeks along already. In ten more weeks, Shannon would look like she was about to explode. And what if I couldn't start the program right away?

"Oh that," said Melissa looking at the paper in my shaky hand. "That's for babies and little kids only. For teenagers, especially in a group home like Shannon, we like to get them into the adoptive home immediately."

This was even scarier than ten weeks. I wasn't ready for Shannon to move in. I was kind of hoping that she'd at least be back in school. But back in school brought me back around to ten weeks. I felt dizzy. Shannon had told Melissa that I was going to quit my job. But that was for the baby. I didn't want to quit for Shannon. She was old enough to stay home alone—but home alone in MY HOME? How quickly could I get my hands on a safe?

Melissa startled me out of my panic.

"I suppose you are curious about the father."

Oh no, I thought. *She knows about the baby. This is the end of everything.* Melissa opened a file, and shuffled a few pages, and said, "We don't know who Shannon's father is." *Jesus; Shannon's father.* How could I have forgotten about Shannon's family? I emitted an unintentionally huge sigh. Melissa looked up from her papers. "Yes," she said, misinterpreting my relief. "There won't be any custody issues from that corner."

Melissa found the page she was searching for. "Back when Shannon's mother was in the picture, she had us track down the man she said was Shannon's father. We were looking to collect some child support. But the guy wasn't Shannon's father. He'd been in prison when Shannon was conceived. When we told the mother, she just said, 'Fuck, then, I guess I don't remember.' That guy had lived with the mom when

Shannon was little. He was a very bad person; Shannon is lucky he's not her father."

"Is there anyone else who could contest the adoption?" I asked.

"No," she said. "When we first took Shannon away from her mother, we tried very hard to get someone in the family to take her. They absolutely refused. A note from the social worker at the time says, 'Unsuitable anyway.' I'm not sure what he meant but my guess is that the relatives were just as shitty as mom."

"How did her mother lose custody in the first place?"

Melissa pulled out several pages from the file. She handed them to me without a word.

I guess there are kids who have worse stories; but Shannon's was plenty horrible enough. Page after page of parental warnings interspersed with bouts of temporary foster care. There was some evidence of physical abuse, but mostly the charges entailed risk of injury and neglect. Mom's addictions were severe; she was totally self-absorbed. The last straw was abandonment. Went off on what she later called a vacation, and left Shannon. Shannon, in second grade, got home from school and found herself locked out of the apartment. She spent the night in the basement laundry room, and went to school the next day in the same clothes. The following day, same clothes and dirtier. Shannon was on the free lunch program, and it was obvious to the teacher that she was ravenous. The school placed a call to family services and they sent Shannon to a shelter. Mom showed up three days later. "Christ," she said to the police, "you'd think the kid would have the sense to knock on the neighbor's door."

The process of terminating parental rights was long, complicated, and nasty. Social workers expected Shannon to be heartbroken or hate-filled. Shannon obliged by being both simultaneously. She was shuffled from foster home to foster home, each interval shorter than the last. I read about fights and theft and vandalism. The vandalism was especially appalling. Broken family heirlooms and burned photographs. By age eleven, Shannon was out of foster care and into state-run group homes. The destruction continued there, but at least could not involve irreplaceable keepsakes. My heart pounded as I thought about my family albums and my precious home. I hadn't witnessed any of this behavior. Shannon was smart-mouthed, but her disrespect hadn't extended to my possessions. I remembered her finger just barely touching the Easter photo on my bureau. Had she changed, or was she saving it up? My little angel salt-shaker had not reappeared.

"We'll have your background check done by the end of the week—but that's just a formality," Melissa said, gathering back the file. We just have to make sure you're not a criminal or a pedophile—or worse."

"What's worse than being a pedophile?"

Melissa unconsciously looked around the room, making sure we were alone. "Being poor."

"Well, I'm not poor."

"Good. Then Shannon can move right in."

"That's so wonderful," I said. "I can hardly wait."

Angela called on Friday to emphasize how important it was that I tell Mom and Mary Ann immediately. Critical as it might have been, it didn't mean that Angela didn't go about delivering the message in her own style.

She said, "Remember after Dad died, Mom talked for weeks about going to visit Aunt Lorraine? And eventually she did go down and visit—and she stayed an extra two weeks. And remember, when she came back she kept saying how lonely Aunt Lorraine was without a new husband? And how, when she finally moved down there, we were already used to the idea?"

Chapter 20

I HAD JUST PICKED UP THE phone to call Shannon when D.J. and Shannon pulled into the yard. Shannon didn't even turn to watch as D.J. struggled to get the mower from the back of the truck, never mind lend a hand. She slid down out of the truck and up to the kitchen door and waltzed in.

I immediately told Shannon that she'd be meeting my family on Sunday. She shrugged and said, "Whatever," but then went to the full-length mirror that hung inside the spare bedroom door, holding her stomach in, then out. She gave herself the finger.

She got a Popsicle and sat down at the sunroom table. A little sunburn across her cheeks and nose helped the black hair quite a bit.

"So where did you go on the Fourth of July?" I asked.

Shannon rolled her eyes a little to let me know that the third degree wasn't part of the deal. "To a party. Like I told you."

I figured I needed to assert myself right away. "Where was this party?"

"In town."

"Where in town?"

"Jesus. At this guy Cole's house."

"Were his parents there?"

"No."

"Were there any adults there?"

"Yeah. Cole."

"How old is Cole?"

"I don't know. Maybe twenty."

"How many kids your age were there?"

She stopped the monosyllabic answers and smiled for the first time. Her face was full of pleasure.

"Just me. I was the only kid there. Everyone else was in college. It was so cool."

I thought this over.

"I'm kind of surprised that D.J. would take you to a party with older kids. He doesn't mind that you're so much younger than everyone else?"

She frowned. "Well, maybe a little bit. He tells everyone I'm sixteen."

I gave her my own frown.

"Okay, so maybe it's because that's what he thinks I am."

"D.J. thinks you're sixteen? In eighth grade?"

"He thinks I got held back a couple of times. Celeste couldn't wait to tell him that." She smirked. "Like I should call his sister a liar?"

"This isn't good," I said. "You need to tell D.J. that you're only fourteen."

Shannon picked up her Popsicle stick. She held it as if it were a pen and gave me a narrow look in an unnerving imitation of Melissa Rodriguez.

"We all have secrets," she said.

Christ. Bribes were one thing. Extortion was another. I couldn't let her blackmail me this early in the project, or by the time the baby came, Shannon would have gobbled up my nest egg, and I'd be washing onesies in the salad spinner.

"I guess I'll have to tell him myself," I said.

I thought for sure she would call my bluff, but she caved.

"Come on, Cynthia. Please." Her voice changed from demanding to pleading in an instant. "D.J. is my only real friend. The only reason anyone is nice to me is because of him. I thought I'd have the whole summer to be kind of normal, but I realized at the party that I only have a few weeks. D.J. is going to find out pretty soon that I'm pregnant and I'll go right back to my life that sucks."

All the toughness fell from her face. It softened me a bit.

"Maybe D.J. will surprise you, and continue to like you even if you are fourteen and pregnant."

"God, you just don't get it." She gave me an exasperated look, like teacher to slow student. "If he sticks by me, everyone will assume the baby is his, and his family will have shits. And if he says the baby isn't his, then all his friends will call him an asshole for liking someone who's already knocked up. He can't win."

Amazing, I thought. How could anyone think she had ever been held back?

"Just give me a few weeks," she continued.

"You're too young to hang around with college kids. It's dangerous."

"I'm okay. I swear, I'm not doing any drugs or booze or anything, cause of the baby." She laughed rather ruefully. "And I ain't gonna get pregnant."

"You could get hurt."

"No way. I've been taking care of myself for years."

I knew I'd regret it, but I relented. "I won't tell D.J., and you can hang around with him here. No parties."

"But that's the best part."

"Well, you can tell him that your mother won't let you."

"That fucking sucks," she said. But there was no anger in her eyes as she got up and took another Popsicle out of the freezer.

Sunday at Angela's. I had casually asked Shannon if she'd like to go to church with me, but she gave me the old exasperated eye-roll that was becoming so familiar. I didn't push it. I picked up Shannon after Mass.

I parked in front of Decision House and started to get out of the car. Shannon flew through the door, hissing, "Get back in the car. Let's go."

She jumped into the passenger seat. "Go. GO!" she ordered.

Caught up in the urgency, I peeled away like the getaway car for some bank robbery. Shannon turned in her seat and shook her fist at the house, laughing.

"Put your seat belt on," I said as we reached the stop sign at the end of the block.

I turned and looked at her.

Shannon had pulled her hair back into a neat ponytail, held by a turquoise scrungie. She had taken off about seventy-eight percent of her eyeliner, leaving her only slightly more made up than Elizabeth Taylor's Cleopatra. All the heavy rings that usually clamped up the sides of her ears were gone, and she wore one pair of large silver hoops in what women my age consider the normal places.

She was dressed in a white eyelet blouse, untucked over a short denim skirt. She wore pink flip-flops and one of those yellow rubber bracelets that usually says something uplifting, although in Shannon's case it might say something entirely different.

"Pretty cute, huh?" she said as I scrutinized her.

I was dressed similarly, in the old lady interpretation. I wore a pale green henley from the shop, and my white denim skirt, about seven inches longer than Shannon's. In place of her big hoops, I had tiny peridot earrings. A gold watch substituted for the rubber bracelet, and bronze ballet flats instead of flip-flops. We were both pretty cute.

"Very," I said. "Who did you swipe the clothes from?"

"Borrowed," she asserted. She looked back towards the house and laughed again. "Fucking LaKisha," she said.

"Will LaKisha kill you when you get back?"

"Probably. But I figure I can pay her off if you give me ten dollars."

Angela lived in a nice neighborhood, in a good-sized Garrison colonial on a street full of similar well-kept houses. Before going up to the door, Shannon stood on the sidewalk and eyed the house.

"Your sister's house is bigger than yours," she said.

"Yes it is."

"Does she have more money than you?"

"I don't know," I replied.

She started up the walk.

"Well," she said, considering. "I'll be nice to her. You know, just in case."

I opened the front door and there in front of me was everything anyone wanted to know about my family. They were all standing in a big semicircle, with balloons and streamers and a big banner across the living room that said, "Welcome Home, Shannon!"

Shannon stood behind me on the threshold. "Jesus Christ," she muttered in my ear.

I stepped in. Shannon seemed stuck in the doorway, and Angela rushed up and took her by the hand and drew her past me into the center of the room. And everyone applauded. They cheered and clapped, surrounding the stunned and stiff teenager, all trying to introduce themselves at once.

I don't think I could have loved them more. I began to cry, picturing the year ahead, when the banner would say, "It's a Boy!" or "It's a Girl!" and there would be happy fighting over who got to hold the baby next.

Someone took the bowl of scalloped potatoes that I was still holding in my hands, and I managed to separate the group into two—Mary Ann's family on one side, and Angela's on the other. And I stood by Shannon and made a more organized attempt at introductions, as Shannon nodded at each name, obviously uncomprehending.

"Don't worry," I whispered, "You'll get used to it."

"No way," she said.

The frenzy finally died down, and everyone went out to the back yard, where there were more balloons and ribbons. And presents. I hadn't seen so many presents since Aunt Marjorie had managed her conceptual miracle and produced Cousin Sheila. Shannon opened a jewelry box from Mary Ann's kids stocked with necklaces and bracelets and earrings. There were fancy socks from Mary Ann, who knew less about what teenagers liked than I did. Karen and Michael and the Seans had chipped in for a fabulous iPod, and they assured Shannon that it was loaded with loud tunes. Shannon unwrapped a skateboard, and I gave her a warning look that clearly said 'Don't hurt that baby,' and she nodded and held it to her chest like it was her very favorite gift. And Angela gave her a photograph of Mom and Dad, in a frame that said "Grandparents."

As Shannon unwrapped present after present, her eyes darted around, as if she expected someone to jump out of the bushes and call a halt to this unexpected windfall. I should have been saddened by her nervousness, but in truth, I was reassured. I wanted her on her best behavior, and I wasn't sure if she could behave and be happy at the same time.

Angela had set up three folding tables end to end, with pink paper tablecloths and vases with white daisies. There were fifteen adults, five little ones, and Shannon. I wanted to make sure I sat next to Shannon, so I could give her a nudge or a little kick if her language got too raunchy or she insulted Mary Ann's dish, or present or— the worst possible scenario—one of her grandchildren.

But Michael grabbed Shannon first, and said, "Come sit with me." And the next seat was the high chair for Max, and Sean-Girl of course needed to feed the baby. Across from them Mary Ann and Frank were already seated. Angela gave me a questioning look as she read the desperation in my face, and she took me by the hand and led me to sit with her several seats down from Shannon. *Oh please*, I thought, *Be good.*

Shannon, awkward and self-consciousness, drummed her spoon against the table.

"So what's your favorite subject in school?" asked Mary Ann, attempting in her Mary Ann way to make polite conversation.

"Chemistry," Shannon answered immediately, and I went for my water.

"Wow," said Michael. "What do you like about Chemistry?"

"That I don't have to take it," she said.

Everyone laughed and Shannon's shoulders relaxed a little and Mary Ann's jaw got tight.

"Do you know what you'd like to do once you finish school?" asked John.

'I'm going into culinary arts," she said, looking at me. "That's cooking," she explained.

"Right," said John. "What's your best dish?"

"Salad," said Shannon. Then her face clouded. "I guess that's not cooking."

"No," said Michael, "but it's definitely culinary. It counts."

"Yeah, that's right," she said nodding with her whole body.

And so dinner progressed.

Karen asked Shannon if she had a boyfriend.

"Sort of. He's going off to college though."

Mary Ann gave me a blistering look that Shannon caught.

"Oh, he's really just a friend," she explained. My heart went out to her for trying to get me off the hook. Then she added. "Anyway, I'm too young to shack up."

Mary Ann coughed.

Angela quickly changed the subject. "Shannon, honey, have you been brought up in any church?"

Shannon smiled, relieved to have a straightforward question. "I've been to lots of churches—depending on who I was living with. Mostly Baptist, since Baptists seem to like to take in kids. But if they can't save your soul right away, they usually send you back. I've been to Catholic Church just like you guys. It's pretty much the same as Baptist."

"How is it the same?" asked Angela.

Shannon put down her lemonade. "Well, they both got the Jesus part of course. And then there's the fainting."

"Fainting?" Mary Ann asked.

"Sure—but I guess not exactly the same. The Baptists faint from all the holiness. Catholics faint from all the kneeling down and getting up."

A considerable howling ensued, mostly from the men. Mary Ann did not laugh. Angela teased her, trying to get her to admit to the humor of it.

"Come on, Mary Ann. You have done it yourself. Just like Mom used to."

Mary Ann conceded. "Mom and I have delicate metabolisms."

"True," said Angela, "You're exactly like her."

"I know I look more like her the older I get. Believe me, I'm worried. But I don't understand how you don't. I was reading an article the other day that said that when siblings get older they look more and more like each other. That it's been scientifically proven. But I don't see a resemblance between any of us at all."

Frank said, "Actually, it's always amazed me that you three girls look nothing alike. I see a lot of your mother in Mary Ann, and a tiny bit of your father in Cynthia. Angela's some kind of throwback to an ancient generation, I think. And there's just no overlap. If a stranger met you on the street, he'd never think you're sisters."

"Well, how about an independent opinion?" said Brian, Mary Ann's oldest. "Shannon, do you think these ladies look like sisters?"

Shannon looked at me and my sisters. She squinted. "No, they're really different."

"Mary Ann, maybe you should write to the author of that article, and say that siblings don't always get more alike as they age," I suggested.

"I should," said Mary Ann.

"You know," said Shannon, still examining my sisters' faces. "There's really a simple explanation. I mean, think about it. It's just as plain as can be that you all have different fathers."

Mary Ann spilled her wine, and the pink paper tablecloth turned red in a spreading circle.

"No honey," she said firmly. "My mother and father were married for years. No other marriages."

"Fuck other marriages," Shannon insisted. "Your mother could have been seeing somebody on the side. Why, Kelly at school has one little brother who's white and one little brother who's black and a sister who might be from another planet."

"No dear," Mary Ann said again, more firmly. "That's not our mother."

But Shannon wouldn't stop, now that she figured she had solved our mystery.

"No offense," she said. "But from the stories that Cynthia tells, your mother could have been, like, bored out of her mind."

Brian, whose altar-boy freckles could never hide the mischief in his eyes, said in a very grave voice, "You know, that could be. Maybe we should ask Grandma how close she really was to Father Casey."

"Brian!" said Mary Ann, and she did indeed look exactly like my purple-faced mother at her most vexed.

"Mary Ann's right," Shannon said to Brian, absolutely serious. "It might be tricky to ask." She sat back and thought about it. Then she smiled. "Maybe you could get her drunk."

Angela leapt from the table and ran into the house.

Oh no, I thought. *Oh no*. It's not possible to bring down a family in ninety minutes. Not even for Shannon.

I excused myself and followed Angela into the house.

The bathroom door was closed. I gently knocked.

"Angela," I murmured. "I'm sorry. I'm so sorry."

A few seconds later Angela opened the door. She had tears streaming down her face and her shoulders quivered.

"Are you all right?" I asked.

"I wet my pants," she said.

⌒⁄⌒

The party regrouped for cake and coffee. The little ones were given slices of watermelon and directed to the far end of the yard to get sticky juice down their arms without contaminating the adults. Shannon chose the kid's group, and instead of being out of place with the grown-ups, she became the wise leader of the gang whose next oldest was seven. I watched her demonstrate her seed spitting technique, which was truly admirable.

She organized a distance-spitting contest and awarded little Madison the prize of one of the balloons, which popped suspiciously in Madison's face. Brian sat down next to me as I watched. "She's exactly the kind of little cousin I always wanted," he said.

"Thanks," I said. "I'm not sure your mother agrees."

"Probably not. Mom always steered me away from kids like Shannon. Didn't want me 'led astray,' you know. But I hope it's not too late for her to be a bad influence on me."

"Please don't say that to your mother. Tell her you intend to be a good influence on *her*."

⌒⁄⌒

The mosquitoes told us when it was time to go. We packed all Shannon's loot into the trunk. Mary Ann needed to reorganize the boxes for a neater fit, and as she moved the smaller items into the corners, she knocked the cover off one of the boxes, and lying with the socks was Angela's silver cake server. She held it up.

136

"How did that get in there?" Shannon asked in a high voice. She took the server and handed it to Angela. "I'm sure we would have spotted it right away, since I can hardly wait to wear those socks."

"Sure," said Angela, giving Shannon a hug, while looking suspiciously into the trunk over Shannon's shoulder.

Mary Ann leaned close and whispered to me, "Are you sure?"

Shannon was quiet for a while on the ride home. Finally she said, "So are you going to dump me now?"

"Of course not," I said.

She snorted. "You know," she said, "you may have that creepy baby-detecting thing going on, but I have superpowers too. I have superhuman hearing. I heard what Mary Ann said to you…that you should change your mind."

"If your hearing is that good, then you know she asked me if I was sure. And I said yes."

"Well, you like them better than you like me, and if they told you to get rid of me, you would."

I glanced at Shannon, but she had her head turned toward the window, and she wouldn't look at me.

"Of course I like them. They're my family."

"Just because they're family doesn't automatically mean you like them," she mumbled at the window.

I thought about her own family, wherever they were.

"Well in my case, it does. And now you will be my family too, and so I'll like you too."

She got quiet again.

"Was this a test?" I asked. "Was all that crap about my mother's infidelity a game to make my family dislike you? To make me choose?"

"You may not listen too much to that old broad, but I bet if your blond sister what's-her-name told you to dump me, you would."

"My blond sister—Angela—would never ask me to. She thinks my life is much too cautious. She thinks I need to screw it up some."

Shannon smiled. "Well, I could do that."

"You certainly could."

She seemed satisfied with that, and we drove in silence a bit.

"Stop the car. STOP!" Shannon suddenly screamed.

I pulled over.

She opened the door, stumbled out to the curb, and threw up.

I grabbed a packet of tissues from my purse, and went over to her, where she was now sitting on the curb, head hanging between her knees. I handed her the tissues, and sat down next to her.

"Does this happen often?"

She wiped her mouth and with the same tissue blew her nose. She tossed it over towards her mess.

"It used to at first, then it got better. Now it's back. Especially in the car."

I pulled a strand of hair away from her sweaty face, and she flinched.

I felt a twinge of something.

"Shannon, do you think you can hold out a few more days? I want to take you to the doctor as soon as possible. But if I take you before you move in, the State might put a hold on the whole thing. I'm sure they'll give me temporary custody any day now. Once I get you in my house, then it'll be that much harder for them to change their mind."

Her head hung lower. "Do you want to get me to the doctor because you think something is wrong with the baby? So that if there's something wrong you can dump me?"

I put my hand on her bony knee, and this time she didn't flinch.

"No," I said. " Remember my creepy baby-detection stuff? There's nothing wrong with the baby," I assured her, despite the fact that I had never had one iota of insight in that area. "I'm not dumping you. I want to take you to the doctor because she can probably give you something to help with the nausea."

She picked up her head and looked at me. She was terribly pale, but beginning to look a little better. "Okay, she said, "I think I can get back in the car."

She stood shakily and brushed herself off.

"I puked on Lakisha's blouse."

"Well, shit," I said, "We'll just have to make it a twenty."

Chapter 21

ONDAY MORNING I SAT AT my desk at Maya Maria's, fretting over the disappointing financial statements. June looked pretty dismal. I had spent too much money on the merchandise. And now one week into July, I had marked everything down and had the double whammy of slow sales and low prices.

The phone rang, and it was Ben.

"Hi," he said. "How was your Fourth?"

"Personally, it was terrific," I replied. "Business-wise, I think everyone left town."

"Good," he said. "Then you can't possibly be busy. Want to play hooky?"

"What?" I wasn't sure I heard him. Business is collapsing and he said 'good?'

"Take the day off. Let's go play golf."

"Golf?"

"Yeah, golf. You've heard of it. 'A good walk, ruined', I think someone called it."

"Mark Twain."

"Yeah, Twain. Did anyone ever tell you that you'd be good at Trivial Pursuit?"

"Everyone."

"So how about it…can you play golf?"

"I can, and I play quite well, if the high score wins."

He laughed. "Think of it as getting your money's worth on the greens fees. So go home, and change into golf duds. I'll pick you up there in one hour."

"Do you know where I live?" I asked, suddenly feeling a little strange.

"W-4."

"Shit," I laughed. "I thought I had a stalker."

"One hour," Ben said. "Bring the paychecks."

The phone rang as I was changing into my cutest turquoise capris and crisp white tee. It was Melissa Rodriguez.

"I'm so glad you're home. I have wonderful, wonderful news. All the preliminary approvals are set. The temporary custody papers will be signed on Thursday. That means Shannon can move in on Friday."

"Oh my God. I can't believe it," I said. And that was certainly the truth, since I couldn't believe that all this had happened, and so quickly. "Oh my God," I repeated. *What was I thinking?* I added, to myself.

"So call Shannon right away, and give her the news yourself," said Melissa. "This is going to be the best day of her life."

I went to the kitchen where I had jotted down Shannon's cell phone number.

The best day of her life. Jesus, that was a lot to live up to.

I thought about my own best day. Maybe five or six months from now. But I will make Shannon a nice life too, I promised myself as I punched in the number. Surely this is a better life than locked in a closet.

It dawned on me as the phone rang that Shannon might want to come right over. I hadn't played golf with a man in probably ten years. I had a right to a nice day too, didn't I?

"This better be important," Shannon growled in my ear.

"It's Cynthia," I said.

"Duh?... Caller ID?"

I looked at the phone as if I could see her Caller ID on my end. "You knew it was me, and you still answered so rudely?"

"Well, I'm busy," she said. She added insincerely, "Sorry."

I thought about what Shannon could possibly be busy doing. I had an unpleasant image of Shannon's face in someone's, um, lap.

"Busy how?" I asked.

"I'm shopping," she said, and I was able to get a breath again. "Do you know how much sheets cost—and bedspreads? I can't even buy a good throw pillow for $20.00."

"Welcome to the land of home furnishings," I said. "And didn't you give that twenty to Lakisha?"

"Oh, fuck Lakisha. She was out when I got home, so I hid the shirt in her pile of filthy laundry. Right where she 'misplaced' it. She drinks like a fish—barfs so often she won't even know the difference."

An interesting conversation, but Ben would be by any minute.

"Well, here's some news. We passed. You move in on Friday."

"Then we've got a lot of shopping to do," she said. Well, maybe not exactly the best day of her life.

"Tomorrow. We're slow at the store, so I'll take the afternoon off. We'll go to that huge shop in Avon and you can pick out whatever linens you want."

"Linens? Do I have to get linens? I want really fancy sheets."

"Okay," I said, not about to correct her or tease her today. "You can get sheets."

There's nothing quite like playing rotten golf on a beautiful day with a cheerful man. I felt ten years younger—and good thing, because I figured that Benson V. Shelter had to be at least that much younger than me.

He came to the back door, not the front, which was friendlier, I thought. He looked like a college kid, dressed in old unpressed khakis and a faded red golf shirt. Obviously doing his own laundry now.

"You shaved!" I exclaimed as I opened the door.

"Yeah," he laughed and stroked his upper lip in a gesture so familiar that it would probably last a lifetime even without the mustache. "The receptionist sat me down on Friday, and told me it had to go. 'Uncool,' she said. I've had the mustache since college. I thought it was very cool...but apparently not."

His look may have been out-of-date, but there was nothing uncool about his car. We drove to the public golf course in a 1964 Chevy Impala SS convertible. Red—riverside red—he called it, with white rag top and white interior. It had a wonderfully blinding amount of chrome, and a trunk that swallowed up our golf clubs with room for seventeen suitcases and one extra large cooler (which was already in there).

Golf was a long formal dance with Ben gliding straight down the fairways, as I made wide semi-graceful circles around him, getting my (his) money's worth from each rough, sand trap, and water hazard.

I never enjoyed a round of golf so much. Maybe there was something to this Florida thing.

143

"You know, with a few lessons," Ben said as we put the clubs back in the car, "you could be terrible."

"Well worth the time and expense."

And we drove to a nearby park and had a picnic lunch. As he opened the cooler, I asked, "Tuna sandwiches?"

He laughed. "No, you are in for a real treat." And he took out cold fried chicken and coleslaw and macaroni salad and big fat pickles, all from Lucinda's Deli, where you can walk in and ask for one hundred meatballs, and they'd say, "with or without sauce?"

"What about Harry?" I said, going for another chicken leg. "You're not going to miss your visit?"

He shook his head. "I'm going later. I'll bring him all the leftovers. He'll be thrilled."

"There's not going to be any leftovers," I warned. "Especially not brownies."

"So you have other vices besides fashion acquisition?"

The store. The sunshine had wiped the impending disaster from my mind.

"I need to talk to you about the store," I said, pushing away my plate. "The financials aren't so good. I've only got one more month to go, and July is going to be worse than June."

"Cynthia," he said, in a soft voice that sounded just like my father's forty years ago, when I entered the city diving competition, even though I had not had a second of training. I had stood shivering by the edge of the pool, crying at my humiliating loss. 'What did you expect?' my father had said at the time, with a mix of kindness and exasperation.

"Cynthia," said Ben. "I may be a lawyer, but I've absorbed a thing or two about the retail business in the last six years. There isn't any profit in June or July. There isn't any profit until Thanksgiving."

"I know now," I said. "I looked at the statements from last year. But this is worse."

"And they say men are competitive," Ben complained to himself as he waved his pickle at me. His face held more of the exasperation and less of the kindness. "Maria grew up shop-keeping. She'd been in the business all her life. Did you really think you would outperform her in one month?"

I did. Christ, what an ego. Where in the world did it come from, after all those dull years at Heritage?

"Okay," I said. "I guess I was a little insane. Worst of all, the deal we struck is a really bad deal—for the store, that is. With margins so small, when I take 5% off the top, I'm really taking the whole profit."

"I know," he said.

I was mildly stunned. "You know? If you knew the store couldn't support a 5% commission, why did you agree?"

He shook his head. "Temporary insanity is contagious."

I reached for the brownies.

"So do I fire myself?"

"No. But cut your commission to 2% and let's see what happens.

Tuesday morning—no customers. About 10:15 the phone rang.

"Does Maui Mango go with Energetic Eggplant?" It was Shannon. She was not in culinary class; she was at the paint store.

"Honey," I said. "You should choose your bedding before your paint color. It's a lot easier to match the paint to your bedding than the other way around."

"So you don't think Mango and Eggplant would go?"

"One's a fruit and one's a vegetable."

"Oh, right," she said. "California Elderberry, then."

Bed, Bath and Beyond was more beyond than either bed or bath. Shannon wanted chocolate peanuts and honeysuckle bubble bath and candles that were shaped like Bambi.

"Later,' I said, putting back the daffodil nail file and the armadillo alarm clock. I wondered if shopping with a toddler was going to be even harder.

In the bedding aisle, quilts were hung in no apparent order. Superman hung next to morning glories. However, the display at the end was lovely—a white four-poster wearing a quilt of delicate violets and pillow shams of hydrangeas.

"Oh, look," I said.

"Yuck," she said.

She walked up and down the aisle, fingering with seeming equality the quilts with monkeys and the ones with roses, the loopy chenille bedspreads and the brown plaid corduroy, the cowboys and the Barbie dolls.

I sat on the gorgeous violet bed, which wasn't a bed at all but a piece of plywood on a stand. My derriere grew stiff and she paced back and forth, considering with a smile or a frown every single offering.

"This one," she finally said.

It was the deepest possible midnight blue—almost black. A good match for her hair, I thought. There were silver moons and gold stars embroidered throughout.

"It's fabulous," I said. "I love it."

And Shannon flashed a quick, brilliant smile. It was gone as quickly as it came, but it was as spectacular as the quilt.

We selected throw pillows –crazy shapes in yellow, green and turquoise and one that matched the little card in her hand that said Maui Mango. Her linens, her "fancy sheets," were orchid, and a six-hundred-thread count to boot. She chose silver curtains that reminded me of crinkled aluminum foil.

She found a pink flamingo lamp, with a tasseled purple shade and a mirror like a sunburst.

With trauma to my charge card, it was off to the paint store, where Shannon rejected both the elderberry and the eggplant, but was completely committed to Maui Mango.

"We have to do the edge stuff too," she said. "That dumb ivory won't work."

"You want to repaint the trim?"

"We have to," she said.

"Well, if we have to…" I showed her a chip of dark blue Southern Evening, "we should probably pick up the color of the spread."

"Are you like eighty years old? It doesn't have to 'match'— it has to 'go,' she said, quoting some TV show that I had watched myself not too long ago.

"That's for shoes and pocketbooks," I said.

"That's for *everything*," she insisted. And we bought a quart of Key Lime semigloss to 'go' with Maui Mango and the midnight bedspread.

We got home and moved all the furniture into the center of the room, where we covered it with an old ivory sheet, from my linen closet that was full of ivory sheets.

As soon as I opened the paint can and started stirring, Shannon threw up.

I opened the windows and brought Shannon upstairs to lie down on my bed.

I did all the painting myself.

Chapter 22

———⟨○⟩———

"HELP!" I HEARD THE RASPY whisper on the other end of the line. I had picked up the ringing phone just as I was reaching for my car keys.

"Jesus Christ," Shannon hissed. "I'm in big trouble."

"Calm down," I said. "What's going on? Where are you?"

"Melissa came by first thing this morning. 'Come on,' she says, 'You need to go to the doctor.' And that's where I am. I'm in the ladies' room at the fucking doctor. The fucking doctor. What the fuck do I do now?"

"Fuck," I said. I couldn't help myself. I sat down hard on the floor.

I had a half-developed plan for this inevitable occurrence. But it wasn't completely fleshed-out and now we would have to ad-lib, and without one or two or nine rehearsals.

"Okay, let's calm down," I said. Taking my own advice, I lay down on the floor.

"Do you think you can cry?"

Shannon may have sounded right on the cliff of tears a second ago, but she instantly dried up. "Shit, no," she said with her usual bravado, "And besides, I could maybe fool the doctor, but Melissa is here too, remember?"

"Right," I said. "Here's what you do. You tell them that you're pregnant. That you were going to get rid of it before the adoption, before anyone knew, but you couldn't go through with it. They'll call me and I'll come right down. I'll tell them that I still want you and I'll adopt you and the baby too."

"Oh, and you're the big generous hero, and I'm the whore."

"No, listen. This puts you in a good light too. That you are a mature young woman who already loves the baby inside her."

"What a lot of bullshit. Everyone thinks you are so wonderful. I think I'll just tell them that this was all your idea."

I stared at the light fixture above me. There was a large cobweb that I had not noticed. I needed to dust. It occurred to me that this was a chance to escape. I could go back to watching the birds. I didn't have to have this alien in my house.

"Tell them," I answered. "I won't deny it. But then they'll know that I am not a hero, but a pretty bad person. There won't be any adoption and you'll go back to Decision House."

"Shit," she whispered. "They're knocking on the door."

"I'll be waiting by the phone," I said. Just as Shannon was hanging up, I added, "I do want you," but I wasn't sure she heard.

I got up off the floor and immediately phoned the store. Not wanting to miss the doctor's call, I left a three-second message on the machine that I had an emergency. Kate wouldn't be in until noon, and she'd be surprised to find the store still locked up, but so what?—we weren't making any money anyway.

I imagined Shannon telling Melissa and the doctor that she was pregnant. Hell could definitely break loose. I could picture Shannon saying that she just didn't care, playing the tough kid, but then that wouldn't jibe with not being able to go through with an abortion. I wished I had the foresight to have already gone over this with Shannon. I had planned to be there during this part of the drama.

Of course, she could tell them that I had planned the adoption to get my hands on the baby. That she was the victim and I was the louse. Which was true, but not the point. I wanted the baby, and I was willing to be really good to Shannon, to provide her with a nice home and some fine cash too. I was the hero, after all, wasn't I?

Why didn't the phone ring? If Shannon spilled her guts, ratted me out, as she would say, I could be in bigger trouble than just blowing the adoption. My scheme could be considered baby-buying. And that was illegal.

I touched my necklace, a long design of miniature dominoes, made out of onyx and mother-of-pearl. I went upstairs and put it back in my jewelry box. It seemed inappropriate; not motherly. I put on a small strand of pearls, but took them off too. I ended up with a tiny gold crucifix. No abortions. I'm Catholic. See?

The phone by my bed rang and I jumped.

"Hello," I said nonchalantly over my pounding heart.

"It's Shannon," she said, and I was surprised that they had Shannon make the call herself. "I've got a problem," she continued, "And Melissa Rodriguez wants to talk to you." There was a shuffle as Melissa took the phone.

"Cynthia, I'm sorry to bother you but it's really important," said Melissa.

"Oh, no," I said, with fear in my voice, "Where are you? Has there been an accident?" To make sure I didn't sound too corny, I added, "Has she been arrested?"

"No, she's okay. Sort of. We're at the doctor's and we need you to join us."

"The doctor's? What's wrong?"

"Just please come over right away. It's Doctor Berg's in the Medical Annex by the hospital. Do you know where I mean?"

"I'll be there in fifteen minutes."

The nurse ushered me into an examination room where Shannon sat on the edge of a table. She was wearing a paper nightgown. She dangled her flipflops from her toes. Melissa Rodriguez sat in a plastic chair against the wall, her purse covering her from lap to chin. The doctor came in behind me and closed the door.

"Okay, what's going on?" I said.

"Shannon?" prompted the doctor.

She looked up. She hadn't cried; I could see that right away.

"I should have known better than to think anything good could ever happen to me," she said belligerently. "Everything is always fucked for me." She let one sandal drop to the floor. "I'm pregnant."

I had thought about what my reaction should be while driving over. I needed to act completely surprised. Although I couldn't be certain whether Shannon had told them that I knew she was pregnant, my best bet was surprise. Even if she had blamed me, there was a good chance that they wouldn't believe her. After all, she was a delinquent and I was the saint who was taking in a troubled child. So I acted as any mother would when confronted with such unexpected news.

"Oh my God," I said. "I am going to kill D.J."

Shannon's jaw dropped for a second, but that's all it took for her to catch on to my strategy.

"It's not D.J.'s. I was already pregnant when I met him. D.J.'s a good guy," she said. "Of course, now I'm fucked with him too."

Melissa got up. "Sit," she said to me. And I sat down in her seat like I felt a bit faint. I did, a bit.

"My God," I said again. I tried to make myself look like my brain was going a mile a minute and not like I was reciting lines. "When you were sick last week..." I let my voice trail off.

"I've been trying not to puke in front of you."

"Why didn't you tell me?"

Now if there was a spot where Shannon would lose it, it was here. My feigned innocence could infuriate her. And although I could see the anger in the narrowing of her eyes, she quickly buried it.

"When I saw that you meant it, about wanting to adopt me and all, I figured I would just get rid of it, and no one would ever know." She looked down at her feet as the second flip-flop dropped from her toe. "But I just couldn't do it. I went to the clinic three times. I couldn't even go in."

She was a genius, no doubt about it. By saying she couldn't even go in, no one could check her story.

Shannon looked up at me. "But if you want me too, I will. I'll do it if I have to."

I touched my crucifix. It was blatant overacting, but I figured I couldn't risk subtlety.

"I could never ask you to do that. I'm Catholic. Babies are a gift from God."

"I'm not even sure the baby's white," Shannon said.

She was more than a genius. Her timing was impeccable.

I smiled. "ALL babies are a gift from God."

Right answer. Melissa's eyebrows loosened like the rubber band holding her ponytail had snapped.

"Look here," the doctor interrupted from where he was leaning against the wall. "I'm not sure where this is going, but I've got patients backing up. If you are deciding to carry this through, not…terminate, well then you need to get Shannon to an obstetrician right away. I've only seen her a few times, and she appears to be healthy. I haven't seen any signs of habitual drug use, but with these types…"

"What?" I turned on him. "These types? Shannon is right here. She's a smart young woman. You don't have to treat her like some invisible imbecile."

I looked at Shannon.

"Get dressed," I said. "I'm taking you home."

That's when Shannon lost it, and real (maybe) tears started to flow.

Chapter 23

SHANNON WAS BRAYING TRIUMPHANTLY ON the ride home. I wasn't sure if this was evidence that she had faked the tears at the doctor's, or just typical of the resiliency of kids.

"Man," she said. "You were great. I thought you were nuts at first to blame D.J., but then I saw how perfect it was. *Of course* you'd say that. And all that Catholic stuff. You left Melissa in the dust."

"Don't celebrate too soon," I warned, but I couldn't help smiling. "I think Melissa was just momentarily stunned by the whole situation. She'll get her equilibrium back, and she'll be wondering what the hell happened, and how much red tape this is going to be. Don't think for one minute this is going to be easy."

"But don't you think I was good too? I figured that if some other poor fucker was in that mess, they'd be blaming the world. It sounded so real to me as I was saying it, and I could see they were buying it totally."

"Yeah," I agreed. "You being surly was some great acting."

"Well, you were great too. You are the best liar I ever met."

I stopped smiling.

I pulled up to Decision House, and we went in together. There was no one around. Shannon ran down the hall and reappeared with a black plastic trash bag. We went upstairs. Her room was horrible; the walls were a combination of torn music posters alternating with fist-sized holes and ugly graffiti. There were three beds somewhere beneath piles of blankets and clothes. The floor was equally strewn with clothes and various trash, wadded paper bags, candy wrappers.

"Nice," I said. "The cleaning lady did a wonderful job."

She threw clothes and shoes and makeup into the bag as quickly as she could.

"Take your time," I said. "We aren't skipping town. I just think we'll have a stronger case if you are already in my house."

"Well, I just can't get out of here fast enough."

"Stop," I said as I saw her put an unfamiliar pair of shoes into the bag. "Don't take the other kids' stuff. Remember that I've got a little money and I'll buy you some nice new things."

"These are my shoes. I swear."

"You wear those pathetic ugly things?"

"Fuck," she said. She took them out and tossed them back on the floor. "I don't need their nasty shit." Shannon turned the trash bag upside down and let everything fall out. She picked a few items from the pile and put them back in the bag.

"Do you have a winter coat?" I asked. Shannon went to the closet, which held almost nothing except for a broken hanger or two. She pulled out a parka. It was dirty green with the fakest of fake fur around the hood. The stitching along the quilting was loose and threads hung along the hem. One armpit was torn.

"Leave it," I said. "It won't fit you by winter anyway."

Shannon looked down at the large plastic bag with a tiny bulge at the very bottom. She swung it over her shoulder.

"That's it," she said.

It wasn't surprising to see Melissa Rodriguez perched on my front steps. But next to her big purse was a big suitcase and next to the suitcase was my mother.

"Jeez, who's the old lady?" asked Shannon as we got out of the car.

Both the ladies and their bags waited motionless as we walked up the steps.

"Hi," I said to two frowns.

"Thank God for Mary Ann," said my mother.

"You had no right to take Shannon," said Melissa.

"I'm happy to see you too," I said, bending down to kiss my mother on her powdered forehead. I took Shannon by the hand and pulled her forward.

"Shannon, this is my mother."

Shannon gravely shook my mother's hand. She smiled in her best interpretation of a normal fourteen-year-old. "Grandma," she said.

My mother winced. If Shannon thought the old lady would melt at the magic word, she was about to learn that osteoporosis was no match for my mother's backbone.

"Girl," Mom said, with a nastiness I hadn't know her capable of, "You have hair like a witch. Are you one of those devil-worshipers?"

"Yeah," she said. "You wanna see my head spin around?"

"Shannon!" I scolded. "She's very upset," I explained to Melissa and my mother, while giving Shannon a burning stare, which I hoped reminded her that we were now in Act II of our drama. "She's been through a lot today."

Suddenly I heard the conversation that was about to take place.

Melissa to my mother: "Shannon just told us that she's pregnant. We're all in somewhat of a shock."

My mother to Melissa: "Pregnant? Shocked? Oh no, Cynthia wouldn't be shocked. She can always tell immediately when a woman's pregnant."

I couldn't let that exchange happen.

I handed Shannon my keys. "Shannon, take my mother into the house. Carry her bag and give her something cool to drink. I need to speak to Melissa for a minute."

Shannon scowled, but grabbed the suitcase. "Come on," she said to my mother.

My mother put a hand on Shannon's shoulder to leverage herself off the step. Shannon looked at her, with something almost like kindness. "Satan's waiting," she said.

I guess I read the kindness part wrong.

I took my mother's place on the stairs.

"I know I don't have the authority to take Shannon," I said apologetically. "But I didn't know what else to do."

Melissa stood and cast her shadow over me. "This isn't acceptable. You need to take her back to the group home, while we straighten this out."

I stood too, and felt for a second like using my height to bully her. But I stepped down, and from the sidewalk I made myself seem a bit smaller.

"Don't you see? If I send her back, she'll think I've changed by mind. That I'm rejecting her after all. She could do something desperate."

Melissa looked away. She sighed.

I gave her a look that I hoped portrayed a combination of pleading and sweetness. "She needs to know that I won't change my mind. That I still want her. No matter what."

"We have rules," she insisted, but not strongly.

"You'll know where she is. She's safe. Isn't that what matters?"

Melissa picked up her bag. She walked a few steps towards her car, and turned back to me.

"If the shit hits the fan, I'm going to say that you promised to take her back. That I didn't know you hadn't."

"Will the group home report her missing?"

Melissa shrugged. "Eventually."

"Look," I said. "I'll call Decision House and tell the director that Shannon is home with me. That you okayed it. But if there's any trouble I'll 'confess' that you didn't know. It's all on me."

"It certainly is," she said.

My mother sat at the kitchen table. There were three placemats out and each one held one of my good water goblets, filled with iced water and a slice of lemon. My mother obviously had waited on herself.

I sat down and took a great gulp from one of the untouched glasses. Music blared from behind Shannon's closed door. Since Shannon had an iPod now, the pounding music was most certainly for effect.

"She's had a hard life," I said.

"That's what she said," my mother responded.

"Shannon said that?"

"No, the other girl. The parole officer."

"Social worker, Mom. Not parole officer."

My mother pursed her lips at me. "So there's a difference?" She made a dismissing little wave with her hand, as if to brush away her mean thoughts. I had seen this gesture a thousand times. "Look," she said. "I feel sorry for kids who've had a hard

life. I really do. But I know what happens to them. They think
that life is rotten and they see no reason not to be rotten too.
Life's tough, they think, and they look out for themselves. No
rules. They hurt other people and they fill the prisons."

I reached over and took her hand. It had that tissue paper
feel. Old person's skin.

"I know that's true," I said. "In most cases. But it's not too
late for Shannon."

"She stole from Angela."

Thanks, Mary Ann.

"That could have been an accident."

"Has she stolen from you yet?"

I looked steadily into her hard blue eyes. They stung me.

"No," I said. "Of course not."

My mother smiled, but the edges of her lips pointed down.
"Of course not," she repeated.

"I need her," I said, which was entirely true, but it gave me
a rotten feeling to say it. "Would you just give her a chance?"

Her big soft chest pushed out so much it rested on the
table. "I give everyone a chance."

I got up and kissed the top of her head. "Come on. Come
look at her room."

I knocked hard on the door, and opened it to see Shannon
sprawled on her bed with a yellow-fringed pillow resting on
her belly. Around her on the bed, she had spread out all her
gifts from last week. Face down was the photo that Angela
had given her—*Grandparents.*

The TV was tuned to some nasty reality show about
piercings and tattoos. The sound was obliterated by the
screeching music. I gave Shannon a little downward motion
with my hand, and she picked up the remote, and pointed it in
some general direction and the music descended to a medium
blare.

My mother looked at the profusion of color. This had been her room when she visited, and she loved the ivory and yellow.

"Isn't this great?" I prodded my mother. "It's so... lively."

"Mmm," she said.

Shannon finally took her eyes off the fascinating ceiling and looked at us.

"Well, I certainly couldn't live with that old boring stuff," she said.

"I see," said Mom. "It must have been horrible compared to your lovely room at the homeless shelter."

"The group home," I corrected.

"Whatever," said my mother and Shannon at exactly the same time.

With a wave of her new magic wand, Shannon re-engulfed herself in noise. We backed out and closed the door.

"She's fourteen," I explained. "Even the best of them are obnoxious."

"She's certainly one of the best of them," Mom agreed.

My mother's suitcase still stood by the kitchen door where Shannon must have dropped it.

"Can I ask you a big favor?" I said. "This is Shannon's first night with me. We need some 'together' time. You know, bonding and all. Could you possibly...?"

"Stay with Mary Ann?"

"Actually, why don't we call Angela? Angela likes Shannon. You've already heard Mary Ann's point of view."

My mother gave me another bitter smile. "Angela likes everyone. She only sees good in people."

"And that's such a bad thing?" I asked.

Mom's smile loosened a little. "Okay, call her."

I picked up the phone. "How did you get here anyway?"

"I had a cab bring me from the airport," she said.

"Holy cow," I said, "That must have cost a fortune."

"It's a drop in the bucket compared to what's ahead for you," she said with satisfaction.

I dropped my mother at Angela's, where she was greeted with a welcome that made me feel mean indeed, for the poor reception at my house. However tactful I had tried to be, I had asked her to leave, for God's sake.

I forced Shannon to come with us, since I wasn't ready to even imagine her alone in my house. She slouched in the back of the car, and wouldn't acknowledge my mother or even Angela. If I had expected her to move to the front seat after my mother was safely stowed away, I was wrong. I felt like a cop with a prisoner.

"Let's go get groceries," I said cheerfully.

"Let's not," she murmured.

"I need food, and I need you to show me what you like."

"How about if you just buy stuff, and I either eat it or I don't. You can let me off at D.J.'s."

"Nope. You're coming."

And I actually had to open her door at the parking lot and pull her out by the arm.

"This is beyond lame," she said. "What if someone sees me?"

"Then walk faster."

But Shannon dragged her heels, moaning behind me, through the parking lot, through the door, through the aisles. She paid absolutely no attention to what I was buying. Even in the cookie aisle, I couldn't get her to pick up a box of Oreos.

"Chicken or steak for tonight?" I asked.

"Just buy something."

It dawned on me that no one had ever given Shannon a choice before, or cared what she liked. Food was put down in front of her, and, as she said, she either ate it or didn't.

So I stopped asking her what she liked and simply filled the cart. She dawdled behind me, pouting like a four-year-old. When we got to the makeup aisle, I told her she could pick out two things, and left her there while I picked up toilet paper and the other stuff that would certainly kill her to watch.

When I got back to the makeup aisle she wasn't there. Shit, I thought, I lost her already. I can't even be a mother for a complete day. I pushed the cart up and down the aisles, wondering if I should go to the front desk and have her paged. But as furious as I was, I couldn't embarrass her (myself) quite that much.

I finally went to the checkout without her. How was I going to tell Melissa that I lost my kid?

I pushed my cart out the door and there she was, leaning against the car, fiddling with her iPod.

"Don't just disappear," I said, relieved and extremely aggravated.

"I didn't just disappear," she said. "I'm right here."

"Didn't you want any makeup?"

"You said to take two things. So I did."

"Shannon!"

"Just kidding," she said.

She sat in the back again as I drove home, but she didn't sulk. She was smiling.

I thought about a strip search, but I just put the groceries away (by myself.)

Shannon was sociable at dinner. Almost excited to be in her new home, but not quite. Moods in kids were wicked, I knew. Moods in pregnant kids...apparently worse.

She talked about buying all new clothes. Now that it wouldn't be a secret, she wanted stuff that made her belly show. So everyone would freak out, she said with a kind of joy.

She scarfed down several helpings of everything.

"See?" she said. "You can buy this again, and I don't have to come grocery shopping ever."

"We can't eat the same thing every day. What about tomorrow? What if you hate the other stuff I bought?"

"Try me."

Tomorrow's dinner. Tomorrow. I had forgotten.

"About tomorrow..." I started. "I don't have anyone available to work at the store tomorrow. I didn't expect you until Friday. I blew it off today, but I'm going to have to go to work tomorrow."

"So?" she said. "Go to work."

"But I can't leave you alone. You'll have to come with me."

Shannon pushed back her chair with a harsh scrape. "No way. Fuck that."

"It'll be fun. You'll see. You can try on everything, and buy whatever you like."

She sneered. "I'm not shopping there. Remember? You agreed."

"But you can't stay here alone," I insisted.

"Why the fuck not? Guess what? I live here now." She gave me her best la-di-da voice. "I think I will be fine staying in my *own* home."

God, this was all way too soon for me.

"Well, maybe someone could stay with you." I hated the idea, but she only had one friend. "Ask D.J. to come over."

"He's going to the Cape with his college friends tomorrow. They're staying all week. She smiled. "Course, I could go with him..."

"Fat chance."

She actually laughed. "So then get used to it."

I laughed too. What choice did I have? "Christ, this mother stuff is going to be hell."

"So what's 'the Cape' anyway?" Shannon said, changing the subject before I could think too much about needing a babysitter.

"Cape Cod," I said.

"Like caped crusader?" she asked.

Was she picturing a whitefish in Batman attire?

"A cape," I tried to explain. A curvy peninsula with a harbor."

Shannon's face was a blank.

"It's a huge beach," I said, giving up on the geography lesson. "In Massachusetts."

"Is that near where you go to the beach?"

"Not too close. I go to Rhode Island."

She nodded. "I went to the beach with one of the fosters years ago. It was in Rhode Island, I think."

"Did you like it?"

"Hot sand, hot sun, freezing water, and about a mile to the bathroom."

"Yup," I said, "That's the place. It's wonderful."

Chapter 24

MY HEAD HAD AN EXTRA pulse in the morning. The floorboards had vibrated all night from the beat of music I couldn't quite hear, but couldn't tune out either.

I tried again to get Shannon to come to work with me. But I couldn't rouse her from her heavy unconsciousness. I figured she was faking it. I thought about the tears in the doctor's office and the probable theft at the supermarket. Maybe after a while I would be able to tell when she was lying, but I didn't have much hope for it.

I left notes everywhere.

'EAT ANYTHING YOU WANT' I taped to the refrigerator.

'USE THE MICROWAVE, NOT THE STOVE' I posted on the stove. But then on the microwave I left 'NO METAL IN HERE'. To be sure, I left plastic dishes and cups right by the microwave.

I left sticky notes on the food in the fridge. 'LEFTOVER CHICKEN', 'POTATO SALAD', 'SALAMI'. I caught myself posting 'MILK' on the milk. I tore that one up.

Then I took a dozen or so of the thumbnail-size notes and wrote 'NO' on each one, and went around the house, posting them on: The computer (although I figured I would eventually lose that one), the china cabinet, the sewing machine, my jewelry box, and several bottles of wine.

I put ten dollars on the kitchen table, along with my spare house key. 'IF YOU GO OUT, LOCK THE DOOR'. I added 'CALL ME FIRST' with the phone numbers of the store and my cell. Then I left the phone numbers by every phone in the house, along with the warning 'ANSWER THE PHONE, BUT DON'T ANSWER THE DOOR'.

I was about to write 'HAVE FUN' as I went out the door, but I had pretty much eliminated any chance of that, so I scribbled 'I'LL CALL YOU' and stuck it to the doorknob. And I went to work and left a screwed-up teenager alone in my house.

At 10:05 as I was just opening the store I got my first call.

"How come you don't have Cheerios?"

"Good morning," I said pleasantly. "You could have picked some up yesterday. We went to the store. Remember?"

"What can I eat for breakfast?"

"Granola."

"Isn't that like kitty litter with nuts?"

"Have toast."

"Where's the bread?"

"In the breadbox."

There was a short silence. "What does it look like?"

"Like a little metal garage on the counter near the refrigerator."

"Okay," Shannon said. The phone went dead.

Three minutes later it rang again.

"Your peanut butter is that crunchy kind."

"Yes, Shannon, it is."

"Is there jelly?"

"Strawberry jam in the fridge. Open the door, look right next to the milk."

"Okay."

Ten minutes later she didn't like the toothpaste. Ten minutes after that she wanted tweezers. And a fluffier towel.

"I'm glad that you can manage so well in your own home," I said on the eighth call.

"Yeah," she said. "I'm doing good."

The new inventory had come in, and I managed to fit in a sale or two between phone calls. I put on some James Taylor and my headache went away. I actually felt pretty good, saying to customers, "That's my crazy daughter again" each time the phone rang.

After lunch—for which I should have had bologna, not salami, and yellow mustard not that brown shit—I answered the next call on the first ring.

"Yes dear?"

"She's here," Shannon said.

"Who's here?"

"The old lady. Your mother."

Christ. "Well, let me talk to her," I said.

"She's out on the porch." With unconcealed glee in her voice, she added, "You said I shouldn't open the door."

"For God's sake, Shannon. Open the door, and let me speak to her."

"I can hand her the phone right on the porch, so I won't have to let her in."

"Shannon."

"All right, all right."

Through the phone I heard the door open and in Shannon's most insincerely sweet voice, I heard, "Why hello, Pauline. Won't you come in? Cynthia's on the phone right now just dying to speak with you."

Which of my private belongings had Shannon been going through that she knew my mother's name?

My mother came on. "Cynthia, is that you? Where are you?"

"Hi Mom," I answered. "I'm at work."

There was a long silence.

"I'm so glad you gave 'bonding' your full effort."

Double Christ. "I didn't have anyone to fill in," I tried to explain. "I'm going to make better arrangements—it's just going to take a day or so."

I heard the pounding underbeat of music. The house was probably vibrating.

"Her first day, and you just *abandoned* her?"

I looked towards the heavens for some help.

"Oh Mom, you're right. I'm sorry. Can you stay there until I get home? I'll come home as quickly as I can."

"Take your time," she said sarcastically.

Forty minutes later I skidded into the driveway. Angela's old Toyota was parked to the left. The house was still standing, but I couldn't be sure anyone was alive inside.

My mother was in the kitchen, making meatballs. An old gray-haired lady in an apron (she knew where I kept everything, even if I didn't even know I had one), gently forming perfect little balls and placing them on a cookie sheet. A sweet domestic picture, except for the volume. The rock music drilled right into your teeth.

"I'm so sorry," I apologized, bending down to kiss my mother on the cheek.

She nodded towards Shannon's bedroom. "She's been in there the whole time. I think she's locked the door. Do you think she's smoking dope?"

"She's fine," I said, "Just bratty. And there's no lock on the door."

"She's probably got it barricaded."

I groaned. "It just sticks. I'll go talk to her. Thanks for making dinner. The sauce smells wonderful."

"Does it? I can't even smell through all this racket."

Shannon's door was not locked or even stuck, although from her window she may have seen me come home, and removed whatever she had jammed the door with.

I started my apologies over again.

"Sorry I took so long," I yelled. "I had customers."

She took the music down a fraction. "Why didn't you tell her to go home?"

"I thought maybe you'd like some company."

"I can't stand her."

"You don't even know her."

Shannon threw a pillow in my direction, but with no force behind it.

I picked up the pillow and walked over to the bed. I sat down next to her and handed her the pillow. Nicely. Although I thought about clobbering her with it.

"I know why she came. To stop you from adopting me."

"Did you ever think that maybe she came to MEET you? That maybe she's actually excited to have another granddaughter?"

"Bullshit," she said. Which it was.

"Well, how about this? The family had a big party to welcome you, and she wasn't invited. Maybe she was just feeling left out? A little jealous of you maybe?"

She let herself fall back onto the bed, her feet still on the floor.

"No one is jealous of me."

"You took her room."

She closed her eyes and smiled. "Yup."

"Look," I said, feeling that I might be making a little progress. "Just humor her, okay?"

She looked up at me. "I've heard people say that but I'm not sure what it means—'humor her'.

"You know, suck up a little. Be nice. Even if you don't mean it."

"Why should I?"

"Because in a few days, maybe a week, she'll be gone and you'll still be here. So you win."

"Damn right," she said pounding the pillow with her fist. She looked at me kind of sideways. "But... if I've already won...why do I have to bother to be nice?"

So there it was. A bribe was due—again. My brain scrambled to think of something through all that loud music. Music.

"Have you ever been to a rock concert?" I asked.

"No," she said and sat up like a little bird waiting for her worm.

"Be nice to my mother and I'll buy you concert tickets. For you and D.J. You can go see anyone you like.

"Good seats; not nosebleed."

"Absolutely."

⌁

"This spaghetti and meatballs is the most wonderful I ever had in my whole life," Shannon said to my mother at dinner.

Chapter 25

*I*T DIDN'T LAST.

The next day, Friday, was the day that Shannon was originally scheduled to move in. We had planned a day of shopping. All for her. She wanted to go to the mall to those shops that were so dimly lit you could hardly see the merchandise, usually because they didn't want you to get a close look at the workmanship. The stores where the music is loud and the clerks are rude. But it was her day, and I agreed with fake enthusiasm.

She was so distracted with excitement at breakfast that she said "thank you" when I passed her the butter. I didn't call it to her attention, since I figured it would not happen again.

I was cleaning up from breakfast and Shannon was in the shower when my mother drove up in Angela's old Toyota. What was Angela thinking, giving my mother such free use of the car? Why couldn't Angela lend her a cell phone instead?

"Hi, Mom," I said, opening the door before she could knock. "What brings you here today?"

She looked around the kitchen, as if making sure than Shannon wasn't about to spring out with the carving knife.

"Well, I figured you were working again, and the kid shouldn't be prowling around here alone."

"She's not prowling," I said, "She lives here. You don't prowl in your own home."

My mother gave me one of her increasingly frequent scowls of disbelief.

"And besides," I said, "Today is my day off."

She looked relieved. "Angela's kids were very easy to babysit for. And Mary Ann's were just a delight."

"Well, my kid may not qualify as a delight, but you don't have to babysit. She's pretty grown up." I smiled. "I skipped the diapers part," I said, enjoying the private knowledge that it was coming soon.

She took a paper towel and wiped the table that I had just wiped.

"Maybe we could all do something together," she said.

Shannon came out of the bathroom wearing my old pink terrycloth robe. It had been in the far corner of my closet, behind the myriad of new clothes that I had acquired at cost from Maya Maria's. Shannon had certainly managed to get a lot done yesterday between phone calls.

My mother didn't see Shannon standing behind her, as Shannon pantomimed hanging herself with the robe's belt.

Shannon needn't have worried though. I was not about to let my mother join us in our shopping day. When I was a teenager, shopping with my mother was a very special kind of hell. Everything I liked was too short, too nasty, too trashy, and too cheap, but not in a money-saving way. We'd spend hours in the store fighting and usually drove home in furious silence, empty-handed. I'd save the experience of shopping with my mother for a day when I needed to punish

Shannon. Besides, I had managed to get Shannon a 3:00 PM appointment with my gynecologist, and I certainly did not want my mother in tow.

I tried to be tactful.

"Mom, that's really sweet, but Shannon and I have a special day planned. We are really looking forward to going to the mall, just the two of us. But why don't we meet up with you for dinner?"

Before my mother could react, the phone rang. It was Kate at the store.

"There's no money," she said. "I'm about to open and I have three dollars and fourteen cents in my wallet."

In my haste to get home, I had taken all the money. We usually left two hundred dollars in the register. Without it, she had no change for the customers.

"I've got it," I said. "I'll bring it right down."

I looked over my mother's shoulder at Shannon's crestfallen face. "I've got to drop off some money. I'll be back in half an hour, forty-five minutes tops. By the time you're dressed I'll be back. We won't lose a minute."

My mother turned and saw Shannon for the first time. She smiled and nodded, like she just knew this would happen.

"No problem," my mother said. "Shannon and I can go shopping together."

Shannon freaked. "Don't make me!" she screamed. "Don't make me get in the car with her! She's too old! She'll croak behind the wheel and we'll drive into a building!" She ran to her room and slammed the door.

My mother disintegrated in small increments. Her jaw went slack. Her eyelids seemed too heavy for her face, and a thousand wrinkles deepened in gray shadows. She quietly picked up her purse.

"Oh Mom, she doesn't mean it," I said. "She's just a kid. She'll come around."

"I'll try to get an earlier flight," she answered, and walked out.

I stormed into Shannon's room ready to explode.

She was in the farthest corner of the room, with her hands planted behind her, gripping the wall. I remembered a scene from an old disaster movie, where an earthquake had ripped through a house, leaving a gaping hole where the floor had once been. A little girl had clung to a tiny section of floor as it crumbled beneath her feet. This was Shannon. I expected a hostile brat. But all I saw was a scared kid.

My anger dissolved.

"I'm not mad," I said, suddenly quite calm. "I know you didn't intend to hurt my mother's feelings. It's okay."

"She's so old," said Shannon.

"Yes she is. But she is not about to die. She's very healthy."

"Old people creep me out."

I stepped into the room, demonstrating that there was still a floor here.

"We'll work on that," I said. "For today, we're still going to have our day of shopping. So get dressed. I'll make a quick run to the store to drop off the money. By the time you do your third coat of makeup I'll be back and then we'll go."

Shannon let go of the wall, and looked down at her white-knuckled hands.

"Can I have a manicure?"

I smiled. I was much better prepared to deal with a selfish teenager than a terrified one. "We'll both get manicures."

I got to Watertown in record time, employing what I call the pre-manic drive mode. Everyone does it once in a while—speeding up on the straightaways, barely pausing at stop signs, going through lights that aren't "too" yellow. I parked crookedly in front of the store, close to the curb, though, if you looked at the front passenger tire only.

I practically threw the bag of money at Kate.

"I'm in a huge hurry," I explained. "Here's all the money from yesterday. Could you just add it to today's deposit, and I'll sort it out tomorrow?"

"Okay, sure," she said. "I gave a 10% discount to two customers to get them to use a credit card."

"Good thinking. Got to go."

I think she said goodbye but I was already out the door.

One down, one to go. Instead of driving home, I drove to Angela's.

Angela led me to Karen's old bedroom in silence. My mother had her suitcase out, and her pile of pastel elastic-waist pants folded neatly inside.

"I'm sorry," I said. "Shannon's sorry. She was in tears when I left."

Mom didn't turn around. "So she came right over to apologize?" she asked sarcastically.

Shit.

"That's my fault. Shannon wasn't dressed; I had to run over to the store. I left without her."

She took all her pastel blouses that matched her pastel pants and put them in the pastel suitcase.

"It doesn't really matter," she said. "You are going to do what you want. You want that brat and you want that store, and I'll just go home and get out of your hair."

"Oh Mom, I want you here."

"I can drive into a building in Florida, and you won't have to miss your shopping day."

"I'll go get Shannon, and she'll apologize."

"She'll kill you in your sleep."

Angela had been leaning against the doorjamb, letting us go at it, but now she stepped between us.

"Do you remember the Thanksgiving when Mary Ann was fourteen?"

"No, Angela, no stories," said my mother, who took a huge white bra from the bureau and tucked it discreetly between the blouses.

"Was that the year she wanted her ears pierced?" I jumped in.

"That's right," Angela continued as my mother ignored her and walked into the bathroom. "Dad said no, and Mary Ann was furious. Wouldn't come to the table for Thanksgiving dinner."

"Funny, what was shocking back in those days." I spoke loudly, but there wasn't too much wrong with my mother's hearing. I'm sure she was taking it all in from the bathroom. "Pierced ears. Now even babies have pierced ears. Lately it's tattoos. I bet the next generation will tattoo their babies."

"That's disgusting and dirty," my mother chimed in from the bathroom. "It's like a label pointing out that you're trash. I suppose that kid has a tattoo."

"No," I said, hoping I was right. "But she'll probably want one and will fume during some Thanksgiving dinner." I nodded to Angela to pick up the story.

"Well, Mary Ann said she would skip Thanksgiving. She had not a thing in the world to be thankful for. Do you remember what you said, Cynthia? You were all of eleven and you said, 'Screw her. I'm thankful that she's locked in the bedroom.'"

"I got two novenas for that comment."

"Well, Dad rather agreed with you. He said that our Thanksgiving dinner might be more pleasant without the crabby teenager."

"He said that?"

"He did."

Behind Angela, my mother finally reappeared and was standing at the edge of the room holding two little bottles of aspirin and antacids. Always prepared. We might not have the right brand in Connecticut.

I'm sure that Angela knew my mother was right behind her.

"And do you remember what Mom said? She said, 'Crabby people need extra love.' And she got up from the table and went into Mary Ann's room. They were there quite a while. Dad gave us each a dinner roll, and told us that we could this once have it before Grace. So we ate our rolls, and waited while the turkey gravy got a skin on the top. Finally, finally, Mom came out with Mary Ann, and they took their place at the table. They both looked like they had just washed their faces. And we said grace, and went around the table saying what we were thankful for. When it was Mary Ann's turn, she said, 'I'm thankful that I won't be fourteen much longer.' And we all said…"

"AMEN!" exclaimed my mother. She walked over to the suitcase, and dumped out the clothes.

"Mom," I said. I have to work tomorrow. I really need you to babysit."

"What time?" she said.

Shannon was lying spread-eagle on the lawn. I stood over her, waving my handbag. She squinted up at me.

"You said you would be right back. It's almost lunchtime. I'm starving. The mall will be closed before we get there."

"It is not almost lunchtime. It's ten minutes to eleven. I believe the mall will still be open."

She popped up and ran to the car.

"Air conditioning," she commanded before I had my key in the ignition.

As I drove, she picked grass out of her hair and let the blast from the vent blow it into the back seat.

Shopping with Shannon was one of those weird reverse deja-vu experiences, where you get to re-live a scene from the past, only now you are playing the other role. Shannon was me, picking out the coolest clothes, and I was my mother, despising everything she chose. Determined not to actually become my mother, I smiled through my clenched teeth until my jaw ached. Besides, I consoled myself, the way the cheap fabrics stretched uncomfortably over her growing little belly, this stuff wouldn't fit for long.

I couldn't get her to even walk into a maternity shop.

"That's for old mothers like you. Young mothers don't wear that shit," she said as she hurried by without even looking in the window. I wondered what young mothers wear when they can't zip their jeans? I'd have to ask one of my nieces.

I did get her to try on something I liked. Shannon was in the dressing room, admiring herself in a skimpy black skirt that she could only barely zip. I brought her a sundress. I carried it in so that she could see only the back.

"A purple sundress? Do you think I'm like six years old?" she groaned.

Then I flipped it so she could see the front. Appliqued down the front of the purple dress was a large yellow thunderbolt.

"I'll try it," she said grudgingly, "...as a favor to you."

She looked adorable in a kinky sort of way, her blue-black hair wild from all the changes she'd already made, the streak of lightning emphasizing her round tummy.

"I'm kind of fabulous," she whispered to the mirror.

We ate in the food court. I bought a cup of coffee and sat at a table that was almost clean. I gave Shannon a twenty, and she went from stall to stall, pointing at selections and counting her change. I watched her drop coins in the tip cup, and wondered whether she was generous or stingy. She returned to me with a tray heaped with teenage delight—pizza, french fries, egg rolls, and a chocolate milkshake. She handed me a slice of pizza.

"You can't live on coffee," she said.

She might be a generous tipper, after all.

As promised, we both had manicures, mine French, hers Transylvanian.

Chapter 26

———◆———

HEN IT WAS MY TURN. The part of the day I had been looking forward to. We went to the gynecologist.

Dr. Sylvia Turner was a few years older than I. She had dark bright eyes and silver curls that unraveled to her collar. She reminded me of the smart standard poodle that walked every day with the antique dealer in Watertown.

If Dr. Turner was surprised to see Shannon, she didn't show it.

I was suddenly at a loss about how to introduce Shannon. *My adopted daughter, my soon-to-be adopted daughter, my new daughter.*

"My daughter," I said.

"Nice to meet you," said Dr. Turner, though she knew I didn't have any children. She shook Shannon's hand.

"I'm pregnant," said Shannon.

"Well," said Dr. Turner calmly, "That's my specialty."

We followed her into the examining room.

"Let's chat a little first," she said. "How old are you?"

"Fourteen. Fifteen in October."

Dr. Turner then asked Shannon the questions I had wanted to ask but didn't know how. "How long have you been sexually active?"

"Not too long. I got knocked up right away."

"When was that?"

"I don't know," said Shannon. "How pregnant do I look?"

I knew that Shannon was pregnant in late May when I met her, and she had told me she was already pregnant when she met D.J. So I could have helped her to pin it down. But I wasn't supposed to know she was pregnant till last week.

"Shannon," I nudged, "we met right after Memorial Day. Were you pregnant then?"

She turned and glared at me, and I tried to look apologetic.

"I'm not sure," she said, and smiled nastily. This from the same kid who just bought me pizza.

I did my best to stay sweet. "Honey, you told me you were pregnant when you met D.J. And you already knew D.J. when we met. So you must have been pregnant in late May."

"If you say so."

"So, do you remember when you met D.J.?"

"After I got pregnant."

The doctor intervened before I could take a swing at her.

"It's okay," she said. "Lots of women aren't sure. The ultrasound will tell us."

Shannon turned her back on me, satisfied. "That's right," she said to Dr. Turner, "I just can't be sure. Like, there were so many times."

"Let's talk about that," said the doctor. "Do you think the father was healthy?"

"I don't know who the father is. I was very popular."

I winced.

"I'm sure," said Dr. Turner, still nonplussed, "But think back a little about all those great guys. Any older men; anybody who smoked or drank a lot? Or did drugs?"

"No, just the usual. Beers and shit. They were all pretty normal, I think. I mean, I didn't fuck any retards or anything."

"O...kay..." Dr. Turner finally had enough. "Time for your exam."

Dr. Turner led us to the examination room, leaving us alone while Shannon stripped down. "I'll be back in a minute. Get comfortable," she said, as if that were possible in a backless paper dress and no panties.

During the exam, Shannon's eyes were shut tight, her body rigid and her teeth clenched. When the doctor gave her hand a little reassuring squeeze, Shannon jerked it away. She may have thought it was me.

Dr. Turner gently probed and Shannon shuddered. Her discomfort was clearly more than that of a young teenager insecure in her body. This was true dread. I wondered whether there was more abuse in her past than what was recorded in her file. I began to doubt her self-proclaimed promiscuity. How could her desire for popularity have overcome this fear of being touched?

She opened her eyes and I smiled and gave her a thumbs up. She reciprocated with a smile that was weak but genuine.

"Done with this part," said Dr. Turner. "Good job."

It only took a moment for her to resume her tough girl façade.

"Is there anybody in there?" asked Shannon.

"There certainly is," she said. "And you're about to see."

And we did. Shannon's belly got prepped with what looked like petroleum jelly.

"Don't you think I already have enough jizz on the inside?" Shannon asked as I hung my head. Dr. Turner finally blushed, and Shannon finally smiled. The ultrasound picture came to life.

"Do you see that?" Dr. Turner asked. "That's your baby."

"It doesn't look like much," said Shannon.

"What do you think it looks like?"

Shannon propped herself on her elbows and considered it. "A cashew," she said. "With a head."

Dr. Turner squinted. "I totally see that," she said. "Although this would be one hell of a cashew." She turned to me. "Grandma, what do you think?"

"Wow," I said.

"You bet," said the doctor. "And here's some more wow." She took a small box with a microphone that looked like Angela's old karaoke player. And suddenly there was a heartbeat—fast, loud, insistently steady.

"That's the baby's heartbeat," she explained to Shannon. "It's completely separate from yours."

It wasn't separate from mine.

I coughed and the tears let go. Shannon looked at me. "Jesus, Cynthia. Get a grip."

"When?" I asked when I could find my voice.

"Shannon, you're about fourteen weeks along. Just like a patient I had this morning. So I'd say right after Christmas."

"See?" Shannon said as soon as we got back to the car. "See how I'm keeping up my end of the bargain? I got a cashew in the oven just like you thought."

"Yes, you are doing great."

"So let's go get a puppy."

"I just bought you all those new clothes."

"Yeah, a shitload. Let's get a puppy."

I turned into the video store parking lot and stopped the car.

"First of all, let's try to make it a dog, and not a puppy. It will be easier on both of us. Second, you have to wait just a little while. A week, tops."

It was already starting to heat up in the car. I turned on the ignition and cranked the air.

"Why?" Shannon said, hollering over the fan. "We have a deal. You said I could have a dog."

"Because I just patched things up with mother. And she's afraid of dogs."

"That old bitch? She isn't afraid of anything."

My turn to yell. "This is my mother you're talking about. Not a bitch. And even the toughest people are afraid of something."

"Not me," she said. "What a wuss."

"Maybe so," I said, preferring wuss over bitch. I stopped the car again, so I could lower my voice and sound reasonable. "It'll just be a few days. Anyhow, that's why we're at the video store. Because my mother is babysitting for you tomorrow."

"Jesus Christ. You should have let her go home."

"I know you're entirely capable of taking care of yourself. This is for her, okay? We're humoring her, remember?"

"Fuck," she said, but she opened the car door. "So what are we doing here?"

We both got out and I put my hands on the hot roof. It felt good.

"Pauline," I said, getting a little smile out of Shannon, "loves movies. Loves. So we'll get a shitload of DVDs, and you won't even have to talk to her. All you have to do is sit in the same room and eat popcorn. She makes great popcorn, by the way."

"And then we'll get a puppy."

"Dog."

"Dog."

"After she goes back to Florida."

Shannon faced me across the car, and put her hands on the roof just like I had. She turned palms upward. She made little "gimme" squeezes with her fingers. "And the concert tickets."

"Okay," I said.

She nodded. "Let's go shopping."

In the video store, Shannon went down one aisle while I stayed up front at the older titles. I took *The Music Man*, my mother's favorite. Shannon approached me and held out her choice. The girl in the picture had a butcher knife in her right breast, and her left eyeball dangled goopily from its socket.

I sighed. "Just this morning you were afraid my mother would drop dead of a heart attack any second. Now this is what you want to show her?"

Shannon widened her eyes and opened her fingers, letting the video clatter to the floor. She pivoted and went back down the aisle towards where I had started.

I slid that gross movie in among some cartoons, and browsed through the newer DVDs. I picked up a copy of a movie I had seen a few years ago. A grandmother reconnecting with her estranged granddaughter. Hell, it couldn't hurt. I tucked it in with the classics.

Shannon returned and handed me her second choice. *The Bridges of Madison County.*

"Good girl," I said.

At the counter, Shannon asked the skinny kid who checked out our movies whether her choice was okay for old people.

"Oh, yeah," he said. "Really old people. It's a geezer romance."

Shannon flashed me a scowl. "It better be some fucking great concert."

Saturday was busy, and women were buying. But they were all very crabby. Or maybe it was me. My mother had arrived one stroke after the crack of dawn, and we had breakfast together while Shannon was still asleep. I showed her how to work the DVD player, and went to work. I hadn't heard from either of them.

I missed one call while I was in the dressing room with a customer, and after that I carried the phone around with me throughout the store. I had it at the register, in the stockroom, in the bathroom. No calls. I was a wreck over leaving my mother and Shannon together for a whole day. Would Shannon tell my mother she was pregnant? I figured she probably would. Then what? How angry would my mother be? I started to call them a dozen times, but each time I ended the call before the first ring.

At two-thirty the phone rang in my hand. My fingers jerked like the phone had delivered an electric shock, and I almost smacked a customer in the nose.

It wasn't Shannon. It was Ben.

"I won't keep you," he said. "But I wanted to ask you to come see my old friend, Harry. He wants to meet Oprah's friend."

"Oh, Ben, that's sweet. I can't do it today though." Ben didn't know about Shannon. It was going to take some explaining, and not on the phone. How I had an instant daughter. "My mother's visiting from Florida," I said instead.

"That's nice," he said. There was a little silence where he might have been waiting for an invitation of his own.

"She's heading back tomorrow," I said, which didn't really explain why I wasn't inviting him over. "Can we visit Harry on Monday, after we do the books?"

"Sure," said Ben.

I felt an uncomfortable pulse in my temple. I shouldn't have any guilt over not mentioning Shannon. I wasn't pretending she didn't exist. I was actually being considerate, not wanting to trivialize the situation when I didn't really have time to explain. She didn't deserve a casual mention, but a thoughtful conversation. Right? That throb could just go away, thank you.

So I called her. The phone rang several times, and I was relieved that Shannon picked up and not my mother.

"So, how's it going?" I asked.

"She's all crying and everything."

"Over you or a sad movie?"

"The movie. I'm being good. But this old broad in the movie, she's like paying her granddaughter to be nice to her. And Pauline's bawling her eyes out… Hey, you know, that would work, you know…paying me."

"I am."

"Pauline could chip in too."

"I'll bring home a pizza," I said.

"No mushrooms."

I could hear "Seventy-Six Trombones" blaring away even as I let myself in the door. I peeked in the living room. They were perfect opposites, my mother soft and round in pale blue—even her hair was pale blue—while Shannon was sharp and all angular black. My mother was smiling, with a bowl of popcorn comfortably balanced on her big soft chest. Shannon had her bowl resting on her little bump of a belly. The look on her face was condescending boredom.

"Hi guys," I said, waving the pizza box.

"Shh," my mother said. "Almost over."

Shannon gave me the usual eye-roll, but didn't get up to help me set the table either.

A few minutes later the TV clicked off, and my mother and Shannon came into the kitchen.

"That was so delightful," said my mother taking her place at the table. "I never get tired of that movie. Did you like it, Shannon?"

"It was pretty corny," said Shannon, licking cheese from her wrist.

"Maybe a little corny," my mother conceded. "But so wholesome."

"Wholesome?" said Shannon. "I don't know. I mean, think about it. That Marian was pretty old, maybe thirty, and she's got this little brother who's about six. And this ancient mother who's about eighty. How does that happen?" Shannon took a bite and chewed and thought. "I think that the kid was really her son, and they were just pretending it's her brother, so the neighbors wouldn't be all shocked."

Here it comes, I thought.

My mother put down her slice, and said softly, as if not wanting to spread gossip, "You know, I have always thought the same thing. Marian was supposed to be a scandalous figure in the town. Because of her relationship with the old rich man. Well maybe there was something to that rumor. It makes the movie that much more interesting."

I moved my pizza to the side, and laid my head down on the table.

"What?" asked my mother.

Mom left right after dinner, given that she would never drive after dark, and notwithstanding that it doesn't get dark in July until after 8:00.

Shannon spent the next half-hour telling me how much I now owed her, that she was a saint, a fucking saint.

"The old lady goes back tomorrow," she said. "I'm going to be a fucking saint for one more day, and then we get a dog."

She went to her room and began shaking the house.

Finally, finally, just after ten, there was quiet. From up in my room I heard the toilet flush, like the old house exhaling one big sigh of relief.

Chapter 27

SHANNON'S CONCEPT OF SAINTHOOD WAS slightly different from mine.

I knocked lightly on her door, and opened it without even sticking my head in. Gently, I said, "Shannon, start waking up. Time to get ready for Mass."

No answer. So I peeked in. She was curled up very small in the farthest corner of the bed.

"Shannon," I said a bit louder.

"Go away," she answered.

"I'll give you a few minutes," I said nicely.

"Get lost," she mumbled.

I closed the door. I went to the kitchen and made coffee. I set the table, and turned on the soft classical music I always listened to on Sunday mornings, to get me in the right church attitude.

Ten minutes later, I went back. I knocked loudly and went in. She hadn't moved.

"Time for church."

Shannon pulled the covers up over her head. "You've got to be shitting me."

I smiled. I employed my most convincing argument.

"Puppy," I said.

"Jesus Christ."

"Yup, that's who we're going to visit."

"No way," said Shannon. She pulled the covers down a bit. I could see the tangle of black-and-blue hair. Her eyes were still closed tight. Her eyelids were red.

"I can't," she said. "I'm sick."

Odds were that she was lying. But her bruised eyes threw shadows against her pale skin. I thought about being fourteen and pregnant. Pregnant with my little grandchild, who I met in its cashew-nut-shell just yesterday.

I knew I was probably making a parental mistake, but I was new at this, and certainly this was just a little mistake.

"Okay," I relented. "I'll go without you. This once. I'll be back a little after eleven. Then we can go to Angela's for dinner."

"Puppy," she said.

⚜

The Breault women were in the pew. My mother furthest in, then Angela, then Mary Ann. I slid in.

I could feel the Breault eyes on me as I knelt and said a quick prayer. *Mother Mary*, I prayed, *give me a sign that I can be a mother. Just anything.*

I sat down with the girls.

"No kid?" Mary Ann whispered. "I thought she said she was Catholic. So where is she?"

My maternal instinct kicked in. Hey, Mother Mary, that was quick.

"I don't see YOUR kids here," I replied.

Angela leaned over and penetrated me with those blue eyes.

"Sorry," I said to Mary Ann, kissing her on the cheek. "Is there a club for frazzled mothers?"

The red-headed lady in the pew in front of us turned around, as did her three red-headed little boys. She stuck her hand out.

"Welcome," she said. "I'm the president."

I came home to a quiet house. I looked in Shannon's room. There were clothes strewn on the unmade bed, and a few on the floor. In the bathroom, a wet towel sagged over the edge of the sink.

I went up to my room and changed into gray linen shorts. There was an empty space next to my black sandals. That's where I had left my old purple flip-flops last night.

I went back to Shannon's room and looked in her closet, and through the discarded clothes. There was no purple sundress.

I thought about it. I called D.J.'s, and his mother explained that D.J. had come home from vacation late last night, but took off about an hour ago.

"She hasn't seen her boyfriend all week," I explained cheerfully to everyone at Angela's. "So I told her to go have fun. No need to hang around with us old folks."

They all snorted. I definitely needed that red-headed lady's phone number.

Sitting in the airport with my mother, she rummaged through her purse and handed me a butterscotch candy.

"So," she said. "What are you going to do about the baby?"

I dropped the candy and it hit my foot and rolled down the floor, coming to rest against a toddler on a leash. He picked it up and put it in his mouth.

"You know? Did Shannon tell you?"

"For God's sake," said my mother, which is wicked swearing for her, "Do you think you are the only one in the family who can spot a pregnant woman?"

"You? Are you shitting me?" I said, just like Shannon would have.

"Watch your language. Of course. Do you think that gift came out of the blue? I just always knew enough to keep my mouth shut. You just blabbered away."

"But you always acted so shocked."

She sniffed. "I like to mind my own business," she said. Though I can never remember her actually doing that.

"So... what about the baby?"

It was obvious to her I knew all along. So I leveled with her. Sort of.

"It's what drew me to her. She's just a little girl herself. With absolutely no one who cares. I wanted to take care of her and the baby."

"And the boyfriend?"

"Not his. Shannon doesn't even know who the father is."

My mother shook her head. "She's a tramp."

"She's fourteen. She wanted to be popular."

"Wonderful. Now she gets to be a mother."

"No," I said. "I get to be a mother."

"I see," she said.

193

"I've always been able to see it," my mother whispered in my ear as I kissed her soft cheek at the security gate. She took her pastel suitcase from me and rolled it toward the conveyor belt. "All those years ago. I saw yours."

She walked away to where I wasn't allowed to go. She turned back to me with tears in her eyes.

"Be a good mother," she said.

⚜

"Let me explain," was the first thing out of Shannon's mouth as I approached her on the steps.

"I'm sure you've had a lot of time to come up with a good excuse," I replied. I stood over her and made sure my shadow covered her. It was as menacing as I could be in linen shorts and a pink lace cardigan.

"No. Really." She turned a sorrowful face up at me. "Saturday was pretty good. I figured I had got in pretty good with old Pauline. So there it was, you know?"

"What?"

"That for sure I'd screw it all up."

There was a certain logic to that.

"So you couldn't leave a note?"

"I wrote a note." She reached in her backpack and handed me a grimy post-it note: *I went out.* "I forgot to leave it."

"You couldn't call?"

"I couldn't call you in church!"

"And after church?"

"I forgot."

"Not acceptable," I said.

"So I'm screwed on the tickets," she said, not asked.

"No shit."

She hung her head, and tucked her arms around her knees.

"It doesn't matter anyway," she said. "I'm probably screwed with D.J. too. We saw Celeste at the park and she spent about an hour staring at my belly. She'll tell him for sure."

Shit. I sat down next to her. "Shannon, honey, YOU need to tell him. Right away, before she can."

She looked at me. "Go now," I said.

She stood up. "I have to go pee first," she said. "I forgot my key."

Forty-five minutes later she stormed back in. Her face was blotchy, her nose running, her black eyeliner like two muddy caterpillars crawling down her cheeks.

"Thanks a fucking LOT," she yelled as she pushed by me. "GREAT Advice. Thanks, MOM." Her door slammed.

She said 'Mom' as if it were the most despicable word she could use.

It was the first time I really felt like a mother. Hated by my teenage daughter. Did motherhood have to be so predictable?

I stood at her barricaded door for several minutes, ready to knock, ready to barge in, ready to remind her that she knew this would happen, ready to hold her in my arms. Ready to send her back to Decision House.

I took my purse and car keys and drove to Wal-Mart. When I got home, her door was still closed, but there was an empty milk carton on the kitchen table.

I didn't knock. I just left the Wal-Mart bag propped up against her door. Purple flip-flops.

Chapter 28

***

BEN OPENED THE DOOR TO an old green Explorer.
"Where's the beautiful Impala?" I asked as I scrambled up and in.

"It might rain," he explained.

I plunked my butt in the seat but stuck my head back out before he closed the door, squinting dramatically. "It's pretty sunny."

"No," Ben said, looking up. "There's a little cloud way over there in the South. The Impala only comes out when there're no clouds at all."

"No use being reckless," I said as he climbed behind the wheel.

"Damn straight," he said.

We drove north, moving further away from the tiny cloud.

"Years ago," I said, "I went to a wedding where the whole wedding party was chauffeured by the antique car club. While we were in church, it started to rain. After the ceremony, we left the church and all the antique cars had disappeared."

Ben nodded. "Naturally. You couldn't leave them out in the rain."

"But the wedding party couldn't get to the reception."

"Not as important as the cars. I'm sure the bride and groom got to the reception eventually."

"I drove them. In my Subaru."

"See? Everything turned out okay and the beautiful cars were saved."

"The bride's gown barely fit in the car."

"And how did the bride feel about that?"

"Cranky," I said.

We drove through the town and into a nice residential burb where the trees made a canopy over the road and the sun flashed between the branches. It was so pleasant it helped me forget about my not-so-pleasant morning.

Shannon had given me the deep-freeze treatment during breakfast. She'd sat down with a plunk that conveyed her continued displeasure with me. With her head practically in her cereal bowl, she went through three helpings of Rice Krispies without a word. The crackling cereal echoed in the silent kitchen.

"I've got a little work to do at the store," I said to the top of her head. "Then I'm going with a friend to visit a very old man who's in a nursing home. He's a genius."

She looked up at me and slowly opened her mouth and let milk dribble down her chin.

"Cute," I said. But I was determined not to get mad. "You can use the computer today. Feel free to surf all the nasty sites you want, as long as they don't cost me anything."

Shannon smiled, and pushed back her chair, scraping it jarringly against the floor. She got up, burped, and sauntered back to her room

But all was not lost. She was wearing the new flip-flops.

✱

Ben pulled up to one of those old residential buildings, low and wide, with dozens of identical narrow windows. The bricks looked as if they were about to crumble into red dust, and indeed, the ground around the building was a powdery red. There were some fading geraniums on either side of the opaque glass doors.

"It's not so bad inside," Ben explained as he saw me attempt to shore up a droopy flower. "I ask Harry all the time if he wants to move, but he likes it here."

Because of his association with Einstein, I had envisioned Harry with wild hair, big brush mustache and an oversized sweater. But he was a polished Buddha, pink and round and completely bald. He wore a black suit with white shirt and a skinny brown tie that reminded me vaguely of Thanksgiving.

Harry had a private room, decorated everywhere with framed photographs. There were pictures of the Taj Mahal and that onion-spired church in Russia. There were family pictures of little boys and girls in cowboy attire, and old men sitting stiffly with heavy-shoed old women. There were photos of Ben and Ben's red Impala. There were pictures of Betty Hutton and Rosalind Russell. There was one wall completely devoted to Oprah Winfrey. But the one that drew my eye was of a shiny young man standing side by side with Albert Einstein.

"I brought you your favorite lunch and a new friend," said Ben.

"My son Benny brings me cheeseburgers," Harry said.

"Your friend Benny," Ben corrected gently, putting the fast food bags down on a small mahogany table that held a crystal vase of plastic roses. "Come sit. This is Cynthia, Harry. She's the lady I told you about. She met Oprah."

"She gave you a beautiful shawl," Harry said to me, remembering a part of the story. "Do you wear it every day or do you save it for special occasions?"

"It was Oprah's scarf, and she wears it on cold nights."

"It's cold in Chicago," he said. "What's your name, honey?"

"Cynthia," I reminded him.

"Have a cheeseburger, Cynthia. Don't eat too many french fries."

"Harry doesn't like to share the fries," said Ben.

"Let's have some music," said Harry, and he walked, heavily on his left foot, then heavily on his right, giving him an aged duck appearance, to a small turntable, circa 1955, and put on a record. Given the atmosphere of all the old photographs, and the heavy lace curtains, I thought I would hear Cole Porter or Gershwin or maybe even Mozart, but the Beatles began to sing 'Come Together.'

I laughed.

"Do you like this?" asked Harry.

"I sure do."

My misperception of Harry as Einstein had persevered even after I had now seen him. Harry was not Einstein's contemporary; he was my mother's. And although my mother's taste had run more towards Frank Sinatra than The Beatles, I can remember her singing 'She loves you, yeah, yeah, yeah' as she frosted the cake for my tenth birthday. There was no reason why Harry and my mother couldn't be Beatles fans. Adults could be cool, but kids can't see it. I'm cool. Shannon just doesn't know it.

"Does she stay with you?" Harry was asking.

"Shannon?" I said automatically, since she was in my head.

"Oprah," said Harry. "Does Oprah ever stay with you? Oprah used to stay with Dr. Einstein once in a while."

"Not Oprah," said Ben. "Marian Anderson. Marian Anderson used to stay with Dr. Einstein."

"That's right. Miss Anderson," Harry said.

"Really?" I asked.

Ben nodded. "Really. Marian Anderson couldn't stay in hotels in New Jersey during segregation. So Einstein offered her his home. She stayed quite often." He got up and went to the wall full of movie stars. He tapped on an old photo. "Come look. Here's Marian Anderson and Albert Einstein."

And there they were, standing against the same floral wallpaper as in the photo of Harry and Einstein. Marian Anderson looked directly at the camera, her eyes serious in her broad square face, while Einstein smiled the shy smile of someone rather smitten.

I hadn't noticed that the Beatles had stopped. But the room was suddenly filled with Miss Anderson's eerie contralto, "Sometimes I Feel Like a Motherless Child." Harry was at the turntable with a rapturous smile and tears falling unchecked down his cheeks.

"No one sings like Oprah," he said.

And we sat and ate cheeseburgers and laughed and cried while Marian Anderson sang spirituals. It was the most delicious lunch I had ever eaten.

As we said goodbye to Harry, he asked Ben, "Is this lady your girlfriend?"

"Yes," said Ben.

"Who's Shannon?" asked Ben before he even started the car.

So I told him about Shannon. Or rather, I told him about a version of Shannon. The idea of being someone's girlfriend after all these years seemed to be crowding out other feelings. Like motherhood. Like honesty.

So I found myself saying that Shannon was the girlfriend of my neighbor's son. That she was in a terrible foster home, needed to get out, needed someplace safe to stay. And that I had taken her in. For the summer, I said dismissively.

"Cynthia," Ben said. "You're a good woman." And he leaned over and kissed me quickly on the cheek.

We were quiet on the ride back to the store. It was a silence not comfortable, not uncomfortable. It was anticipatory.

Ben pulled into the alley behind the store and parked next to my car. He kissed me a real kiss then. More than friendship, less than lovers. It was also anticipatory.

He waited in his car while I started mine, like men do, making sure you are safely on your way. So I pulled out of the alley and he followed me the first block and then turned right towards the highway. In my rearview mirror, he held up his hand in a wave or a salute. I went around the block and pulled back into my parking space in the alley. I stopped the car.

It wasn't like a romance novel where his kiss had made me all swoony, and I couldn't drive. I just needed a minute.

It was nice to think that something might come of this. Ben was intelligent, sincere, funny, caring. I had forgotten to want those things, but now they were showing up and reminding me—reminding me that I might even want a man. But if Ben were all those things, then wouldn't he be the kind of man you could be honest with? Years ago, an acquaintance who was trying her hand at computer dating told me that she had more luck when she changed her bio from 'mother' to 'cult member.' Are all men afraid of children? I didn't think so, but then again, I had instinctively downplayed my connection to Shannon.

A nice man had kissed me. In the quiet car, I heard him say, "You're a good woman." I heard Mom say from the backseat,

"Be a good mother." I turned on the radio to drown them out. The Beatles sang out, "Lady Madonna."

"Okay, okay," I said to my mother and the Beatles. "I'll make it up to her."

Chapter 29

—⟡—

D.J. WAS SPREAD-EAGLED ON THE back lawn. There was no sign of Shannon. I sat down next to him.

"What do I do?" he asked. "I'm so screwed." He flung his forearm over his eyes. "I want to go to college."

"So go to college," I answered.

"But what about the baby? My parents are shitting bricks. Shannon says she won't have an abortion."

I leaned back a bit. "Wait a minute," I said. "Do you think the baby is yours?"

"I want to go to college," he repeated.

He took his arm away from his face and squinted up at me. "What did you just say?"

"Shannon was already pregnant when she met you."

D.J. jumped up. "I'll kill her."

I got up too, but with a little more effort than D.J.

"No," I said, "Let me."

As I turned to the door, I saw Shannon's face in the window. She shrugged her shoulders in an 'I-don't-care' attitude, but her eyes were a heartbreaking mix of fear and sorrow. Lady Madonna.

I sat back down.

"Yeah," said D.J., fists clenched. "Better that I do it."

"Sit down," I said.

I had just been dishonest with a man for less reason.

"D.J., she's just a scared kid, and you're her only friend in the world. She's so afraid of losing you."

"Well, she certainly guaranteed that."

My anger veered instantly to D.J. It was that maternal thing kicking in again. It was amazing how something you didn't even know you had can suddenly and completely take over.

"Just a minute, Mr. Perfect. The fact that you thought the baby was yours means that you were having sex with a fourteen-year-old kid. Let me think—can't you go to jail for that?"

He dropped to his knees and then fell forward on his elbows. He buried his face in his hands and mumbled something into the grass. I think I heard the word, 'college'.

Having frightened him enough, I put a hand on his shoulder.

"It's okay," I said. "Nothing is going to happen to you."

"Tell that to my parents."

"No, you will."

D.J. sat up and hugged his knees. He looked eleven years old.

"How?"

"You are going to tell them this: That the baby isn't yours, and you aren't having sex with Shannon—because, believe me, you aren't going to be having sex with her from this moment forward—but that you are her friend, and she needs a friend right now."

"That doesn't sound too bad."

"No, it's good. Your parents will like it. And you are going to get to practice it right now—because you are going to go in the house and say the exact same thing to Shannon."

He shook his head. "I can't be her friend. I hate her."

"No you don't. You are about the only person in the world who likes her."

"You like her."

This surprised me. But it was true. I did like her.

"When you first met her," I asked D.J., "what did you like about her?"

He looked up at the sky and smiled.

"That first day, she was being harassed by these assholes. I really hate those guys. You know the type. Morons who don't even know how stupid they are."

An image came immediately to mind of my old boss. "Morons with a superiority complex."

D.J. laughed. "No kidding. Anyway, I said she was my girlfriend just to shut them up. I put my arm around her real loving like, and walked her out of that park. She never said a word. We got in the truck and went for a ride. We went all the way up Route 8 to where it ends, and then just turned around and rode back. She was just quiet the whole time."

"And you liked her."

He plucked a blade of grass out of the lawn and tossed it in the air. "Man, do you know what most girls are like? I mean, they never shut up." Realizing that I was, in fact, a girl, he peeked up at me. "No offense," he said. "But they talk about their feelings constantly, like they're taking their pulse or something, and when they're not for like a split-second, they expect you to. Shannon likes to just sit with you. Do you know what she finally said when I dropped her off? She said, 'Nice Truck'. That was it."

"So you liked her."

He nodded. "The next day after school I drove over to the junior high where Celeste goes, and waited across the street. When Shannon came out, she walked right over to my truck and climbed in. She wasn't surprised to see me; she didn't even look around, you know, and spot me. She just walked straight from the school door to the truck. It was weird, sort of. And we drove to Kent Falls and climbed the rocks and shit. And she didn't even walk around with me. She went one way and I went the other. But when it was time to leave, she just was right there."

"Do you talk more now?"

"Yeah, sometimes. She talks a little about songs on the radio. Or about what some asshole did in school. She knows a lot of assholes. Mostly, though, it's like being alone without being alone."

A good definition of companionship, I thought.

"So you like her?" I nudged him again.

"Yeah, I guess." But he shook his head. "But not like 'forever' and now there's a baby."

"I'm going to take care of Shannon and the baby. And Shannon knows it's not forever. She's resigned to the idea that when you go off to college you'll find a girl your own age."

"You think so?"

"I know it. So what would be so hard about being her friend—her only friend—for the rest of the summer?"

He got up and brushed the grass from the seat of his jeans. "Okay."

"So go in and tell her. And tell her that I've changed my mind and that you two can go to a rock concert after all. Go in and look for a good show on the internet." I smiled. "Not too far a drive," I added.

He walked towards the house, but turned back to me.

"She talks about you sometimes," he said.

"Does she think I'm an asshole?"

"Not all the time," he answered.

I lay back on the lawn. Well, I had promised to make it up to her. *How's that?* I asked John, Paul, George, Ringo and Pauline.

<hr/>

I fed both of them, because that's what mothers do.

Notwithstanding my cheeseburger for lunch, I served hamburgers and corn on the cob. Shannon's corn eating method was loud and slurpy, eating from the middle and out in some pattern that I couldn't fathom. D.J. went back and forth like a typist. He mowed the lawn the same way. I tended to start on the left and go around and around like peeling an apple. The leftover tension made us critical of each other's corn-eating style.

D.J. escaped as quickly as he could.

"Thanks, Cynthia," he said as he bolted towards the door. He looked back at Shannon and softened a fraction. "I'll pick you up at nine tomorrow and a bunch of us will go to the beach."

Shannon frowned. "I can't wear a bathing suit. All your friends will see that I'm knocked up, and you'll be mad all over again."

"Well, fuck them then. I'm okay with you being knocked up. Okay?" he said loudly, more to me than to Shannon. And he slammed the door on the way out.

My hero.

I must have been partially forgiven, because later that evening, Shannon shut off the screaming (literally—it must have been a slasher movie) television in her room, and came out and watched TV with me in the living room. I silently handed her half of my orange, and she picked off every little bit of white membrane and carefully made a little pile on her knee. We watched a decorating show. They were redo-ing a bedroom.

"It's better than it was," Shannon said towards the end of the program, "but it's still pretty boring. Mine is better."

"I agree," I said.

At the end, the homeowners were tearfully thanking the decorating host.

"What crap," said Shannon. "Furniture shouldn't make you cry."

"I think it's just the idea that someone cares about them."

She thought about this. "But they're not exactly homeless. And they're not broke, obviously. They could buy new stuff if they wanted. And they're married. Like, don't they care about each other?"

"You've got a point. But sometimes it's difficult to see what's right in front of you. You don't appreciate it."

"Ungrateful pricks."

I looked at her. "Shannon, why did you tell D.J. that the baby was his?"

"I didn't really. He just assumed. He started yelling about fucking college, and how I ruined his life. That it was all my fault. Like his dick didn't have anything to do with it."

"Well, um, his dick didn't have anything to do with it."

"That's just timing. It could have. He was such an asshole. He *deserved* to suffer. At least for a little while."

I may have a mean streak myself, because I silently agreed with her. But I said, "I think you should forgive him. He just needed a little time to get used to the idea. He still wants to be your friend."

"Yeah, that's what he said. He said he couldn't be my boyfriend anymore, but that he could be my best friend."

"Are you okay with that?"

She shrugged. "Like I have a choice?... But hell, I figure I can still hang out with him, and everybody will still see me with him. I'm going to pretend like he's still my boyfriend, but let everyone know that I'm willing to cheat on him. That'll be cool." She got up and her neat little pile of orange scraps scattered on the oriental rug. She didn't see them.

"Is it too late to go out and buy sunglasses?"

D.J. arrived at the crack of 9:25. Shannon opened her bedroom door and jumped out, announcing her presence with a "Ta-DA!" She wore a short yellow flouncy skirt and a lime green halter top that had a ruffle at the waist. She had caught up her hair in a banana clip and then pinned the ends under—a sort of modern French twist. She had her usual thick eyeliner, but had rouged her cheeks with bright pink circles. Purple flip-flops and a dozen bangle bracelets stacked in a rainbow of colors completed her look. She didn't look too pregnant; she looked adorable. It was going to be very hard indeed for D.J. to stay mad at her, which I'm sure was the whole point.

I turned to D.J. "So what time will you be home?"

"Well, we usually leave the beach around four, but we like to stop at this place that has really good fried clams."

Shannon made a little gagging noise. It was actually pretty similar to the noise I make when someone mentions clams.

D.J. laughed. "Don't worry, kid. They've got great fried chicken too."

"Eight o'clock at the latest," I said, waving my finger at him in my best imitation of a mother.

Shannon picked up the beach bag I had packed for her last night, making sure she had towels and sunscreen and a heavy sweater. Although everything I own is just old-lady awful; Shannon had borrowed some dark cat's-eye sunglasses, and she put them on and smiled at D.J. With the pointy shades and her black hair pulled up, she suddenly took on a Holly Golightly glow. This is what Holly Golightly would look like today. Still invulnerable on the outside and fragile on the inside.

I handed her two twenties. "Since D.J. is your friend now and not your boyfriend, he shouldn't have to pay for everything," I said.

She grinned, waving the money at D.J., and made a gesture like she was going to tuck the money in her bra, then relented and put it in the zipper pocket of the beach bag.

"What a good Mom," she said in her lilting insincere voice. She opened the door.

"See you at midnight!" she said.

"Eight o'clock!" I hollered after her.

Another slow day at the store. I was beginning to see that there was a major flaw in this country's retail system. I had wonderful stuff to sell to affluent stylish women, but affluent stylish women didn't have time to shop. I wanted to work regular hours, and go home early, but affluent stylish women were working those same hours that the shop was open. Why was I open when they weren't here? Out-of-work women could come during the day, but they didn't have any money. Old retired ladies could come during the day, but it seemed like all of them—except me—didn't care too much about what they wore. I could sell a little bit of stuff on the weekends to affluent stylish women who weren't scrambling like geese trying to get their groceries and banking and cleaning done, all while trying to be wives to their husbands and mothers to their kids for a few hours.

I tried on one of the necklaces, and appraised myself in the mirror. My hair looked exceptionally cute today.

So I did the logical thing. I phoned Ben. The receptionist said he was in court, but put me through to his voice mail. I left a message asking him over for dinner tonight.

He called at lunch time.

"Are you a good cook?" he asked.

"Not especially," I said. "But I make up for it in portion size."

"But if the food's not good, why would I want a lot of it?"

"Because it's the American way."

"Okay," he agreed. "What time?"

Ben rang the bell at exactly seven. He came to the front door. It was sweet and friendly that he had come to the back door when we played golf. But ringing the front door was a date. A real date.

I was wearing the raspberry sundress that Ben had rather admired. I felt like throwing open the door with a "Ta-DA" like Shannon had this morning. But since this was a real date, I opened it with dignity, although I did give my hair a little shake so Ben could appreciate how nicely it had come out today.

He was wearing a polo shirt in gray-blue, and khaki cargo shorts. He had thick soled sandals, and the long unbroken line from his knees to his feet made him look very tall indeed. His calves were nicely shaped and just hairy enough to be masculine, not Cro-Magnon. He didn't have those skinny ankles some men have—you know, white bony and hairless from all those years in socks. He had, in fact, better ankles than I did.

In the crook of his left arm he cradled a bottle of red and a bottle of white wine. In his right hand, he had one of those purple slushy drinks with the built-in straw they sell at the Seven-Eleven.

"You said stuffed sole on the phone. But you could have changed your mind, or the sole could be stuffed with roast beef, so I brought the red too." He smiled.

"Very practical," I said.

"And I brought this for your houseguest," Ben said, holding out the purple cup. "I don't know what teenagers drink, but this looked disgusting enough."

I flinched a little at the word 'houseguest'. I was ashamed of the way I had minimized my relationship with Shannon, and wasn't exactly sure how I was going to put it right. I had spent most of the afternoon coming up with explanations that didn't make me sound shallow or worse—lovestruck. But all the excuses I had invented made me sound both. *Gee whiz, I really like you, so I thought I would pretend I didn't have a kid.* I was hoping something would inspire me during dinner.

"Thanks," I said, taking the cold sticky cup. Ben followed me back to the kitchen. I stuck the drink in the fridge.

"Shannon went to the beach with her boyfriend, but she'll show up eventually."

"How old is she?" he asked.

"Fourteen. Before you say it, I know that's really young to go off to Rhode Island with a boyfriend. He's a bit older though, and a good kid. Very responsible. I've known him his whole life. And she's had a tough week. And I owed her a favor."

"That's a pretty long explanation," Ben said. There was almost a question mark at the end of the sentence.

I looked at the ceiling. "I'm afraid I'm not doing it right."

Ben smiled. He leaned his hip against the refrigerator. "Does anyone do teenagers right?"

"Oh, my mother. My sisters."

"I don't know them yet, but your mother had it easy, right? I mean you were a perfect teenager, weren't you?"

"I was." I did a quick calculation of the couple of months I was a dream child. "About twelve percent of the time."

"Cynthia the Accountant," he said. "Show me what's for dinner."

So I opened the oven and showed him the stuffed filet of sole.

"I didn't stuff it with roast beef," I said. "But I couldn't make up my mind between crab meat, spinach and cheese. So we have two of each. Stuffed sole trio."

"You didn't lie about portion size," he said, and I wondered if he was implying that I lied about other things. Of course not. Guilt was making me paranoid, like The Tell-Tale Heart. Maybe I should just blurt it out and lie down in the gutter with Poe. We ate in the dining room, with my best china and silver and my favorite wine glasses. I had put some daisies in a blue vase, and after the initial effect—I got an appreciative head nod—I moved them to the far end of the table.

"My father used to like to have breakfast in the dining room," Ben said. "Made him feel like fifties TV. Robert Young, he said."

"Did he wear a suit to breakfast, with a pocket handkerchief and cuff links?"

"He did. He was a lawyer."

"Just like you."

"Not exactly like me. He was successful."

"You're successful," I said supportively. "You have your own law partnership."

He picked up his wine. "Ah, it's not the same. Roger and I were friends in law school. We went into business together with a rather unique partnership. We each do what we want, and we bill our fees separately. We are only a partnership so we can share the receptionist, clerk and office space. Roger is mostly real estate, and I'm mostly... well... free."

"Free? Are you legal aid? Like the court-appointed attorneys in the movies?"

"No. Actually court-appointments would be more successful. The state pays you. I just have a hard time billing people when I do easy things."

"What's easy about law?" I asked

Ben laughed a little embarrassingly. "Almost everything I do. I mostly help old people—with wills and estates. It's really easy. Most old people just need a standard will, and someone to help them with their taxes and their health care. And they usually don't have a lot of money, so I don't charge much."

"How about Harry? He's not broke, is he?"

"That's the other side of the dilemma. Harry's got a decent nest egg. But my job is to preserve it. So I feel very guilty charging him a lot."

"Are you sure you're a lawyer?"

"That's what my dad always asked." He took a sip of wine and frowned. "And Maria."

I felt bad that I had reminded him of Maria, but I found myself slightly satisfied that I had reminded him that she was shallow.

"Do you like what you do?" I asked.

He looked at me and said, softly and seriously, "I do."

"I spent twenty-five years making pretty good money doing something I didn't care a thing about. It's nice to have the money, but I'll never get those years back." I gestured with my glass to encompass the room, the meal, the company. "Now, I do what I like."

Ben leaned back in his chair and looked out the window.

"Do you remember what summers were like when you were a kid?" I asked.

He put his hands behind his head, elbows out, like you do when you are relaxed and reminiscing. He closed his eyes. I could see him picturing himself –maybe on his bike, or playing ball.

"Do you remember how long the summer was?" I continued. "How long each day was? Well, I have a theory. The days were long because each minute was filled with so much pleasure. So you enjoyed all those minutes and they all added up and minutes really are a long time. I mean, just count to sixty— it's pretty long. But when you're an adult, the days fly by if you aren't doing anything you like. You can't remember any individual minute because there's nothing memorable about it. So they just disappear. And so does the day. And day after day just disappears."

Ben opened his eyes and nodded.

"Well now my days are long again." I said.

"Some people complain about how time drags on."

"Not me. I love it when time slows down."

Ben took his napkin off his lap, folded it, and placed it on the table. He stood up and came over to me. He leaned over and kissed me. He didn't press. He just touched his lips to mine and allowed them to meet for quite a long time. Then he went back to his chair and placed his napkin on his lap.

He raised his glass. "Here's to slow, memorable minutes." I blushed.

"By the way," he said, "you lied to me."

My blush drained away. *Oh no. Not so soon.*

He held up a fork full of sole. "You are a really good cook."

Ben had made me breathless in two different ways in the space of a few moments. I took a sip of chablis while my heart recovered.

"It's that comparison thing again," I said. "You can't live up to your father's lawyering and I can't live up to my mother's cuisine."

He smiled. "Maybe we can surpass them in new, naughty ways."

And the kitchen door slammed.

"She's home," I whispered, though I didn't know why I sounded guilty.

I excused myself and went into the kitchen. Shannon was standing at the fridge. She'd already found the purple drink and was sucking it down with the refrigerator door still open. She was sunburned and her shoulders bore little white lines where the strings of her bathing suit had been. Seawater had given her hair that mermaid dreadlocked look.

"Did you like the beach?" I asked.

"It was better than I remembered," she said.

"I have company," I said. "Come meet my friend, and you can tell us all about it."

She followed me curiously to the dining room.

"Shannon," I said, "This is my friend Ben."

Ben stood up and came to Shannon and shook her hand, very formally.

"Nice to meet you, Shannon," he said, almost bowing, but I guess it just looked that way since he was so much taller than she.

Shannon looked puzzled and slightly annoyed.

"So what was the best thing about the beach?" I prodded.

She just stood there and stared at Ben.

"The beach?" I asked again.

She twirled the straw around to soften up the icy bottom of her drink, and then slurped up the last of it.

"I guess the best part was this kid Flaine—he was such a prick, and what a stupid name—his parents must be morons just like him—anyway, he got stung by a jellyfish. He was bawling like a baby. An ambulance had to take him away. I think he wet his pants even. I came close to peeing in my pants too—I was laughing so hard."

"That certainly sounds like fun," I said dryly.

"Why don't you sit and have dessert with us?" asked Ben.

Shannon stiffened and glared at him. "I don't think I need an invitation to eat in my own house," she said.

I had already experienced how quickly her mood could change, but I was mortified that she showed it to Ben so soon. He didn't react though; it must have been all the legal training never to look surprised.

"You're right," he said calmly. "That sounded kind of rude." He didn't actually say which one of them had sounded rude. "Cynthia," he turned to me, "Do you have dessert to share with us?"

"Absolutely, I said. "Sit, Shannon." And she did sit down, albeit with her arms crossed in suspicion. I hated to leave them alone for even the few seconds it took to go to the kitchen, but I didn't have to worry, because not a word was spoken while I rushed in and out with plates and cheesecakes and cherries.

I gave them generous helpings and they occupied themselves with a concentrated eating effort. My relaxed meal was gone. I tried to start up a conversation.

"So what made this Flaine prick such a prick?" I asked as if that were the normal language of the house, for in the last week or so, it had become pretty much the case.

"Oh you know the type," answered Shannon. She looked hard at Ben. "You know, the kind of pricks that think they own the place."

Ben refused to take the bait. "Yeah, I know. Always trying to boss you around."

"You got that right," she said.

"Didn't work though with the jellyfish," Ben pointed out.

Shannon narrowed her eyes down to two large streaks of eyeliner. "Some animals you can't boss around. They sting."

I needed to jettison this uncomfortable subtext.

"Jellyfish come out when the water's warm. This is pretty early for warm water in Rhode Island. Did you think the water was warm?" I asked.

"No, I froze my ass off," she said dismissively, keeping her eyes focused on Ben. She leaned towards him. "Are you like Cynthia's boyfriend?"

He leaned back and smiled at me. "I think maybe I'd like to be."

She snorted. I had always thought that grown-ups all look about the same to kids—old. But I was wrong. She cocked her head, her voice sweet, her smile nasty. "How did you guys meet?" Shannon asked him. "Did you go to school with Cynthia's nephew?"

Ben went for the wine.

Shannon pushed back her chair. "Gee, thanks for the wonderful dessert." And she strode out of the room and shortly the music started to reverberate.

Ben looked at the empty seat where Shannon had been. "Holy shit," he said.

"Yup, that's my kid," I said.

He put his elbows on the table and held his face in his hands, like he was waiting for story-time to begin. "Tell me again why you took her in?"

This was my opportunity to set myself straight with him. But honesty is an elusive place, and I only got halfway there. "Don't judge her too quickly," I said. "I know she can be quite nasty... and she is most of the time. But a tiny bit of the time, she is just a scared kid. Someone needs to take care of her. I don't want you to think I'm crazy, but... I like her."

"You like her," Ben repeated, not asking a question, just considering the idea.

"Well, not right this minute of course."

We did the dishes without much talking; the music had gotten progressively louder, and it was just easier not to try to converse. I brought the dirty dishes in from the dining room and he stacked the dishwasher in a lovely logical way. Nothing was crammed in, but there seemed to be no wasted space either. "Did you ever think about becoming an engineer?" I asked loudly in his ear, the way I used to flirt at bars when I was in my twenties.

I walked him out to his car.

"I'm sorry if Shannon was a little bratty," I said.

He leaned his butt against the car, put his hands on my hips and pulled me to him.

"It's okay," he said. "I don't want to date Shannon. I want to date you."

I laughed. "Shannon might be closer to your own age," I said. "What grade did you say you were in?"

We kissed quite a long time in the dark summer night. I felt young.

When I walked back to the house, I thought I heard the back door close quietly.

Chapter 30

———⟡———

SHANNON WAS SUPERFICIALLY REPENTANT THE next morning.

I sat quietly with my coffee, watching Shannon pour Cheerios into a bowl. She filled it to the very brim, and then added a few more, making a little mound in the center. As she poured in the milk, the Cheerios overflowed and floated onto her placemat like the empty life preservers around a sinking ship.

"Oops,' she said. "Sorry."

"While we're apologizing…" I said.

She tapped an escaped Cheerio with her forefinger, and it stuck. She popped it in her mouth. She then went around her bowl and tapped the rest of the loose cheerios. She held up her hand with the five little sticky circles at the end of each finger. She smiled, and waved her Cheerio'd hand. I didn't smile back, and she licked off the cereal and wiped her hand on her shirt.

"Okay," she said. "I know he's your friend, and it doesn't matter what I think."

"No, it doesn't. It doesn't matter because in this house, we're nice to everyone."

"Tell that to Bean."

"Ben. And he was very nice to you."

"He invited me to dinner, like it was his own goddamn house."

"He was trying to include you."

She shrugged. "It didn't sound that way to me." Then she softened and looked at me from under her eyelashes. "Maybe I'm all mixed up in the hormones, what with me having a baby for you and all."

I figured I'd accept that for an apology. I knew she was bound to play the pregnancy card often in the next few months. But I found that I didn't really mind. It served to remind us both of the bargain we had made. And I had forgotten, at least momentarily. There was a baby. I needed to keep my focus on the prize. But it would be nice to have two prizes, wouldn't it? I stared into my coffee cup and saw Ben kissing me in bed, with a baby asleep in the next room.

I looked up and saw Shannon watching me with alarm, as if she had seen my daydream exclude her.

I stood up.

"Guess what we're going to do today," I said.

"What?" she asked, rather exasperated. I think she probably thought I would march her over to Ben's office and make her apologize.

"We're going to get a dog."

"Holy shit!" she said and tipped over the Cheerios box.

We drove over to the local Animal Rescue shelter. Mary Ann once adopted a cat from this place. It was a pretty nice cat too—good-looking and friendly enough in that snooty cat way.

Shannon and I walked in and immediately set off every dog in the place.

"Jesus," said Shannon. "Can you imagine that every one of these dogs wants to come home with us?"

"Let's pick the quietest one."

A woman in an orange smock approached us. She had tragic dog eyes and a tiny feline nose. Born to work here.

"I'm Kathy," she said. "Have you come here to adopt one of our little critters?"

"Yeah," said Shannon. "An adoptee looking for an adoptee."

Kathy looked confused but laughed politely anyway. She had sharp little mouse teeth.

"A dog," continued Shannon. "We need a dog."

"Not a big one," I added.

"Oh, we have some sweet dogs right now. Do you want a puppy or an adult? Sometimes one of our seniors makes a lovely companion for a teenager."

"I already have a senior," said Shannon. She smirked at me. "And a puppy on the way." Kathy was completely addled now, and Shannon was on a roll. "So I think something in the middle."

Since the puppies didn't have their full voices yet, and the seniors didn't have the energy, we walked down the noisiest aisle. There were some huge dogs whose expression was either mean or terrified. These were dogs left in that condition by mean or terrified owners. Some of the medium-sized dogs didn't seem so bad, but they tended to be howlers. There were two small dogs at the end of the row.

One was adorable. Some kind of Bichon Frise mix. White curly hair, big round eyes—sort of a Harpo Marx type. He wagged his tail and his little butt wagged too.

"How about this one?" I asked Shannon.

But she had already fallen in love. The other small dog was a mongrel of the worst kind. Part Chihuahua maybe, part some awful kind of terrier. He had long thin wisps of hair in some places, but was nearly bald on other spots. The spots where an animal could use a little hair, if for modesty's sake alone. And his eyes! Or rather, eye. One eye looked at us in despair. The other eye looked at the light fixture on the ceiling.

"I like this one," said Shannon.

"What's wrong with his eye?" I asked Kathy.

"He had a tumor. The doctor got it all. Benign, but it made his eye bulge out. He's blind, of course, but it doesn't bother him at all. The other eye is perfectly okay."

"Does he bang into things much?"

"Well, he tends to veer right when he walks," Kathy said.

"I like him," repeated Shannon. "Let's take this one."

"Shannon, look at him. Don't you want a cute little dog like this little curly one here?"

"No." Shannon looked at her pathetic pick. "Everyone wants the cute one," she told him. She turned back to me. "That cutesy dust-mop will have a home by noon. No one will want this guy. He needs us."

And she opened the cage and took out the bizarre creature. He shivered in his baldness and tried to climb inside her shirt.

On the drive home, Bizarro sat on Shannon's lap, and so I had a nice long ride with the bulging eye profile.

We stopped at one of those big box pet stores where animals are welcome to come right in. For what purpose, I'll never know; maybe you can train them to push the shopping cart. We bought a collar and a leash, and three kinds of dog food. Plus a bowl and a little bed, and God help me, a little purple outfit with sequins.

Later at home, Shannon kept the dog on her lap during dinner.

"Did you decide on a name?" I asked.

"Carlos."

"After someone you know?"

"Well, one foster I was in, they had this kid..."

"And his name was Carlos?"

"No, it was Ryan. He was a real prick. But he had a nice dog. The dog's name was Chico. He died. Carlos will be like Chico's little brother."

I looked in on Shannon before I went to bed. Despite the brand new dog bed, and my absolute ban, Carlos was in bed with her. He was curled up around her growing belly. I wanted nothing more in that moment than to lie down with them, and put my arms around these two strange souls. But I closed the door and went up to my room.

Shannon was actually pretty good at taking care of the dog, except for when she forgot to feed him, or when she left him out in the pouring rain, or when she sat on him, or when she shut him up in the closet by accident, and he peed on her new shoes. Those are certainly normal mistakes that any kid can make. Although usually not in the first two days.

Chapter 31

*T*HE VERY NEXT TIME I saw Ben I slept with him. Saturday at the store was relatively busy, considering how bad most of the summer had been. We sold some summer clothes to women who just wanted something new for the last few weeks of summer. And we had some early birds looking at our first fall shipment.

Shannon called in the early afternoon. It seemed that D.J. was taking his sister and her friends to the movies that evening. He had called to invite Shannon.

"Can I go with these guys to the movies?" she asked. "I still have a little money left from the beach."

I was very impressed—impressed that she asked me, and impressed that she didn't even ask me for money.

"Who else is going?"

"Celeste and her moron friends," she answered. But underneath her contempt I sensed a vein of excitement. "It's some vampire movie, and the fuckers are actually dressing up like Halloween. It's goddamn July."

"So you're not going to dress like a vampire?"

"Hell no," she said. I pictured her intense black hair and magic marker eyeliner, but I kept that thought to myself.

"Sure," I agreed. "Tell D.J. you can go."

Five minutes later the phone rang again. Kate answered, and gestured to me.

"It's Maria's husband," she said, handing me the phone.

"Hi, Ben," I said, walking away from Kate's curious gaze and her unwelcome reminder of his marital status.

"Are you by any chance free tonight?" asked Ben.

"It turns out that I am. Shannon is going out to a movie."

"Great," he said. "Would you consider some heavy petting followed by a light supper?"

I knew that Kate couldn't hear him, but her eyes burned into my shoulder blades regardless. "That would be okay with me," I said with as much businesslike manner as I could manage through a sweltering blush.

"Your place or mine?"

"Mine. I want to be there when Shannon gets home. Plus, I'm babysitting. I now have a dog."

"Jesus Christ, Cynthia. A kid and a dog...I can't keep up with you."

"I intend to make it very difficult for you to keep up with me," I whispered into the phone.

"Can I come over now?" he asked.

"Seven-thirty," I answered.

I thought the day would never end. I needed to get home as quickly as possible, and discreetly doll myself up, which in this case meant getting as young as I could. That would take some doing, and I didn't really want Shannon to know my intentions. In the best scenario, I could be Shannon's mother, cheerfully seeing her off on her Saturday night date, have Ben arrive just after she'd gone, do our heavy petting, eat our light supper, and have him depart before Shannon could come home and insult him. How hard could that be?

Kate watched me all afternoon, or at least it seemed that way to me. I wondered if she was still in touch with Maria. What was wrong with everyone that they made me feel so guilty?

We still had some cute summer things in inventory. I abandoned the customers to Kate and tried on a sweet pale aqua camisole and a white eyelet skirt. I looked forty if I squinted, but of course I couldn't squint because then I had crow's feet. But close enough. I also took a short cardigan sweater. It was yellow and black in a bumblebee stripe, with a delicate green lace placket down the buttonholes, contrasting crazily with the sportiness of the stripes. It was much too young for our customers, which is why it hadn't sold. I thought it would be adorable for Shannon. And if she absolutely refused to wear clothes from my store, well, I'd just bring it back. No sales final (for me).

I calmed myself and slowly and casually closed up with Kate.

"Big night?" she asked as I recounted the money I had already miscounted twice.

"My kid has a date," I said. "I want her to have fun, but I also want to read her the riot act before she leaves the house."

We finished locking up.

"I didn't even know you had a kid," said Kate at the door.

"I just got her," I said, and turned out the light.

✐

Just like me, Shannon was nervous and pretending not to be. She wore a short black skirt with a little black tee, which was tight around her belly. It crossed my mind that maybe she had decided to dress up vampire-style after all, but I didn't dare ask her.

"You know," I said, trying not to sound too horribly like a typical mother, "the air conditioning in movie theaters is cranked up really high. I have a theory that if they ever let the theater warm up, everyone's shoes would stick permanently to the floor and they'd all have to leave barefoot."

And she laughed. I made my kid laugh.

"So you may be freezing without a sweater," I continued. I handed her the bag. "I won't be insulted if you don't like it, but if it's any consolation, all my customers hated this sweater. So it may not be too awful."

Shannon held up the strange bumblebee and lace sweater. I wondered what had possessed me to buy that for the store anyway.

"Not awful," she agreed. She pulled it on and jumped up for a fleeting glimpse in the living room mirror, then ran into her room to get the full effect. She came out trying to chew off the tag while still in the sweater.

"Do you want a little supper?" I asked, and was relieved that she didn't—they were going to go out early for pizza, because they certainly weren't going to be caught dead seeing a vampire movie before dark. Yea for vampires. But I could hardly tell her she could stay out as late as possible.

I kept thinking about my own new clothes, and my hair and my makeup and the sheets on my bed, as I waited impatiently for the other kids to arrive. I had told Ben to come at seven-thirty. It was close to seven before D.J. drove up in his mother's SUV. There were four kids in the car already. D.J. jumped out and ran to the back door. He was not dressed as a vampire.

"You look cute," he said to Shannon.

"New sweater," she said. And she smiled at me. She really did.

"What time will you be home?" I asked D.J.

"Celeste's friend Nick has the earliest curfew. Eleven-thirty. So we'll drop him off first, and then Shannon if that's okay."

"Well," I said, trying to sound reasonable and not plotting, "Since Shannon lives so close to you, don't make a special trip for just her. It only makes sense that you leave her for last." I added, "But by midnight of course," since what I had just said sounded so odd.

"For sure," he said, and they were out the door.

I knelt on the sofa by the window and watched as Shannon climbed in the back seat with the other kids. Doors slammed and they drove away. I scooped up Carlos, who was pacing at my feet, and sat for a moment. I was a little overwhelmed by the normalcy of it all.

And the doorbell rang.

"Hi," I said, opening the door. "You just missed Shannon." I tried to make that sound like it was something regrettable.

"Would you think that I was a terrible person if I told you that I saw her getting into the car as I turned down your street, so I drove around the block until they were gone?"

"Not so very terrible," I said. I realized that I was still holding Carlos.

"Ben, meet Carlos. Not exactly ready to enter the beautiful dog contest."

Ben scratched Carlos' ear, the one above the bad eye, so as Carlos looked up, his eyes for a second matched in a very unfortunate way.

"He's not so bad," said Ben kindly. "I've seen worse."

"When was that?"

He laughed. "I can't quite recall," he said like politicians (and lawyers) do.

I put Carlos down and he immediately ran into Shannon's room and jumped on the bed. He made about seven circles before he lay down on her pillow.

Ben looked at me. "Has anyone told you today how beautiful you are?"

"You'd be the first."

"I'm a lucky guy," he said, and he kissed me.

So much for the new outfit I never had a chance to change into.

I stood back a bit, put my hands on my hips and said, "How'd you like to go right to bed?"

"Oh boy," he said slowly.

We went upstairs, and without any hesitation, I took off all my clothes. I stood before him. My fifty-year-old body didn't embarrass me. I had learned in my first year of college not to be ashamed of my body. When you took your clothes off, men were so happy. There was never any criticism.

"Jesus," he said, and he was very quick getting out of his own clothes.

He stood with his body just brushing my nipples. Then he moved me slowly over to the bed. I let myself fall backwards and I let My Self fall completely away.

Ben made love like he kissed, gently and earnestly. He asked my body long sweet questions. Somewhere in the process I had a passing thought about how long it had been since I had done this. No matter. One doesn't get rusty in sex. It's like meeting an old dear friend—the conversation just picks up where you left it.

He didn't collapse afterwards, the way some men do. (But I'm not criticizing that ferocious style of lovemaking either, that insane frenzy that exhausts—I was already thinking about trying it soon.) He straddled me, sitting back on his heels, studying me without touching me, smiling.

His body was different than it looked in a suit. He was lean, not skinny, with a strong frame. He had large smooth shoulders. There has not been enough written about the beauty of men's shoulders.

I saw his back in the mirror behind him, and laughed in surprise.

"You have a tattoo!"

"Oh my god," he said, "Where?"

I gave him a light cuff to the forehead with the palm of my hand. "Wise guy."

"You don't like it?" he asked.

"I'm not exactly a fan of tattoos. Skin itself is so beautiful. But I don't hate them either. It's just doesn't seem to match you somehow."

"Yeah. I was talked into it. I'm glad it's somewhere I can't see."

"A dragonfly? Does it have some special meaning?"

"Not really. It was a compromise. A similar shape to the dagger she wanted."

Suddenly I was shamefully aware that I was in bed with another woman's husband. He read it on my face. He swung his leg over and lay next to me. We both looked at the ceiling. He took my hand in both of his.

"Cynthia. We all have a past."

"I know, I know." I sighed. "It's just that your past is so… recent."

"So it is." He propped himself on his elbow and looked at me. "What do you want to know?"

"Nothing," I said instinctively. Then I changed my mind. "No, wait."

He lay back down and put his hands behind his head. "Ask," he said.

"How old are you?"

I could feel him smile. "Forty."

"Thank God. I was very concerned that you might be still in your thirties."

"I'm glad to have spared you that particular trauma."

"How old is Maria?"

He paused. "Maria is thirty going on nineteen. We met six years ago. She was so intense. She craved excitement. I loved it at first, but it exhausted me. I just can't live my life at such a crazy pace. Not continually. I was hoping that with time she'd calm down just a little. I thought the store might do it...she grew up in her mother's shop in Mexico. And she was good at it. But it didn't settle her down. It bored her. I bored her, I guess. And there was Roger, going through his own midlife crisis. They took off to Key West to live like Hemingway."

"Hemingway wasn't very happy."

"I know," he said. "She's not a bad person. She's a very good person. We just aren't a good match." He closed his eyes. "I miss her though."

It was an odd conversation to have with my first lover in a decade, but I found myself reassured that he spoke about her kindly.

He shook himself from whatever memory he was in. "Okay," he said, "your turn."

"Fifty," I said.

He laughed. "No, I already know that. Don't think I didn't check out your employment information. Remember that first day we met about the store? You said you were retired. I couldn't believe you could be sixty-five, so I checked you out. Believe me, if you are relieved I'm forty, think about how relieved I was that you weren't sixty."

"Yikes," I said.

"No kidding." He leaned towards me and his face became serious. "Here's my real question. Shannon isn't just here for the summer, is she? You don't buy a pet for a houseguest."

I conceded. "No, you don't. You buy a pet for your kid." I met his eyes. "I'm adopting her."

Ben sat up straight and looked at me. "Wow," he said.

"That's everyone's reaction."

"It's such a huge step."

"It's even huger than you think." I sat up next to Ben, took a deep breath and let him have it. "Shannon's pregnant."

"Holy shit." Ben cocked his head a little, confused. "So why did you tell me she was here for the summer?"

"I guess because it's such a scary thing."

"Are you scared?"

I turned to him and smiled. "No."

He fell back against the headboard making a slight thunk with the back of his head. He picked his hands up once, then put them back down. He seemed to be literally framing his thoughts.

"Cynthia, Shannon's so young. I don't mean to criticize your religion or anything, but do you really think she should have this baby?"

"It's not that," I replied. "I think I'm a fairly good Catholic, but I don't really believe that the Church—or me, for that matter—should force someone to have an unwanted baby. I'm actually glad that abortion is legal. It's not a religious thing. I want the baby."

By saying, *I want the baby*, rather than *I want Shannon and the baby*, I came as close as I could to the truth. A subtle distinction, but the best I could do. A semantic truth.

Ben got out of bed and paced back and forth.

"Why do I always pick crazy women?" he said mostly to himself.

"It's not crazy," I said. "Women become mothers. It's a pretty common occurrence, I think."

He stopped pacing. "But you're about to become a mother and a grandmother at the same time."

"Yes, I am."

"Grandma," he said, more like a question than a title.

I tried to be lighthearted, but it came out more serious than I intended. "Does it make you want to put your clothes back on?"

He stood at the foot of the bed. He regarded me, sitting still naked and hopeful on the bed in the thankfully dim light. Massive moments passed. He put his hands on his hips.

"Nope," he said.

Ben climbed onto the bed and pulled me down. "I should be running out of here as fast as I can," he whispered, "but suddenly I feel pretty hot."

My earlier wish for feverish passionate sex was granted a lot sooner than I had expected. We consumed each other with a delirious urgency that left us both laughing and panting and begging each other to stop.

The kitchen door slammed to the tune of "Jesus Fucking Christ!" Then another door slam. Shannon's bedroom.

"Oh no," I said. I looked at the bedside clock. It was nine-fifteen. "This is not supposed to happen."

Ben rolled off me and looked at me with maddening calm. "Your teenager is predictable?" he asked.

"I need to go and make sure she's okay. I'm sorry. I'm sorry." I pulled on my bathrobe and raked my fingers through my hair. I ran to the door, and ran back to the bed. I kissed Ben on the forehead. "Wait right here." I said.

I stumbled down the stairs, toweling myself off with the hem of my robe.

Her door was closed. There was no thundering music. I knocked lightly and went in.

Shannon was sitting cross-legged on the bed, her head down and her hair forming a curtain around the strange little dog in her lap. She didn't look up when I came in.

I sat down next to her, and she shrugged my hand away when I tried to tuck back her hair. My hand hung awkwardly midair, so I petted Carlos instead.

"So tell me what happened," I said.

"They're such assholes," Shannon said.

"What happened?"

When she finally looked up, her eyes were swollen and her black eye makeup was smeared not only around her eyes, but also on and under her nose, where she had wiped her nose with her smudgy hand.

"We went for pizza. I thought it was going pretty good, you know. They all were being sort of friendly. Then Nick leans over to me and says in my ear, 'Since you're already pregnant, how about some free pussy?'"

"That asshole punk!" I could feel myself getting red. "What did you say?"

"I said, 'Sure, why not? Let me just tell Celeste that we're going out back for a few minutes to screw.'"

"Ha!" I said, "Good for you!"

"No, not good for me. Nick called me a liar and a bitch. And Celeste told everyone that I had tried to trick D.J. into thinking it was his kid, just to ruin his life. She said it was her turn to ruin mine."

"Where was D.J. through all of this?"

"Oh, he was being cute with some titty waitress. By the time he's back at the table, I'm pouring my coke down Celeste's neck."

"That's pretty bad," I said, not specifying which part.

"Everyone hates me," she bleated.

"Is D.J. really mad at you?"

She smiled ruefully. "Yeah, but I think he's even madder at Celeste. He was furious that she told those holes that he ever thought even for a second that the baby was his. He told them that they could all walk to the movies, and call their fucking moms to bring them home. And he packed me up and drove me here. He was real mad but he did laugh when I told him that Nick could fuck the pizza instead, since I squashed it right in his fucking crotch."

"So all is not lost," I said encouragingly.

Shannon crumbled as rapidly as she had perked up. "But D.J.'s going away. And now for sure everyone hates me." Then she hunched her shoulders and toughened up like I had seen her do before. "But I don't care. Those assholes can go to hell."

"You'll make new friends once school starts," I said. I heard the front door close softly. I hoped that in Shannon's misery she hadn't heard. But her eyes narrowed and she refocused her anger.

"You think you know everything. Well, I know a few things too. I know whose car was in the driveway. Do you think I'm stupid? Do you think I don't see that you're in your bathrobe at fucking nine o'clock?"

"Oh, Shannon," I said, trying to soothe her.

"You sure want to be my mother," she hissed. "You're just like her."

I stood up. "Ben is a nice man, and we're adults. And I do want to be your mother."

"We'll see about that," she said.

I went back to my empty room. Ben hadn't waited for me. He had straightened the room and turned out the light. There was no evidence that he had even been there. Maybe my first instinct was right. Children were too scary for men.

I brushed my teeth and scrubbed my face. I took a towel, ran it under very hot water and washed my vagina and legs and breasts. I put on my dowdiest nightgown. I would just be a fifty-year-old grandma. Just what I always wanted.

I crawled into bed in the dark, but a minute later sat up and snapped on the light. Under my pillow was Ben's business card. He had written on it. *'Tomorrow.'*

Chapter 32

———⟨∿⟩———

W ITH BEN'S CARD TUCKED UNDER my head, I expected to dream about sex. But I didn't. I dreamt about babies.

In the morning, I lay in the quiet considering my baby. Up to now, I had not let myself think about it. It was an inherited superstition. My mother had never allowed a baby shower in our house—not for herself, and not for Mary Ann or Angela. She advised my sisters to try not to think about the baby until it was actually here. Too much could go wrong. I had first-hand knowledge of the truth of it.

But my dreams had been filled with the sound of baby laughter. A hungry chubby baby was sitting in a high chair, kicking its little feet and clapping its hands while I made airplane noises with a spoon full of applesauce. And for the first time since I met Shannon—for the first time since I had been pregnant myself—I let myself think about it.

I wondered how soon we would know whether it would be a boy or a girl. I rather wanted a girl, since that's what I knew from growing up in a house full of them. But I had also seen how trusting and loving little boys like Max could be. A boy would be okay. I could learn to play catch or dig worms. Shannon had said, maybe truthfully, that she didn't know if the baby was white. I pictured a brown baby with black curls and those beautiful greenish eyes that biracial people sometimes have. Then I pictured Angela's delicate blondness and pink cheeks. It would be such a sweet surprise to finally see. I wondered what Shannon looked like as a baby. Maybe she had a picture.

I got up feeling better, determined. I picked up my bathrobe and hung it in the closet. I didn't want a continuation of last night. So I dressed quickly in jeans and a tee shirt and brushed my teeth.

Shannon was at the table, drawing with her finger in the toast crumbs. She didn't look up when I sat down. She nudged the strawberry jam with her elbow, and the jar toppled from the table and smashed on the kitchen tiles.

"Oops," she said.

"That's one big sticky mess for you to clean up," I remarked.

"I'm sick," she said, and bolted into the bathroom.

I knew I should leave it. Wait her out. But I picked up the pieces of the broken jar and threw them in the trash. I scooped up the spilled jam with a paper towel, and wiped the area with the cleanser. I'd probably have ants. They'd march down in hordes from Massachusetts by tomorrow morning.

I heard the toilet flush. I counted to ten and walked into her bedroom.

"I said I was sorry," she said immediately.

"No you did not. But listen to me: You can be as mad as you want over last night. I'm on your side on this one. Remember? But go ahead and blame me if you want. It won't make a difference. Those kids will still hate you. And you still live here. And — we have a deal, and I don't care how bad you feel. We still have a deal. I've kept my end. You have a new room, new clothes, a TV—a dog for God's sake. Now it's time to keep your end of the bargain."

"I'm keeping my end," she whined. "I'm getting fatter every day!"

"You have to do more than just have a baby. I have to adopt you. It has to be legal and final. And that's not going to be easy if everyone thinks you're miserable. Melissa could send you back. So you're going to be happy if it kills you."

I thought I might get a smile out of her, at least a hint of a smile, but she just grimaced.

I pressed on. "So we are going to go to church this morning, and then we're going to Angela's for Sunday dinner. Just as if we like each other. So, pretend, God damn it."

"Can I bring Carlos to Angela's?" she asked.

I pictured the mangy threadbare creature crawling into Mary Ann's fastidious lap.

"Sure," I said cheerfully. "We'll swing by after church and pick him up."

Even Angela looked a little dismayed to see Shannon slip into the pew beside her. 'Dismay' didn't do justice to Mary Ann's reaction. Shannon was wearing cut-off jeans, a yellow racerback tank top, which emphasized quite dramatically the purple satin bra straps underneath. She had three blue-black braids, one hanging down each side, and a bonus braid in the back. The right one sported a pigeon feather. She had extra eye makeup, although before this morning I would have doubted that it could have even been possible. No lipstick or blush though—she had covered her face in makeup much lighter than her now-tanned skin. And sometime over the past week she had gotten a henna tattoo on the back of her right shoulder. It read 'Cuidado.' I think she found the word on the passenger side sun-visor in my car.

She had appeared in my bedroom in that getup. "Ready for church?" she had asked.

I bent down, wiping an invisible spot from my shoe, regaining my composure, although I wasn't quite sure whether I was keeping myself from laughing or weeping.

"Perfect," I said. "Let's go."

And now in the pew, seeing the consternation of my sisters, I felt rather smug about my fabulous tolerance. *They may not remember what it's like to be the mother of a teenager. But I know something about motherhood now too.*

The subject of the sermon was 'Turning the Other Cheek'. Shannon looked as if she were about to scream. I leaned over and whispered in her ear. "Bullshit. Stand up for yourself." She looked at me, stretched her gum around her tongue and blew a little bubble.

When Shannon got up for communion, Mary Ann reached for her to try and sit her back down. I was instantly certain that my mother had told Mary Ann about Shannon's pregnancy.

I spent the rest of the service figuring out the right strategy with which to make the belated announcement.

Angela scooped Carlos out of Shannon's arms, declaring him to be her new sweetheart. Mary Ann took the cake box from me, declaring it to be *almost* as good as homemade.

There were no men in the house today. Both husbands had gone off fishing.

"I thought we needed some girl time," said Angela. So either my mother or Mary Ann had told Angela too.

I let them awkwardly avoid the subject through dinner. Angela and I discussed how many pairs of black shoes one really needed—pumps, ballet flats, stacked heels, and boots being our agreed-upon decision, although I argued without convincing her that black sandals were also required—while Mary Ann watched Shannon feed Carlos under the table.

Finally annoyed by the trivial conversation, Mary Ann asked Shannon, "So what were you and Cynthia whispering about during the sermon?"

"I don't remember," said Shannon. "Was there a sermon?"

I spoke up. "I don't always believe in turning the other cheek, and I was telling Shannon that she didn't have to either."

"In church? You're telling her in church to go ahead and fight?"

"Not fight necessarily. But last night she stood up to some kids who were being very mean to her, and I think she did the right thing."

"Easy for you to say," Shannon said, picking up the argument from last night. "I don't have any friends and now I never will."

"Those kids don't decide for everyone."

"Yeah they do."

"They don't decide for you," I insisted. I heard my voice get a little shrill, a little like my mother's. "I'm sure there are other kids who can choose their own friends without consulting Celeste and Nick."

Angela put down her fork. "Do you remember Jackie, my roommate in college?" Mary Ann and I nodded, and Angela smiled at Shannon. Oh, story time.

"Well," Angela started. "Jackie had it pretty tough when she was in high school. When she was fifteen, her mother died, and her father disappeared."

"Was she murdered?" asked Shannon. "I'll bet the father did it, and that's why he disappeared."

"No," said Angela. "Not murder, just rotten cancer. But Jackie's dad couldn't handle it. He went off to California. He said he would come back for her but he never did. Jackie had to go live with her grandparents."

"Cynthia's almost old enough to be my grandmother," Shannon observed in her kindly way. Angela ignored her and continued.

"Jackie's grandparents had a bakery in New Haven. They lived over the bakery. It was a neighborhood that had gotten really run down. But the grandparents had always lived there—even their parents before them lived there. And in that neighborhood Jackie was confronted with some very nasty people. She walked to school terrified, she went to her classes terrified, and then she walked home terrified. This went on for months. Then all of sudden Jackie figured something out, and everything got better."

"What did she do? Run away? Buy a gun?" asked Shannon.

"Nope," answered Angela.

"I know, I know," said Mary Ann, caught up in the story. "She gave everyone stuff from the bakery, and then they liked her."

"No," said Angela, "Though that's not such a terrible idea. There's a problem, though, with bribing people. They get used to it, and then you have to give them more." She gave me her sternest look. "That can get very expensive."

"I'm sure it can," I said, forwarding the look to Shannon. She grinned and picked up Carlos and put him on her lap.

"So what's the answer? What did that girl do?" asked Shannon.

"She made friends with the toughest, meanest kid in school. And everyone was nice to her after that."

"But how did she make friends with such a tough dude?" asked Shannon.

Angela leaned back and smiled. "Because Jackie was a lot like you. She was smart and funny, and she made this tough guy laugh. And he didn't have any real friends, so he was very happy to have a good friend like her."

"Um, Shannon," Mary Ann interrupted. "I think Carlos needs to go out. Could you take him outside right away before he has an accident?"

Shannon gave me a bewildered look, but didn't argue. She picked up the dog and they went out.

"Angela," Mary Ann said as soon as the door closed. "I don't think that it's a good idea to encourage Shannon to make friends with hoodlums."

"I think for once I have to agree with Mary Ann," I said. "Kids today can have a lot more problems than when you were in school."

"I'm a teacher," said Angela. "I know what kids are like. But I also know that that the toughest kid in eighth grade is most likely the loneliest."

"Or maybe the most likely to take an axe to his parents," I observed.

"I don't think you're giving Shannon enough credit for making good choices."

We looked out the window where Shannon was pathetically tangled in Carlos' leash.

"Like choosing that creepy dog?" asked Mary Ann.

"No," Angela said emphatically. "Like choosing Cynthia." I loved that woman so much.

"Let's have dessert," I said. I went and knocked on the window, beckoning Shannon to come in.

Angela brought out my store-bought cake, remarking sweetly though pointedly that she understood how I might not have had time to bake, now that I was a mother. I didn't volunteer that I was having uninhibited sex at the time usually set aside for baking Sunday dessert. But I did take her busy-mom comment as the cue she was obviously offering.

"Well," I said, "Shannon and I have some news. It's very serious but it's also very happy news. Shannon is expecting a baby."

My sisters tried to act surprised but the look they exchanged gave them away.

"When?" said Angela.

"Right after Christmas," I said.

"You're only fourteen," Mary Ann said to Shannon.

"Oh, I'll be fifteen by then," Shannon said with a smile.

"That's still hardly old enough to be a mother," Mary Ann almost shouted.

I intervened. "Shannon and I have already decided. She will be the big sister and I will be the mother. Everything will be fine."

"Fine?" asked Mary Ann. "You're going to be a mother to a promiscuous teenager and a newborn. You? With no husband, no experience?"

"Every woman who becomes a mother has no experience at first. You did it. And Shannon is not promiscuous—she just made a big mistake."

"And both of you are going to turn that mistake into something wonderful, I know," said Angela.

The conversation became a tennis ball being volleyed with increasing severity across the table by Angela and Mary Ann. Angela talked about the magic of babies and how I would be fantastic and Mary Ann slammed back with the tragic consequences that were sure to ensue. It was like one of those cartoons with the little angel on one shoulder and the devil on the other. Shannon and I sat and waited. I put a second slice of cake on Shannon's plate. She looked at me and circled her finger around her ear in the gesture that means 'cuckoo'. I didn't even know kids still made that sign. She grinned at me, like we were on the same side. The sane side.

I jumped in when Mary Ann was making the point that this was much, much more than I had bargained for.

"Hold it," I said. "Think about what you just said. With my so-called *'talent'* (and I made little apostrophes in the air around 'talent', even though I hate when people do that), don't you think that maybe I knew exactly what I was in for? I've known Shannon was pregnant from the start. I want Shannon *and* the baby." I smiled at Shannon. "Shannon is giving me the family that I always wanted. We're going to be a real family, with a mom and a kid and a baby."

"And a dog," said Shannon.

"And a dog," I agreed.

"But no husband," said Mary Ann.

And just as suddenly, the Cynthia-Shannon team fell apart. The amusement that had been on Shannon's face evaporated.

"Oh, since we're doing all this sharing shit," said Shannon, "why don't you tell them the rest?" She sneered at me. I had no idea what set her off, and now she was about to tell my sisters that I was paying her for the baby.

But that's not what she said. "Maybe Cynthia's going to have a husband after all," she said. "Hasn't she told you? Cynthia has a boyfriend."

A little crumb of cake fell out of Mary Ann's mouth. "Who?"

"It's not that serious," I said as dismissively as I could. "I've had a couple of dates with Ben Shelter. Just casual." Angela looked at me puzzled, not quite sure where she'd heard that name. "Ben; from the store." I added.

"The owner's husband?" Angela asked innocently.

"Husband?" shrieked Mary Ann and Shannon in unison.

Shannon stood up, and Carlos tumbled to the floor. "That creep is married?" she screamed. And for the second time in one day, she stomped off and the bathroom door slammed behind her.

"They're separated," I said to my sisters. "She moved to Florida. Months ago. And it's only a couple of dates. He's nice..." I trailed off.

Angela got up and patted me on the back. She patted Mary Ann a little harder since Mary Ann was choking a bit on her cake.

Angela packed up all the leftovers for me. ("You might be too busy to cook," the full-time teacher said to her retired little sister.) I coaxed Shannon out of the bathroom and into the car. Just as I was pulling out of the driveway, I caught a glance of turquoise on Shannon's wrist. I slammed on the brakes.

"That's Angela's bracelet!"

Shannon looked at her wrist as if discovering that particular body part for the first time.

"Shit,' she said. "It was on the sink in the bathroom. I just tried it on." She looked me straight in the eye. "Gee, I guess I forgot I was wearing it when you dragged me out of there."

"You're putting it back RIGHT NOW. Hopefully without anyone knowing you 'forgot it.'"

I walked her back into the house.

"We both decided we needed to hit the bathroom one more time," I said lamely to Angela. Shannon had just spent twenty minutes in that bathroom, but Angela didn't question me.

"You first," I said to Shannon. I gave her my best threatening glare.

And when it was my turn, I made sure that bracelet was back on the sink.

"My Lord," Angela said as she kissed me goodbye for the second time. "Your life has gotten interesting."

Chapter 33

WHEN I WAS A TEENAGER, I worked one summer at the local amusement park. At midnight, when the park closed, all the teenage employees would open some bottles of Boone's Farm apple wine and ride the roller coaster. It was an old classic wooden coaster, creaking slowly and dramatically up the steep incline and then catapulting down and around the traditional design. It wasn't crazy-scary, not like the modern coasters today—it was the ancient rails and rotting wood threatening to collapse at any moment that provided the excitement. One loose and rusty bar held us in. We'd take big gulps of cheap wine and close our eyes. By the middle of the summer, we knew each clank and lurch and swerve. But still we rode. At once thrilling and routine.

So was August with Shannon. The month was hot and dry, as expected, and we settled into a drama as predictable as the screeching brakes at curve three of the coaster.

On Mondays, after the store's paperwork was completed, Ben and I would go to visit Harry at the nursing home. We'd lunch on cheeseburgers and fries and listen to Marion Anderson and the Beatles. Ben and I would then drive to the Thomaston dam, where there was a tiny secluded glen in the middle of some pine trees. A place he had found on his bicycle as a kid. Now a nice place for a little romance. We'd linger an hour or so, and then drive home to have dinner with Shannon. Shannon's mood was invariably some version of lousy, from sarcastically nasty—

Ben: "This chicken is delicious."
Shannon: "Is it as good as your wife makes?"

To simply inappropriate—

Ben: "How was the movie?"
Shannon: "The fuck parts were cool."

To disturbingly cruel—

Ben: "How's Carlos?"
Shannon: "He has cancer."

Ben's response was always the same. "Good one, Shannon," he'd say, and go back to his dinner, nonplussed.

Shannon's general anger would continue into Tuesday. Luckily, I went to work. Shannon had dragged a couple of lounge chairs from my cellar to the farthest corner of the yard, where there was a little shade from the neighbor's big maple. She'd go out there with her iPod right after breakfast and she'd still be there when I got home from work. Sometimes Carlos occupied the second chair; often it was D.J., with Carlos by his feet. Shannon and D.J. had made up almost immediately after the pizza incident. They probably would have eventually anyway, but I speeded up the process a bit by promising D.J. a new laptop to take to school if he resumed his friendship with Shannon. I would watch the two as I prepared dinner. They'd lie motionless in the heat, sometimes exchanging a word but more often silent. They'd come in for a silent dinner and then take off in D.J.'s truck. I didn't deceive myself into believing that they were no longer having sex. After all, as Nick had so nastily said, there were certainly no consequences now. But I pretended not to know. I didn't want her to be alone, and besides, it made the rest of the week more bearable.

Shannon would be a bit more pleasant on Wednesday; she'd sometimes speak. And on Thursday I'd take her out after dinner for ice cream and she might smile once or twice.

Friday was our best day. We'd shop. D.J. only came once to mow—the grass was so parched in the heat of August—and that day we stayed and watched him mow before we went shopping. I'd buy her jewelry and makeup. We weren't having a lot of success with clothes. Sean-girl had shown Shannon how a rubber band through her waistband buttonhole could give her a little more room in her pants, but we were running out of rubber bands big enough. Shirts were a little easier— she didn't mind showing off her growing belly. She liked the stares she was beginning to get.

We went to a different town to shop each Friday in August. West Hartford, Avon, Clinton. The best shopping excursion was to New York City. We got up early and took the train. Shannon was so excited and overwhelmed by Grand Central I thought for a second she would hold my hand. We went to every cheap hip shop in Manhattan. We even found a store for teenage mothers-to-be. We stocked up until we couldn't carry any more. She told me loudly on the train home that the day she got knocked up was the luckiest day of her life. The briefcase-laden businessmen across from us looked carefully out the window.

If Friday was my best day with Shannon, Saturday was certainly my best day without her. She and D.J. would go to the beach. I'd go to the shop for our busiest, most profitable day, and come home to Ben waiting for me on the porch. We'd take Carlos for a walk, then go up to my room for leisurely happy lovemaking. Our conversations centered around books, politics, and childhood memories. What was better, toast or English muffins, thunderstorms or snowstorms, JFK or RFK? Whatever side I'd take, he'd argue for the other. We'd move our best arguments to the kitchen table and still be discussing Joan Baez versus Judy Collins when Shannon would bang the screen door to announce her return. "You again?" she'd say to Ben, and I could feel the heat of her sunburn and her rising anger as she stomped by me to her room. The music would gush from her room like the rising water filling the Titanic, and Ben and I would retire to the lounge chairs in the back yard.

On Sunday morning, I'd call my mother and Shannon would get on the extension and declare dutifully that she was being good and eating lots of healthy food. Then off to church and dinner at Angela's. We'd both pretend our world was flat and steady, and we were just as normal as anyone, which maybe we were.

But for all the predictable highs and lows of the familiar August roller coaster, there were of course the minor interruptions, sudden jolts and minutes of sheer pleasure or, more often, terror.

Not terror, but certainly not pleasure, was the breakage. There was an increasing frequency of accidents. Glasses and plates hit the floor with curious regularity.

"Jesus!" I'd holler. "Carlos walks around here barefoot, and he's practically blind!"

"Sorry," she'd say—to Carlos.

Before long I surrendered and bought a picnic set with plastic plates, bowls and cups. I'd need them for the baby, anyway, I told myself.

I also took to sifting through the trash before I brought it out, because there always seemed to be forks and spoons in there. I went to the restaurant supply outlet and purchased three dozen sets of cheap tableware. But the drawer still seemed to be emptier every week.

Shannon's moods could and would change in a second. The bad moods were easier to predict. There were certain words I learned to avoid: school, friends, fat. We'd be having a nice ordinary breakfast and a song would come on the radio, and it was all slamming doors and curse words. I didn't know the exact trigger, but I learned to eat breakfast without the radio. The good moments would come out of nowhere and tweak my heart, but were gone as suddenly and mysteriously as they came. If she helped with the dishes on Wednesday, I could be sure on Thursday that she would insist that she had never wiped a dish in her life, and wasn't about to start. She got a case of childish adorable giggles one day when I fed Carlos a piece of steak from my fork. But a few days later when I did it again, she said, "That's totally gross," and left the room.

"Is she bi-polar?" I asked my sisters.

"It's drugs," said Mary Ann.

"It's insecurity," said Angela.

Chapter 34

"**I**T'S HORMONES," SAID DR. TURNER.

We had an early morning appointment on the third Thursday in August. Shannon was in her nineteenth week of pregnancy. Her belly was now adorably obvious. Since I had dragged her out of bed and hustled her into the car before she was fully awake, she hadn't had time to slather on the makeup, and with all her trips to the beach, she looked young and healthy. She now actually looked like a good match for D.J. Only he was about to leave.

I was determined not to embarrass myself with an emotional display this time. But just looking at the baby magazines in the waiting room caused me to mist up just a bit.

"What the fuck?" asked Shannon. "Are you starting that shit again?"

And I willed my tears to dry up.

In the examining room, Shannon changed into a Johnny and sat on the end of the table. She looked nervous. I caught my reflection in the paper towel holder over the sink. I looked nervous.

"You look great!" Dr. Turner declared as she walked into the room, and got one of Shannon's rare remarkable smiles.

"I'm feeling pretty good," she answered. "No more throwing up."

Shannon looked vacantly at the ceiling during the examination as Dr. Turner pressed and poked and measured.

Then the ultrasound.

"Hey," said Shannon, rising up on her elbows, "it sort of looks like a baby."

That was the end of my self-control. I cried all over again, probably harder than I had the first visit.

Dr. Turner patted my hand. I patted Shannon's hand.

"Shannon," asked the doctor, "Do you feel anything moving in there yet?"

"I think so, sometimes," she said. "Just a little. Is it supposed to be like popping popcorn?"

"It is exactly like that."

"Well, maybe I'll name it Orville."

"Do you want to know if it's a boy or a girl?"

"Yes!" we said in unison.

Dr. Turner smiled. "Then you should pick a different name than Orville."

A girl. I didn't think I could cry any harder than I was already crying, but my god, tears can really gush.

"Cynthia," the doctor said gently. "It's okay. Lots of mothers aren't exactly happy that their teenage daughters are pregnant."

I sobbed. "It's so wonderful. I'm going to have a daughter."

Both Dr. Turner and Shannon stared at me.

"A daughter and a granddaughter," I corrected. "This is the family I've always wanted."

Shannon's eyes went flat. It was too late.

In the car I tried to apologize.

"I'm sorry, Honey," I said. "You know that you're my daughter too. And a good one," I added.

"You can cut the 'Honey' bullshit," she said. "I know the deal."

We drove in silence. I could see her counting the passing cars with little nods of her head.

"How about if we stop and I'll buy you something—earrings, maybe?"

"Sure," she said indifferently.

We had one unannounced visit by Melissa Rodriguez in the middle of the month. She stopped by on a Thursday, so weekly hostilities were on the wane. Shannon and I expected this would happen sooner or later and we had already decided our strategy. Except for our secret deal (the BIG secret), we were going to tell the absolute truth. That way we wouldn't have to try to keep our stories straight or try to remember later what we had said.

So when Melissa asked Shannon what was best about her new life, she said, "Three things—Carlos, shopping, and food." Asked the same question, I said, "Not eating alone. I love having someone across the table from me at mealtime."

Melissa also asked us what was the hardest adjustment, and Shannon said that it was definitely being watched all the time. "Cynthia is so nosy. She wants to know everything." My answer: "The noise level."

Melissa left satisfied.

The week before school started, I made an appointment with Shannon's principal and homeroom teacher. I can't take credit for being so organized or thoughtful—Angela had suggested it.

I explained to Shannon that I wasn't going behind her back, and that she could come if she wanted, but she said she would rather snort nails, and I took that as a no.

So I went to the school on a hot Friday morning. Teachers were washing desks and moving chairs and hanging pictures. I didn't realize that all teachers did that by themselves. I thought it was just Angela.

Mr. Mancini was exactly the same guy as Mr. Wells, my own principal back in junior high. Not just the same type; the same guy. He had a neat comb-over and a single eyebrow, and high elbows coming out of his wide short-sleeved shirt. Mrs. Strong was the soft and sweet African-American version of Angela.

They were surprised by my call. In the two years that Shannon had been attending the junior high, there had not been one call, note, or meeting with anyone regarding Shannon. Her file was thin, but it told the same story as her thick Social Services' file. She alternated between hostile and withdrawn—hostile mostly with the kids, withdrawn mostly with the teachers.

The principal expressed a little alarm (and perhaps defensiveness) by my asking to meet concerning Shannon's 'special needs'.

"By 'special needs'," asked Mr. Mancini, "do you mean that Shannon has a learning disability? We haven't seen any evidence of a disability."

I thought back over the last several months. I hadn't seen any evidence of a learning disability either. Of course, I hadn't seen any evidence of a book, either.

"No, I don't think she's learning disabled," I said.

Mrs. Strong jumped in. "No, no, she's really smart. Smart enough to pass without ever doing any work at all. Ever."

I smiled. "I'll see if I can't get her to do some homework once in a while."

"You can try," said Mr. Mancini.

"Anyway, to get back to why I called…"

"Oh yes," he said, "you really are to be commended for taking Shannon in. It's a wonderful sacrifice you are making."

I tried not to squirm.

"Why I called…When I said that I wanted to discuss Shannon's special needs, I meant her immediate issue. Shannon's pregnant."

The pair looked at me with some sympathy but not much surprise.

"So what happens?" I asked.

Mancini described for me the three alternatives. Some kids get home-schooled. The town provides the tutor. This is for kids whose family doesn't want anyone to know they're pregnant. But of course everyone does. Then there is a program for pregnant girls up at the high school. Junior high girls can go up twice a week and join those classes. Highly recommended, said the principal. Then of course, they can just go on as they are, and the school will make some accommodations for their condition.

"Are there any other pregnant girls this semester?" I asked.

"Two," he answered. One opted for home schooling, but the other girl was going up to the high school for afternoon parenting classes.

"Shannon could go with her," suggested Mrs. Strong. "That would be nice for both of them." I doubted it, but I figured it would be helpful to have her know something about babies.

I didn't really want her home-schooled. For one thing, I really didn't want her home. Also, I knew that she might opt for tutoring to avoid kids like Celeste. But I wanted her to stand up for herself. Hiding out at home wouldn't help,

"It's her decision," I told the principal, but I knew I would only let her choose whether or not she wanted the parenting classes. "So I'll talk to her and let you know."

Shannon was out in the lounge chair with a towel over her face. I picked up Carlos off the other chair and sat with him in my lap. I explained to Shannon about the parenting class at the high school.

"Who's the other girl?" she asked through the towel.

"Someone named Gina."

"Gina Chase? No Shit. She's not even allowed to wear makeup."

"Well I guess someone liked her anyway, as strange as that may be. Anyway, she's going to go up to the high school on Wednesdays and Fridays for parenting class, and you could go with her."

"I got a better idea. You take the fucking class. You're the parent."

"I'm not going to make you," I replied calmly. "I'm not sure if I want you up at the high school anyway, what with all those older kids."

Bingo.

"You can't exactly stop me. What kind of mother would you be, not letting me take parenting classes?" Shannon finally pulled off the towel and looked at me. "What classes do I get to skip?"

"P.E. and social studies."

"How do we get to the high school?"

"I offered to share the driving with Gina's mother."

"She has an even better car than you."

"Really? Well, I'll think it over. I might let you."

"I'm going," she declared.

This mother stuff wasn't so hard.

Chapter 35

―――――✦―――――

THINGS STARTED TO GO REALLY wrong in September. On Labor Day, D.J. packed up his things, including the new laptop I had surreptitiously bought him, and stood by his tarp-covered pickup in front of the house. Shannon stood woodenly on the porch, refusing to go down the steps to say goodbye.

I went down to him and gave him a kiss.

"Don't feel guilty. It's time for you to go," I said.

"I know," said D.J. "I'm excited, but I feel kind of bad showing it."

"Just go!" Shannon yelled from the porch.

D.J. strode over to her and she put her hand on the doorknob,

"I'm not leaving forever," D.J. said. "I'll be home at Thanksgiving."

"Yeah," she said. "You'll probably bring home a girlfriend."

"I doubt it. But if I did, and she didn't like you, I'd drop her like a hot potato. I'd make her walk back to Boston, like I made Nick walk home from the movies."

"I'll be enormous by Thanksgiving."

"I'll rent a crane to get you into the truck," he joked. But she wouldn't smile.

"I'll call and text," he said.

"Don't bother," said Shannon.

D.J. gave up and walked back to the truck.

"She'll be okay," I said as D.J. climbed into the truck. "So you have fun at school."

He started it up. As he pulled forward, Shannon ran down the steps.

"Wait!" she cried.

D.J. slammed on the breaks. He reached out the window for her hand, but she pulled it back. She looked up at him from the curb.

"Wear a rubber," she said.

Shannon stared out the window at the kids congregating across the street.

"I'm not going," she said.

"It's the first day of school," I said calmly. "Of course you're going."

"Nope. I changed my mind. I want to be home-schooled."

This stopped me. "How'd you hear about home-schooling?" I asked.

"I called Gina. Her parents told her she could stay home and have a tutor. But she thought they just wanted to keep it all a secret. She decided to go to school to screw them."

In part, I was dismayed to have Shannon learn about tutoring. But there was another part of me that was sort of happy. She had called a kid. Maybe she had a chance to have a friend.

"Well, you don't have any secrets either," I said. "So there's no reason to stay home."

"I'm not going." I peered out at the kids from behind the curtain. Celeste was there, and a scrawny boy about the same age, and a couple of kids who might have been a little younger.

"You aren't saying that you're afraid of Celeste?" I prodded.

"Look at her. Giggling with Nick. They keep looking over here. They're just waiting to get me."

"That ugly skinny jerk is Nick? The guy with the beak?"

"Oh, go ahead and laugh. You don't care."

"I care. I care enough to want you to go out there and face them."

"I'm not going," she reiterated.

"Look, there're some other kids there too."

"I just can't," she whispered.

Suddenly I was fourteen and Paul Deacon was calling me "Ape Girl" as I hunched over my books and ran for the bus.

"I'll drive you," I said. "In my BMW," I added, "which, by the way, is a hell of a lot nicer than what Mrs. Chase drives."

As if on cue, the bus came and picked up the kids, leaving me with no choice anyway. I steered her by the shoulders towards the back door.

Shannon locked her knees. "I can't go. There's no one to take care of Carlos."

I scooped up the dog from the kitchen table, where he was licking the egg remnants off Shannon's plate.

"No problem. I'll take him to work with me. He'll be good company."

I managed to get them both in the car, Carlos a lot happier with the ride than Shannon. I wished she could just hang her head out the window and enjoy the breeze.

There were kids and adults and busses and cars all around the school. It didn't look intimidating. It looked nice. I'd go.

Shannon looked out the window and didn't move.

"Do you see anyone you know?" I asked.

"Gina. She's over there by the basketball hoop. Red hair."

Gina was a skinny girl with freckles and glasses. She looked like the kind of kid they get to play the nerd in the movies. She looked about ten. Mrs. Chase must have been pretty surprised.

"Here's what grownups do—like when they go to a party and all of a sudden they feel very self-conscious. You pick out a person—like Gina—and you walk very deliberately straight towards the person you pick out. It makes you look very confident."

"So I get out of the car and run over there?"

"No... walk pretty slow. But don't hesitate either. You know exactly where you are going. And remember, you've got those great New York clothes, and fresh highlights and a manicure. You are the most stylish person in this whole school."

"Jesus, what a load of crap," she said. But she got out of the car and walked right to Gina.

I pulled away but not too far. I watched for a while. Shannon and Gina seemed to just look at each other. They didn't speak. I didn't want to spy exactly, I just wanted to make sure Shannon actually went into the school. Finally the bell rang and Shannon and Gina walked in, side-by-side but still silent.

At work, I gave Carlos one of the bulky Peruvian sweaters that had been drooping from its hanger the first time I came to the store. He made a nice little bed for himself by circling about thirty times, and nested in. I had only four customers all day, and no one said a word about a little ugly dog in the corner. I liked having him there. It gave the store an avant-garde bohemian feeling. I decided I'd take him every day.

I waited for Shannon to call, maybe swearing, maybe screaming, to come and get her, but my phone didn't ring. At three-thirty, when I knew I wouldn't be disrupting a class, I called her.

"I'm home," she said. "You don't have to check up on me."

"How was your first day?"

"It sucked."

"How nice," I said.

"You really brought Carlos to work?"

"Yup. That's the benefit of being the boss. He likes it here. He's happy."

"Well he's the only happy one in this family."

"I'll bring us home a pizza."

"That won't do it," she said, and hung up. The nice thing about cell phones is that no one can slam one down in your ear.

According to Shannon, ninth grade was just as lame as eighth grade.

"The only difference," she said with a mouthful of pizza, "was that I was wearing nicer shit."

"That counts for something," I said encouragingly.

She waggled her head in that 'so-so' manner. "Emma Gleason asked where I got my shirt, and she gagged a little when I said 'New York.' She's even more popular than Celeste."

"It must have been nice to make her gag." I observed.

"Yeah, that was okay. And everyone knows that me and Gina are knocked up, and that we're gonna go to the high school for classes. That was the coolest part."

"And how was Celeste?"

Shannon put down her pizza and took a long swig of milk. She pursed her milky lips.

"She was just a bitch. But I don't care anymore. Emma Gleason likes my shirt and I get to go to high school instead of Social Studies. So fuck Celeste."

"See," I said, picking up the dishes, "School's not so bad."

She got up and gave Carlos her pizza crust. She looked at me from the doorway. "Don't kid yourself," she said. "It blows."

And she turned and strode back to her room, with Carlos trotting behind. The door slammed and a few seconds later the music blared.

Not so bad, I thought.

And blow it did. Just as Shannon had said, I was kidding myself.

Encouraging Shannon to attend the parenting classes was a big mistake.

First, there was Gina. Although she looked like she just stepped out of a Peanuts cartoon, she was a little girl whose sole motivation in life was tormenting her mother. Her pregnancy appeared to be her biggest, most deliberate torture. But there was no aggravation too small to be inflicted. Even her fresh face was meant as a defiant gesture to her carefully made-up beauty pageant mother. And her hostility seemed to serve as inspiration for Shannon. Together they cut classes, missed curfews, and sent their mothers on wild goose chases.

"Did I say McDonalds? I meant Burger King."

"I'm sure I said the movie got out at eight."

"No, I told you that Mrs. Chase would pick us up."

"My cell phone must have died."

Maybe Gina's mother deserved it, but it was more probable that, like me, she was just the designated enemy in some teenage game. Both kids got enormous entertainment out of adult exasperation. My initial relief that Shannon had found a friend disappeared very quickly, and I found myself wishing she were alone again. When she was friendless, at least she spoke to me.

Then of course there was the high school itself. I had pretended to disapprove of Shannon going up to the high school as a ploy to make her want to go. I should have realized the truth in my own words. Surrounded by the high school kids, Shannon got tougher and surlier, which was quite a feat. Although Shannon and Gina were not allowed to go over to the high school alone, and so still needed their mothers for their ride, they insisted on taking the school bus home from the high school after parenting class. I'm not sure what transpired on that bus. But Shannon left for school fourteen years old, and on Wednesday and Fridays, she returned eighteen years old.

And speaking of eighteen years old, Shannon found a new boyfriend at the high school.

Shannon insisted that he was not her boyfriend, just a friend.

"Trust me," she said. "At this stage, no guy is exactly getting hard for me."

His name was Lucas Barrow. I'm sure he was a direct descendent of Clyde. When Angela had advised Shannon to make friends with the toughest kid in class, she meant ninth grade. But Shannon eagerly interpreted that advice to include the toughest kid to ever stay in school as a means of avoiding prison.

Lucas was blond, and good-looking I suppose, if you go for Hitler Youth type. His buzz cut revealed a three-inch scar at the back of his head. He got it 'just fucking around,' he informed me, whatever that meant. He had hand-drawn tattoos inked into his knuckles, and always had a cigarette about to drop an ash. My only consolation was that he didn't have a car.

As diplomatically as possible, I broached the subject of what Lucas might see in Shannon.

"How does Lucas feel about your pregnancy?" I asked at dinner one night. "He doesn't mind that you're carrying some other guy's baby?"

"He's cool with it," Shannon replied. "He says it shows that I don't listen to nobody."

"He's got that right," I agreed.

"Yup," she said, as usual completely oblivious to my sarcasm. "And it shows how cool he is too."

"I see. How about his family? Are they also cool with it?"

She put down her fork, and sighed. She looked at me in irritated condescension, like Mary Ann used to when she had to explain something that should have been obvious.

"I just told you, we don't answer to anybody. His family— and he's got 'em by the truckload—parents, steps, halfs—you name it, we just act like they're invisible. And they treat us the same. It works; you should try it."

Lack of wheels didn't stop Lucas from hanging around my house, pretty much constantly. It must have been extremely easy to ignore his family—he was never there.

I would have given him some credit if he had a least trudged crosstown on foot, but he was always bumming a ride from someone. And then of course the only way to get him to finally go home (usually after dinner) was to drive him myself. Shannon and Lucas would sit in the back while I was chauffeur. And they were good at pretending I wasn't there too. This was one of their little tricks that actually worked in my favor though. I heard snippets of their dreadful conversations so I at least knew what to expect. Maybe I would have been better off not knowing. I heard words like Probation, and Anger Management, and Scoring, and Wasted, and the worst word of all—California.

I couldn't bear the thought of Shannon taking off with this dick, and with my baby. So as her behavior got worse,

I got nicer. I fed them, drove them around, bought tons of snacks and sodas, smiled instead of screamed. I even gave Lucas cigarette money a few times. I could just hear Angela warning me that the problem with bribes is that they keep escalating. But if Shannon ran away, even if she eventually came back, I feared that the State would never finalize the adoption. And I'd never have my legal granddaughter.

I tried nudging her to other boys.

"Wouldn't it be nice to have a boyfriend your own age, who you could see every day at school?" I said one morning as I was dropping her off.

"One of these idiots?" Shannon asked, nodding her head towards the passel of teenagers loitering under the basketball hoop.

"Yeah, one of those nice young guys. I see Timmy Driscoll—his mother goes to our church. And she shops at my store. They're a really nice family. And he's cute."

She snorted. "I'm sure Mrs. Driscoll would be extremely happy to have her little Timmy dating your pregnant charity case."

"I could talk to her. Tell her what a nice kid you are."

Shannon gave me her famous eye-roll.

"First of all, I told you that Lucas is not my boyfriend, just my friend. Second, none of the junior high guys or any guy for that matter is going to be dating me while I'm knocked up. Guys just don't really get hot for pregnancy." She stopped and looked back at the boys. "Except for maybe one. But he just wants the shock value."

I looked over at the boys, wondering which one was interested in using Shannon to hurt his family. Maybe I could run him over.

She continued in a voice that had lost its belligerence. "I thought about it though. He's cute and popular. But you know, it seemed kind of mean. Like… you know…mean to *me*."

I closed my eyes and gathered up my emotions. Sometimes I almost liked this kid. "It IS mean to you," I agreed. "In just a few more months you won't be pregnant anymore. You'll be as pretty as before, and smarter by a long shot. You'll find a boy who will be nice to you."

"I had one for a little while."

"Yes you did. D.J. was very nice, but just a little too old for you, and so he had to move on ahead of you. But you'll find someone."

She shook her head and rearranged her face from sad to hard. "I sure will," she said. "Gina says that all the boys will want us once we drop our kids. They know we're giving candy."

Goodbye, tender moment.

Chapter 36

EN AND I STOPPED GOING to the shop on Monday mornings. Instead, he came over to the house where we could have some romantic time unencumbered by teenagers. We had, for about five seconds, considered having sex at the store—there was just too much Maria there to even brush lips.

I dropped Shannon off at school, with my bag of work stuff in the back seat, but then returned home where Ben was waiting on the back steps. I gave him a key, but he said it felt impolite to go into my empty house, and I liked him all the more for it.

We took our time on Mondays. "Energetically lazy," Ben called it, or was it "Lazily energetic"? Either way, it was comfortable.

We started with coffee and the newspaper. He read the front page and reported to me what was going on in the world, and I would tell him how wrong his interpretation was. Then I summarized what mattered in the sports page, and he'd tell me how badly I'd misunderstood.

Once we had emptied the last of the coffeepot, we drifted upstairs for some sex that was somehow both energetic and lazy. My bedroom faced east, and in the crisp September light I will admit that I worried that my body wouldn't compare well to twenty-year-younger Maria's. But Ben seemed pleased with what he discovered. I think he saw with his fingertips, not his eyes, and we were both content.

We showered; not together. This was satisfactory to us both. I have always been uncomfortable with tandem bathing. I don't want to be romantic then—I want to be clean. Ben didn't relish awkward positions on slippery floors. So he gladly lounged in bed while I showered. Then I could do my hair and makeup while listening to him slosh around behind the curtain. He was tall enough to peek at me sometimes from over the curtain rod. I loved having him watch me open my mouth slightly as I put on my mascara. I don't know why opening your mouth helps you darken your lashes. But it is sexy when someone naked watches you do it.

I'd pack up Carlos and follow Ben to the nursing home. I just couldn't leave my car in the driveway. Shannon got home from school right after three. I didn't want her to know I hadn't gone to work. This was my private time.

So I drove behind Ben watching the back of his head. I could tell by the way he moved that he was singing to the radio. I switched around the stations trying to find the same song by the rhythm of his nodding. Then I sang too.

Harry was just as delighted to see the scruffy dog as to see us.

"Harry, this is Carlos," I introduced.

"Hi, Careless," Harry said. I didn't know whether he was consciously making a joke, or didn't quite understand the name, but it didn't really matter, because within a few minutes Harry was calling the dog Mickey, and later Skipper, and even

Elsa, depending on whichever place in his life he happened to be in.

It was obvious that Harry was wandering more and more away from the present. He sometimes recognized Ben— "Benny"—although he often called Ben "Doc". We didn't know whether Harry thought Ben was one of the doctors at the nursing home or whether it was some older memory.

And Harry thought I was his wife.

"Abbie," he said, "I miss Rehoboth Beach." He walked up to a hazy photo of two skinny people squinting in the bright sun, and shook his head.

"What did you like best about Rehoboth?" I asked.

"That's easy," he replied. "The dolphins. What did you like best?"

"The sunshine on the water," I said, playing it safe.

"Abigail, let's go to Delaware again this summer."

"That sounds really nice."

Harry winked at me. "But don't forget—no high heels. Remember when you got your heel stuck between the planks in the boardwalk? We just couldn't free that shoe. So you took off the other shoe and placed it right near the stuck one. And you said, "That way if someone else can free it, they'll have a pair."

The scene was vivid, timeless and completely charming. Harry and Abigail, young, laughing. Watching the dolphins leap from the waves in the sparkling sunlight. The shoes left side by side on the boardwalk. If I could have an alternate existence, I might choose that moment. It was a lovely memory, and Harry had given it to me as a gift.

As we left, Harry said to me, "Cynthia, Don't forget what the fortuneteller said."

It wasn't until I was back at the car that I realized he had called me Cynthia, not Abigail. Did he have a message for the real me, or was this just another mixed up part of Harry's brain? I wanted to go back in, but Ben had already started his car, and was shrugging his shoulders in a question. I didn't have much hope that Harry would remember the fortuneteller the next time.

If only wonderful days always turned into wonderful evenings. But we had to go back and have dinner with Shannon and Lucas.

Do people still use the word 'churlish'? I can't quite think of another term to describe the surly, snarly, uncouth lump that was Shannon at the dinner table. I had thought it horrible enough before. Adding Lucas into the place settings encouraged a new level of rudeness from my little girl. She sat with her face two inches from the plate, the better to shovel in the chow and make a getaway.

On the other hand, Lucas was smug and over-polite in the way that reminded me of the kids in the old "Our Gang" series. Alfalfa, perhaps, but with a mean streak. Lucas liked to point out that Ben was an unwelcome freeloader, completely unaware of the irony of his own second helping.

Lucas also seemed obsessed with determining just how much money Ben might have. I think Shannon had already told him I was loaded. So he wanted to determine whether she had hit the daily double.

"So all these old bastards pay you to watch their money?" Lucas asked.

"That's sort of right," said Ben in the calm voice which I thought was way too civilized. Ben really needed to apply a good dose of "Shut Up" once in a while (of course, I never did either).

He put down his fork and opened his hands in the kind of offering pose that I see schoolteachers use.

"What I do is help preserve their assets. Look at it this way. Say a guy is seventy years old, and he has $200,000. That sounds like a lot of money, right?"

Lucas made a kind of grunt.

"Okay," Ben continued. "But say this guy lives to be ninety. So he needs that money to last twenty years. So how much does he have to live on in each year?"

Lucas just rolled his eyes, but Shannon seemed a little interested behind her hunched shoulders. I could see her doing the math with her fork in the gravy.

"Ten thousand," she mumbled.

"Right," Ben said, pleased. "And that's not a lot. That barely buys food and heats your house. And what if you get sick? And what if other people—like maybe not-so-nice people in your own family—want to take that money from you? I make sure that old people have everything they need and no one steals from them."

"Let me get this straight," said Lucas. "People just give their money to you and then just TRUST you? And some of 'em are so senile, they don't even remember they gave you the money? Pretty sweet, I'd say."

"Sounds like you may end up in jail,' said Shannon.

"What happens," I asked, "if someone wants their money for something that isn't a very good idea? Do you say no?"

Ben gave me an approving but serious nod. "That's a really good question. And a hard one."

Lucas snorted. "No, it's easy. You say, 'take a hike—it's not your money anymore.'"

Ben's face slowly changed into something that was part anger, part hurt. I'd only seen that face once before, the first time I met him, when he was still bruised by Maria.

"When I first started practicing," he began, and looked at me and said as a kind of 'aside'—"I can tell this story because it is now part of the public record—one of my first clients was a wonderful smart old lady named Catherine. She had a nice nest egg, but she wasn't a millionaire or anything. One day Catherine came to me all excited with a business idea. She wanted to open a drive-in theater. Drive-ins were already a thing of the past—just about every drive-in in Connecticut had closed a long time before. But Catherine wanted to open a new one. She had all these really sweet memories of her and her husband packing up the kids and sitting in the car wiping breathy fog from the windshield, listening to those tinny speakers. 'Families would do that again,' she said, 'I know they would.' I didn't agree and I told her so. She could lose everything, and then what would she do with the rest of her life? But she explained that she was nearly eighty, and didn't care if she died broke. She wanted to have some fun.

"So I helped her do it. She bought some land and we paved it over. We found a company that still sold projection equipment and big screens and speakers. And she opened her drive-in. After some initial curiosity and enthusiasm, it failed pretty badly."

"Figures," said Lucas.

"What happened then? Did she have anything left?" I asked.

"She had a little. I made sure she hadn't spent every penny. But she died suddenly, and it all became a mess. Her family sued me. Turns out her kids lived in California, and she hadn't told them that she had started the business. When they found out, they claimed that I was negligent by allowing her to pursue such a risky idea." He looked at me and shrugged his shoulders. "So what do you do? Do you tell people that they can't spend their own money?"

"That's what I friggin' said," brayed Lucas.

I came to Ben's defense. "But it was her money and she wanted to. You were right to let her decide. Surely the law was on your side."

"No," said Ben. "I lost."

Shannon finally spoke up. "So Lucas is right and you were wrong," she crowed.

"No, I was right."

"Let me clue you," Shannon said meanly. "You LOST!"

Ben shook his head and said quietly, "Just because you lose doesn't mean you weren't right."

Shannon laughed. "What fucking world do you live in?"

Ben slammed his hand on the table. He stood up. "It was her fucking money!" he yelled. He stormed out the back door. I heard his car start and screech away.

When Shannon and I returned from bringing Lucas back to the loony bin, um, to his busy and populated home, Ben's car was back at the curb. I could see his shadow out back, longer than the old lounge chair he was stretched out in.

"Jesus, that's creepy," whispered Shannon. "Do you think he killed himself?"

"He's fine," I said. I took Carlos from her, and handed her my purse and keys. "Go inside," I said.

I dropped Carlos gently onto Ben's lap.

"Hi, Careless," he said.

I lay back in the other chair. "I thought a little dog therapy might help."

Ben looked up at the stars. "Do you have any stories where you wish you could change the ending?"

"A few."

Ben absent-mindedly petted Carlos. "I really loved that old lady," he said after a while.

"Was she devastated when the business failed?" I asked.

"Actually, she wasn't. She was pretty philosophical about the whole thing. 'It was fun while it lasted,' she said." He laughed. "And it was fun. I ran the projector sometimes on the weekend. You should have seen that rich old lady serving up hot dogs."

I sat up. "You worked there?"

"Yeah, as often as I could. I loved it there."

I thought about this. "So you worry that you gave her the money because it was something you wanted to do?"

"A little. But I know that she had a really good time. What better way to spend your money?"

"And she didn't end up broke."

"No. The family sold the property. High end condos. They all became millionaires. I'm the one who ended up broke."

"What?"

"You know, the lawsuit. The judgment against me was pretty big. I was just starting out. My father thought I had shamed him. He thought, maybe rightly, that it was a miracle I wasn't disbarred. I couldn't go to him for the money."

"What did you do?"

"It was Roger." I could feel Ben look at me in the dark. "Yeah, that Roger. He was a real estate attorney after all. He put together the condo deal. They all made a bundle. He paid my judgment out of his take. 'Shit happens,' he said. 'But it doesn't have to stink.'" Ben laughed, and I could hear the sadness in it. "So I can't even hate the guy who took off with my wife."

I considered it.

"You could dislike him intensely," I said.

He reached out and took my hand in the dark.

"Okay," he said.

And we lay side by side in the chilly night, looking at the thousands of stars above us.

Chapter 37

HEN I STOPPED FOR GAS the next day, twenty dollars was missing from my wallet. I had bought some milk on Sunday, and paid for it with a fifty, so I had two twenties, a five, and a couple of singles on Sunday night. I hadn't spent a penny on Monday—I had been with Ben all day. And here I was on Tuesday with not quite enough money to pay for the forty dollars' worth of gas I had already pumped. I handed the clerk my credit card, smiling casually outside while inside I seethed.

We had a good day at the store, and I smiled at the customers as I rang up their purchases, and inside I seethed. By the time I got home, I was one big seethe.

I made supper and ate with Shannon in a silence that was not unusual, except that it came from me, not her. As she was about to get up from the table, I let her have it.

"I handed you my purse last night, and now I am missing twenty dollars. That's quite a coincidence, don't you think?"

She shrugged. "I guess," she said. "Where could you have lost the money?"

"Somewhere between the car and your bedroom," I answered.

"No way," she said. "I didn't take it. Maybe you spent it and forgot."

"I didn't spend it."

"Maybe that old geezer you visit took it. He probably ate it with his hamburger and didn't even know it."

"Harry didn't take the money. Ben didn't take the money."

"Are you saying Lucas took the money?" Shannon asked in a voice high-pitched with a phony innocence.

"Shannon," I said, with my voice getting lower as hers rose, "Don't ever steal from me again."

"Jesus Christ," she hollered as she stormed towards her room. "I didn't steal from you. It's fucking horrible and unfair that you won't ever trust me!" She turned and looked at me. "What kind of mother doesn't trust her own kid?"

And I remembered saying the exact words to my own mother, when I told her I was going to spend the weekend with my girlfriend, when my boyfriend was idling his car half a block away. And that's how I knew it was a lie. I had wondered weeks earlier if I would ever be able to tell when Shannon was lying. Well, I had conquered that mystery.

I followed her into her room.

"I am going to consider this an advance on your allowance," I said. "So you'd better make that money last till the end of next week."

I turned to leave.

"Bitch," Shannon hissed quietly behind me.

The bedroom door slammed as it had so many times over the past few months. But this time I got to be the slammer, not the slammee.

I went up to my bedroom and picked up the phone.

"Angela," I begged. "Tell me a story."

"Sure," she said. "What kind of story?"

"A story about how rotten Karen was when she was a teenager."

"Mmmm," said Angela. She was quiet for a minute, but I could hear her smiling. "Okay. How about this? When Karen was a junior in high school, she decided that she would no longer bring a lunch to school. Lunch was for babies. So I made her a nice sandwich, an apple, cookies, and put it all in one of the nice little bags I bought especially for lunches, just like always. I told her she was going to take that lunch, and I didn't care that the other girls didn't eat lunch. She picked up that bag and carried it out with her. When she got to the street, she turned back, saw me in the window, smiled, and dropped the bag down the storm drain."

"Nice," I said. "I am beginning to feel a little better."

"And how about if she did it every day that week?"

"I feel five times better. How did it turn out?"

"Oh, I guess it ended in a draw. I stopped making her lunch, so she thought she won. But I started putting a dollar bill in Michael's lunch every day, and he naturally bragged about it to Karen. 'But you don't want lunch' I said when she complained, 'so I am giving the money I am saving to Michael.' Sometimes it's kind of fun to make your kids furious."

"It's okay to take revenge on your kids?" I asked.

"It's an absolute requirement."

"Did she ever call you names?"

She laughed. "Here's a good one: Remember when I took that Spanish course at Pilgrim Community College? It had been a long time since I was a student. I aced the exam, and I was very proud of myself. John took us out to dinner and he toasted me. 'To an A in Spanish' he said. And Karen held up her glass, 'To Pilgrim Community, whose curriculum caters to morons!'"

I hooted. "No shit! What did you do?"

"Sometimes you just have to be philosophical. I decided to be happy that she knew the word 'curriculum.'"

I had let my weekly lunches with Gwen lapse through the summer, and so I was surprised and happy when she called me at work. I was stocking up for the Holidays, which of course started in September, and Kate and I were both at the store. "She's asking me to lunch," I said to Kate, pointing at the phone.

"If you don't mind if I abandon you for a while, I'll bring you back something."

"Go," she said. "Bring me lots."

I left Kate holding both the fort and Carlos—literally, in Carlos' case—Kate had a tendency to carry him around for hours. The odd-looking little mongrel seemed to have a calming effect on everyone. I often dropped Carlos in Shannon's lap when she was being particularly bitchy. I can't say that she didn't stay bitchy, but she didn't get worse.

Gwen was sitting in our corner booth at Wah Lung. She did a little drum roll with her chopsticks when I walked in.

"Hi," I said, trying to slide into the booth, but getting hooked on the rips in the plastic upholstery. I picked up my butt and hopped into the center. "What's new?"

"Oh my God," Gwen said. "You can't believe how exciting the insurance business is. Why just last week we repaired one thousand windshields."

I laughed. "Jesus, I've missed you."

We had lo mein and pepper steak while she caught me up on the latest Heretic gossip. There was a little snarky news on who was sleeping with whom, but as usual, the main gossip was about who was excluded from what meeting. At Heritage, not getting invited to something strategic was as good as a commercial in the middle of the Super Bowl that proclaimed your career was over.

"So," said Gwen over pale tea in chipped cups, "What's new with you?"

"Big," I said. "Bigger than windshields, if you can believe that. I'm adopting after all."

Gwen warmed her hands around her cup. "Truthfully, I heard that. I mean, Jim heard that. At a meeting of state social workers. A caseworker was very proud of placing a tough kid. And that this kid was pregnant too."

Gwen looked at me and her face was full of worry. "It's why I called you. Jim is concerned. He remembers that you wanted to adopt a baby from a pregnant teenager. And now he hears that you are adopting a pregnant teenager." She frowned harder. "I'm so afraid you are going to hate me, but Jim's worried. About your motives. That you only want a baby, and you're just using that kid." She looked down, peering into her cup. "Is this the same kid?" She added, in a whisper, "Don't hate me."

I could feel my tonsils throb against the pulsing heart in my throat. I had forgotten that someone knew I had wanted to adopt a baby. Just a baby.

"It's the same kid," I admitted. "And I do want the baby. I'll admit it. But babies, as Jim told me, are always wanted. The baby would be just fine without me. But this kid has nowhere to go. I'm giving her a good home."

It was the explanation that Shannon had used to select Carlos over the cute little happy dog. But it was true, too.

Gwen leaned towards me, nodding her head, anxious to see me in the best light. "That's what I told Jim. I told him no matter what you were thinking when you got into this, you're a good person, and you will be a good mother to that kid. That she'll be better off. Right?"

"Absolutely," I said, jumping on my own bandwagon. "This kid—Shannon—she's had a horrible life. And now she will have a home and a mother. And I'm going to see to it that she gets a good education. She's really smart."

"See? You sound like a proud mother already, bragging about your kid. You're a good mother."

"I am. I am. I will be. Please, please ask Jim not to say anything. I'll prove to him what a good mother I can be to both the baby and Shannon."

"You love her. Right? I can tell Jim that you love her?"

I thought about this. I did my best to look Gwen in the eye, and I almost succeeded.

"Of course. Of course I love her."

I'm really trying, I said to myself as I drove back to the store.

Kate and I exchanged armloads. She got a big bag of everything greasy, and I got Carlos.

When I got home, Shannon was not there. She was supposed to come home immediately after school, part of her punishment for stealing. But I decided I'd be reasonable about this. All teenage kids do this, and she's had a tough life and now she's full of hormones.

I cooked up pork chops, like I gave her the first time I had her over for dinner. When our deal was struck. Maybe it would serve to remind us of how far into this we had come.

I ate by myself with my eyes on the door. Maybe she got hit by a car. I wished she got hit by a car, so I wouldn't have to be angry with her again.

She strolled in as I was just about to put away the food.

I pointed to the stove. "I've got pork chops and applesauce," I said pleasantly.

"Yuck," she said. With no explanation, she picked up Carlos and went to her room. A TV game show shrieked through the closed door.

I'm really trying, I said to myself.

Our visits to Dr. Turner became more frequent as Shannon's belly got bigger. We had regular after-school appointments every two weeks once the weather got cooler. The sonograms—sob-o-grams, Shannon called them, because I no longer even tried to contain myself—showed a real baby now.

Seeing this large-headed, thumb-sucking being that Shannon was creating filled me with tenderness not only for the baby but for Shannon as well. She was making my dreams come true, and I wanted to love her. I had promised to try. But any display of affection, especially after a doctor's visit, was rejected. It was clear that she resented how much I loved the baby, and I really couldn't blame her, but she wouldn't let me love her too, not even a little. She winced when I touched her and sneered when I called her dear or honey.

I tried the direct approach after our doctor's visit at the end of September.

"Shannon," I said. "You are doing so fantastic. I love you so much for giving me the family I've always wanted."

"Shit, You're owing me, not loving me," she said. "And I'm not doing anything. It's just happening to me, is all."

I could see the truth in that—life now was something that was just happening to her. She took no active part in baby-making. She only possessed two attitudes, passive and hostile.

I couldn't seem to get her interested in actually joining the baby and me as a family.

I tried to engage Shannon in name discussions, but except for names chosen expressly to infuriate me, she refused to participate.

"How about Phoebe?" I asked over dinner one night.

"How about Feeble?" she replied.

"You told me you wanted to name the baby," I reminded her.

"I guess I'm just gonna have to see her first. She doesn't look like a human being yet. She looks like a pig. We could call her Babe."

"Hmm, Babe," I said thoughtfully, as if Babe Breault was under serious consideration, and not just an attempt to keep our miniscule conversation alive. "Did you ever hear of Babe Didrikson? She was a great athlete of the thirties and forties. The first female superstar."

Shannon put down her milk and looked at her stomach with dismay. "That's what you want? A jock? Don't get your hopes up. She's coming out of my body, remember. I can barely waddle."

"Oh honey, that's not true. You waddle great!"

And I got a tiny fragment of a smile.

Of course, on cue as moment-spoiler, Lucas appeared at the door. He managed to open it (without knocking), fumbling to hold his bag of chips, can of coke, and cigarette in one hand. That would be supper unless I fed him. And I was so looking forward to those leftovers.

Shannon immediately changed her face to match his scowl. I changed mine into 'disapproving mother.' Our momentary connection vanished as thoroughly as the leftovers.

"Shannon," I said, glaring at Lucas's cigarette, "Tell Lucas what the doctor told you today."

"What? That my twat was going to get big enough to pop the baby out?"

"Shannon, watch your mouth. Lucas, don't smoke around Shannon anymore."

James Taylor was singing "You've Got a Friend" with Carole King and me. We sounded pretty good. October was starting out wonderfully.

On Monday, Ben and I had paid our weekly visit to Harry, and I had a surprise for him. The month before I had sent off an email to Oprah Winfrey, describing Harry, including his friendships with Einstein and Marian Anderson. I expressed his admiration for Oprah, and threw in my brief meeting with her at O'Hare. I hadn't expected too much in response, maybe a form email saying 'how nice, etc', but a few days ago I had received a large padded envelope in the mail. In it was a 4" by 6" framed photograph of Oprah. She was standing in a large yard, with an even larger house in the background, presumably hers. Oprah had a smiling dog at her side, and over a lightweight dress she was wearing a large winter scarf. It wasn't the scarf I had rescued for her at the airport, but the intention was obvious. She had taken that picture just for Harry. She had written in the top left corner, "To Harry: It is an honor to be your friend. Oprah."

Harry's reaction was even better than I could have imagined. I wanted to hang the picture on the wall, but he wouldn't part with it. He hugged it to his chest. He wouldn't let it go to eat his cheeseburger.

And then there was Ben's reaction. I confess that I had this at least partly in mind when I first wrote to Oprah. We left Harry still cradling the photo and drove to my house for some amazing afternoon delight. It is good to be adored, even if only temporarily.

The usual edgy dinner with Lucas and Shannon couldn't spoil our mood. The kids were fixated that night on dying. If you had AIDS, would it be murder to intentionally infect someone else? Sure, thought Lucas, but who cares?

"I mean, if I was dying, I could take out as many fuckers as I wanted. What are they going to do? Execute me? I'm dying already." He nodded smugly at Shannon.

She agreed. "I would commit as many crimes as possible. And I would get a credit card and just buy everything. I'd tear up the bills."

Like Angela's deliberate choice years ago to view Karen's insult as a measure of her education, I decided to regard the conversation as an intellectual discussion of ethics.

"I'm not really afraid of everlasting punishment, but I think I would rather lie on the beach than steal stuff I won't be needing anyway." I said.

Ben joined in. "I'd want to spend all my time with the people I loved."

Shannon glared at him. "Well, I certainly wouldn't waste my time spending one minute with assholes."

And she got up and left the room. Lucas smiled proudly and followed her to the living room, where I could hear sniggers and the slaps of high-fives.

"Gee, that was fun," said Ben.

"Who cares?" I asked, still in my good mood.

"Not me."

And we left the house and went out to his car, where we made out like teenagers. If my acquired teenagers were watching us from the window—well, who cares? Not me.

"I think I know why you have such fond memories of the drive-in," I said, wriggling out of my bra.

Tuesday was a continuation of good luck and good spirits. We were busy at the store. Almost all my fall inventory was gone, and new merchandise for the holidays was coming in and going out the door as fast as I could order. I was almost at break-even now. If Christmas was good, we might make a little profit.

And that morning I may have experienced a small miracle. Shannon and I were sitting at the table, eating our breakfast in our usual silence. I saw a delicate change in her face. She closed her eyes and her jaw relaxed into a vague smile. Mona Lisa in Cleopatra kohl.

"Do you feel it?" I asked gently. "Is she kicking?"

"No shit," she said. "I think you're going to get your jock after all."

As usual, I misted up a bit, and Shannon looked at me with disdain.

"For a price," she said, "I may let you feel it."

Then the little miracle. Shannon shrugged and said, "What the hell." And she took my hand and placed it on her stomach. There it was, like a kitten under a blanket.

But that little wondrous kick wasn't my miracle. It was Shannon taking my hand.

So that's why I was singing along with JT and Carole. All three of us oldies, singing like we used to in the seventies. I was in the back room unpacking new corduroys and thick sweaters in rich winter shades. I pulled on a wine v-neck over the olive sweater I was wearing. It was still early in the morning; I usually didn't get any customers until noon, so Kate wasn't coming in until then. I was surprised when I heard the door open.

I pulled off the sweater, hollering in the friendliest way I could holler, "Be right there!"

I patted down the static in my hair, and walked out to the store to see a woman holding Carlos in her arms.

She was striking. Tall and thin, her olive skin tanned to perfection, her dark hair shining with youth and health. She wore a violet dress, just tight enough to make a man fall down. The dress stopped at her knees, where black high heel boots took over. I'm really tall, but I didn't know that anyone made boots that long. She wore thick silver jewelry, the kind that was hand-hammered by a sensitive artist.

Then there was her face. Deep brown eyes and red lips, high cheekbones, straight intense brows. She was completely perfect. I fixated on the slight little bump at the bridge of her nose. A flaw, I thought, but in reality, it was a perfect little bump.

Maria.

"Hello," I said.

I could see in her face that she knew who I was.

She petted Carlos, who had already put his head on her breast.

"Kate told me you brought your dog to work."

"He's good company, and the customers seem to like him."

She gazed around the store. "It looks nice," she said.

I had thought until that moment that it looked nice too, but now it suddenly looked middle-aged.

We stood there without saying anything for a very long minute.

"Would you like some tea or something?" I finally asked.

"No thank you."

I looked at that little bump on her nose. Maybe she thought it was ugly. Maybe she worried every day that she wasn't pretty.

"Umm, are you visiting or are you back?" I asked awkwardly.

"Back, I think," she answered, stroking Carlos's ear.

"Oh." Jesus, how stupid I sounded. "Look," I said, "if you want the store back, I guess that's okay. I was going to be leaving in a month or so anyway," I said. "I'm going to be a grandmother." My god, that was even stupider. Did I really need to tell this young woman, my rival, that I was old?

"I know. Kate told me that you had a pregnant kid." Maria looked at me. "So you're leaving the store. Are you planning on leaving Ben too?" It was kind of a mean thing to say, but she didn't really sound mean. She sounded kind of sad.

So she knew. Did Ben know she was back? He certainly hadn't acted like it on Monday. She might have gone right to him before coming to the store. Of course. She wouldn't come here first. Why would she check out the store instead of her husband? And what had he said about me? Or maybe it had been Kate. I hadn't told Kate that I was seeing Ben, but she could have figured it out. She often seemed suspicious, now that I thought about it.

Maria looked down at the little dog in her arms, and gave him a little gentle hug.

"What's his name?"

"Carlos."

She smiled. "At least his name fits the store."

I laughed, and a little wave of tension dropped away. "You know, I never even thought of that."

Maria handed Carlos to me.

"I love him," she said, and I knew she wasn't talking about the dog anymore.

"I do too," I said. We regarded each other in silence and we suddenly realized that we weren't really enemies. We were two women in the same place.

"He's a lucky man," I said.

She smiled at me. Her face was lovely even filled with regret.

"I can see that," she said.

I grabbed the phone while the breeze from Maria's exit still ruffled the merchandise. But as I dialed I realized I couldn't think of a sentence that wouldn't make me sound petty, scared, whiny, angry, demanding. I couldn't find an adjective I actually wanted to sound like, except maybe 'mature' but I couldn't find any mature words to say. So I hung up.

Customers came in and I waited on them with a rude lack of attention. When Kate showed up at noon, I turned the customers over to her, and went back to the storeroom to unpack sweaters that wouldn't be insulted by my silent inconsideration.

Around 1:30 the phone rang. Thank god, he's calling, I thought.

But it wasn't Ben.

"Mrs. Breault," the unfamiliar voice said. "This is Ray Cerniglia. I'm the security manager at Wal-Mart. We have your daughter here. She and her friend forgot to pay for a few items they forgot were in their pockets."

"Pardon?"

"Maybe I was too subtle. Shannon Miller. Shoplifting. Can you get here faster than the police?"

And here I thought Maria had ruined my good mood.

"I'm in Watertown, but I'll be there as quickly as I can. Please don't call the police," I begged.

"I'll wait half an hour," he said.

I ran out to the front, and explained to Kate and her curious customers that I had a family emergency. "Lock up," I hollered as I fled out the door. It wasn't until I was on the street that I realized that I had gone out the front door, and it would be quicker to go back through the store to access the back lot where my car was parked. But I couldn't face Kate's curiosity. So there went the first minute out of the thirty the security guy had given me.

I drove fast, but halfway there it started to pour. I could hardly see through the pathetic wipers. So I slowed down and watched the minutes tick off on the dashboard.

I wished I had asked who she was with. Her friend, or I guess I could say, accomplice. I rather hoped it was Lucas. I would finally have a good reason to forbid Shannon from seeing him.

I got there in twenty-one minutes. As I ran through the rain to the door, it occurred to me that there is a Wal-Mart in just about every town in Connecticut. What if I had the wrong store?

The cashier directed me by simply pointing to the security office.

Shannon sat in an orange plastic chair. She didn't look at me when I stormed in.

"Mrs. Breault?" asked a youngish man who stood up when I walked in. Although probably not quite thirty, he already had a good start on a middle-aged stomach.

"Yes," I said, not bothering to correct the missus part. "Shannon's my daughter."

He sat heavily back down and gestured me into an old wheeled office chair in front of his metal desk. I sat with my back to Shannon.

"The other kid's mother already came and took her away. You're lucky I'm a sympathetic guy. I'll let your kid off the hook too. Like the pretty mom explained, two young pregnant girls—well, their hormones have 'em all messed up. Not thinking straight."

So it was Gina. Not Lucas. And I was thinking straight enough to note (and rather resent) that Gina's mom was the pretty one. I guess I was the old one. And this guy hadn't even seen Maria. I didn't stand a chance.

"Thank you," I said. "I appreciate your generosity in this situation. Shannon is having a hard time with her pregnancy, and her judgment is not great right now. But at heart she's a good kid, and it won't happen again."

"Just between you and me," he said, as if Shannon weren't sitting right behind me, "if she wasn't pregnant, the cops would already have her. Come down hard the first time, nip it in the bud, that's my motto—let her spend a couple of hours at the police station. Then I might agree that it won't happen again."

I rose. "Thank you so much." I took Shannon by the shoulders and steered her out of the room, out of the building, and out to the car.

She didn't say a word for most of the ride home.

"What the fuck were you thinking?" I finally yelled.

"Gina said we could get away with it," she whined. "That nobody would notice, and if they did, we could cry about being pregnant and scared, and they'd let us go." She stopped short and sort of smiled. "Which they did."

I pulled into Dunkin' Donuts. I parked and turned in my seat to face her. She was red-faced and her eyes were tight.

"You are nuts to listen to Gina. Gina has nothing to lose. Her mother will make excuses and take her home and she'll get grounded. You are the one with something to lose. If that guy had called the cops, then what? You're not my kid yet—we've got three more months. The state could decide that a few years in juvenile detention might be good for you. Did you ever think of that?"

"Then you'd lose your precious baby!"

"I'm not talking about the baby!" I shouted. "I'm talking about you. You could go to juvie jail. Locked up."

JUST WHAT I ALWAYS WANTED

Shannon's face turned from red to white. She suddenly got small and she collapsed into tears. "I didn't even want to," she blubbered. "I didn't even want to cut school. I wanted to be good. I really did."

I leaned back in my seat. I could see in my rearview mirror an old lady glaring at me for hogging the parking space. I started the car.

"I believe you," I said, which was almost true.

She was silent for a while as I drove through the rain. Then her anger rose again.

"And Jesus, she sucked at it. Gina was the worst shoplifter you ever saw. She was so fucking *obvious*!"

The light was red, and I threw my hands up in the air, a good alternative to putting them around her neck.

"You just don't get it," I screamed. "Gina WANTED to get caught. Stealing crap from Wal-Mart wasn't what she wanted. That wouldn't get a rise out of her mother. A call from the police would really make Mom shit her pants."

I drove on. I heard Shannon say "Fuck" over and over again under her breath as she thought it through.

A couple of blocks from home she started to cry in earnest. "Gina wanted to get arrested, and she didn't care whether I did too. She didn't care if she fucked up my life."

Friendless again, I thought. "Oh, Shannon. Gina didn't deliberately want to hurt you. She's just so caught up in her own misery, she doesn't think about anything or anyone else."

"I'm always the one who gets fucked," she cried.

Ben's car was parked in front of my house. As I pulled in the driveway, he got out of the car. He had Carlos in his arms. I had forgotten the poor creature at the store.

Shannon grabbed Carlos and raced through the rain to the porch. She buried her sobs in his thin little coat while I unlocked the door. She ran in, slamming the door behind her.

Ben and I stood on the steps. It rained harder than ever.

"I stopped by the store,' he said needlessly.

"You're not the only one."

"Maria told me," he said. "Why did you say she could have the store back? Did you think that was your decision?"

Christ, he was mad *at me*?

"I have a crisis," I said. "I can't talk right now."

Ben took my hand but it was easy to pull it free in the slippery rain. He took it back, hooking his fingers around my bracelet.

"It's okay," he said. "We'll all be okay." He leaned down and kissed me lightly on the cheek, and turned and ran back to his car.

I went in. Shannon's door was closed. There was no blare of TV or music. My house was as quiet as it had been before Shannon moved in. I didn't much like it.

Carlos was in the living room shivering on the sofa. I took one of my best towels from the bathroom and dried him off. I carried him to the kitchen and gave him a slice of bologna. I gave him a hug. His problems were easy to fix.

The raindrops dripped down my forehead as I made myself a cup of tea. For some reason, I didn't feel like getting dry. Cold and wet seemed the appropriate condition for the moment. I thought more clearly when my physical state matched my mood. I was miserable inside and out.

An hour later, there was still no sound from Shannon's room. It felt like midnight, but it was just after four. I began to worry that perhaps she had killed herself. It was unlike her to not have dragged Carlos in to share her misery. I was her legal guardian; if she died, would I be at fault? Maybe they'd arrest me. Maybe I wasn't thinking so clearly after all.

I went upstairs and dried what had not dried itself and put on some warm clothes. I took a big bath towel and threw it in the dryer for a few minutes. Then I went to Shannon's room.

She was lying on the bed, facing the wall. I sat down beside her, putting the warm towel over her, and she let out a croaky sob.

"I got arrested once," I said.

"I don't believe you," she murmured to the wall.

"I was eighteen. It was Saturday night, the sixteenth of August, about 10:30. We were in the back parking lot of the old clock company. My boyfriend and my best girlfriend and some other guy. Smoking pot. Grass, we called it back then. You'd think out there in the dark, we could have seen the cops drive up. We were so stupid. The cops called another police car and they took us to the police station—the boys in one car and the girls in another. I was terrified. And then they called my father. Then I was really terrified."

Shannon turned over and looked at me, her face changing from doubt to surprise when she saw that I was telling her a true story.

"You have no idea how hard it was to face my father at that police station. He was the most proper man in the world. Serious, hard-working, law-abiding. Like something out of the Bible. Or maybe some old-fashioned Western movie. He bailed me out and took me home. He never said a word. He never said a word for two weeks. My mother made up for his silence. You should have heard her."

Shannon smiled a tiny break-through smile. "I can picture that. Did she hit you and swear at you?"

"My mother didn't hit. But it probably would have been easier. She swore at me for the whole two weeks that my father didn't speak to me. I don't know which was worse." I stopped and considered it. "My father's silent treatment, I guess. I couldn't bear his disappointment."

"So what happened? Did you go to jail?"

"I got really lucky. That guy that I didn't even know—the dude who was with my girlfriend—well, his father was a cop. He made it go away."

"Shit, you were worse than me," she said with satisfaction.

"At that moment I guess I was. But the point is that I really could have screwed up my life. I was about to go off to college. What if the charges hadn't gone away?"

Shannon sighed. "You probably would've ended up like my real mother. What a fuck-up."

"We both got lucky—you and me. When you get lucky like that, you can't waste it."

"What's that supposed to mean?"

"Don't screw up again."

Shannon pounded the pillow. "It was goddamn Gina's fault."

I took the pillow and smoothed the dent away. "I could have said the same thing. It was my boyfriend's pot. But you know what?—I wanted to do it."

"I didn't."

"But you went along with it," I prodded. "Don't you think you should own up to some of the responsibility?"

She shook her head. "Oh no, I know that game. I take responsibility and then I get punished."

I wondered what in her history led her to that conclusion. Whatever it was, she probably had good reason to think so. But this was now.

"Honey," I said. "You're going to get punished whether you own up to it or not."

She stood up. "That's not fair," she said. "You said you understood."

Now that Shannon was standing, I took the opportunity to put my head down on the pillow. I closed my eyes.

"Shannon, I understand exactly how you are feeling. I've been there." I opened my eyes. "But now I also know exactly how my parents felt."

I stood up and looked down on her. "And you're grounded." I walked to the door. "You're grounded until your birthday."

"What!" Shannon was about to stomp her foot like a toddler, but caught herself, and ended like a horse pawing the ground. "That's three weeks away. You only got two weeks!"

"I would have been punished a whole lot longer but I went away to school."

"When can I go away to school?"

"When you're eighteen. Would you like to be grounded till then?"

"Shit." She said.

"And since you won't be going anywhere you won't need an allowance. And I will bring you to school and pick you up. No bus; no high school classes."

"I can't even learn how to take care of the baby?" she complained.

"Whatever you didn't learn I'll teach you when the baby comes. Oh, and when you get home from school you will not go in your room where you have all these nifty entertaining gadgets. You will sit at the kitchen table and do your homework or read a book until dinner." This was a good way to find out whether she could even read.

"Three fucking weeks of prison!"

"Three fucking weeks." I eased off a bit. "On your birthday you get a completely clean slate."

"And a present? You're not going to screw me out of a birthday present?"

"You screwed yourself. But you get a fresh start then. I'll get you a nice birthday present."

I started to leave. "Wait a second," said Shannon. "How are you going to pick me up from school every day? You have to work."

Yeah, there's that, I thought.

"I don't think I'll be working much anymore."

"You're going to quit work because of me?" she asked.

"Yes," I lied.

I left her room, and went to the kitchen to start supper. Shannon came out about twenty minutes later. She got out a head of lettuce and started peeling off leaves. She took out the salad spinner.

After a silent dinner, we each went to our respective rooms. I imagine we did the exact same thing—brooded about how unfair life was.

I wanted to call Ben, but I didn't dare. What if Maria picked up the phone? If they were already back together I didn't want to know that today. I could call his cell; Maria probably wouldn't answer that. But I couldn't be sure. I pictured him kneeling on the bed, straddling her naked body like he did mine, his cell phone on the nightstand. The image was so vivid that it suddenly struck me how unclear it should have been. I had never been to his house. I wondered why that was. Had Ben deliberately tried to keep me out of his previous life? So that it would be easy to go back? Or was it me?—maybe I didn't want to know that he had a whole different life out there. I certainly had shown no curiosity. I hadn't even realized until now that I had never even been in his neighborhood. If we managed to stay together despite Maria's return, I would make sure I became a part of his world.

Of course, that was unlikely. I had seen her. She was breathtaking. And nice, and smart. And young. I was nice and smart too, of course. And sort of pretty. Not breathtaking. And not young. And I had a teenage werewolf in my house and a baby on the way.

You don't necessarily get everything you want in life. I'd concentrate on the baby.

I went downstairs around midnight and I could see the outline of light under Shannon's door. She was probably on the phone bitching to Lucas. I opened the door quietly. She was sound asleep. As I was about to flick off the light, I thought that perhaps she didn't want to go to sleep in the dark tonight. She may be a thief, but she was also still a little girl. I left the light on and closed the door.

Chapter 38

HE SILENT NIGHT TURNED INTO silent morning, with a silent breakfast and silent drive to school. Shannon finally spoke when I followed her out of the car and walked up the stairs towards the huge metal school doors.

"What are you fucking doing?" she cried. "Do you have to ruin all of my life?"

"Listen," I said, not breaking my stride, "You didn't just get in trouble with Wal-Mart yesterday. As surprising as it may seem, they noticed at the high school that you never showed up. I had a message on the answering machine when I got home. So unless you want to get suspended as well as grounded—which will pretty much be solitary confinement for the next few months—then just shut up and look sorry."

And she closed her mouth and followed me into the principal's office, head down.

Mr. Mancini was dressed in the same short-sleeved shirt, although the weather was much cooler than the August day we first spoke. He smiled, not unkindly, but I detected a certain amount of I-told-you-so at the corners of his mouth.

"We have a problem," I said, as he gestured us both into some ancient chairs in front of his desk. "As I'm sure you are aware, Shannon skipped her parenting class at the high school yesterday." I didn't mention Gina. Her mother was so good at getting her off the hook; let her come in and flirt her skirt off. "We both know that Shannon is no angel," I continued, watching her expression change from phony sorrow to defiant. "But this time, I feel partially at fault. Shannon hates those classes. She feels out of place with the older kids, and frankly, though she is too tough to say so, I think she may be the target of some bullying. She's already going through so much right now"—and here I paused and gave her my most motherly angelic smile—"that I think throwing her in with those older kids may have been a mistake. Some of them are pretty hardened." I felt satisfaction using that word, 'hardened.' Nobody hears that word without silently adding 'criminals.' "So anyway, I think it's best that we just keep her here at the junior high, where she's with kids her own age, and where she gets the strong guidance that you and her teachers provide."

By the time I got through, Mancini was smiling and nodding. Any thought that he may have had that Shannon needed to be punished for skipping school was gone.

"Sure," he said. He smiled indulgently at Shannon. "Shannon, you don't have to go up to the high school if you don't want to. You stay right here with us."

And he walked us down the hall to the door. Shannon went out to join the other innocent youths and I walked back to the car. As I was getting in, she ran up to the car door and said, "You should think about the movies."

"You're welcome!" I yelled as I drove off.

I had an attack of nerves as I drove to the store. My imagination escalated with increasingly irrational images of Maria taking back her life—her life that had become my life. I envisioned walking into the store this morning to find Maria unpacking my (her) new merchandise, leaving me to creep off wondering whether the past five months had ever happened. I scooped up Carlos and sat him in my lap for the last mile to the store. I think he knew his position was illegal; we shivered together.

The store was dark and exactly as I had left it. But I wasn't comforted. She'll come walking in any minute, ordering me out of her store. When the phone rang, I screamed.

It was Ben. "I'm so glad you're there," he said, and I knew I wasn't the only one with a reckless imagination. He apologized—he was sorry that he criticized me, and sorry he didn't call sooner.

"I have court in a minute, or I'd be there now," he reassured me. "How's Shannon's crisis?"

"Ongoing, but down a notch."

"I want to hear all about it, but I've got to go in right now. Can I take you out to dinner?"

"I'm grounded," I answered.

"Huh?"

"I mean, Shannon's grounded, but I know I can't enforce it unless I stand guard. So I'm grounded too."

"I'll come over after work," he offered.

"God, she'll be furious."

"Excuse me," Ben said. "But if she's being punished, why would you care?"

"Good point," I said. "But I don't exactly want her listening in on our conversation either."

"Excuse me again," he said, "but she can eavesdrop over that ungodly unmusical din?"

"Good point again. Come after dinner—she'll have the volume cranked up by then."

"Okay. We need to talk. Gotta go." And he hung up.

Men should be forbidden from using that sentence—'*We need to talk.*' All the reassurance I had felt in our banter immediately evaporated. *We need to talk* means *I'm breaking up with you. We need to talk* means *I'm going back to my wife. We need to talk* means *I don't love you.*

Kate called in sick. I wondered what that meant. Was she out with Maria? At 2:30, I locked up and went to get Shannon. I worried some more on the ride. If Maria showed up at the store now, and saw that I had irresponsibly closed early, she'd have further reason to want to take the store back. Adding to my dilemma was the fact that I didn't really want the store anyway.

I just didn't want Maria to have it. Among other things.

I got to the school just as the kids were escaping. Shannon was about to board the bus, but she reluctantly got out of line and dragged herself over to the car. She got into the back seat and lay down.

"Jesus," she said. "This is going to be the longest three weeks ever." Even Carlos avoided her.

At home, I sat her down at the kitchen table, gave her a glass of milk, and instructed her to do her homework.

"I don't have any," she said.

"Read a book."

"I don't have any."

So I went to the bookshelf in the living room and looked at what I had. I tried to remember what I liked at that age, but I didn't have any romance novels. I found the next closest thing.

I handed her *Jane Eyre*. She measured the heft by juggling it from one hand to another.

"This looks important," she said, "and not in a good way."

"You might like it," I answered. "It's about a girl like you. A poor orphan—mistreated and unloved."

"Oh, that's me all right." She cracked it open just a bit, and peaked inside, as if snakes might jump out.

"I loved that book. I was a little older than you, but if you're smart, you might be able to read it anyway," I challenged. "I'd love to read it again. You can read it aloud if you like."

"You're pushing it," she said.

"Okay, just read."

She was silent a few minutes. "I hate the first page," she informed me.

"Read more."

It was early to start supper, but I had to do something while I supervised her. I started to make meatballs. That would take a while.

Fifteen minutes later Shannon said, "These stupid people took her in just to torture her. There's lots of foster parents like that."

Not me, I thought. Please, don't let her mean me. I took two chocolate chip cookies out of the cupboard and put them on a napkin near her milk.

She didn't comment further, and she talked about her birthday during dinner. She couldn't make up her mind about what she wanted.

"Would you like a party?" I asked.

"Who'd come?" she said. She didn't sound angry; she sounded resigned.

After dinner I let her go to her room. She didn't take the book with her, but that would have been asking too much. She hadn't thrown it into her spaghetti—that was enough.

Ben came about seven. We sat in the sunroom and closed the door. It was cool, so we wrapped ourselves in a blanket. Not quite cuddling though. We were both nervous and stiff.

"So what happened with Shannon yesterday?" Ben asked.

"Gina and Shannon ditched school. They went to Wal-Mart and got caught shoplifting."

"Shit," he said. "I mean, it's not like murdering someone— lots of kids try it—but it can become a mess. Did she get arrested?"

"Nope. Gina's mom flirted away the problem."

"So you don't need a good lawyer?" he asked.

I smiled. "Not for Shannon. But I do need a good lawyer." I nudged him with my foot. He didn't tense up. A small positive sign.

"My turn," I said. "So what was your week like?"

He ran his fingers through his hair. "The doorbell rang Tuesday night. Maria was standing there with her suitcase."

I tried to find a breath somewhere. "So she stayed?"

"No. I stepped outside and talked to her on the steps. She couldn't even tell me why."

I made tiny little braids out of the fringe on the blanket. "So where is she now?"

"I'm not sure," Ben said. "Maybe with Kate."

And Kate hadn't said a word when we worked together Wednesday. She probably knew that Maria had come by. I couldn't blame Kate though. Maria's her friend. I'm just her temporary, substitute employer. Maybe I'm just a substitute all around.

"Are you getting back together?" I asked.

"She ran off with my best friend."

"That doesn't really answer the question."

"I don't think I can love her again," he said.

"I met her, remember? She's beautiful. And she didn't seem like a bitch or a whore, even though I was hoping she would be. She was kind of nice," I admitted sadly.

"She ran off with my best friend," he repeated. "So not that nice. You're nice." He looked at me and shrugged his shoulders. "You suit me."

Jesus, that wasn't much of a declaration, but I found a little spot inside of me was thrilled anyway. I tried to smother that feeling.

"But I've got a juvenile delinquent and a baby on the way." I didn't really understand why I was arguing Maria's case.

Ben took my hand under the blanket. "You know," he said, "some women have children and a loving relationship too."

"But I'm new at both those things. And those other women don't have Shannon."

He looked at the door.

"I'll admit she's a challenge," he said. Quite loudly he added, "Look at it this way. You need a good lawyer to keep her out of prison."

Within a few days I learned the nasty secret of punishment—that is was harder on the parent than it was on the kid. Shannon alternated between repentant and repulsive, and either way, I was miserable.

Driving her to school in the morning wasn't too horrible. She regarded afternoon pickup as complete humiliation, and it would have been so easy to relent and let her take the bus home, but I couldn't back down. I'd sit her down at the table after school. Usually she sat with her arms crossed in defiance for at least ten minutes before she'd pick up the book. Sometimes she'd read with interest; but sooner or later I would see her gouging at a word with her fingernail.

I'd sit beside her and read myself. It sounds companionable, but it was tense and tiring. It was a relief to start supper, which Shannon would either eat or not eat with no discernible logic. Finally excused, she'd go off to her room with an emphatic door-slam, and un-music (as Ben called it) would break the awful stillness.

"Did you ever un-ground your kids because you couldn't stand it anymore?" I asked Angela.

"Absolutely not. It's against the parental code. You must pretend you are enjoying her torture."

"Well, this is going to be the longest three weeks of my life."

"Oh, it'll get worse," Angela said cheerfully.

I had told my sisters Shannon was grounded for cutting class. I saw no upside to telling them about her shoplifting. Nevertheless, my mother called the second night.

"Put her on," she said.

And I heard familiar yelling reverberating through Shannon's head.

"Was Grandma unhappy?" I asked innocently as Shannon put down the phone.

"No," said Shannon. "She's just thrilled. She wants to get on a plane right now so she can sit me on her lap."

"How nice."

"Maybe I should have reminded her about how you were a pot-head."

"That would have been very helpful."

"I'll call her tomorrow."

Nineteen days to go.

On her remorseful days, Shannon would come out of her room in the evening and sit with me while I watched TV. She'd rub her tummy and sigh. She'd laugh with me when the show was funny, or pretend to cry a little if I misted up during the tearjerkers. But she couldn't sustain it. Sooner or later she'd blurt, "Christ, this show sucks." And she'd saunter back to her room with a bag of potato chips.

Chapter 39

MY ROMANTIC LIFE LIMPED AWKWARDLY through these long days. I convinced a reluctant Ben to turn the store back over to Maria. I knew that my afternoon imprisonment with Shannon was temporary, but I just couldn't go back to the store.

I met Maria late Sunday evening. I was dressed in my favorite casual look, faded jeans and a black vee-neck sweater. Maria was spectacularly dressed in faded jeans and a black vee-neck sweater. She was gracious but unenthusiastic as I handed her the key. I suspected that she viewed the store as the initial step in reclaiming her old life. I looked at it more like a consolation prize. She could have the store—I wasn't about to give Ben back.

Maria halfheartedly offered to keep me on to help during the Christmas rush.

"I don't think that would be such a good idea," I said.

"Me either," she admitted, "but it seemed like the right thing to say."

"And if I had said 'yes'?"

"Dios, que lio! A real mess."

"Yeah, thanks anyway." But I could see in her eyes that there was more than politeness in her asking me to stay. If I had agreed, she'd know that my interest in Ben wasn't that serious. So now she knew where I stood.

"Your little grandchild will need you soon," she said, reminding me of our age discrepancy.

I made good on my promise to myself to become a part of Ben's life. On Monday, after we visited Harry—who was having a bad spell, and only pretended to recognize us as he ate his cheeseburger—we went to Ben's house.

He lived in an old neighborhood, and his house was one of those split-levels considered modern, even avant-garde, in the sixties. His back yard was pretty, but looking a bit neglected at this time of year. Leaves were strewn on the unused picnic table.

Inside, the house was immaculate. Not cleaning-lady, or even wifely immaculate, but the kind of impeccable neatness that is uniquely masculine. There was nothing on the kitchen counters. There was a single pad and pen by the phone in the living room. The nightstand held one small alarm clock. The only sign that the place was lived in was an open downturned book on the kitchen table.

The color was the evidence that Maria had once lived there. It was Mexican at its most beautiful. Yellow kitchen with a blue tile table, terra cotta living room with green leather furniture, a stark white bedroom with a wrought iron bed and a sunrise of red and gold everywhere.

"Wow," I said. "Shannon would love this."

Immediately, I squirmed with regret. I didn't want Ben to think I was asking to move in.

"Only if I moved out," he laughed, filling the awkward moment.

"It's very beautiful." I stood in the bedroom and turned slowly, taking it all in. "It's so …energetic. But how do you relax?"

Ben took my hand. "You close your eyes."

We lay down on the rough woven bedspread. He must have had the bed specially made—as tall as he was, he had several inches to the iron footboard. We closed our eyes. But it didn't work. It wasn't my room. It wasn't even Ben's room. It was Maria's place, and I didn't belong.

I swung my legs over, and sat looking out the window. He turned on his side and held me around my waist.

"We can re-paint," he offered.

"I think it goes deeper than that."

"We all have a past," he reminded me. "And this is mine. It's part of me."

I stood up, straightening my skirt. I leaned down and smoothed his hair. He looked so much younger in this young room. "It was easier to pretend that you were brand-new."

He got up and led me silently down to the basement. There were boxes of books and shelves and dishes. He reached into one box and handed me a framed photograph. His college self smiled widely as he draped his arm around a tiny young girl.

"All this," he gestured to the boxes, "is me too." He tapped a box. "This one has my train set from when I was ten. This one is college stuff. Those lamps are from my old apartment. And that is my first girlfriend," he said, pointing to the picture in my hand. "Maria made me put it all away."

He kissed me on the forehead.

"I don't believe in 'brand-new'," he said. "I think you bring it all with you, and that's okay."

I looked at the sweet open faces in the photo.

"What was her name?"

"Kathleen."

"The love of your life?" I asked.

"You're all the loves of my life."

"Fair enough," I said. But it was a good thing I had to go pick up Shannon, because I wasn't quite ready to join all those memories in that bed.

The next day I started to feel a little sick. It was bound to happen sooner or later. I hadn't even had a cold for more than a year. I drove Shannon to school feeling slightly queasy, and by the time I picked her up, I was sweaty and feverish.

"Christ," she said, climbing into the car, "You look like shit."

"Some kind of bug, I guess."

And in the solicitous way of teenagers she asked, "What am I supposed to eat for supper?"

Shannon apparently didn't starve, because the next morning she peeked into my room. I could barely focus, but it seemed that she had more makeup and less skirt than usual.

"Take the bus," I groaned. "But you're still grounded, so come home right after school."

"Don't worry," she said. "I'll be fine." She didn't ask whether I would be.

I called the doctor later in the morning. "There's flu going around," he said.

"Flu? In October?"

"Yup. Drink lots of water. You'll feel better in about three days."

I had dreams that the room was a big Mayan pyramid, painted in bright Mexican yellow, only it was upside down and so kept swaying on its tip. A big fire roared in a fireplace

I don't have. I stripped down to my undies and fanned myself with my blanket. Later I put on a sweatshirt over my pajamas, then a robe over that, and shivered under two extra blankets.

I woke to bells ringing in a big church. But it was the phone.

"Hi," said Ben.

"I'm sick," I said, hanging up.

The church bells rang again.

"What's the matter?" he asked.

"Flu."

"In October?"

"The early bird special."

"I'll come right over. I'll bring soup."

"Don't you dare," I said. "I can't look at soup and you can't look at me."

"Come on. I can take it."

An image from Harry's gallery popped into my swirling head.

"Albert Einstein, 1953," I said. "Only in a pink fuzzy bathrobe."

"I'll call you tomorrow," said Ben.

Shannon actually came home right after school. I heard the kitchen door open, immediately followed by the refrigerator door.

Sometime after it got dark, she tiptoed in and sat on the bed.

"Ugh," I said. "Don't bounce around like that."

By the light from the hall, her face looked soft and serious. She leaned over me and put her hand on my forehead.

"Gross," she said. "You're all greasy and sweaty."

"Shannon, don't get too close. I don't want you to catch this."

She jumped up quickly, and I shuddered with nausea.

"Do you want anything to eat?" she asked from a safe distance.

"No. Truly no."

"Okay," she said and started to leave. My head cleared slightly.

"What will you have for dinner?" I asked.

"There's not much left," she said. "I ate the hotdogs yesterday. And the rest of the bread for breakfast. There's cereal and a little milk. But I'm saving it for tomorrow morning."

I thought about her mother leaving her alone to fend for herself when she was just a little girl.

"Call for a pizza. Have it delivered."

"Really?" she asked, kind of excited.

"Yes," I said.

She grabbed the phone by the bed and asked for the number of the local joint, the one where she poured soda over Celeste. She ordered a large pizza with meatballs and olives. I didn't know she liked olives. She put her hand over the phone and whispered to me, "That way I'll have some for tomorrow, in case you're still fucked up." Her face clouded a bit at their response, and she handed the phone to me.

"They want to talk to an adult."

I took the phone in my clammy hand. "My daughter is ordering pizza. She's a good tipper. Please deliver it right away."

To her I said, "Take a twenty from my wallet...and five for a tip." As she started for the stairs, I added, "I know exactly how much money I have," even though I didn't have a clue.

I never heard Shannon leave for school the following morning. I woke about ten, with Carlos breathing softly on my neck. He looked happy to see me open my eyes. I was weak and lightheaded, but not feverish. I plodded down the stairs with one hand gripping the banister and the other holding my stomach.

The kitchen looked like I had abandoned it two months ago, not two days. The table held bowls and plates and forks in a precarious stack. The sink was filled with every glass I owned, including a few that I didn't even recognize. I opened the refrigerator to find a pizza box crammed into the shelf, and the stuff that was usually on that shelf, butter and relish and the like, in the vegetable bin. At least Shannon hadn't just thrown it all away. Open and mostly empty cans were on the counter: tuna, soup, beans, pears. Carlos's dish held the remnants of what looked like tuna.

Carlos had relieved himself by the kitchen door. I cleaned that up first, while he hung his head.

"Not your fault," I consoled him, as I took him outside and hoped no one saw me with my dirty clothes and wild hair. He squatted quickly and I hustled him back in.

I made tea and took it into the living room, so I could avert my eyes from the mess for a few minutes more. The living room was redecorated with microwave popcorn bags and paper plates filled with pizza crusts. I ended up in the dining room, which had been spared from the tornado.

I sipped the tea though I found I no longer wanted it. Finally I went back to face the kitchen. I got a trash bag and threw away everything paper, plastic, or old food. Then I stacked the dishwasher; not everything fit, I'd have to do another load, but it was an immediate improvement.

I went back to bed.

Ben called around one.

"I'm a little better," I reassured him and myself.

"What do you need?" he asked. "I'll come over."

I swallowed my pride. "I'm scary to look at, but I need everything. The cupboard is bare… I need milk and cereal and bread, and stuff that teenagers eat. And dogs. Carlos has been eating tuna fish, but even that's gone."

"I'll stop at the store and be there in an hour."

"I'll try to shower," I said.

"Wash your face and brush your teeth, and I'll take my chances."

Fifteen minutes later the phone rang. I figured Ben was calling for more instructions on the groceries. But it was Angela.

"It's recess, so I only have a minute," she explained. "I called last night. Shannon said you were sick and that maybe you would die."

"I've got the flu, but I'm a little better."

"Want me to come over tonight with some stuff?" she asked.

"Ben is coming now and bringing everything we need. We're okay, but thanks."

"Ben, huh?" She was quiet for a minute, but I didn't offer any explanation. "Okay, okay," Angela said. "I trust you. Just take care, and not just of your flu. I'll call later in case he forgot something. Men are notorious for getting distracted at the supermarket. They forget the necessities and you end up with pickled pigs' feet and brussels sprouts. Gotta go… Jennifer, put that down."

I immediately fell asleep and awoke to Ben's light touch on my cheek.

"You didn't even lock the door," he said.

"Burglars are afraid of flu," I said.

"I put everything away and cleaned the mess," he bragged.

"I picked up," I insisted.

He rolled his eyes, "Yeah, good job." He patted my hand. "You go back to sleep. I'm going to take Carlos for a walk."

"Could I ask you a really big favor?" I tried to look sweet even though I figured I was fairly disgusting.

"Anything."

"Don't take this wrong or anything, but could you be gone by the time Shannon gets home from school? I haven't got the strength for any drama."

His look was gentle, but he shook his head. "You need to accept me with all my baggage and I need to accept all of you too, even Shannon."

"How about if we start when I'm feeling better?"

He smiled. "Go back to sleep. I'll deal with Shannon. I'll even feed her."

"I don't know," I said, but I didn't have the energy to argue about it. I closed my eyes.

His lips brushed my hair.

When I woke up it was getting dark. I smelled something cooking. I tried to concentrate on where I was and what time it was and what that smell might be. I finally remembered Ben.

I got up and washed my face and brushed my hair. I put a little baby powder on my hair and brushed it again, hoping it would look less grimy. I changed into a nicer bathrobe.

Ben was in the kitchen, tending a big skillet of chicken, broccoli and rice.

"Hi," I said. "I lived."

"I'm so glad," said Ben.

I looked around and realized how quiet the house was. "Where's Shannon?" I asked.

"She's not home yet."

My stomach lurched. I looked at the clock. It was almost five. "No, that can't be. She's supposed to be home by three."

"I'm sure she'll be home any minute," said Ben, like everything was fine, like Shannon was just a normal kid at cheerleading practice. I opened my mouth and crazy came out.

"It's your fault," I cried. "She saw your car and took off. I knew this would happen. You should have gone home. I wanted you to go home."

I started picking up the dishes that Ben had laid out on the kitchen table. He stopped me by holding me firmly by the shoulders. He took the dishes from my hand and put them back. Maneuvering me into a chair, he pulled up his own chair and sat down opposite me, knees touching.

"Cynthia," Ben said, "I know you're sick and now you're worried and angry. But Shannon is a teenager, and she's not going to do everything you say or everything she promises. It's normal. It's nothing that we can't handle." He lost his gentle look for a moment. "And it's not my fault."

I turned my head away from him. It irritated me somehow that he said that 'we' could handle this. I knew that I should have been comforted, but I wasn't.

And suddenly she was home. Shannon threw open the door, and stomped in. She had a big brown bag in her arms, and a plastic bag dangled from her elbow. She kicked the door closed behind her. She looked triumphant.

"Where have you been?" I cried. "It's so late. You are supposed to come home right after school."

The pride vanished from her face. "I bought groceries," she said. She looked at the pans on the stove. "I guess it was a waste of time."

I should have said, 'how thoughtful' or 'that was such a responsible thing to do' or at least, 'thank you,' but I said, "Where did you get the money?"

She slammed the big bag down on the table, rattling the dishes. She let the bag hanging from her arm drop to the floor with a thud.

"I didn't steal the money, and I didn't steal the food." She glared at me. "Lucas lent me the money."

"Lucas?" I asked in disbelief.

"Yeah. Lucas got a job." She walked away from me, and went down the hall. She turned and came back. "Lucas got a job—and a car!"

A car. Lucas has a car. I jumped from the chair, and raced (as much as you can race with slippers on one end and a fever on the other) to the bathroom. I threw up.

I sat on the bathroom floor with my cheek resting against the tub. The cool porcelain soothed me. I thought I might stay there quite a while.

I heard Ben and Shannon. He asked her what kind of car Lucas bought. As if that mattered. What was he doing? Acting like Dad?

He said to Shannon, "Cynthia is really sick, and was very worried about you."

"Yeah, sure. Not so sick that she couldn't have a little screw."

"Shannon, shut up. I don't really care what you think about me, but you'd better be respectful towards Cynthia. Look how she's taken you in. Cared for you. She didn't have to do that. She loves you."

"Jesus Christ," yelled Shannon. "Loves me? Open your eyes, you moron."

I couldn't let this conversation continue. I staggered from the bathroom, and they both stopped and stared at me.

"Shannon, I apologize," I said. "It was very mature and responsible for you to buy groceries. I appreciate it. And I'm not mad that you were late. It's okay." She gazed at the ceiling but I could see just the slightest relaxation in her shoulders. "Could you give me a minute with Ben? And then we can all have something to eat."

"Take all the time you want," she said, "Lucas took me to McDonald's." She strode past me towards her room, and I gave her arm a little pat as she walked past. She brushed it off her sleeve like it was dust. The door slammed, but not as hard as it does sometimes. I'd be able to patch things up later.

I sat down and hung my head. "I apologize to you too," I said to Ben. "My brain is not quite working."

"Don't keep me out," Ben said. "I feel like I am totally separate from what is going on with you. Like I'm an escape from your life, not a part of it."

"I'll let you in." I wasn't sure I meant it. "I promise," I said, mostly to myself. I looked at the plates and the food now gone cold on the stove. "I can't eat anything."

"I'll put it away," he said.

I got up and looked in the bags that Shannon had left. There was milk, bread, cereal, peanut butter, orange juice, saltines, and three cans of Campbell's chicken soup. In the bag she dropped on the floor were six cans of dog food.

"Go to bed," said Ben. "I'll straighten up and call you tomorrow."

"We can be a family tomorrow," I promised.

I woke up a little after nine pm. The fever was gone and I was famished.

Downstairs the kitchen was quiet and clean. All the dishes were put away. There wasn't even anything on the draining board. In the refrigerator were Ben's and Shannon's groceries, and some containers with the food Ben cooked tonight. He had put a sticky note on one container—*This came out good. I took some home.*

I looked in the cupboards, and saw the saltines and soup. Carlos pattered in, and looked at me hopefully.

I knocked lightly on Shannon's door, and peeked in. She wore her earbuds and I could hear the tinny faraway rattle of drums. On her big tummy was a familiar book. *Jane Eyre.* I knocked louder and she looked up and pulled one earpiece aside.

"Carlos and I are going to have some chicken soup. Do you want some?"

She shrugged her shoulders. "Yeah, okay," she said. She pointed at the book. "In a minute," and my heart made a tiny little leap.

I wasn't sure how hungry any of us really were, but I opened two cans, and put the saltines on the table.

Shannon came to the kitchen in her PJs. Her makeup was gone and her hair was in messy braids. She was hardly more than a baby. With a baby coming soon.

"You know," she said, "If I was Jane, I would be saying to Rochester, what the fuck is going on in the attic?"

"Girls weren't very assertive back then," I said, handing her a bowl of soup.

"No shit."

In the corner, Carlos lapped noisily at his soup. Shannon slurped with the same gusto. I took tiny spoonfuls and it didn't seem too bad.

"This is good," I said.

"Sick people are supposed to eat chicken soup," she informed me.

I went to the fridge and took out a package.

"Look at this," I said, handing it to Shannon.

"What the hell is it?" she asked.

"Knockwurst," I said.

"I don't even know what that is."

"German sausage," I explained. "Ben bought it. Men don't know a thing about what to eat when you're sick. I think chicken soup is a much better idea."

"What's up with him anyway?" she asked. "He's even weirder than usual."

"I think he just wants to take care of us a little bit."

She sat back. "We can take care of ourselves."

I smiled. "Yes, we can. But it's nice that he wants to."

"It's creepy," she said. "Let him get his own family."

I knew it would come out pretty soon, and as long as we were being the Cynthia-Shannon team for a moment, I confided in her.

"Ben's wife has come back."

Shannon slurped a single noodle and stared at me. I corrected myself. "She's back in town, anyway, and she wants to come back."

"Good. She can have him. I never liked him anyway."

"You've made that perfectly clear." I put down my spoon, and crumbled some saltines in the bottom of my bowl. "The thing is, I like him."

Shannon took a few saltines and crumbled them in the bottom of her own bowl, watching as the crackers absorbed the last remnants of the soup.

"So what are you going to do?" she asked. "Lucas knows some guys who could beat the crap out of her."

"Thanks. That's a very nice offer, but I think I'll pass. I guess I'll just tell him I want him to stay with me, and see what happens."

She picked up Carlos and put him on the table, letting him lick the bottom of her bowl. I didn't say anything.

"What does she look like?" Shannon asked.

I sighed. "Think of the prettiest, most glamorous movie star in the world. Right? Okay, well, Maria's even more beautiful. And she's about twenty years younger than me."

"Fuck," she said. "Good luck with that."

Chapter 40

O F COURSE, THE NEXT MORNING Shannon was outraged that her purchase of the groceries didn't relieve her of the last week of her punishment. She was stunned when I refused to recognize her complete redemption as evidenced by Campbell's chicken soup.

"I am astounded at your unfairness," she said, although I admit that this is not a direct quote. I have translated her actual words, "Are you fuckin' shittin' me?"

So I explained that although her good deed was very thoughtful, and I was in fact glad that she had ignored her curfew in order to make sure we both had something to eat, a nice gesture does not atone for theft.

"Of course it does," she argued. "People get paroled all the time. If I can't get something good out of it, why would I bother being good?"

"Because it makes you feel good," I answered.

"What a load of crap,' she said.

"One more week," I said pleasantly.

Ben came over for dinner and we reheated the food he had prepared the previous day. It was quite delicious and I was impressed by his culinary expertise.

Shannon wouldn't touch it. "I can't eat this shit," she said, and when I glared at her, she quickly amended, "It must be the baby," and rubbed her belly. "I'll just have a bowl of cereal." She got up. "In my room."

"Good," said Ben after she left. "I am totally losing patience with her."

"Sometimes she's nice," I said. "She was really sweet last night."

"After I left."

"Well, yeah. But eventually she will be nice in front of you." I smiled. "By accident of course, but you might witness it."

"I'm more likely to witness an alien invasion," he remarked.

"This is an alien invasion," I said. But he was not amused.

Shannon's birthday was not a disaster—from Shannon's point of view.

I relented and bought her a laptop. For one thing, I wanted to give her something that would really wow her, and indicate that all was forgiven. But also, I couldn't think of anything else. Every time I asked her what she wanted, she'd bring up an idea more outlandish than the last. "A pony," she said once. "A trip to Hawaii." "A raccoon coat." And once, though I have no idea why: "Acorn squash."

So I went to the computer store, and picked out a flashy purple laptop. I had the geek advisor install some controls. One that prohibited access to porn sites, and one that prohibited online purchases. I figured I wouldn't tell Shannon about either one. She may happily surprise me by never trying to do either of those activities, in which case, she didn't need to know I didn't trust her. And if she did try, I'd be glad I had them.

I did have the guy download a couple of horrible and popular games; ones that, although disgusting, weren't entirely unacceptable. I may be able to stop Shannon from viewing pornography, but I couldn't stop her from being a kid. A few grisly games seemed about right.

He also sold me a wireless router so we'd have internet access throughout the house. He gave me complete installation instructions that I would never remember. I hoped Ben might have another hidden talent.

Hardly any of the cute clothes I bought Shannon for school fit anymore. Shannon had taken to wearing Lucas's shirts over sweatpants. So we went out the night before her birthday and bought a few new outfits. It wasn't easy. Many of the clothes Shannon tried were so awful I had to admit that the sweatpants were better. We finally settled on maternity jeans and cargo pants, with a couple of tent-shaped tees. One had Bob Marley's picture—Shannon didn't know who he was, but he looked cool enough. We added an empire waist gray hoodie and an almost flattering violet pullover. We were exhausted and ready to call it a night when Shannon found a long sleeved black tee that actually said 'Love Hurts' across the baby bump. Assuredly the least tasteful purchase I have ever made, but I just laughed defeatedly and handed over my credit card.

I took Shannon and Lucas out to dinner for her birthday. Their choice was the big Chinese buffet. I readily agreed since both pregnant Shannon and starving Lucas could eat like elephants and an all-you-could-eat option seemed wise. When we walked in, we saw a long table filled with rowdy teenagers.

"Oh look," said Lucas with a phony innocence. "These kids are friends of mine."

"Can we go sit with them?" asked Shannon. "Then it would really be almost like a birthday party."

I knew it was a set-up, but I was stuck. I let them go, and took a booth in the corner where I could watch them.

The kids were foul-mouthed, loud, rude, and got worse when Lucas joined them. They terrorized and insulted the skinny pony-tailed little girls who brought drinks and cleaned tables. They tossed food at each other and dipped their dirty forks into the serving pans. They added hot sauce to chicken and ice cream to the lo mein. Shannon built a totem pole with chicken fingers and when it toppled to the floor, one of the boys ground it into the rug.

I had only just started to feel competent with the whole Mom thing, but I now found myself both mortified and paralyzed.

One disgusted customer finally went over to the group and asked them to behave.

Lucas looked up and said, "Why thank you, sir, for the suggestion." Then he sucked out the meat from his crab leg and dropped the shell at the man's feet.

I watched a couple of boys take the cans of whipped cream from the sundae bar. That was enough for me.

"Time to go," I said, grabbing Shannon by the wrist. Lucas insisted on staying with the other kids, and I was relieved to leave him behind.

I handed two fifty-dollar bills to the worried wrinkled lady standing at the register. "For the mess," I whispered.

Time for another car lecture. These were becoming common, and I wondered if all mothers used the confines of the car to let loose.

"That was horrible," I yelled. "You were horrible."

"Oh we were just kidding around. It was nothing."

"Why were you so mean to those waitresses? I don't know that I've ever seen you so mean."

Shannon turned to me. "Those girls came over from China. They have it a lot better over here. They don't have anything to complain about."

"Those girls are just like you. You had a bad life and now you have a better life. How would you like to be treated like that?"

She slumped down in her seat. "How do you know I'm not?"

At home, Shannon's new laptop was set up in her room, with a bright yellow bow on top. Ben was gone. I wasn't sure whether he wanted to surprise her or avoid her, and I wasn't sure how I felt about either scenario.

"No shit!" Shannon whooped when she saw the computer. She moved the mouse and the screen came to life. "Strangulation Mania! Jesus Christ. Lucas is going to be so bumming that he didn't come home with us."

By the computer was a little box. Inside were earrings, big black hoops and from each dangled what looked at first to be freshwater pearls. But on examination they were tiny skulls.

Shannon held them up. "Thanks. These are cool."

"I didn't buy them," I confessed. "They must be from Ben."

She made a face and said, "Then yuck."

"You know," I said with a shrug, "You could like the gift and still hate the giver. It's sort of like using someone for your own ends."

She dangled the skulls by her ears, sizing them up. "Okay," she said, "That's what I'll do."

Chapter 41

ALL OUR ARGUMENTS OVER THE next two weeks were about Lucas, and most specifically and often, about Lucas's car.

As soon as she was no longer grounded, Lucas started to pick Shannon up after school. They'd pull into the driveway—later each day—and Shannon would clumsily unload herself from somewhere inside the crowded vehicle. Lucas's car consistently contained a shitload (and I use that word accurately) of kids. Now that Lucas was driving, he seemed to have accumulated a lot of friends. They could have been the same guys that trashed the Chinese restaurant, but it was hard to tell. They almost looked like the same punk over and over again.

I told Shannon I didn't want her in that car. She told me I was ruining her life.

"I want to see his driver's license. And his insurance," I demanded more than once.

"You never needed to see D.J.'s insurance," she'd fire back.

"I knew D.J.," I'd answer.

"You know Lucas."

"Yeah, that's what I'm afraid of."

Once, when I was asking again for his credentials, I added to the list. "I want to see his license, his insurance, and his probation report," I said.

"Jesus Christ. A couple of fights and everyone is on your case forever," Shannon responded.

"You mean I'm RIGHT? He's on probation?" I was close to shrieking.

She stared at me as it sunk in. "Fuck. That's not fair. You tricked me."

"So now that I know, tell me the rest of it. What was he arrested for?"

Dragging it from her, syllable by syllable, Shannon revealed that Lucas had been in three vicious fights within a six month time frame. He was 'going through shit', she explained without explaining. So he was on probation and 'forced' to sit through anger management classes.

"He could just kill that guy who runs the anger management program," she said without irony.

"Doesn't it worry you that he might explode when you are there?"

"Nope," she said.

I could see she completely meant it. We were so different. I once had a hairdresser who was going through a wicked divorce. She voluntarily enrolled herself in an anger management course in an effort to control her wild emotions. This was exemplary. I understood that. And yet I found a good rationale to switch salons. I didn't want angry scissors anywhere near my hair.

And I didn't want Lucas's anger anywhere near my developing baby. But unlike the lack of parking spaces near my old salon, I couldn't find a good excuse to forbid Shannon from seeing Lucas. It was hard to argue that he was too old; D.J. was even older. And Lucas hadn't been in trouble recently. On top of it all, he seemed to like her, and she needed at least one friend.

So although I complained about him constantly, I didn't outright forbid her seeing him. When my nieces and nephews were teenagers, they changed partners every other week. Shannon and Lucas were bound to fight sooner or later. My fervent wish was that he would just dump her. If she did the dumping, he might be angry, perhaps violent. But if she was the dumpee, then she'd be the angry one—and she already was.

But how I loved our doctor visits. Although they were a reminder to Shannon that I was using her for my own happiness, I couldn't contain that happiness. The baby glowed on the screen like a holy vision. And I swear her heartbeat was a little faster when I touched Shannon's stomach.

Towards the end of October, Dr. Turner told us that she thought the baby might come early.

"Girls your age often don't carry to term. You need to take good care of yourself," she said to Shannon.

"I don't think I should go to school anymore," Shannon volunteered.

Dr. Turner shook her head. "Nice try. Just get a lot of rest. If you want to give something up, try junk food."

I didn't take it so lightly. "They'll both be okay though, right? If Shannon should be on bed rest, I'll keep her out of school."

"Relax, Grandma," said Dr. Turner. "You've got at least a month before we need to worry about that. Maybe two if Shannon's careful."

"If I jump around a lot, can I fart the kid out now? I wouldn't mind getting it over with," said Shannon.

"Absolutely not," laughed the doctor. "It will be better for you and the baby to go as long as you can. Don't worry. The time will go by fast."

"Boy, are you wrong! This is like the most boring movie I ever sat through." She looked at me. "It's like 'Sleepless in Seattle'."

"I love that movie," I said.

"Yeah, I know. Like a dozen times, I know."

I felt like a family at that moment.

Dr. Turner asked, "Do you have any names picked out?"

"Apricot," said Shannon.

"No way!" I protested.

"But that movie star you like, she named her kid Apple."

"Yeah, that's why Hollywood kids are so fucked up."

Shannon threw back her head and laughed from her jellied-up big belly.

And I knew that there was no better sound in the world than hearing your kid laugh.

On the drive home, Shannon was quiet. I paused at an intersection to let a funeral procession drive by.

"Lucas says," she started, (and how I hated all the sentences that started that way), "Lucas says that I need to make sure that I get lots of your money if you should die. That it shouldn't all go to the baby."

I pulled out behind the last funeral car. "Shannon, don't worry, it's already taken care of. I have a lawyer for a boyfriend, remember?" I patted her knee. "You'll get lots of money." I thought about Lucas for a second. "As long as I'm not murdered."

"Okay," she nodded. "I'll ditch that plan."

We both watched silently as the hearse pulled up in front of the church.

"What happens though if you die and I'm still a kid?" she asked. The casket was being removed by white-gloved old men. She answered her own question. "I suppose if I've got lots of money, somebody might want me," she sadly speculated.

"That's taken care of too," I said. "If anything happens to me, you and the baby will go live with Angela. She's okay with that," I added. "She likes you."

"Shit," said Shannon. "Could I go there now?"

And my sweet afternoon turned sour.

⌁

It wasn't too long before I regretted giving the store back to Maria.

A good part of my motive had been a desire to keep her busy. If anyone was going to have free time for Ben, I wanted it to be me. Of course, now I had too much free time. Ben had a day job; and now I didn't.

I knew as soon as the baby came, I would be busy again. But with Shannon in school, and Ben locked in a complex probate challenge, the days were as long as 'Sleepless in Seattle.' When I had first retired, I loved the long lazy days. Now I paced and watched the clock.

I took long walks with Carlos. The weather was getting cold, and I dressed him up in his sequined sweater and we roamed the neighborhood. He was used to being held, not walked, and most days I had to pick him up and carry him after the first quarter mile.

And speaking of sweaters—that was another reason I was sorry I had relinquished the store. I irrationally coveted that purple sweater I had been trying on the day Maria walked

335

in. Giving up the store meant I really couldn't shop at Maya Maria any more. That was unfair. I had stocked that place with beautiful clothes—it was my own private wardrobe—and now I was embarrassed to shop there. I became obsessed with that sweater. I called the wholesaler and described the item. They told me the closest retailer was in Springfield, and I drove all the way up there one morning. The sweater was strangely unattractive.

Besides our Mondays with Harry, Ben and I started to go out one night a week. Ben insisted that we needed adult time together. We did, of course, but still I was hesitant. The worse Shannon behaved, the less I wanted to leave her alone. And her behavior was truly worse. I blamed the out-of-control hormones. She hated whatever I cooked, missed school twice a week, refused to attend Mass at all, and to my horror (not to mention Mary Ann's), she pierced her eyebrow with a safety pin.

"We need to escape from Shannon-land," said Ben. So we'd go out to dinner someplace very, very quiet. And all through our civilized dinner I worried about what might be happening at home.

Shannon took to calling me constantly on the evenings I went out. "Don't answer it," Ben said by the third call. "She's just trying to spoil our evening." He was right. There was never any real emergency. But how could I be sure?

"In the linen closet," I said. Next call: "I'll buy some tomorrow." And, "Yes, I will take you to the hospital if you're still sick when I get home." (Which she never was.)

Ben's smile got thinner.

"It's just a stage," I assured him.

"How do you know?"

"Because we're adults and we can outlast her."

"Yeah, but she's younger—she may outlast us."

"She doesn't have the attention span."

At the next ring, he grabbed the phone away from me.

"Twenty bucks if you don't call for the rest of the evening," he said.

I snatched the phone back.

"Forget that," I said.

"Make it twenty-five," said Shannon, "and you don't even have to come home. You can fuck all night."

I ignored her comment. "Just remember, this is a one-time deal," I said. "There won't be a next time."

"Next time let's make it thirty," she said, and signed off.

I looked at Ben, who was grinning smugly.

"That's just wrong," I said, attempting to scowl. But my smile leaked through.

His broadened. "Yeah, I know. But I'm desperate."

"My sisters tell me that bribes are dangerous."

Ben nodded and sipped his wine. "I think your sisters just want you to suffer through your kid's adolescence the same way they suffered."

"I'm sure I'm suffering more," I said.

"So when I am going to meet these all-wise sisters, anyway?"

I shrugged. "I'm a little afraid of their disapproval. Shannon already told them that Maria is back."

"Jesus," said Ben, shaking his head. "Hasn't anyone in your family ever gotten divorced?"

"Aunt Lorraine. Repeatedly. And, well…me."

He put down his wine and looked at the ceiling. "For crying out loud, Cynthia. How many more secrets do you have?"

My glass was empty, so I picked up his wine and took a swig. "It's not a secret. It's just so long ago that I don't even think about it anymore."

He took back his glass and considered it. "Well, that's how I want it to be for me," he said.

"Give it twenty-five years."

"Ha," he said. "I think I'm going to be okay in about twenty-five minutes."

⁂

Although Shannon had given me permission to spend the night, she was still up when I came home at eleven. She was watching TV in the living room, with a very big bowl of ice cream under her chin, the quicker to shovel it in.

"Where's the money?" she said, holding out her hand.

I handed it over. "This is from Ben, not me. Any further negotiations will have to be with him."

"I'm beginning to like him better already," she commented.

"He certainly knows the way to your heart."

"Yup. Cold cash."

I sat down next to her, and dipped my finger into her ice cream. I let Carlos lick it off.

"You're certainly in a good mood," she observed. "I guess the way to your heart is a good lay."

I laughed. "No, a good scampi."

She rolled her eyes, and I kissed the top of her head. She didn't flinch.

⁂

Her good mood continued through the next morning. She cheerfully ate her Cheerios, and gave an awkward twirl to model her "Love Hurts" tee shirt. "They may send you home from school," I warned.

"That's my plan," she said.

When I pulled up to the curb at the school, she slumped down in the seat. "I can't go in," she whined.

"Are you sick?" I asked.

She grimaced. "No, I can't go in. I can't get through the door."

I smiled. "You are the hottest pregnant girl in the whole school."

"There's only two of us."

"Well, you are sooo fuckin' cooler than Gina!"

She giggled. "No shit." And she clambered out and made a big show of squeezing through the door.

But good moments are just moments. When Lucas drove up at the end of the afternoon, hostilities recommenced. It was lucky we had electricity and not oil lamps like Jane Eyre. Shannon would have certainly torched the house. She had to make do with coat throwing and door slamming.

The latest demand came as we finished supper, which, although the ham steak was her favorite last week, had apparently become shit tonight.

"I think I should get half of the twenty thousand as soon as the baby comes," Shannon said as I got up from the table.

I wasn't going to take a spin on that carousel. "Good idea," I said. "I'll set up a trust that you can have when you turn eighteen."

"That's not what I mean," she said.

"Gee that's too bad." I said, scraping the remains of her plate down the disposal. "But won't it make you feel nice and secure to know it's there?" I asked.

"Shit, no. It's going to make me crazy."

"Then by all means, let's set it up tomorrow."

"I really hate you," she said.

But she didn't *really* hate me. The *really* part didn't take hold until I started getting the baby's room ready. Every piece of stenciled furniture, every wall hanging, every baby blanket made her that much more furious. I tried to placate her, make her feel included.

"Why don't you help decorate? Your room looks so nice; we could pick things out together."

And I dragged her along shopping, where I chose Maurice Sendak and she chose Bram Stoker. Shannon put a painting of day-glo skeletons in my cart and I took it out.

"I thought you wanted me to help," she said.

"We are not raising Rosemary's Baby," I said.

"Huh?" she said.

Still I tried to encourage her. "We don't have to go too babyish. We can go bright and funky like your room."

She put black towels in my cart. I took them out.

"Why don't you just give it my stuff and move me into the attic?"

I winced a bit when she called the baby 'it', which she had begun to do with regularity.

"Do you like the name Amelia?"

"How about anemia?"

Well, she knew that word. I could be happy she had a good vocabulary.

She put a pillow embroidered with marijuana leaves into the cart. I took it out.

In the cart were some baby sheets and a cow jumping over the moon. I left it in the aisle. "Come with me," I said.

I took Shannon next door to a small coffee shop. Most of the tables were the tall sort with high uncomfortable stools—I wasn't sure Shannon could lift her belly that high. I found the only normal, though un-level, table with regular chairs, and plunked Shannon down. "Wait here," I said.

I came back a minute later with a hot chocolate for her and a coffee for me.

"We need to clear up a few things," I started. Shannon cupped her hands around the cup and blew softly at the whipped cream, paying me no mind.

"I've been straight with you from the beginning. I told you from the start that I wanted a baby. So you have no right to be mad that I'm excited about the baby. That's what I wanted out of this deal from the start." She still didn't look at me. "And do you remember what you wanted? Remember your list? I'm giving you what you wanted, aren't I? Did you have on that list anything about me loving you more than I love the baby? Did you expect that?"

Shannon sneered. "I didn't expect love at all. And good thing."

"Good thing," I repeated sarcastically. "Look, I want the baby. I love the baby." I put my elbows on the table and leaned towards her. "But even though that's true, it's also true that I'm adopting you. For real. You are my daughter too. I'm not going to abandon you for the baby. You are a real part of this family."

"Yeah? Which part?"

"Your part is obnoxious teenage daughter. You're very good at it."

She dipped her middle finger in her whipped cream and held it up to me.

Chapter 42

———⟨∿⟩———

"SO DO YOU SEE HER much?"

We were having tea at my kitchen table after visiting Harry. Harry was feeling much better; it was Ben who seemed a little lost. But it might have been me.

"We've talked a couple of times."

In the last two weeks, I had become paranoically focused on Maria. I compared myself to her constantly. I saw every line in my face in the context of Maria's perfect complexion. When I dressed in the morning, I wondered what she might be wearing. And once, well maybe twice, I drove in an adolescent mania by Ben's house, only to see a strange car in the yard. It must be Maria's car, I thought. It was newer than mine.

I tried to keep the fear out of my eyes. "Do you think you will reconcile?"

"Maria would like to try. But no. I can't."

"Why?"

"She thinks I'm boring. I'm only going to bore her more as I get older."

"But since I'm as boring as you…?"

He put his cup down rather hard. "Stop it, Cynthia. I didn't say that." His voice softened. "You seem to like me the way I am."

I almost cried out in relief.

"I do," I said. "I'm sorry that I'm so crazy."

"Speaking of crazy, how's Shannon?"

"Totally off the hormonal deep end. Hates me, hates the baby."

"She's jealous of the baby."

"Oh, big understatement."

"I don't think she realized how much she'd care about you."

I shook my head. "Care about me? Oh no. She's now asking on a daily basis if she can go live with Angela."

Ben got up from the table. "I have to go," he said. He bent and kissed me on the top of my head. Half out the door, he turned and said, "Why is it that you think that no one could love you?"

Wait, what just happened?

"Aren't you staying for supper? Are you coming back?" I hollered. But he was already gone, and I hadn't really hollered. I hadn't even spoken it. Shit, I hadn't even thought it until about twenty seconds after his car was gone.

I put my head down on the table. It seemed to me that he had mentioned love. Could I have misinterpreted the conversation? Maybe I said something horrible that now I didn't even remember.

I looked at the four steaks thawing on the counter. Lucas always joined us for Monday night dinner. I tried to give Lucas the benefit of the doubt and attributed his presence as a desire to even the playing field. He didn't want Shannon ganged up on. But I recognized the overwhelming probability that the opposite was true. Lucas and Shannon enjoyed ganging up on Ben. I was not in the game, forced to be neutral by my love for Ben and my need for Shannon.

Well, I'd cook the four steaks anyway. Ben might come back. If not, Lucas and Carlos would be happy.

It was four-thirty. School let out at three, but Shannon never came home directly after school anymore. I couldn't even start cooking until she came home, because I never had any idea of when that would be. I went to the living room and turned on the TV. A cooking program came on, and I dozed off right away.

I woke just after six, and Shannon still wasn't home. I called her cell phone, but got voice mail. I figured her caller ID warned her it was me, but also reminded her she better come home. She and Lucas sauntered in about half an hour later.

"Where have you been?" I said. "Do you know how late you are? I didn't even start dinner yet."

"Relax," she said, which of course made me more furious. "Lucas and I ate already."

"You ate? You didn't call?"

Shannon gave Lucas a look that signaled she was about to give me the story they'd concocted. "I told you this morning. At breakfast. You were half asleep, but you said okay. I told you."

"You certainly did not."

"Hey," said Lucas, "Where's your young stud?"

I wheeled around to him. "Good one, Lucas. Now go home. Now."

"Jesus," protested Shannon. "I told you. I told you."

Lucas just laughed and said, "See you, honey," and left.

Shannon shook her head like she was humoring a senile old lady.

There was something about her that was different. I stared at her and she turned quickly, moving towards her room.

"Stop," I said. "Turn around."

And I saw it. The safety pin she'd been wearing in her eyebrow had been replaced. Instead there was a gold tie tack, the edges delicately scrolled. It was my father's tie pin. My mother had given it to him for his wedding suit. Aside from his wedding ring and a St. Christopher medal, it was his only piece of jewelry.

"Where did you get that?" I screamed. I reached for it, and she jerked back. "Take that out right now. Give that back!"

"What the fuck is the matter?" she asked. "I found this in the attic, with a bunch of old crap."

"That's not crap. That's my father's. It's mine. Give it back."

"Jesus Christ!" Shannon unscrewed the little tip, and slammed the pieces down on the table. "Yup, that belongs to your family. The one that I'm such an important part of!"

She started for her room, but turned around and ran out the back door.

I let her go. She got on her cell-phone in the driveway, and a few minutes later Lucas pulled up. I was ready to go out and block the driveway to keep her home, but they didn't go anywhere. They sat in the car. I watched them, their arms animated by the streetlight in what looked like a huge bitch session.

I put the steaks back in the fridge, and took out the bread and peanut butter. No lover, no kid, no nice dinner. I ended up eating the peanut butter straight off the knife.

I went upstairs and sat in the dark. Shannon came in around nine and I heard the refrigerator door open.

Shannon refused to go to school the next day. Her stomach hurt, and her head. She hugged her breasts, which were now way too big for a fifteen-year-old, and a small measure of pity joined in with my anger. I ended up with enough empathy to let her stay home, but not enough to want to spend the day with her.

"I need groceries and stuff. Are you okay if I leave you by yourself?" I asked.

"What would you do, hold me on your lap?"

I left.

It didn't take long enough at the drugstore and supermarket, and I wasn't ready to head home. I drove to the nursing home. It wasn't kindness that led me to Harry. It was selfish of me, but I hoped he was a little vague. I needed to escape; perhaps I could be Abigail for just an hour.

"Hi, Cynthia," he said. "Where's Benny and Careless?"

I was stuck in my life. I handed him a bag from the bakery. "Benny's working and Carlos is with my little girl."

I was just in time for Oprah, and we sat together and watched as Oprah interviewed a young man who had saved a child from drowning.

"I always wanted to do that. Save someone," said Harry.

"That would be wonderful," I agreed. "Knowing someone is in this world just because of you."

"And I could meet Oprah."

"Maybe the President too."

"Oh, I did that," he said. He handed me a doughnut.

"You did? Which one?"

"That tall guy."

His clarity dwindled and I found myself comforted to stay for a few minutes in a safe cloudy place. We ate doughnuts and drank cider and he held my hand.

"Do you remember the fortuneteller?" I asked.

"At the dolphin place," Harry said.

"That's the one," I said, encouraging his memory. "Do you remember what he told Abigail?"

He put his forehead near mine and whispered. "Sure," he said. "There's only two kinds of people in the world."

"What kinds?" I whispered back.

"Yours and not yours."

We sat quietly, heads touching, and I thought about Ben and Shannon and the baby.

"How do you know which is which?" I said quietly.

"Which is what?" asked Harry.

I wiped the sugar from his cheek and kissed where the sugar had been.

⁂

I sat in the car for a while. I didn't know if the words were from the fortuneteller or from Harry, and I didn't know if they were platitude or profound.

I checked the groceries in the back seat. No ice cream. They'd be okay. I phoned Shannon.

"What?" she said groggily.

"I called to see how you were doing."

"I was sleeping."

"Will you be okay by yourself for a little while longer?"

"I WAS SLEEPING."

"Sorry. I'll be home in an hour or so."

⁂

I walked into Donovan & Shelter. It surprised me that it was very sleek and modern. Sharp angles, black lacquer. I expected TV show lawyerliness, with mahogany and oriental rugs, I guess.

NANCY ROMAN

The receptionist matched the decor. She had black pointed hair and a mirrored necklace.

"I don't have an appointment," I explained, "but I am hoping that Mr. Shelter can give me five minutes."

She asked my name, and her expression changed when I told her. Was I the subject of gossip here at the office? She was probably another of Maria's allies that would make a phone call as soon as I was out of earshot. But perhaps she was glad that Ben had found someone new. Nah.

Ben poked his head from an inner door. His eyes were full of question marks but they were not angry questions.

He had a small conference table in his office, and I took a seat there. He sat opposite me.

"Well, hi," he finally said.

"I don't want to interrupt your work. I'll just be a minute." I said. I shrugged; it was exaggerated and awkward. "I'm smart enough to know I made you mad yesterday, but I think I am too thick to quite understand why."

He leaned toward me, offering his hands. Then he changed his mind and sat back, adding distance between us.

"For the last couple of weeks, ever since…well, you know…everyone is telling me that I should reconcile. Try again. Forgive. Take her back. Stay married. Blah, blah, blah. It's tough enough to listen to. But when it comes from the woman I think I'm in love with…"

Ben stopped. He shrugged his shoulders, mirroring me. He waited for it to sink in.

"Holy shit," I said.

He sighed. "So why aren't you encouraging me to stay with you?"

"It doesn't seem fair. I'm committed to Shannon and the baby."

"So you can't commit to me too?"

I shook my head. "No, that's the easy part—committing to you. It's that I can't expect you to commit to Shannon too, just because I am."

He grabbed his head like he would tear out his hair. "Jesus, Cynthia. Shannon is not the problem. She's a brat—and sometimes, a lot of times, it gets to me—but she's a bratty kid, not a monster." He raked his fingers through his hair. "Do you think you're the only one who can stand her?"

"Do you think you could stand her for three more years?" I questioned.

"Honey, I'm not sure I can stand YOU for three more years. But I can stand you now. Isn't that enough?"

I answered quickly and quietly. "Yes."

"Do you want me to go back to Maria?"

"No way."

He took my hands and pulled me up from the chair. "Then go home to your bratty kid and I'll see you tonight. Are those steaks still good?"

Chapter 43

MY MOTHER AND HER SISTER didn't come north for Thanksgiving. Aunt Lorraine had a big celebration planned with a new beau; it wouldn't surprise me if she were married again by Christmas. My mother, always frugal, decided she would wait until Shannon's delivery date got close. Then she would come up to take charge—excuse me, *help*—when we brought the baby home. I was unhappy about both her Thanksgiving absence and future great-grandmotherly presence.

I was sorry that she would miss Thanksgiving. I had promised Ben he would meet my family. I knew he'd love Angela—everyone does—but I needed my mother to explain Mary Ann to an outsider. When someone met my mother, then MaryAnn became an 'Oh, I see'.

Further, I was dismayed by the thought of my mother overseeing my new baby. Certainly she knew more about babies than I did, and she had become quite sanguine about Shannon, but I had dreamt too long about holding that baby all day and all night. She was to be my baby at last. I didn't want to share.

And finally, with Shannon's hostility threatening the impending finalization of her adoption, the anticipation of the new baby, and the stress of holding onto Ben while Maria seemed increasingly beautiful and sad, I was already juggling too many sharp knives to handle even the slightest distraction.

My mother didn't come home for Thanksgiving, but D.J. did. Shannon had given me no sign that she and D.J. had been communicating at all. But Wednesday afternoon, as soon as Lucas drove Shannon home, she jumped out of the car, surprisingly agile for almost eight months along, and ran into the house. Lucas sat in the car for several seconds—I think he was stunned by Shannon's abrupt disappearance—then he gunned the engine and took off.

Shannon changed her clothes. But not the comfortable sweats that allowed her belly to hang out. She put on a pink (pink!) maternity sweater that brought a memory of Angela's daughter-in-law, Sean-girl. I didn't remember Shannon receiving anything from either Angela or Sean. But there was Shannon, rosy and pink, with a jeans skirt and adorable striped leggings. She ate nearly nothing and planted herself by the living room window.

By about eight, the house seemed to shake with nervousness. I sat down beside her.

"You know," I said, "there's always a ton of horrible traffic on the night before Thanksgiving. I'm sure D.J. is just stuck in some big traffic jam."

"Go away," she said.

I continued to sit by her side for quite a long time. Her pink sweater moved a little as the baby kicked, but the rest of Shannon stayed still. Headlights came down the street about nine fifteen. D.J.'s truck sped past our house and pulled into his own drive. The taillights went out and the porch light went on. Shannon craned her neck and watched D.J. hug his mother and go into the house. The porch light went out.

"It's so late," I said. "D.J. must be exhausted. He's probably going straight to bed. He'll come by in the morning."

"Go away," she said.

And I did. I sat upstairs by the window in the baby's room, where I could see D.J.'s house. The lights went out about eleven. I heard Shannon lock the kitchen door.

D.J. did come by in the morning. Shannon was at the kitchen table, picking at her toast, still wearing the pajamas that my mother had sent her. They had a hugely expandable drawstring waist, and a gaudy flower pattern that reminded me of hospital curtains.

"Hi," D.J. said casually as I opened the door.

Shannon looked up with a mixture of desperation, adoration, and anger.

"When did you get in?" she asked.

"Sometime last night. I went out with some guys at school, so I got a pretty late start."

"Right," she said sarcastically.

"Do you want some juice or coffee?" I asked.

"No, I gotta go. I'm meeting up with some kids, and we're going to the football game."

Shannon looked startled. I had no idea what, if anything, he had promised her.

"Well, you better go then," she said.

"You look good," he said. "You're really pregnant," he said stupidly. "But cute too," he added belatedly. "I gotta go. I'll see you this weekend for sure."

And he was out the door.

352

I looked at Shannon. The tears were standing in her eyes. "What a prick," I said.

She shook her head. "No. He's not."

*

Ben was coming by to pick us up to go to Angela's for Thanksgiving dinner. He called to ask what to wear, which I thought was very endearing.

"We don't dress up much," I said. "Wear that nice grey sweater that makes your eyes look really blue."

"I have a sweater that makes my eyes look blue?"

"You do. Jeans are okay. Jeans a little loose in the waist, because you will be eating vast quantities of every possible food on the nutritional pyramid."

*

It took some coaxing to get Shannon dressed. She didn't want to go. I convinced her that D.J. would be busy all day at his own family's holiday, so there would be no possibility that he'd call or come by.

"I can't get these leggings on," she cried, coming out to the kitchen with one leg half on and the other dangling from beneath her skirt. "I don't know how I did it yesterday. They are fucking impossible."

I sat her down and started over, putting her feet through and pulling them up to her knees. Then she stood up and together we tugged and pulled them over her tummy.

"How in the world will you go to the bathroom?" I said, exhausted and sweaty.

"I cut a hole in the crotch," she said

"How about your underpants?"

"What underpants?" she said.

I considered her fairly short skirt. "Pick the table with the longest tablecloth," I said.

Shannon laughed, but she was sullen again by the time Ben drove up. She balked when I wouldn't let her bring Carlos. I explained that with so many of the little grandchildren around, he would be too agitated.

"Tell me again what I am supposed to like about this stupid holiday," she said.

Three tables were set at Angela's. Our generation was to have the dining room. Two folding tables in the living room held the kids and grandkids.

"Christ," said Shannon, "I'm not fifty and I'm not thirty and I'm not five. This is going to be such fun." She looked at Ben. "You might want to sit here with the younger guys," she observed.

Angela and MaryAnn were scrambling in the kitchen. I pulled Ben in and made introductions. He smiled with his head a little tilted and slumped his shoulders slightly. It occurred to me that he was trying to look old. I dropped my dishes off and brought him out to the den where the men were planted in front of the inevitable football game. I whispered to him, "It's okay if you look a lot younger than me; it makes me seem pretty damn alluring." John took Ben's bottle of wine and handed him a beer instead. "See you later," I said.

Back in the kitchen, Angela just said, "Hmm."

MaryAnn said, "Is he Catholic?"

Eventually, everything was ready and we gathered in the living room before sitting down to eat. There wasn't enough room to all eat together, but we stood together to say grace. MaryAnn started our traditional round of what we each had to be grateful for.

"I'm thankful that everyone is here, safe and sound," she said.

"I'm thankful that our family is getting bigger and better," I said.

"With more to come," added Angela, smiling at Shannon and her own pregnant daughter Karen.

"I'm thankful for turkey," "stuffing," "mashed potatoes and gravy," "pumpkin pie," said the men one by one in what had become the traditional testosterone response.

Ben's turn. "I'm thankful that I do not have to eat my mother's awful cooking, God bless her." Funny and safe, I was happy with that.

Shannon knew that she was supposed to be thankful to be part of our family. Everyone looked at her and willed her to say it. She resisted. "I'm thankful we're almost done with this shit," she said. She took her seat and helped herself to the mashed potatoes.

By the time dinner was half over I was exhausted with trying to watch both of my charges. I kept half my attention on Ben and my sisters' reaction to him. That part seemed to go well. But I kept straining to see or hear what Shannon might be up to. From where I was seated, I could only see a corner of Shannon's table, only Michael and Karen. Karen's expression was particularly interesting, in an unsettling way. I could see the effort in the stretch of her neck as she tried to find common ground with her new and also-pregnant cousin. Michael's jaw got tighter and tighter, and I began to wonder how any turkey could get through the set of those teeth.

I wished I had insisted that Shannon sit with my sisters and me. My sisters had already been through the miserable teen years; I think they'd recognize this unpleasant stage. On the other hand, their kids were still young enough to believe that they had been perfect. They were probably appalled that the eccentric but essentially sweet kid they had met this summer had turned into the one from The Exorcist.

I couldn't hear much above my pounding headache on the ride home. It seemed that Ben was saying it was a wonderful Thanksgiving, and Shannon might have slightly disagreed.

She was already texting someone as we opened the door, and she went right to her room, the better to text and computer chat at the same time.

I sat down at the kitchen table, not able to go further. Ben put away our share of the leftovers while I put away a fourth glass of wine.

"Would you mind terribly if I sent you home?" I asked. "I just don't have it in me to get romantic."

He laughed. "I hate to disillusion you as to my sexual prowess, but that much food keeps even my youthful body from getting frisky." He kissed me at the door, but he was careful to prevent our tender stomachs from touching. "I'll be recovered by tomorrow," Ben said. "All my frisky parts too. Would you come over and spend the evening? The whole evening?"

"I can't," I said. "I can't leave her."

"Yes, you can."

"I can't."

He frowned. I thought about leaving Shannon. I should be able to. Why not? I was so tempted. It would be sweet not to have a teenager—just for one night.

"I'll come and spend the evening, but I can't promise to spend the night. Let's see how it goes." If D.J. came over, she'd be happy, and happy to see me gone.

"You need a life too. When the baby comes, you won't get many chances for a quiet romantic evening."

He kissed me gently twice, my left eye, my right eye. He touched my hair.

"Okay," I said.

Chapter 44

———— ❦ ————

.J. came over the next day, but it seems that his idea of spending time with Shannon included telling her about all the great plans he had that didn't include her. He was meeting some buddies for lunch. And that night he had another Thanksgiving celebration with his mother's side of the family. Saturday was some great party that was going to be awesome. To none of these events did he think of inviting Shannon.

"Sunday," he said. "Let's go out for a ride before I head back to school."

"Whatever," said Shannon, and he was gone.

"You were right yesterday," she said. "He's a prick."

I handed her a piece of pumpkin pie, even though it wasn't quite eleven in the morning. I took a slice for myself too.

"I wasn't right," I said. "I'm sorry I called him that. I think he is just so caught up right now with being a big-shot college man that he doesn't even know how obnoxious he sounds."

"Well, it's real fucking obnoxious."

"He'll get over it. He'll come back to earth again in a few months. You know he's basically a nice person."

"I don't know why I ever liked him. He can go fuck himself." She took the remainder of her pie, and ate it in one big gulp. Then off to some version of anti-music in her room.

My sympathy, although encompassing poor Shannon, was predominantly focused on me. Yesterday I had been ambivalent about spending the evening with Ben, but my anticipation had grown into a romantic frenzy during the night.

I couldn't abandon Shannon on the same day that D.J. had. I lounged in my perfumed bath and considered strategies to get out of the house. Ben had certainly brought my youth back—all the way back to adolescence.

I saw Shannon sulking in front of the open refrigerator around four.

"Honey," I said. "Ben has invited both of us over for dinner. It will do you good to get out."

"No fucking way," she politely declined.

"He has a really nice house and a big TV."

"Good for you; have a swell time."

"I couldn't go and leave you alone," I protested.

"Yes you fucking can. I WANT to be alone."

And that easily, I was off the hook. I didn't feel very good about it.

About six, as I covered my best lingerie with my lowest cut sweater, Shannon waddled into my room in her increasingly duck-like sway.

"Lucas and his buddies are going to the movies, and he wants me to go with them."

It was awful. This was the reprieve I was looking for. I didn't have to leave a lonely kid alone. But it was also Lucas and his penitentiary-bound buddies. Shannon was fifteen and almost eight months pregnant.

"Oh, Shannon. I don't like those guys."

"It's the MOVIES," she argued. "The worst they can do is throw popcorn." She laid on the guilt. "You're going out anyway."

"This isn't a good idea," I said.

"I'll come home early; I promise. I'll come straight home after the movies." She gave me her most sweet and pleading smile, and I said yes to a very bad idea.

"So, did I get the seal of approval from your sisters?" Ben asked.

We were lying in sort of a quilt sandwich in front of his fireplace.

"Yes, they had very nice things to say."

"Like what?" he said, looking up at the ceiling like he was outside counting stars.

I propped myself up on an elbow and frowned. "Don't tell me you are one of those insecure guys?"

"I definitely am."

"Well, Angela was quite taken with you. She said you were very handsome, and smart, and witty and that you had very kind eyes."

"Did she say they were very blue, and I wore the perfect sweater to bring them out?"

"Oh yes."

He batted his eyelashes in great big flutters. "And what did MaryAnn have to say?"

"She said you were very tall."

He threw his forearm over those blue eyes in distress. "That's not a very ringing endorsement."

"With MaryAnn, it can take a while to win her over."

"How long?"

I thought about it. "After I got divorced, she told me one day while we were washing my mother's windows that it was probably for the best. It was five years after the divorce was final."

"Five years."

"Minimum."

Back in my purse, somewhere behind the sofa, my phone started playing Stardust.

"Leave it," said Ben.

"I can't." I looked at the clock. It was just before 10:00. "She's probably just calling to let me know that she's home, just like she promised."

"She's calling to spoil your evening, just as she promised herself."

I got up and dug through my purse for the phone.

"Come home!" she cried. "Come home now. It's just awful!"

My heart starting jumping. "What's the matter? Are you okay? Are you in labor?"

There was no answer. I could hear loud voices in the background. Angry voices. Then another voice came on the phone.

"Who is this?" he demanded.

"Who is *this*? Put Shannon back on the phone right now."

"Is this her mother? Well, this is Detective Eaton. There's been an incident at your house. We need you to come here right away."

I was already trying to dress one-handed. Ben held me by the elbow while I stepped into my panties. "What happened? Is she hurt?"

"I don't think she's hurt. Come right now."

He hung up. I immediately began to cry. "Jesus. Jesus." I fumbled with my buttons.

Ben took me by the shoulders. "Don't panic. I'll drive you home and we'll take care of whatever it is." He unbuttoned my shirt and re-buttoned it correctly. He ran his fingers through my hair, and grabbed my coat.

He drove through town as quickly as he could. He was efficient and careful, I think. I took a tissue and cleaned the blurred traces of passion from my eye makeup.

There were several cars in my yard, and three police cars— two on the street and one on my lawn. Kids were everywhere, some jumping from one foot to the other and yelling at each other. Others were huddled in silent clumps. Shannon was on the porch with a large police officer. I pushed past the kids and ran up to her.

"What happened?" I screamed.

"I didn't mean to," Shannon cried. "I never meant any of it."

"What?"

"When Lucas picked me up to go to the movies, I told him you went out. So he said, 'Let's have a party' and I didn't think it would be bad. I thought it would be okay. But he kept calling guys, and they called other guys, and it got horrible. They were making a big mess and breaking stuff, and … it was awful. I didn't mean it."

Ben broke in. "So the neighbors called the police?"

"No," said the cop. "They should have."

"I didn't want you to know," Shannon continued. "And I didn't know what to do." Her voice cracked in a big sob. "So I called D.J."

"Where is he?" I looked around.

"I just wanted him to help me kick everybody out and clean up before you got home. But Lucas and D.J. got in a big fight." She shook with fear.

"Oh my God."

The cop continued. "The Lucas kid knifed the other kid. That's when someone called us."

"Oh no... where is he? Where's D.J. now?"

"Ambulance took him already," the cop said.

"It's not my fault!" Shannon shrieked.

Ben stepped between the cop and Shannon. "This is no one's fault," he said calmly. "Kids fight. Do you know how seriously he was injured?" he asked the cop.

"Not for sure. There's lots of blood but sometimes that doesn't mean much." He turned back to me. "So did you give permission for your kid to have a party?"

"Don't answer that," said Ben, but I was incapable of answering. I saw for the first time that Shannon was covered in blood.

"My god, Shannon. Look at you! Is the baby all right?"

And Shannon, already on the cliff of hysteria, jumped off. "THE BABY? Oh, is the baby okay? What about me? What about this big blob around your precious baby?" She pushed me away from her. "Why don't you two just have your own baby and then you wouldn't have to BUY MINE? I want my MONEY RIGHT NOW!"

Everyone heard it. The cop heard it. The kids heard it. Ben heard it.

Chapter 45

.J. LIVED. THAT WAS THE most important thing. Everything else unraveled.

By Sunday, when it became apparent that D.J. would pull through, Shannon tried halfheartedly to retract her accusation. She said she never meant that I had schemed to buy her baby; she was just crazy and afraid. But she really was too crazy and afraid to keep her usual tough façade. Melissa Rodriguez, covering her own ass with her client in trouble, visited Lucas in jail. Lucas knew the truth and gladly snitched. Shannon had told him about our deal weeks ago—it was at his suggestion that Shannon had demanded half the money up front. It didn't take long for Gwen's husband to come forward as well, relating his suspicions that I wanted a baby and not a teenager. Shannon buckled when confronted with this evidence. But there was no problem, she unfortunately insisted, since she was happy to get adopted and sell me the baby. Melissa packed Shannon's things and took her away. No one would tell me where.

Lucas didn't fare too badly. It turned out that one of his many parents knew a good lawyer and Lucas was able to plead out as a juvenile, and get some not-too-terrible time at a progressive facility for troubled youth.

I knew a good lawyer too, but he wouldn't speak to me. The goddamn caller ID warned Ben not to pick up. I borrowed Angela's phone but as soon as he heard my voice, the line went dead. I don't think I could have explained myself anyway. I don't think it was the act of baby-buying that destroyed Ben, but the revelation that I had been lying to him for so long.

He did, however, as a man who lived his life protecting others, send a decent lawyer my way. And I needed one. This sweet but practical older man convinced the State not to charge me with baby-buying. With Shannon recanting and her primary corroborator being of doubtful character as he sat in jail, there really wasn't much evidence. I was glad I hadn't gotten around to setting up a trust for Shannon with what would certainly look like a down payment. And the Department of Children and Families didn't really want to further publicize how eagerly and quickly they had forked over a little girl. There were a couple of sensational stories in the local papers for several days, and that was enough for the State's Denial-And-Blame Department to jump in and bury the issue. (On the subject of newspapers articles, it was rather amazing how many of my high school classmates could be rounded up in such a short time, and how many of them knew at sixteen that I was irresponsible and dangerous.)

D.J.'s parents weren't so eager to forget. By February, they filed a civil lawsuit claiming I had allowed dangerous minor delinquents to go unsupervised, resulting in the near death of their son. I instructed Ben's lawyer friend, who'd been negotiating settlements for forty years, to give them whatever I had. I offered my nest egg to fund college education for

D.J. and Celeste. I didn't care. If they wanted me to pay for their graduate schools and weddings too, I would have agreed. "You know how much I have," I said, "and that's what I am prepared to give them." I didn't care. The lawyer nodded and went off to spend my money.

I wasn't sure I would ever be able to face D.J. or his family again. I was glad the snow covered the yard. I didn't think I could bear to see the grass grow. I figured I would sell my sweet little house come spring.

My family clung to Shannon's feeble recantation as only they could. Of course I never agreed to buy the baby. I just wanted to give Shannon and her baby a good home. Shannon was 'disturbed'. It was all a tragedy. My mother wanted me to move to Florida—or change my name. Mary Ann wanted me to find someone else—the State, the newspapers, Lucas's family—to sue. Angela came closest to the truth. She sat with me on a very quiet Christmas Eve. She told me a story.

When cousin Sheila got her first nursing job, there was a horribly obese woman on her ward. She was very near death. When a patient died, it was the nurses' job to clean up the body and prepare it for transport to the morgue or funeral parlor. "Prepping" they called it. Everyone hated this task, especially in cases of morbid obesity. Before starting their work every day, the staff would go over all the cases. The supervisor would say, "Let's keep Mrs. Fatty alive just to the end of this shift, so the night nurses will have to prep." Then the night nurses would say the same thing. Each shift did everything possible to keep Mrs. Fatty alive so they wouldn't have the unpleasant task of dealing with her body. So, eight hours by eight hours, the poor woman stayed alive. And eventually she recovered. "So you see," said Angela, "the nurses saved her life, even though their motives were very selfish."

Right after Christmas, I got a job. My pension came every month, but with the upcoming settlement, I would no longer have enough to live on for twenty or thirty years. So I took a part-time job with an accounting firm, doing the books for small businesses. I had the option of working from home, and I mostly did. It would probably have been better for me to get out, but I was having trouble facing anyone, since the newspaper had detailed my ignoble story with great relish. Besides, Carlos needed me. He cried and paced incessantly after they took Shannon away, so I called Melissa and asked her if I could give Carlos to Shannon. "No pets," she said, and hung up. So Carlos was mine. I didn't restore the baby's room to an office. I just closed the door, and worked at the kitchen table with the little dog on my lap.

Harry died at the end of March. I had continued to visit him, just not on Mondays. He could no longer identify the people whose photographs filled his walls. He called Einstein the *funny old guy* and Oprah *the dog lady*. Sometimes he thought I was Abigail but mostly I was someone he was happy to meet for the very first time. The nursing home was kind enough to call me when he died.

The funeral was small, so there was no avoiding Ben. I shook his hand like a respectful stranger. I thanked him for introducing me to a good man. "I wish he had been my father," said Ben sadly, and I went home and cried for my own loss of both good men.

Chapter 46

———◦◦◦———

SPRING WAS LATE. IT WAS April before the snow melted.

On Holy Thursday, driving back from the supermarket loaded with supplies for Angela's Easter dinner, I saw her. She was hanging with a clump of kids on the town green. She had cut her hair down to her scalp, and dyed it platinum. But there was no mistaking her. She looked both bored and defensive, like the first time I saw her on my porch steps. She was smoking a cigarette.

I pulled over by the open space near the fire hydrant. I got out of the car and just stood there on the sidewalk. Eventually, Shannon looked my way. She was motionless for a second, and I thought I saw her mouth an obscenity. Then she broke off from the kids and walked over.

"So?" she said.

"You look really good," I said. "And skinny."

"Yeah. You never saw me with a waist."

I faltered. "How's school?" I asked.

"Lame. How's Carlos?"

"All right, I guess. He spends a lot of time walking around in circles."

"He always did that. You can get him to stop with a cookie."

"I'll try it."

We stared at each other. A women with a baby carriage motioned for us to clear the sidewalk. We watched together as the carriage passed by with its hidden treasure.

"How did it go?" I asked, and she knew what I meant.

"It was fucking hard, but the baby came out after about a gazillion hours."

"Is she okay?"

"Yeah. She's good." She waved her cigarette in a general southerly direction. "She got adopted by these people who've been waiting for a baby for seven years. Or seventeen. Whatever. I got to meet them. They seemed nice. They were like delirious."

"That's great," I said. And I found that I meant it. "And how about you? Where are you living?"

She snorted. "I'm back at Decision House. It sucks. But what the fuck."

"I like your hair. It's very sophisticated."

"I used this stuff—supposed to make you really blond. I guess I used too much. My hair all broke off." She ran her hand over her stubble. "So I had the barbershop give me a buzz."

"Well, I like it."

Shannon threw her cigarette butt in the gutter. "I gotta go," she said. She turned and started walking back to the kids.

"Wait," I said.

She turned back.

"What did she look like?"

Shannon looked inside herself for the memory, and her smile was serene and beautiful and wise. "Like D.J."

"What?"

She met my eyes and waited for my comprehension to catch up. "Yup."

I leaned against the car because my legs were suddenly wobbly. "Why didn't you tell him?"

She rolled her eyes in a gesture too familiar to me. "I did. YOU were the one who told him it wasn't his."

"For God's sake, Shannon! That's what you told me. Are you sure?"

"Shit. That's right. I'm just a big whore." I saw the start of tears, but she held them by looking at the sky. "Well, I'm not. I never slept with anyone else. Only him."

"You should have told me. You should have told HIM."

I took a step towards her but she pulled back.

"I didn't want to fuck up his life. He was the only person in my whole life who was ever nice to me." She shrugged. "And then I ended up fucking up his life anyway."

She turned her back and walked quickly away.

"I'm sorry," I whispered to the space where she had been.

The truth of it stung me, and continued to sting. The only person in her life who was nice to her was D.J. Not me. Certainly not me.

I drove my food over to Angela's and left it on her porch.

That night, I sat in Shannon's room while Carlos walked in circles.

I opened the closet and looked at the tangle of empty hangers. Most of the clothes I had bought her would be too big now. I should have bought some smaller things that she could wear now. The dog rummaged through the back of the closet and came out with a little toy. I looked closer. It was a little angel salt-shaker.

I crawled into her bed about midnight, and Carlos jumped up and trembled next to me. I took him in my arms and we shivered together through the night.

I woke before dawn, with Carlos wriggling for the usual reason.

It was cold out in the dark, waiting for Carlos to finish up, and I found I was no longer shivering. I was clear and calm like the pre-dawn air.

I got Carlos a sweater and a cookie, and I grabbed a soft gray leather jacket from my Maya Maria retirement package. I drove through the deserted silent streets.

I sat at the old picnic table and watched the sun come up. A little after seven a light came on in the kitchen. A while later Ben opened the door and looked at me for a good long time. Then he closed the door.

I didn't care. I'd parked in front of his garage and blocked him in. If I had to sit all day I would. If I had to pound on the door, I'd do that too.

But a few minutes later he came out with two mugs of coffee. He was wearing jeans and an old tee, and moccasins without socks. He had thrown on an old raggedy bathrobe for warmth. It was a faded brick color that perhaps had been burgundy in a previous incarnation.

He put a mug down in front of me and sat.

"Hi, Carlos," he said.

The little dog wagged his tail and climbed into Ben's lap. He pushed his nose into Ben's hand.

"I need a good lawyer," I said.

There was a heavy sigh of exasperation, or maybe even disgust. "Isn't Martin working out?" Ben asked.

"Martin is fine. But I don't need a negotiator. I need an advocate."

"I can't help you," he said.

"I want to fight for custody."

"You want the baby?" he asked, incredulous.

"The baby is fine. She has a good home. I want Shannon back."

"So you can introduce her to some new sperm?"

I took a breath. He wasn't going to get rid of me with insults.

"I deserve that. I know. But for the record, Shannon was already pregnant when I met her. I didn't arrange that."

"You just arranged the acquisition."

"Yes, I did. And a home for Shannon too, which she didn't have."

"Just like Mother Theresa."

"Just like a mother." I stood up. "Ben, I want her back."

"I can't help you," Ben said. He put his cup down hard, and a little coffee splashed out. "No one will let you have her back now."

"You can do it. You can make them understand. You know how to make people understand."

He shook his head. "*I* don't understand."

"I just wanted a family."

"So you went out and bought one."

He was right. I did. But I didn't feel ashamed.

"It was the best money I was ever going to spend. Ben, it was a family. I was fifty years old, and I'm older now, and I want a family. I want Shannon."

"What does Shannon want?"

"She's just a kid," I said. "A kid that has never had anything but misery. She doesn't know what she wants. I know what's best for her." I held out my hands to him. "I'm her mother."

He looked at me and I saw the slimmest palest flicker of kindness. Not quite understanding. Acknowledgment maybe. Enough for now.

"You'll lose," he said.

I probably will lose. But Shannon won't. For once in her life she'll see that someone will fight for her. That's she's worth fighting for.

I'll fight for her. I'm her mother.

About the Author

An English Major with an M.B.A., Nancy Roman is a financial executive who likes her day job. She lives in Connecticut with her husband and several well-nourished cats.

Just What I Always Wanted is her first novel.

Follow Nancy At

http://notquiteold.wordpress. com

60976208R00227

Made in the USA
Middletown, DE
18 August 2019